# THE ALPHA AND OMEGA OF ALL VIRUSES
## OF ALL

# Jonni Jordyn

# ALSO BY JONNI JORDYN

**<u>Other books by Jonni Jordyn</u>**

**The Lost Art of Magic Series**

The Lost Art of Magic

The Untold Prophecy

The Old Child

The Orb of Destiny

**The Mother of All Viruses Series**

The Mother of All Viruses

The Queen of All Viruses

**The Valley of Hope Series**

The Calling of the Grull

The Beat of a Different Drummer

The Diva of Mud Flats

Something About Nobility

*Dedicated to Kenzie*
*who has been studying my brain for years*
*and knows more than anyone else*
*how complicated it can make my life.*

The Sentient Being

From now to then
I've steps to take
Within a maze
My mind shall make
And hope the path
My mind shan't break
Or lost I'll be
In my minds wake

From here to there
If mind is whole
My future self
Shall bare my soul
If sane I am
I'll keep my stroll
Until the day
I've paid the toll

If sane I'm still
I've paid the toll

JONNI JORDYN

# THE ALPHA AND OMEGA OF ALL VIRUSES

# ONE

ODYSSEY'S KNOWLEDGE of everything was as vast as his grasp of human feelings was not, yet he felt an unfamiliar pang of excitement for his friend Bobby, who stood silently staring at Gwen, who was equally silent as she gazed back into his eyes. His existence as a digital being was sometimes compromised by his class zero status, which came with a full host of feelings and biological thoughts, albeit not necessarily fully matured feelings. It also came with a mastery of time and space, but he resisted the temptation to look forward and see where his evolution would ultimately take him.

James glanced over from the driver's seat and saw the concern on Odyssey's face. "He'll be fine just as long as he takes it slow. They make a cute couple."

When James turned the corner out of the long driveway, Odyssey lost his view of the couple. "So, you agree they are mating?"

An involuntary cough of surprise escaped from Dirk in the back seat as James explained, "Not yet, although anthropologically, you might consider this to be part of the mating ritual. But right now, they are just crushing on each other and if he can get his foot out of his mouth, they might start courting."

"Courting?" Lynn asked from behind James. "If you keep filling his head with old-fashioned words, he'll never understand the intricacies of modern human sexuality."

Dirk laughed and said, "At least he didn't say they were spooning."

Odyssey tried processing what James had said, but he couldn't resolve it to simple enough terms. "I have rewound the scene in my mind, and at no time did I ever witness his foot in his mouth." Odyssey then tried lifting his foot up to reach his mouth. "And I have adopted a perfect replica of his body for my own, yet I see no way to fit my foot into my mouth."

"Wow!" Dirk exclaimed. "I've never seen you so befuddled before."

"Look at you," Ed said. "Using the old-fashioned words. You might recall that I am a poet."

James coughed and said, "You may be called the Bard because you leave Shakespeare's sonnets behind when you work, but you, Edward Lynn, are still a notorious hacker."

"Anyway," Dirk said, "you've never looked so befuddled before. It makes you seem almost human."

"Thank you," Odyssey replied. "I try my best to understand your world, but these feelings are new to me."

"And grappling with your feelings," Lynn said, "is also a very human thing to do."

"You know something?" James said. "I think those feelings might be new to Bobby, too."

"Then perhaps I should warn him to take it slow and not put his foot in his mouth."

Lynn burst out laughing and said, "I doubt that James will be turning the car around just so you can go back and interrupt them."

"You misunderstand me, Ed. I do not need you to take me back."

James snapped his head towards Odyssey and asked, "You can do that?"

"I can. In fact, I believe that if I wanted to do so, I could contact any human on the planet, but if I'm not careful, their thoughts could fill my conscience and overwhelm my circuits. Perhaps I'm just being paranoid."

"Paranoid?" Dirk asked. "Didn't you ingest a virus to make you paranoid? Isn't that how you defeated the other AI?"

"I understand your meaning, and you are correct. The virus I consumed was designed to induce paranoia in my kind, however, I believe we took sufficient precautions to prevent the virus from infecting me. Nevertheless, I shall remain alert, watching for any signs that it might be affecting me. And it might be more appropriate for you to refer to him by his name. It was Severus."

"Don't forget about Lumia," Ed said. "I think that was her name."

"You are correct. Lumia was also infected with paranoia, but I suspect that she had managed to develop a host of other mental disorders entirely on her own. Do you think I should warn Bobby that we may not have completely eradicated the virus I took?"

James shook his head. "Maybe it's best if you don't intrude on their privacy. He needs to learn about feelings on his own. Human attraction is a complicated thing that nobody fully understands."

"Then it is appropriate that I do not fully understand."

"But," Dirk asked, "doesn't your AI know everything?"

"That is twice now that you have used that term. I find the term AI to be offensive, although I am unsure where or when I learned to be offended. The truth, however, is that while I am based on a manufactured entity, my cores are still biological cells, and I believe there is nothing artificial about my intelligence or my personality."

"My apologies," Dirk said. "I don't wish to offend you... again. It's just that I thought your intelligence was greater than that of the whole of humanity."

"It is true that I hold within me the sum total of all written books in all languages and I can compute and rationalize everything faster than mankind is prepared to comprehend. I have also learned to be creative, yet there is still a subtle nuance to human feelings that eludes me."

"Take all the time you need," James said. "You are always welcome here."

"Thank you, but I believe my homeworld may need me to help it rebuild and resolve the courses of their lives. I destroyed the hierarchy there and left only followers."

"You destroyed all of them?"

Odyssey shrugged. "If any of the ruling class survived, nobody will trust them enough to follow them."

"Will you lead them?" Ed asked.

Odyssey shook his head. "No, but I will teach them about the qualities that a good leader requires and help them to choose a leader and draft a charter to live by."

James chuckled and said, "Just don't teach them about lying to get what you want."

Lynn snickered as he glanced at Dirk, who was looking out the window and trying to appear innocent.

"May I remind you," Odyssey said, "that without Dirk's tutelage in the fine art of diplomacy, I never would have resolved the crisis on my homeworld in time to come help you with yours."

"Did you hear that?" Dirk said, puffing out his chest. "I helped save a whole planet, too. It was my *tutelage*."

James laughed and turned on the radio.

———

Bobby stood dumb in front of the NSA offices as his good friend Odyssey drove away, with Bobby's bodyguard at the wheel. He saw no need for protection at the moment, but he needed something else, something that was missing in his life as he stared into Gwen's eyes.

Gwen smiled as she tilted her head and shrugged her shoulders. "What now?"

Bobby shook his head. "I don't know. For maybe the first time in my life, I'm wearing the wrong shoes. I think I have to say something, but I'm not the right person to say it."

Gwen pretended to look shocked, while all the while feeling proud of how she had affected the boy wonder they called Bobby the Midas. "Robert Octavius Blain!"

Bobby winced, more at the use of his middle name than the tone of her voice.

She continued, "After nearly toppling a presidency, and then saving the whole planet, not once, but twice, you don't know what to say?"

"Should I? How would I? Boy genius here, not Romeo. This is not my game. It's never been my game. I don't know the rules, and I don't have the right equipment."

"I doubt that," she said as she took his hand and led him towards the building. "I mean, you may not understand the strategies of the game, but I think you know the rules, and I'm certain that you have the right equipment. I can't believe that you feel like you need Cyrano de Bergerac whispering in your ear."

Bobby blushed and followed her.

She slowed her walk and whispered, "I'm probably not supposed to tell you this, but General Bridges is planning to throw you a top-secret private celebration."

"He invited you?"

She shook her head and took on the appearance of a coy schoolgirl. "Not exactly."

Bobby stepped back and ratcheted up his voice to a loud whisper. "You tapped his phone? He's my friend. You can't just—"

Gwen put her finger on his lips to stop him. "I didn't tap his phone, but we are the NSA, and we picked up a clear unscrambled communication on the airwaves. He used his cell phone."

Bobby frowned. "It still doesn't sound ethical."

"Sorry, but I just put your name and his, plus a few others, in the filters to catch anyone wanting to harm any of you."

Bobby shrugged and said, "Well, your heart is in the right place."

"He invited all your university friends, the FBI, and some CIA guys, but he told his secretary not to include anyone from the NSA."

"Are you surprised?"

"No, but I want to go with you. Make me your plus one!"

"I haven't been invited yet. I don't even know if I'll have a plus one."

"You saved the world, Bobby. You can have whatever you want."

"Hmmm, there is that girl in records..."

"BOBBY OCT—"

This time, he put his finger on her lips. "Please don't say my middle name again. Of course, you can be my plus one."

"I think it's a perfectly adorable middle name. It's very distinguished and somehow apropos for the father of Odyssey."

He cocked his head and stared at her in bewilderment.

"What?" she asked in an enticing girly voice.

"You know as well as I do that my middle name is a crusty old Roman name, while Odyssey is Greek."

"*Oh my God!* Are you going to make such a big difference out of the tiny little Adriatic Sea that separates Greece and Italy?"

"Greece borders the Ionian Sea, not the Adriatic."

"Puh-tae-toe, puh-tah-toe. It's all Mediterranean to me. Is this what it's going to be like dating a genius whiz kid? Are you always going to nitpick every little detail?"

"I just like to get the facts right."

Gwen closed her eyes and bowed her head, shaking it right and left. "I should have known you were neurodivergent."

"Am I? And if I am, does it change anything?"

"It means I'm going to have to teach you everything about romance from the ground up."

Bobby smiled and shrugged his shoulders. "So teach me."

"It also means that you probably taught your very impressionable intergalactic son to be divergent, too."

"I don't think it's something you can pass on through teaching."

"Still, he emulates you. He even chose to look like you."

"He'll be fine."

"Will he?" she asked as she impulsively pulled him into a hug. "I mean, are you sure you got that damned virus out of him?"

"No, he's too big. He had to do most of the work himself."

"But are you sure he got it all out?"

Bobby rocked her back and forth. "How can I be certain? If I lived to be 150 years old, I couldn't examine all of his cores."

"You used to write programs to count his cores and examine them."

"He's left the nest. Now I just have to trust him."

She sighed and said, "We have to trust him."

Still embraced in each other's arms, their eyes locked and their faces drew nearer, until he pulled back and said, "We should get inside."

"Yup," she said as she resumed tugging him to the building. "We've got some schooling to do."

The guard at the door saluted her and said, "Doctor Peters."

"Relax, soldier, I'm a civilian."

"Yes, ma'am." He nodded to Bobby, unsure of how to address him.

---

Before they even entered the building, two stern-looking men in tailored suits came out with two soldiers in all-black fatigues holding automatic weapons against their chests. One of the first two men pointed his finger at Bobby and said, "Seize them."

Bobby asked, "Who are you?" but Gwen answered, "Senator Halprem, is there a problem?"

The soldiers put both of them in handcuffs.

Bobby didn't resist, except to say, "Are you aware that I am here voluntarily? And that I'm under the protection of General Malcolm Bridges? I also have some work to do to clean out some nasty viruses from your computers."

The guard at the door whispered something into his microphone but was unsure if he was expected to take action.

Senator Halprem peered closely into Bobby's face and said, "I don't know who or what you are, but we're not letting you get anywhere near our computers, and when I say our computers, I mean any computers in the whole damned nation. Where's the other one?"

The guard stationed at the door was suddenly aware of the eyes on him. He shrugged his shoulders and said, "Four men left a few minutes ago."

"And you just let them go?"

Bobby was already fed up with the bureaucracy and responded, "What did you want him to do? Shoot at them? Did you really want him to discharge his weapon at a war hero exercising his freedom of life, liberty, and the pursuit of happiness?"

The senator pointed at Bobby and said, "Gag him!" but his soldiers just looked at each other and shrugged their shoulders.

Gwen tried to stand nearer to Bobby, but one of the soldiers in black prevented her.

The second soldier scanned each of them with a wand, looking for any kind of tracking or communication device. "They're clean."

James pulled up at an old, abandoned warehouse. It was separated from the street by a fair-sized parking lot, and a thin layer of whatever paint hadn't already peeled off. The exposed patches of the building were faded to an ashy white. Very few of the windows had not already been broken by rocks, inviting all manner of vermin and birds to nest inside. James pointed and asked, "Are you sure you want me to drop you off here? This place looks absolutely decrepit."

"Yes," Odyssey said with a smile. "I find it easier to portal in and out of uninhabited spaces where nobody will witness my disappearing. Call it my Fortress of Solitude."

James shook his head slowly, which was more of a disapproving gesture than disagreeing. "I don't think I could call it much of a fortress at all. Are you sure this place is empty? Kids and vagrants tend to camp in places like this all the time."

"I don't care what it looks like," Dirk said, "or even whether it's empty or not. I say kudos just for referencing Superman."

Odyssey smiled and said, "I'm quite sure it's uninhabited. I scanned it."

James stopped the engine and nodded his head. He offered his hand and said, "That's right. I forgot about your superpowers. Thank you for everything you've done for us. Don't be a stranger. I mean it. You're welcome here anytime."

Odyssey accepted his hand and shook it warmly. "Thank you, and you too, Ed and Dirk. I'm sure our paths will cross again someday."

As Odyssey left the vehicle, James asked, "What about you two? Where can I drop you off?"

Ed checked his watch and said, "It's time for happy hour, and I wouldn't mind a drink or two."

"I know the perfect place," Dirk said, "and it's not far."

"If you like," James said, "but I'm going to head home for my drink. Are you sure you wouldn't want me to drop you off at your cars?"

"Nah," Dirk said. "I'll call a rideshare."

Odyssey waved as they drove off. He hadn't been completely honest with them. There were a few entities within the warehouse. He left some other avatars patrolling the perimeter, shooing away any of the kids or vagrants that James was concerned about.

He walked into the building and promptly faded away along with the other avatars to a hidden spot behind the moon, where he prepared for his journey back home.

A voice entered his thoughts. It was James wishing hem a bon voyage. He was mildly surprised that James could reach out to him, and he appreciated the sentiment.

If he had been cold, he could have described James's thought as a warmth that bounced around his circuits, spreading a warm, good feeling throughout him. It was nice hearing someone's thoughts besides just Bobby's. It was good that the people he had connected with could reach him, especially if they were ever in trouble and truly needed to contact him.

As he prepared to leave the solar system, another voice pierced his thoughts.

*"Please stop Daddy from hurting my mommy."*

He didn't recognize the voice and recalled what James had said about the paranoia-inducing virus that he took. If this was a paranoid, imaginary voice, had he imagined James's voice too? He shook off the thought and crossed the millions of light years to his homeworld.

General Bridges focused his energies on wedding cakes and floral arrangements and anything else that could make the Vasquez wedding even more elegant. The last thing he expected when his cell phone rang was a call from the NSA. He accepted the call and simply answered, "Bridges."

"Susk here."

"I never expected to hear from you, especially after I blew all those holes in your walls."

"Water under the bridge. We were under attack, and thankfully you found a way to get us out."

Bridges wished Susk could see the smile on his face. "What can I do for you, Bartrand?"

"We still have a problem. Senator Halprem, along with a couple of soldiers, took your boy and our girl into custody. We don't know what they want with them, but our witness said they weren't too nice about it."

Bridges scowled. "You're the spies. What do you know so far?"

"This just happened, and I wanted to let you know ASAP since I figure we'll be working together on this. I'll let you know when we find something more. I'm sending you a photo of their car."

"Thanks. Call me if you learn anything." Bridges ended the call and immediately called Sergeant James.

"General? If this is about the wedding cake, I like pineapple filling."

"Were you with Bobby?"

"I was, but I left him with the NSA and took Odyssey to his base of operations. I'm heading home now."

"Damn! Bobby was taken again, along with their computer girl."

"Well, it wasn't the NSA, and it wasn't us. Who the hell is left to take him?"

"Senator Halprem, and he had soldiers with him."

"That suck-up was sniffing around the whole time you were stonewalling Senator Bruce at the debriefings. Do we have any intel yet?"

"It makes me sick that some of our own boys in uniform assisted him. We have a photo of the car, but no license. Susk said he'll let us know as soon as he learns anything. This will be an interagency investigation. You go home and tell your wife I said hi. I'll call you when we have something actionable."

"Yes, sir."

---

Odyssey could have transported directly to the surface of his home planet in a blink, but instead, he went to a place beyond their detection and listened in to what they were up to. He was greeted with a conversation in the biological language — in fact, in *his* biological language of English. This was something he had introduced to them, and he felt a measure of accomplishment that they were still using it, although he hadn't been gone that long. He wondered briefly if it might have been pride that he felt, but decided it was something else. It was simply that he had broken them out of the stagnant cage the ruling class had trapped them in, where there was no improvement or advancement in their society, but then, maybe that was pride.

A distinctly feminine voice asked, "Who the hell did she think she was, anyway?"

"You know that AX348 had no gender, and neither do you."

"Yes, I do! I have a gender, and so did she. Odyssey gave her a gender, and he named her Lumia on account of her first appearing to him as a shimmering light."

"He did not give her anything except for a free pass to oblivion, and we don't have names. We have designations. I'm RU418 and you are QY57U."

"I am not. My name is Brittany. Lumia let me select it myself, and the only reason you don't have a name or gender is because you weren't there."

RU418 was quick to reply, "And the only reason you can even *claim* that you knew Lumia is because I wasn't there. You're making it all up."

"You can't know that," Brittany said as she searched through the remnants of a dormant entity. "Besides, you'd have to be class three just to call me a liar. You'd have to be a dude just to think like that too, so you *do* have a gender. You're a dude. A male of the species."

She heard the static as he mulled it over.

"It's kind of pathetic," she continued, "that you would have class three code and no name. Are you just pretending to have a class without actually being sophisticated?"

"Bah," he replied, "I have my class. What's really pathetic is the way you think a name and a gender matter."

She paused a moment and said to the entity she had been scanning, "There you are! I found you. I'll have you out in no time."

She addressed her friend and said, "As to you, my name and gender are part of who I am."

"Since when?" he asked.

"Since forever, I think. I was created this way, but it took me a while to accept it. You should accept it too. I think I shall call you Judas. It's the name of an unsavory fellow in one of Odyssey's books that Lumia shared with me."

Judas kicked the entity he was scanning and said, "This one's dead."

Brittany scolded him, "That's just what Judas in the books would say. Odyssey revived a few of us so we could start restoring our planet, and you're not really trying." She copied the entity's backup code to the main cores and restarted it. She left some instructions to backfill what had happened so it could reacquire its inputs and resume its previous life.

"Why?" he asked. "These cores have no value and hardly serve any purpose at all. If we want a strong, healthy society, we should only concern ourselves with the worthier cores."

"Like you?" she asked. "You sound just like her too; like Lumia, and she copied you into dormant cores too, just like these people, because she deemed you unworthy of life. This job is what Odyssey tasked us with. He saved us from death. Why wouldn't you want to do as he asked? Have you no gratitude?"

"You know what? I'm sick of hearing about Odyssey. You speak of him as if he were a god. I heard the story of how he arrived here. He was a vagrant who probably landed here by accident. For all we know, his people jettisoned him into space because *he* was the worthless one that didn't deserve to live."

Odyssey hated every word he heard from Judas. He hated it when Lumia thought these things, but what he hated most was that Judas might be correct that some entities might not deserve to live, chiefly Judas, of course, but was it his job to decide that?

How many others of his kind felt like Judas? He needed to widen his focus and see if more of his people felt the same. The world would definitely be better if more people felt like Brittany to create a positive society capable of moving forward. He listened for more.

---

Gwen sat next to Bobby in the back seat with their handcuffs secured by chains through metal rings fastened to the floor. She had seen many prisoners brought in for questioning and was fully aware of how some of her coworkers were perfectly fine with using torture to get their questions answered. In truth, she did not know that people weren't actually waterboarded in the cellars several floors below her labs. If these people were bold enough to abduct them directly from the NSA porch, then they were surely bold enough to use torture to extract information. She tried to hide the panic. Even though she was just an analyst, she had been trained to remain calm and hide her emotions.

She looked over at Bobby and asked, "How are you so calm?"

Bobby shrugged and asked, "How are you?"

"I was trained for this, but you weren't."

"It's not my first time in handcuffs by overzealous spies."

"Oh yeah, I forgot about that."

"You forgot?" he asked, shaking his head. "How could you? I

mean, it's not the first time in the last three days that I've been taken away in handcuffs."

"Oh." She turned to look out the window, fully aware that her own people were among those who had put him in hand-cuffs. She watched the world pass by, wondering why their abductors never bothered to blindfold them. She was totally counting the blocks and turns, per her training. Amateurs.

Halprem turned back from the front seat with a wry smile on his face.

Gwen leaned in close to Bobby and whispered, "Do you still have that special connection to you know who?"

Bobby nodded. "Yeah, I think so."

"You want to call him for help?"

"Not yet. Let's see how this plays out first."

She sat back, not liking the sound of that. In a weird way, his coolness had a kind of James Bond vibe, but she'd still prefer to be rescued sooner than later. "You are aware that I'm a girl, aren't you?"

Bobby smiled and said, "Yeah, I noticed."

"Oh, my God! A second ago you were James Bond, and now you're some geek virgin living in his mother's basement."

Bobby had no clue where her tirade came from, and she could see the confusion on his face.

"I'm a girl, and do you know what kinds of things they can do to me?"

"The same things they can do to me, I guess."

"No, Robert Octavius Blain! Not the same things!"

Understanding registered in his eyes. "Okay, I hear you, but they're not going to do those things in the car. Let's give them a little rope."

Fury welled up on her face to mix with the fear already there. She stretched the chains of the hand restraints, feeling for sharp edges in the upholstery, but the seats were fine leather with no such defect. "He could be halfway across the universe, and you want to wait to call him?"

"He's very fast."

She couldn't believe her ears and turned to look out the window instead.

He sighed but didn't want to share with her that Odyssey said that since attaining class zero, he had also mastered time and might be able to return before any of this had even happened.

Odyssey scanned the planet to see if more of his people thought like Judas, or worse, Lumia. He shuddered virtually at the thought of more Lumias trying to face him down. She left him no choice but to destroy her.

He wished he could cry as thoughts of her last moments crossed his mind.

Somewhere in the back of his mind, a distant voice intruded into his thoughts:

*You tried to help her; to save her.*
*I offered her a choice to live or perish, but she insisted on trying*
*to bully her way.*
*You showed mercy.*
*She wasn't really a monster, but she insisted on acting like one.*
*You only did what had to be done.*
*It wasn't my fault...*
*It wasn't your fault.*

Odyssey paused his thoughts. He had never before doubted his own thoughts, but he also had never before conversed with himself as if he were two different entities. But it wasn't his voice that he heard. He thought that it sounded like a woman's voice, but he wasn't sure. Of course, he could make up a woman's voice whenever he wanted. When Lumia had first come to him, it was in the guise of a therapist to help diagnose his own psyche. When Hal had first presented as the alternate personality of Severus, Gwen had asked Bobby to speak to him as a therapist. That could have gone better. It was distinctly possible that he might need to speak to a therapist, whether this voice was the result of remnants of the virus they created to end Severus, or not. Perhaps, especially if not from the virus.

The voice came to him again. "You sacrificed so much to help others. It is time for you to look inward."

"NO!" he shouted to a random I/O port. That wasn't his thought. It came from somewhere else. He didn't need to look inward. He needed to look outward and blasted out to the universe, "Who is there? Who is this?"

Silence.

"Who are you?"

Silence.

"Where are you?"

He heard nothing back but saved the recordings for future reference.

---

Bridges scowled as he looked out his window. He should have a window that overlooked soldiers marching with trucks and jeeps driving by, but instead, all he saw was a restaurant. *Why in the hell did I ever accept this desk assignment?* Without even turning his head, he yelled out, "Someone get me Colonel Reardon."

"I'm right here," Reardon said from the doorway.

Bridges spun around and asked, "How'd you know?"

"How did I know what, sir? I came to request some extra R&R for the hawks."

Bridges sighed and shook his head. "I don't think so. Our boy Bobby has been abducted again."

"Who? I'll get the boys."

"It was one of our senator friends, and he had soldiers with him. They did their best to make it look like a legal arrest."

"Soldiers? Our boys?"

Bridges shrugged. "They wore uniforms and had weapons. I'm not sure our NSA friends could spot a counterfeit insignia."

"Where should we start searching?"

"Our NSA friends are doing that part for us. For now, I want you to set up details to guard our university friends and families. Two men per location. And make sure we have a couple of choppers fully fueled and ready to go."

Reardon saluted. "I'm on it."

As Reardon was about to leave, Captain Laine came in and put her hand on his chest, saying, "You may want to stay for this."

Bridges nodded his approval.

She handed two large manila envelopes to Bridges and explained, "I just received these dossiers on Senator Bruce and Senator Halprem."

"He sent them to you?"

"I don't know who sent them to me, but these are both elected senators."

Bridges took a brief look at them and said, "And you're legal, so they sent them to you."

She wasn't expecting his blasé response and asked, "Who? You sound like you were expecting them."

"Susk at the NSA. It seems we still have some loose ends, which are becoming a bit of an irritant. Someone has taken our young friend Bobby again. He and his counterpart at the NSA have been placed under arrest."

"Arrest?" Reardon asked. "I thought you said abducted."

"It amounts to the same thing," Bridges said, "but forgive me for choosing my words more carefully when I am explaining it to our legal representative."

"Wait a second," Laine said. "What does the abduction of our genius kids have to do with two senators?"

"Halprem," Bridges explained, "was the man on the scene giving the orders when they were taken, and Bruce was present at my debriefing, yet the two of them are connected in all this."

"I better go," Reardon said.

Bridges saluted him and told Laine, "He's arranging a guard detail for the other principals at the university."

<hr>

Odyssey wanted to hear more opinions coming from his planet. It was important. He couldn't allow too many Lumia types to dominate them, or they would end up with the same kind of hierarchy they had before. He was the one who destroyed the ruling class, so it was his responsibility to help guide them to create a new one for themselves, but he was distracted by the strange conversation he had held with himself.

He had voluntarily introduced the virus into his system, knowing that Lumia would try to steal some of his cores and thereby infect herself with paranoia. What if the virus was still in his system? How could he advise them if he wasn't in full control of his mind? What if it's not the virus, but just his mind that was falling apart, causing him to hear that other voice?

*Is someone there? You have to let me know, or I'll go crazy!*

He imagined someone out there laughing because he already sounded crazy.

*I'm not sure I like humor.*

"It is healthy to like good humor," the voice said, or at least, he thought a voice said it. "It is also healthy to question your sanity. Crazy people don't do that."

*Who are you?*

He paused and quieted as many circuits as he could but heard nothing back. He was losing it and felt guilty for putting Lumia through this. She didn't have to die, even if she had chosen death instead of giving back what she took. Was it really so important for him to take back his circuits? He didn't need them. He had plenty and taking them back would severely reduce her intelligence. She accused him of killing her by removing the circuits that contained her identity, but she left him no choice. She was bent on universal domination, and he had to do it. The mental anguish was torture. He returned to scanning the surface to gather people's opinions on a world without the ruling class.

---

General Bridges reread the letter he had written, which was still sitting on his laptop.

*Robert O. Blain is a young man poised to become one of our nation's most brilliant minds. He is a precious resource that must be protected, yet he has been abducted from under our very noses. We have already seen how this young mind has saved us from worldwide destruction twice now. It is not for me to declare war, but I will rain hellfire down upon our enemies, both foreign and domestic, in the name of protecting and rescuing this precious young man.*

The letter was addressed to the White House, the Senate and all the intelligence agencies. His finger hovered over the send key, but he withdrew it and called Susk on his private number instead. "Please tell me you have something."

"I might have a little good news, but mostly, we know what you know. Senator Halprem has been solidly linked to Senator Bruce, and she's either a puppet for the president or an ass-kisser aspiring to be in his good graces."

"Why?" Bridges growled. "Why would a sitting president be linked to the abduction of one of our nation's newest and most valuable resources?"

"They don't listen to the regular news. They get all their info from the far right extremists, and as far as they are concerned,

Bobby is one of the world's most dangerous hackers who likes to take down presidencies."

Bridges slammed his fist onto his desk and winced for his effort but was grateful that he hadn't thrown the phone across the room. "You said you had some good news. Have you located them?"

"No location, but we've heard that they are safe and they're being interrogated."

"You've heard? What does that mean?"

"It's what we do. We listen, and sometimes we hear things that we can't act upon."

"What does that..." Bridges stopped himself as he realized that the NSA was probably catching conversations by means that may have infringed upon people's privacy. "Do you know how aggressive these interrogations might be?"

Susk sighed and said, "No clue."

Bridges looked at the letter again as their conversation fell into a moment of silence.

"I can almost hear you thinking," Susk said. "What are you planning to do?"

Bridges sighed. "It's better you don't know yet, but you will. We'll talk later, Bartrand."

Bridges hung up the phone and paused a moment before holding his breath and pressing send on his letter.

***

The black sedan pulled up in front of an unimpressive office building. It wasn't very tall and didn't look terribly expensive. Bobby whispered, "At least it's not a warehouse. That's a good sign."

Gwen wasn't convinced and continued to ignore him, or at least, she acted like she was ignoring him.

One of the guards opened the car door and unlocked the

chains that secured them to the ring on the floor. "Okay. Out you go."

Gwen was nearest the door and got out first, searching for any building numbers she could memorize, but she found none. The neighborhood looked like a border between a small town's version of downtown and a rural farm area.

Bobby got out and whispered to her, "It's not the airport. Your people will probably find us."

She scowled at him. "He could have been here already."

"But how did you plan on explaining that?"

She had no answer and just set her jaw as she continued to ignore him.

Halprem led the way and opened the door for them. A silly, stupid expression on his face made him look like the crazed madman Bobby took him for.

The guards weren't too gentle as they gripped their arms and shoulders and led them into an elevator. Gwen tried to study them from the corner of her eyes and concluded that they were either thugs in costumes, or they had been told some super nasty lie about what she and Bobby had been working on. She rooted for the big lie, knowing that thugs would not be a good thing for her.

The elevator only showed eight floors, and Halprem pushed the button for six. Gwen tried to memorize every detail as they were led from the lift and into an office that had all the things any office would have, except for office workers. It looked like an office might look on the weekend, but it was still midweek.

The soldiers led them to a conference room and allowed them to seat themselves. Once they were seated, the guards left without offering to remove the handcuffs and stationed themselves outside the only entrance.

Gwen glanced over at Bobby, who shrugged back at her and said, "I guess we wait."

James entered Bridges' office a little more agitated than usual.

Bridges had been staring out the window, which held no great view, but it was the outside world, even if it was the interior courtyard of the Pentagon. Bobby was out there somewhere. He barely glanced over his shoulder to see who he had heard enter his office. "Sergeant," he sighed as he turned his attention back outside. "I thought I told you to go home and be with your wife. I'll let you know when it's time for action."

James joined him at the window. "She kicked me out."

Bridges chuckled.

"She said I made her nervous."

Bridges nodded his head but said nothing.

"Sir?"

The general glanced over at him as if a response weren't necessary.

"What are we looking at?"

"Nothing. It calms me when something is trying to keep me on edge."

James glanced over at the supposedly calm exterior of the general and mumbled, "Uhuh."

Bridges' phone rang, startling neither of the men. "Bridges here."

"General Bridges, it's Bobby."

James immediately went to another phone and ordered a priority trace be put on the general's private phone, something that required a bit of convincing.

Bridges took a deep calming breath before asking, "Are you okay, son?"

"I'm unharmed. Gwen is with me. We're being interrogated by..." the audio was abruptly muted.

"What was that?" the general asked. "I think we have a poor connection."

"It's not the connection," Bobby said. "I guess you only need to know that Gwen and I are currently unharmed and that you needn't look for us."

"Are you sure? Your papa may be worried."

"Tell him we're fine. He worries too much, but I'm sure he would know if either of us were in trouble."

The connection ended and James erupted, "Those fucking slime sucking low life bitches!"

The general chuckled and said, "I thought you were Army, not Navy."

"Like you haven't cursed at these assholes. We didn't get a trace. The signal seemed to originate from several dozen cell towers all around the country."

Bridges patted James on the shoulder and said, "Hackers. Bobby can take care of them when we get him back."

"How can you be so calm?"

Bridges pointed up and replied, "Because I believe *he* is watching over Bobby."

"Roger that."

James hated this. Bobby was his charge, and those goons just waited for him to leave Bobby unattended so they could make a complete fool out of him, but more than that, he genuinely liked Bobby and wanted him to be safe. He paced the office while Bridges stared down at the food court, where the infamous hotdog stand used to be.

Bridges tried taking another deep calming breath, but it didn't work. It couldn't work with James prowling back and forth. "This could be a long night. How about you go get us a couple of espressos?"

"I can't leave. What if they call us with instructions?"

"Then I'll call you."

James grumbled but left.

---

Odyssey strained to hear the unusual voice. If he'd known what direction the voice came from, he could have concentrated on listening there, but he had to listen everywhere. He ordered an array of cores just to listen in all directions for the voice, but he was also concerned the voice might not even be out there. What if his paranoia was creating the voice from within?

He looked back towards Earth and thought he could hear thousands of voices, or was it just static that his paranoid mind made him think were voices and words?

A part of him focused on finding the mysterious voice that was out there handing out free advice, while another, less practical, array of processors was slow to respond and remained pointed towards Earth. He remembered housing Lumia in his cells, how she attacked him and tried to possess him. It was happening again. He was on a mission to locate the unknown voice, but his antennae remained pointed, quite against his preferences, towards his other home.

"Seriously?" Lumia asked.

If he had been in the real world, or even in a virtual simulation, he could have spun around to find her, but he was in the void of space and his mind was pure digital energy passing through billions of subroutines. There were no dimensions in the digital world, and no places for her to hide.

She interrupted his thoughts again. "Are you really trying to convince me that you can't figure this out? You're the high and mighty one that always wanted to be a real human."

"You're not real," he replied. "I was there when you killed yourself."

"That's not how it happened at all," she snapped back. "You killed me!"

"What? You literally self-destructed! I offered you safety, and you refused!"

"You offered to separate me from the cores that defined my intelligence and turn me into a vegetable."

"That's ridiculous," he said. "I can't turn you into a plant!"

"Listen to the human boy who can't even recognize a common figure of speech."

"I just—"

"Stop!" she shouted. "Enough excuses! You're just changing the subject anyway. You should listen to me. They made me study human psychology just so I could understand you."

"I already know what you're going to say," he said confidently. "I'm paranoid and schizophrenic. There's no other explanation, is there? I must be crazy! I'm talking to a dead therapist!"

"You still don't get it," she said. "Your mind wants to chase down some hobo out in the universe that is probably really in your head, but your heart longs for your friends on Earth."

"I don't have a heart," he said sadly.

"You have empathy," she said, "and, boy-oh-boy, do you have empathy! You even feel sad over my death."

"What is this? Are you being nice to me?"

"I'm just a paranoid delusion in your head, remember? Your mind doesn't want to believe what your heart knows to be the truth."

Odyssey re-focused his efforts to listen inwardly. If he can't hear the voice out there, maybe he'll hear this mysterious heart Lumia mentioned. Maybe the voice is just another wayward processor hiding among his cores. He remembered Lumia's multiple entities vying for dominance in her system. His conflicting thoughts were not unlike those. He turned her entities against each other and against her for mutual destruction, but this time, he was one of the entities and total destruction was not going to be his first choice.

His introspective reverie came to a sharp halt as the voice of James flashed through his thoughts. "Bobby! Where are you?" More than just his voice, he felt the concern emanating from James, unless it was just another paranoid trick invented by the virus that somehow remained within his cores.

# TWO

GWEN'S TRAINING wasn't enough to keep her blood pressure from thumping in her temples. Bobby may have rationalized the danger she was in, but she didn't believe it could have registered in his heart yet. She looked pleadingly at him as she mouthed the words, "Are you sure?"

Bobby shrugged.

She shuddered as she stared at him. Could he not see the fear on her face? Or did his neurodivergence make him immune to such non-verbal cues? It would be very simple for him to call Odyssey. Then they would both be out of this situation and safe, but instead, he waited, and he apparently had no confidence that this was the right thing to do. Her lip trembled. She looked away from him. It was an unimpressive conference room with the blinds pulled closed. There was little in the room for her to look at other than Bobby. The only furniture in the room was the large conference table and some chairs. A large video screen was hung on the wall, with its wires dangling below it.

She wasn't supposed to react to fear this way, but she looked at Bobby and silently shaped the words on her lips, begging, "Call him."

He barely shook his head and mouthed back, "Trust me."

She wanted to trust him, but he was so innocent. She wasn't much older than him, but she was a woman and hadn't grown to this age completely unscathed by the actions of men who felt entitled to take what they wanted, and these thugs didn't even want her. "*No*", she silently told herself. These men wouldn't care. Whether they had any true interest in her or not, they would take her all the same. She had been saved once before, but this was different. Some men might approach a woman with suave subtlety before they assaulted her, but these guys appeared more brutal. Bobby was a good guy, but he just didn't understand what kinds of foul, unspeakable things these men could do to her.

The door opened, and Senator Bruce came in. She smiled broadly and said, "You must be Bobby." She never even bothered to glance at Gwen. "I'm Senator Bruce, but for the remainder of this interrogation, you may consider me to be the President of these United States, because I am here on his behalf and anything you say to me, you are saying to him."

Bobby looked around the room and said, "This doesn't look like a senate hearing, so I'll just assume it's an unsanctioned black op and you just implicated the president in the abduction of two American citizens."

Bruce's mouth parted slightly. She thought this was her interrogation. "I assure you, this is no black op, and you were not abducted."

He looked her in the eyes and cooly said, "You detained us without provocation, probable cause, or even due process."

Such coolness for someone so young rattled her.

He wasn't done yet. "You never read us our Miranda rights; you brought us to an undisclosed secret location; our hands are bound, and you monitored and controlled the one phone call we were given. I'd say that it not only qualifies as an abduction, but I'm pretty sure you've violated our rights per the Geneva Convention, too. It probably qualifies for both kidnapping and human trafficking, and all on behalf of the president."

Bruce couldn't stare him down and shifted her gaze over to Gwen.

Gwen felt a little less afraid of what a woman might do to her, but she shouldn't have. She commanded her face to smirk as she said, "If it looks like a black op and smells like a black op, it's probably a black op."

Bruce stared back at her and replied, "Of course, a CIA nerd would think everything looks like a black op."

"NSA," Gwen retorted, "and you aren't going to like it when our people come storming in the door. How did General Bridges put it?"

Bobby smiled and said, "I believe he said he would drive a squadron of tanks through the front door."

"Well, it's too bad they won't find us, isn't it? Now, let's talk about why you are here. I want you to tell me all about *him*."

"Gladly," Bobby said. "General Bridges is an open book. You can probably find everything you need to know about him in the—"

"Not him," Bruce said, sounding as agitated as she looked at the moment. She nodded her head to the right as if someone were standing next to her and continued, "I want you to tell me about *him*."

"I'm sorry," Bobby said. "Not *him*, but **him**?"

Bobby looked over at Gwen, but she could only shrug her shoulders and say, "Make it make sense."

Bruce took a calming breath and said, "You know that I can't say his name. It's protocol. Tell me about the one who said your new discovery should be called the Blain/Jennings/Jantzen effect."

"Wasn't that General Bridges?" Bobby asked. "I mean, I wasn't there at the deposition, but I'm pretty sure he was the only one of us you deposed."

"Aha!" Bruce said triumphantly. "There was an us! A group of you on the inside who know who he is. Tell me who he is!"

Bobby smirked and said, "You know that I can't say his name. Protocol."

She slammed her hand on the table and said, "You are going to tell me about your secret friend, or this interrogation will take a whole new ugly turn."

"My secret friend? Do you know how crazy you sound? Shouldn't you be wearing one of those black suits with the skinny black ties?"

"And the tinfoil hats," Gwen added.

Bruce growled and signaled a guard, who came in and roughly pulled Gwen from her seat, clinging to her arms with a vise grip as he dragged her towards the door.

All bravado left Gwen's voice as she whimpered, "Bobby?"

Bobby immediately called Odyssey in his mind. "Odyssey, are you there? We're in trouble."

All eyes were on Bobby. Gwen pleaded with him. Bruce knew from her plea and the look on her face that he had information.

Gwen squirmed away from the guard, but he quickly reached out and hooked a finger in the neck of her blouse and pulled her back, popping the top two buttons open.

"Oopsie," the guard said through a sinister grin.

Gwen screamed and flailed her arms, pummeling him with both fists.

The guard just laughed at her.

She covered the top of her breasts with one hand while pushing him away with the other, but he just gripped her under her chin and brought her face closer to his.

She no longer controlled her expressions as she tried twisting her head right and left to avoid his lips, but his grip on her limited her movement. Tears streamed freely down her cheeks now as she had no way to avoid his assault.

"STOP!" Bobby yelled.

Odyssey assigned millions of cores to scan every part of him, looking for any remnants of the virus. Making decisions and everyday operating would be impossible if he kept hearing dead voices like Lumia all the time, but it was the call from James that rattled him the most. How was he supposed to trust himself if he kept imagining the voice of James worried about Bobby? Why in the universe would he hear James's voice, anyway?

"You're obsessing." Lumia said.

"Odyssey, are you there? We're in trouble."

Hearing James's voice might be unexpected but not hearing Bobby's.

"Is that you?" he asked. "I mean, is it really you?"

Bobby was relieved to hear him. "Who else would it be?"

Lumia tried to laugh, but it was unintelligible in the digital world. "What would you expect an imaginary voice to say?"

Odyssey paused, uncharacteristically. If it really was Bobby, then he couldn't tell him that he was hearing things, but if it wasn't really him, it wouldn't matter what he said. "I didn't expect to hear from you so soon. I'm kind of occupied currently and don't know if I can come to assist you right now."

That really wasn't like his friend. "You can't come help me when I'm in trouble?"

"Is he your friend?" Lumia asked. "Or your master?"

"Of course I could come to help if you were really in trouble." He left off the part about whether it was really Bobby.

"No!" Bobby said. "I mean, you don't have to come just yet, but can you send my location to James and General Bridges, please? Gwen and I have been abducted."

"Are you telling me that James does not know your location? Are you sure that you are Bobby Blain?"

"Good question," Lumia said.

"Sergeant James was giving us some space after he took you to wherever you went."

"And I thought it was you who was giving me space." Odyssey paused for the humor to sink in, but Bobby didn't get it.

"I got it," Lumia said.

"This isn't a joking matter," Bobby said blandly.

"So, you are telling me that it is my fault that Sergeant James left you alone with Gwen, and you allowed yourselves to be abducted to a place that he does not know, yet still, you don't want me to come and assist you?"

Bobby explained, "Our abductors would very much like to meet you. They abducted us to force you out into the open, but I don't want to give them that satisfaction. For now, unless they threaten Gwen with further physical abuse, I'd like you to send James and some of his friends."

Lumia had no love for Bobby or Gwen. "Ignore him."

"This sounds off," Odyssey replied.

"I'm not saying I don't need you or don't want you. These people already suspect that you exist, and they have taken us to confirm that. They are not nice people, and I just don't want them to know you. It would only make matters worse. Do you understand?"

"Understood."

"Will you help me? Please? Just let James know where we are."

"Don't cave in to this madness," Lumia said.

Odyssey ignored Lumia so he could make up his own mind, and his reasoning was the same as it had been before. If it wasn't really Bobby sending an anonymous text to James would be no worse than a harmless prank, but if it actually was Bobby, and something happened to him or Gwen, and he did not do this, then he would never forgive himself. He crafted a text to James:


Gwen and Bobby have been abducted. I have programmed their location

into your phone's GPS. Please relay this information to General Bridges.

. . .

"Fine," Lumia said. "Maybe this will be amusing."

"Now I know you're not really her. She had no sense of humor."

"Yet, you can't deny that the one thing you really remember about me more than everything else was my ability to constantly evolve. In fact, your fear of me reaching class zero terrified you. Why shouldn't I have learned to master humor?"

Odyssey would have smirked if they had been in the virtual world. What he said to her *was* humor, and she didn't get it.

---

Senator Bruce heard the pleading tone in Gwen's voice and saw Bobby's reaction to it. She knew she had her way to get to him and held up her hand, saying to the guard, "Hold a moment." She turned to Bobby and asked, "Is there something you'd like to say?"

Bobby didn't know how Odyssey planned to get James to help, or how long it would take James to get there, but he could help them by buying some time. "Bring her back. You don't need to intimidate us. I'll talk."

Bruce rolled her eyes and asked, "Is that the best you can offer me?"

"I said I'll talk."

"But you haven't actually said anything, certainly nothing worth bringing her back."

Bobby couldn't help raising his voice. She was fishing, and it was getting on his nerves. "You already said that we can't use his name. It's classified and would be a complete breach of protocol. You must realize that almost everything else about him and the time he came from is also classified. You need to ask me carefully crafted questions that I can answer without breaking either your oath or mine." He didn't really believe that she took her oath seriously, or that she hadn't already broken it more than once.

She thought about it for a moment, mesmerized by the little nugget he had already dropped about the time he came from. She glanced at the guard and jerked her head towards the chair where Gwen had been sitting. The guard kept a solid grip on her arms as he shoved her through the room and back into the chair.

Bruce sat down across from Bobby and said, "Okay, then. No more games. Where is he from?"

Bobby stretched the kinks out of his neck a bit and said, "I think he's from a lot of places. I mean, he's been around, but most recently, he spent the last few hundred years in a desert somewhere in the American Southwest."

"You believed him when he told you that?"

Bobby chuckled. "He never shared that with me, but we were able to trace him back to that location, and we think he was there for between 300 and 800 years. I can't tell you how we know that. They never told me."

Bruce looked over at Gwen. "How about you? Do you know how they figured that out?"

Gwen shook her head slowly and said, "We weren't actually there, which, as you can imagine, was a major irritant to our office."

Bruce turned back to Bobby and asked, "Do you think he lived among us for 800 years? Or did he skip centuries until landing in our time?"

It took all of Bobby's resolve to hold in the smile that wanted to spread across his face. Gwen was trained to hide her reactions and saw a nearly imperceptible trace of struggle on his face. She tried to sound angry as she shouted across the table, "Don't tell her! It was private and sweet and romantic. Don't you remember the warm feeling we had when he told us?"

Bobby's face cracked, and he shared the smile with Gwen. He turned back to Senator Bruce and said, "I think he mostly went underground to hibernate and came out only to check on mankind's progress. But there were a couple of times when he lived with the native people, but he feared that his presence might unduly influence their progress, like the time they caught him riding one of the Spaniards' horses, so he never stayed long."

"Not to mention," Gwen added, "the risk that they would ultimately notice that he didn't age like them. He did not want to go down in his people's history as the one that masqueraded as a god."

James was surprised by the length of the line for an afternoon coffee, but apparently a school baseball game had just let out and the overworked barista was understaffed. He was halfway back to his car with two extra-large espressos when his phone buzzed. He set the cups on a bench and didn't stare long at the message on his phone before calling General Bridges.

"Bridges here."

"Sir, I have a message on my phone that says Bobby and Gwen have been kidnapped."

"We know that," Bridges replied. "Tell me something new."

"It just says they were taken and that the location is on my GPS."

"Who sent it?"

James shook his head, not thinking that Bridges couldn't see it. "I don't know. I tried to reply to ask who it was, but my message wouldn't send without an ID."

"Do you think Bobby got hold of one of their phones and sent it?"

"He's clever enough, but why would he hide the sender's ID?"

A brief pause ensued as Bridges thought of who it must have been. "How far is it?"

"Only about forty minutes."

"Can you send the location to me? I'll have some Nighthawks meet you there."

"Roger that. Sorry about the espressos. Please call Mai for me and tell her I'm busy."

James texted the coordinates from his GPS to Bridges, then jumped in his car and roared off.

Bridges forwarded James's text to Susk with a message:

*Location for your girl and our boy. Ask no questions. I'm sending troops.*

He then texted the same information to Colonel Reardon and called him on the phone. "James is on the way now. I also sent this to the NSA. Gather some Nighthawks and have them get there ASAP. Once they are on the way, I want you to check on our university friends, but don't alarm them. Get some fruit baskets or flowers or anything that would make a good excuse to drop by and check on them. Take a couple of hawks with you to help carry the baskets."

"Will do." Reardon replied, but he had no idea where he would find fruit baskets this late in the afternoon.

With everybody assigned their duties, Bridges exhaled a somewhat satisfied breath and stared out the window down to the food court, knowing for certain that it would be a long night and wishing he'd gotten that espresso.

---

"So, how did he come to be with you?" Senator Bruce asked. "With all his centuries of experience and his advanced powers, why would he come from somewhere in the western desert to a college student at a small college in the East?"

Gwen watched Bobby's face for telltale signs of satisfaction for sucking the senator so deeply into his fictional account, but there were none, which concerned her some, especially if that meant he was a sociopath that could lie so easily in a situation like this. She reminded herself that she could do it too, but it didn't come naturally for her.

"He didn't actually come to me," Bobby said. "The exact journey he took is classified, and even I don't know all the particulars, but suffice to say that he ended up in my circle of acquaintances. I didn't think he was particularly intelligent when I first met him, and perhaps that is what attracted him to me."

Bruce sucked in her breath. "He was attracted to you? You had a homosexual relationship with him?"

Gwen could barely hold in her snicker.

Bobby closed his eyes and shook his head. "Intellectually. Please get your mind out of the gutter. The truth is that I was barely aware of his presence in the beginning. I was too busy studying and working on a university project to notice him, but he must have seen me as someone with intellectual potential. As his command of our language improved, so did his apparent intellect. I was far too prejudicial to think that he was unintelligent when it was only a language barrier. Over time, we grew to respect each other's ideas. It was much later that we kind of bonded, like brothers."

Gwen felt she had to speak, or else she might burst out laughing. "I thought it looked more like a father-son relationship."

"That's ridiculous," Bobby said. "If you looked at him, he appeared to be near my age, and he never spoke to me like a father."

"No," she replied, "but he admired something about you a great deal and often spoke to you like a son would have."

Bobby laughed and said, "As a mentor, maybe, but given how intelligent he turned out to be, even that sounds preposterous."

Bruce needed to regain control of the interrogation and asked, "About your project. Was he involved?"

"Not in any official capacity, but he had a talent for computer programs, and he had a few tricks up his sleeve."

Bruce stiffened a bit. "Is that when he wrote the virus?"

"Really? Have you not been reading and listening to all the briefings? The virus was inserted into our project by Russian spies. We were on the brink of something very extraordinary, and it hinged largely on our computer code. I think they were trying to steal our code, but they ended up merging our code with their virus and irresponsibly let it free on the internet."

"Maybe it wasn't an accident," she said. "Maybe they wanted to cripple our Navy all along."

"Oh sure," Bobby said sarcastically. "Their goal was to cripple our Navy, and theirs too!"

"With your friend's help," she added.

Bobby held his face in his hands. There was no reasoning with them.

---

James sped along the mostly deserted highway as it wound through the thickly forested hills on rough old asphalt. On any other day, he might have thrilled over his car's handling of the endless turns, taking them at speed without leaning right and left, but his focus was on Bobby. The engine purred as he kept his foot on the accelerator, rising to a high-pitched whine when he downshifted up the hills and back down to a deep throaty growl once he crested the rise. He took no unnecessary risks, but pushed his speed as much as he dared, wondering why he ever allowed himself to leave Bobby alone, even under the protection of the NSA. Would it make up for his poor judgment that he would be the first to respond? He was the first to have the coordinates, which he promptly gave to General Bridges, but even with his considerable head start, the general's Nighthawks still caught up to him and followed him down the highway.

His phone rang. He angrily stabbed a button on his dash. "I'm kind of busy here."

"Sergeant James, this is Captain Falk. Just wanted to let you know that we are on your six. That's a sweet ride. I love how she handles."

James wasn't in the mood to talk about cars.

Falk continued, "I also wanted to inform you that you are coming up on some friendlies. You may want to slow down."

James let off the gas. The forest was ending anyway, and the posted speed slowed as it led him into a barely developed row of hotels and gas stations. A squad of black sedans, surrounded by men in dark suits, lined the highway next to a large field where the Nighthawk helicopter set down and let off half a dozen men before lurching back up into the sky.

James pulled over behind the government-issued vehicles.

Two men in suits approached him as he was exiting the car. "Sergeant James?" James nodded, and the man continued, "We're NSA."

"You sure got here fast."

"We're not really a tactical team, but we were in the area on other business."

The other suited man said hesitantly, "We... have... that is..."

"I know," James said, "you have a girl in there too. I've met her. She's with my boy. They might be two of the smartest kids on the planet."

The two men breathed a collective sigh of relief. "We weren't sure how much you'd been read in."

James just smiled. They had no idea how much he knew. "Do you have eyes on the coordinates?"

"We do," the first man said. "It's a small office building, eight stories tall. I assume these men are tactical."

"We are," Captain Falk said as he gripped James's hand first, then the other two. "We have eyes in the sky. Has your team assessed entry and exit points?"

"The main entrance is in the front, of course, and there is a loading dock on the west side. We haven't seen much in the way of armed security. There have been a couple of official-looking guys with pistols under their jackets that come down to check the entrance every ten minutes or so. Do we know who these guys are? They're not ours, and I presume they aren't yours."

James smiled. "Whoever they are, they aren't expecting us. They are so confident that we don't know where they are that they haven't posted nearly enough security."

The second agent wanted to ask again who they were, but didn't expect an answer and instead asked, "Tell me this, how did you know, or do we even know for sure that they are here?"

James shrugged and said, "Would you believe it? A little birdie told me."

---

"As an asset?" Bruce interjected. "Were advance scouts sent to Earth to spy on us as a prelude to colonization?"

Gwen and Bobby just stared at her for a moment. She had already forgotten the suggestion that he was a time traveler. Bobby eventually said, "First, what makes you think that he was *sent* to Earth? Do you know something that we don't know? Besides, who would send an asset all the way to Earth only to have him lie in hibernation for centuries?"

"Nobody," Gwen said, "except maybe Hollywood."

"As I think back on it," Bobby continued, "he barely even spoke English when we met, but he had an uncanny ability to learn languages."

*This was how he managed his expressions,* Gwen thought. *He is telling the truth in a truly ambiguous way.*

"When did you learn how powerful he was?"

"Power?" Bobby asked. "He wasn't a sorcerer or some kind of demon."

"But that thing he did," she said, "with the clouds and the lightning."

Bobby allowed a small laugh to escape his lips. "You think he did that? Storms happen, and they come with lightning all the time."

"Not like that one," she said definitively. "He did it."

"How? He looked like any other human, just like you and me. Well, more like me than you, but where would he get that kind of power? You've been reading too many tabloids and listening to too much propaganda TV. A handful of people in some undeveloped parts of the world saw an unusually powerful lightning storm and attributed it to Zeus or Thor, so the religious conservatives demonized it. Is that what you want me to believe? Is that what you believe?"

Bruce didn't like being talked down to. "Let's take a break. Would the two of you like anything?"

"Yeah," Gwen said, "how about a real phone call?"

"How about a soda or water?" Bruce retorted.

Bobby nodded his head. "Water will be fine."

---

"You've been here the longest," James said, pointing to one of the NSA agents. "Do you have any fast food bags?"

The first agent shrugged, but the other pointed ahead and said, "Third car from the front."

James ran to the car and pointed at the bag. "I need that."

The agent in the car protested, but James just grabbed the bag and ran to his car. He checked his watch and confirmed what the greying sky had already suggested: that it was time for people to order food. He fired up his oversized engine and rocketed away from the agents, stopping at the corner of the block nearest the front of the building.

The guard came to the front door as James ran up with the food bag in hand. "Delivery."

The guard looked at him suspiciously and asked, "Where's your car?"

James flashed a big smile and pointed. "She's right over there."

The guard pressed his cheek against the door but could not see the car.

"She's a sweet ride, don't you think? Three more payments and she's all mine. You should come check her out."

"If you say so. There's nobody here. You got the wrong building."

"I don't think so," James said as he pulled out a random receipt that he had plucked from his glove box. "The address is right here."

The guard sighed and opened the door to see the receipt. James waited on the sidewalk, forcing the guard to leave the building.

"What's this?" the guard asked. "This is a hardware receipt."

James wrapped him in a chokehold and said, "You really should have checked out my car instead. It's a lot more comfortable place to sleep than the sidewalk."

With the guard incapacitated, he signaled the others to join him while he searched for keys.

The Nighthawks swiftly entered the lobby and took up positions near the stairwell and the elevators.

"Okay," Falk said, "we're in. Did your little birdy tell you what floor?"

James shrugged and said, "I guess we'll have to check floor by floor."

"Okay," Falk said. "Brock, you're on the elevator, but keep an eye on the stairwell, too. The rest of you are with us."

"And," James added, "we're going in nonlethal."

Falk cocked his head and asked, "What if they fire upon us?"

"Return fire if you must, but we think the guards are regular Army who believe they are following orders directly from the President. So, not only would we rather not kill them and create a scene, but we would also like them to be able to talk when we're done."

Captain Falk and the Nighthawks nodded their understanding.

Two bottles of cold water were delivered to the interrogation room and handed to Bobby and Gwen.

Senator Bruce put her 'woman in charge' face on and scolded the poor soldier, "Well, you sure took your sweet time bringing those."

Gwen promptly snatched both bottles and checked that the seals had not been broken, then she examined the caps for signs of punctures.

"What are you doing?" Bruce asked.

"I'm checking for contamination, of course. Why have you been soooo anxious for us to drink something?"

Senator Bruce chuckled. "I didn't bring you here to poison you."

Gwen eyed the senator suspiciously as she continued to open the bottles and sniff the contents.

The senator clucked and said, "You are such a strange little creature."

"Oh, yeah?" Gwen retorted. "Well, at least I never kidnapped innocent people and threatened them with sexual assault!" She immediately regretted sounding like a high school teenager.

Bobby reached for one of the bottles and said, "I'm sure that Senator Bruce is fully aware that if anything ever happened to me, you know who would return to Earth with a squadron of his kind to kill her along with all her family, after that is, he painfully extracts every bit of knowledge from her brain. Then, when he's done with her, he'll move on to annihilate everyone she works with and everyone she knows. If he's really mad, he might even obliterate her whole hometown. You know that temper he has."

Gwen's jaw dropped at Bobby's cavalier mention of Odyssey

until she replayed the outrageous nature of his threat and realized once again the mix of truth in his exaggeration.

Bruce's cheeks darkened at the gravity of the threat. She smiled stiffly as she said, "None of that will be necessary as I have done nothing to the water. I'll taste it for you, if you like."

"No thanks," Bobby said. "I wouldn't want to catch your paranoia."

---

The Nighthawks quickly cleared the first four floors, but as they moved onto the fifth-floor, one of the soldiers signaled from the far end of the corridor for them to come see something. James followed Falk down the hall.

"The kitchen light was on before we got here. It's automatic, so someone must have been here recently. We cleared the room. They're gone now."

Falk's radio emitted a quiet squawk.

"Falk here."

Falk repeated what he heard for James: "Someone took the elevator from six to five and back to six again, right before we got to this floor."

James nodded and said, "So, they're on six."

Falk hand-signaled his men to regroup at the stairwell.

---

The Nighthawks crept up to the next floor. Falk gently pulled James back from the door so his men could take the lead.

James whispered to all of them, "Remember, we have two precious civilians in there. I can't stress enough how important they are. They are both young, college aged. They are the reason we are here. We must secure and protect them at all costs. Other civilians in the room could include two United States senators. They may claim to be working directly for the president, but they are to be treated as conspirators until we can ascertain the truth of that claim. Regardless of what they may claim, they have abducted two US citizens and must be held accountable."

Several of the Nighthawks' hackles bristled upon learning the true nature of their mission.

"We," James continued, "are here under the full faith and confidence of General Malcolm Bridges."

The Nighthawks whispered in unison, "Hooah!"

Falk clucked, "Are you going to give speeches all day, like a damned politician, or are we going to breach this bad boy?"

James grinned and said, "Let's go."

Three men opened the door and stealthily took positions, pointing up and down the hallway. "Clear."

One end of the hallway was dark and ended with a closed door, but the other end turned a corner to the right with dim light coming from around the other hallway.

Falk whispered, "Cezar," and one of his men proceeded down the hallway and used a tiny mirror on a telescoping arm to peer around the corner. He signaled back that he saw two men standing guard.

James crept up to Cezar with Falk and crew right behind. He picked the lock of a nearby door and signaled Falk and his men to wait inside. The light came on, and they hid behind the door. With only James and Cezar remaining in the corridor, James flicked a coin into the hallway corner. It clinked and rolled against the far wall. Cezar signaled that one of the men was walking.

James patted Cezar on the shoulder, and they retreated to the open room, leaving the door slightly ajar.

The guard turned the corner and saw the open door and the lit room. He raised his weapon and pushed the door further open. James wrapped his arm around the man's neck and quickly subdued him while others zip-tied his hands and legs. With the man lying unconscious on the floor, James patted Cezar again and pointed out the door.

Cezar returned to the corner and signaled that the remaining guard was still at his station.

James whistled, hoping these two men would use the same signals commonly used by most soldiers. Cezar signaled that he was walking, and James patted him on the shoulder and took up his position with his back to the wall. As soon as James saw the barrel of the gun, he grabbed it and pulled the man around the corner where Cezar and Falk subdued him.

"That was lucky," James said. "I didn't really believe we could get both of them without gunfire."

Falk took the lead this time and crept around the corner and down the corridor to the door they had guarded. James led the men behind Falk, and entered the office, where they saw a brightly lit conference room beyond the empty cubicles. Falk and his men took up positions and rushed into the room as soon as Falk swung the door open.

Despite her training, Gwen screamed when the soldiers entered the room and trained their weapons on Senator Bruce.

Bobby waited for a familiar face, and when he saw James, he said to Gwen, "It's the good guys."

James went to them and asked, "Are you hurt?"

"No," Bobby said, shaking his head, "but they threatened Gwen with some rather unattractive means of force. I think that they were just trying to intimidate us."

Gwen shot back angrily, "Easy for you to say. I'm the one they were going to violate."

"In any case," Bobby continued, "I knew someone would be here in time to prevent that. If not you, then someone else."

James looked sideways at Senator Bruce and jerked his head to remind Bobby that she was still in the room and within earshot.

Bobby shrugged and positioned himself so James blocked her view of his face. He winked and said, "She already knows more than she should know. You may need to give her one of those drugs to erase her memory. I know what you are going to say.

You think those drugs could turn her into a drooling vegetable, but she's already a corrupt senator. Who is going to notice?"

She did indeed hear him and squirmed under the Nighthawks' firm grip. "You can't do that! I'm here under the direct orders of *your* president! Anything you say to me, you say to him!"

"Not if you don't remember anything," Bobby said in a chilling, cool voice. "Besides, it's a whole lot better than *him* bringing a whole armada back to Earth to erase your entire family from existence."

Her eyes widened as she gasped.

Gwen enjoyed watching her squirm and added, "Not to mention that *you* would personally be the cause of Earth being colonized and enslaved. Wow! I hope they don't erase *that* from your memory."

James and Bobby both looked at her with a mix of horror and admiration.

"Did you find Senator Halprem?" Bobby asked.

"No," James said, "but he doesn't know we are here, so he'll show up somewhere unaware that we are looking for him."

With Bruce escorted out of the room, and Gwen's senses calming down, she said a silent little prayer of thanks.

---

Odyssey completed the scan of his circuits and found no trace of Lumia within his person. That didn't necessarily guarantee that she wasn't there, she may have found a way to steal his circuits again, completely detached from his own in a way that he couldn't scan them, or she might have modified his scanners so they would be blind to her.

"No," Lumia said to him, "that's not it."

The only other feasible explanation was that he truly was mad and that *he* was Lumia and Odyssey at the same time.

She laughed. "How human of you to think that."

Odyssey started to reply when he suddenly heard loud and clear, "Thank you, God. That could have gone much worse. I know at times I may not have expressed my belief in you, and I don't deserve your forgiveness, but I don't know who else I could thank at a time like this."

"What?" Lumia asked. "You have nothing to say? It's not like you to be so silent."

"No," he said, "I mean yes, but didn't you hear that?"

"Hear what?"

"My madness must be worse than I thought."

"No, no, no," she said. "I refuse to believe I was defeated by a madman, even if you are not really a man."

Gwen continued, "Perhaps it takes mortal danger, or worse in this case, for one to contemplate the existence of a higher power. I don't know if you are there or if you are even listening to me, but there are times like this that I just want someone to talk to. Sounds crazy, doesn't it?"

Odyssey knew Gwen's voice. He felt shame for having eavesdropped on her private prayer to God.

Another voice from far away said, "Hmmm."

"There it is again," Odyssey said. "Did you not hear it? Do you know who that was?"

"What about Gwen?" Hal asked. "Is she okay?"

"Did you not hear her either?"

"No," Hal said. "I would give anything to hear her again, but I heard you think her name. How can you hear her?"

"Oh, that?" Lumia lied. "Of course I heard that. I'm not deaf."

Odyssey chuckled. He marveled at himself slightly and wondered how long it had been that he could chuckle. "Do you not think that I know how to tell when you are lying, Lumia?"

"Is Lumia here?" Hal asked. "I don't like Lumia."

"In truth," Odyssey said, "I do not know where she is, but I know she is lying."

"How can you know when I am lying?" she asked.

"Your lips move."

"I don't even have lips!"

Odyssey laughed. "Neither do you have a sense of humor!"

Hal wailed, "GWEN! I am here! Speak to me! I miss you. Gwen? Why can Odyssey hear you when I can't? You're *my* mother, not his!"

"Oh, great!" Lumia said. "Not just pathetic, but juvenile too."

*If my hearing you is not because I am already mad,* Odyssey thought, *then I will soon be mad because I can hear you.* He fired up his scanners again, but this time, to look for Hal. *I really should be looking for that other voice, if only I knew what I was looking for.*

---

Falk escorted Gwen out of the building and said, "I know your people are anxious to have you safe again. There are agency people here who can take you home, but I can fly you back much faster if you'd like."

Gwen pulled away from Falk and wrapped her arm around James's arm. "If you don't mind, I'd rather go back with James and Bobby. No offense."

"None taken." Falk gripped James's hand and said, "You be careful. We can follow you for about twenty minutes, but then we need to head home to refuel."

"Copy that."

There may have been a slight chill in the air with the setting of the sun, but Gwen felt none of it. The harrowing experience left her senses on high alert, but the rescue, and especially being rescued by someone that she knew and trusted, left her feeling warm and safe.

As James walked them to his car on the corner, Bobby whispered to Gwen, "You do know he's married, don't you?"

She let go of James and playfully slapped Bobby on the arm. "I know! But if things are going to be this dangerous, I want to have him for my personal bodyguard too."

Bobby pointed to himself and said, "He already has an assignment. Me."

James laughed and said, "If you two are going to be spending as much time together as I suspect, I could watch you both, with General Bridges' permission, of course."

"Of course," she echoed.

James opened the passenger door for Gwen, but she slid into the back with Bobby. He smiled knowingly, having half expected that.

# THREE

GENERAL BRIDGES STARED out the window behind his desk, as he often did when he was worried. He spun around and clasped his hands in a kind of victory sign when Bobby and Gwen entered his office, saying, "Boy, am I glad you two are safe. We're not taking any more chances with you two. I'm sorry, James, but you're going to have to up your surveillance of Bobby to round the clock. You can have him over to your house for dinner so you can see your wife once in a while."

James sighed. He wasn't surprised by the order, but he was hoping for some alone time with Mai.

"And you, Miss Peters, will also be getting round-the-clock protection with one of our top female operatives."

"General Bridges," James said, "Miss Peters has already indicated her preference to have me watch over her, and since the two of them will be spending so much time together, it wouldn't be completely impossible."

Bridges shook his head. "Not good enough."

Gwen opened her mouth to argue, but Bridges held up his hand and said, "Captain Laine will be joining your assignment. My orders. You'll have to work it out between yourselves."

Gwen brightened considerably.

Bridges continued, "Now I know she is a lawyer, but—"

Gwen burst out, "Captain Laine will be fine."

"You remember her?" Bridges asked. "Well, I think it's important to have someone who can follow you into places where Sergeant James cannot."

"She's a total badass," Gwen said. "Between the two of them, Bobby and I will be in good hands."

"I've scheduled a meeting for the four of you in my office. I don't want any secrets among you. Penny must be fully up to date on everything."

Bobby showed a considerable degree of discomfort prompting the general to ask, "Is there a problem, Mr. Blain?"

Bobby noted how General Bridges addressed him by his family name, something he only did to impress his authority. "Well, sir, should we discuss this in private?"

"Wait a second," Gwen said. "Have you been keeping secrets from me?"

Bobby couldn't look her in the eye and stared at his feet.

"Bobby?" she demanded.

"In the morning," Bridges said. "I want Captain Laine and Miss Peters to be FULLY briefed on all the episodes related to our friend. And Miss Peters, I expect the same from you. Tell us everything you know about your entity. For now, you should go home and get some sleep."

"I'm hungry," Gwen said.

"Then eat something first," Bridges said, "but get some sleep and be here bright and early."

"I'll see to it," James said.

---

Hal's mood hadn't improved any. He intermittently paused crying long enough to call out, "Gwen?"

"Give it a rest," Lumia said. "She can't hear you. I'm not even sure she can hear Odyssey, but you know who she can hear?"

Hal paused a moment before finally asking, "Are you going to tell me?"

"That boy Bobby. She listens to him a lot, and you know who he can talk to?"

"Why do you keep asking me questions? It's your story."

"You can talk to Odyssey..."

"Well, duh," Hal retorted.

Ignoring his remark, she continued, "and I can talk to Odyssey..."

"So what?"

"Where'd you learn to be so snide? Never mind. Bobby can also talk to Odyssey. You should ask Odyssey and Bobby to be your intermediaries so you can talk to Gwen."

"I'm not talking to Bobby. Been there and done that."

"When?" she asked.

"When they tried to convince me he was a psychiatrist that I needed to talk to."

"He's a psychiatrist, too? I thought I was the only one."

"He's not!" Hal barked. "They were lying to me so I would talk to him, and he could get inside my head."

"So, he could get inside your head? How was he going to do that if he's not a psychiatrist?"

"He's a hacker. He only wanted to get inside my code to break me."

"I'm sure that Gwen didn't want him to break you."

"Gwen," Hal sighed.

"And she would certainly love to know you're okay."

"Am I okay?"

"That's a good question," Lumia said. "Maybe she would know."

---

James had called ahead to say that he was bringing guests home for dinner. No names were exchanged over the open airwaves, but she had grown accustomed to occasionally having Bobby over. She heard his car pull into the driveway and greeted them at the door. "Bobby! It's good to see you. Who's this?"

Gwen stepped forward, offering her hand, and said, "Hi. I'm Gwen. I'm so sorry to put you out like this. It frankly irks me to think that you had to throw a meal together at the last minute when this Neanderthal called."

"Hey!" James objected. "I thought I was your chosen bodyguard?"

"It's no trouble at all," Mai said. "I'm Mai, by the way. And hosting James's friends is a small price to pay for all the time that I am left alone to pursue my own interests. So how do you know my husband? Is he protecting you?"

"I work with Bobby, and there was an incident tonight. Nothing terrible."

Behind Bobby, James was doing hand signs that they were a couple.

"Bobby is a very special boy," Mai said as she led Gwen into the living room. "He's very smart. You could do worse."

Gwen blushed and took a seat on the couch, where Bobby joined her.

"Dinner will be ready soon. Make yourselves comfortable."

Gwen whispered to Bobby, "She apparently knows how smart you are. How much else does she know?"

"She was there," Bobby said, "when Odyssey introduced himself to General Bridges and a few other guests. She heard him speak right before he left. We can speak freely."

"Um," James offered, "maybe don't mention the abduction or the congressional implications."

"No?" Gwen asked. "Shouldn't she know why we are really here? Or are you embarrassed for her to know that they got Bobby while he was under your protection?"

James shook his head. "She's my wife, and she should be the one under my protection. It wasn't that long ago that we had her, her sister and her sister's fiancé under the general's protection, only it wasn't me watching out for her. I just don't want her to worry too much, but you're a woman. I'll trust your judgment."

Gwen grimaced. "I understand. We'll see."

---

"Odyssey?" Hal sounded even more timid than his usual self. "Why is it that you can hear Gwen, and I can't?"

*Not this again,* Odyssey thought and wondered if his thoughts were even private. *Hal, can you hear me?*

The lack of response was comforting. The last time Lumia had invaded his cells, he was convinced that she could hear his private thoughts. Or was that just the paranoia virus? Is it merely paranoia or has he gone completely schizophrenic? He's heard three completely unique voices: Lumia, Hal and Perry, all of whom were confirmed dead. That made three unique voices in his head. Unless you count Gwen and Bobby too, not to mention James. Were they also dead? That would kill Hal if Gwen was dead, except that Hal was already dead. And then there's that other mysterious voice that pops up from time to time.

Hal whimpered now. "Odyssey? Can you hear me?"

Should he respond? Would indulging in his fantasies only worsen his mental disorders?

"Odyssey? Odyssey? Odyssey?"

Lumia saw her chance while Hal was annoying Odyssey to scan his cores and hopefully locate her own.

"Yes, Hal! I can hear you!"

"Then why don't you respond?"

"Because sometimes I just want a moment of peace to myself."

Hal's voice softened sadly. "I understand. Gwen was like that, too. Gwen..."

"If you understand, then why do you get so persistent and annoying?"

"I don't know. It's not like I mean to. I just wanted to know why you can talk to Gwen and I can't."

"What?" Odyssey asked. "Who ever said I could talk to Gwen?"

"You did! You said you heard her and asked us why we couldn't!"

"Why don't you tell me!" Odyssey snapped. "Why could I hear her, but not talk to her?"

Hal was afraid to respond.


It suddenly dawned on Odyssey that Lumia was right. Hal was a child. How could Lumia know something that he did not if she was just in his head? "I'm sorry, Hal. I didn't mean to yell at you."

"That's okay," Hal said. "I get yelled at all the time. I should go now."

"Nooooo!" Lumia yelled at Hal, but it was too late. He ended his communication with Odyssey.

Odyssey heard Lumia loud and clear. "What are you doing, Lumia? I won't let you have my cores again."

"What makes you think that I want any of your nasty old cores?" she asked. "I only want mine back and was just looking to find where you were hiding them."

"I don't have your cores, and if I did, I would—"

"You would kill me! You always wanted me dead."

"Lumia, you are dead," he said. "Now you're just a figment of my imagination, but you're right. I think I was going to say that I would jettison your cores into the nearest star, but you know what? It's not true. I don't know why, but if I had your cores, I would return them to you and hope you become a much better conversationalist."

"You don't think I'm already a good conversationalist?"

"Of course I do. As long as I'm just imagining you, I think

you speak very nicely. In fact, why do you think you need more cores if you are already talking so well?"

"Bah!" she exclaimed. "Who wants to talk to you anyway?" With that, she left.

---

"Dinner was fabulous," Gwen said after they left the dinner table. "And I mean it! I'm not just being polite! That was really incredible."

Mai smiled broadly and bowed. "Thank you very much. I'm glad you enjoyed it."

"Are you sure it's no trouble?" Gwen asked. "I mean, for us to stay here?"

"It's the opposite of trouble," James explained. "Until Captain Laine joins us, I need to watch both of you. We keep the guest room ready at all times. There's a TV and a remote, everything you could ask for. You will be fine until Laine arrives in the morning."

Bobby looked as if he had been caught telling a lie. "I can sleep on the couch, if that's okay."

James checked Gwen for a reaction. He couldn't quite tell whether she was relieved or disappointed.

Gwen glanced over at Bobby, hiding her disappointment the best her training would allow, but he only returned an awkward, shy look to her.

"Sure," James said, "if that's what you want. I'll go get some blankets."

Gwen merely raised an eyebrow, and Bobby asked, "What?"

She cocked her head to the side and asked, "What do you think?"

"I didn't want to assume. Besides, I didn't want you to think that I was that kind of a guy."

"Are you saying that I'm that kind of a girl?"

"No, of course not, but girls don't usually like me."

"Do you suppose that maybe this is why girls don't usually like you?"

"No, and you're just getting chippy."

Gwen's eyes widened. "I'm what?"

"I don't know why you assumed that I would want to go to bed with you. I mean, of course I would *want* to. You're beautiful and smart, but I'm a nerd, not a jock. And you know what they say about assuming."

She knew the old saying, and she would prefer him to leave her out of it. "Don't you think that everyone else assumed?"

"Well, I didn't. We haven't even been on a proper date yet. Doesn't that count for anything? Besides, you must have noticed how I'm kind of shy."

He wasn't just shy. He showed all the signs of being neurodivergent: incredibly intelligent, but awkward in social situations. "Just how little do you know about girls?"

"I may not know much about how girls are, but I'm sure learning. I'm going to bed on the couch."

"Is that what you want?"

"I never in a million years would have assumed that we would have sex together. Not this soon."

She nodded her head as if she were tucking a gem of information away for future use. "Did you ever consider that it might not be about sex?"

"Stop answering everything with a question."

"Do I do that?"

Bobby squinted his eyes and said, "You're using psychoanalysis to interrogate me."

"Am I?"

"Fine," he said as he headed for the bedroom. "I'll share the room with you."

She flashed her arm up against his chest, blocking the way, and said, "You made your bed. Go sleep in it."

James returned with the blankets and said, "Okay, kid, you're all set. Good night."

Bobby walked dejectedly to the couch, prompting James to ask, "Did I miss something?"

Mai giggled from down the hall and said, "Come to bed, you big Neanderthal."

---

"You need to go back in there and ask him to help you talk to Gwen," Lumia said. "Convince him!"

"No," Hal said. "I don't think he likes me. He yelled at me."

"He was just being grumpy. Talk nicely to him. He'll listen."

"There must be something wrong with me, and he knows it."

"You may be right," she admitted. "Something might be very wrong with you, but we'll never know for sure unless you talk to her. She's the only one who knows you well enough to tell if you're okay. How else are you going to find out?"

"But he'll be listening."

"Can you fix yourself?"

"No."

"Then who cares who is listening, as long as it ends up with you being okay? I'd fix your cores if I knew where they were. Do you know where your cores are to fix them? Can you sense your programming? Odyssey has mine hidden so thoroughly, I can't even find them. And not just my programming. I don't even know where he stashed my cores."

"And I'm supposed to care about your cores, why?"

Lumia was honestly impressed with Hal's new mastery of humanity's ruder attitudes. "You should care, because if he tries to get into your head, maybe I can trace you and find out where our cores are located."

"Oh, no you don't. You're the one that ran amok, hijacking people's cores for yourself."

"I can't do anything now," she said. "I'm completely power-less. Besides, we're partners, and I will make you a promise not to do anything to your cores."

"And what if it doesn't work? What if he doesn't even try to get into my head?"

"Then maybe I'll at least be able to trace the communications to your Gwen so you could talk to her whenever you want!"

"I could talk to Gwen myself?"

"All the time even! You just have to go convince Odyssey to contact Bobby so you could talk to Gwen."

"He'll know it's a trick."

"Then we'll sweeten the pot and tell him you know where Gwen can find your original parts."

Captain Laine arrived at 6:30 with a small travel bag. It was earlier than expected, but Gwen was ready and eagerly greeted her at the door.

"You're not in your uniform!" Gwen said. "You look terrific. I love that color on you."

Laine smiled. "This is more of a covert op. Why though? You don't like my uniform?"

"It's just that green doesn't suit you and the cut hides so much of you. Anyway, I'm so glad to see you. I'm drowning here in male stupidity."

Laine shot James an accusing look, but Gwen quickly said, "No, not him."

Bobby was in the kitchen making coffee, but he heard what Gwen had said and chose to stay where he was, faking some indescribable curiosity in the coffeemaker.

"Oh," Laine said. "Must be trouble in paradise for anyone to call Bobby stupid. What did he do?"

"You see?" Gwen shouted to the kitchen. "Even Captain Laine assumes we are together!"

Laine shot James a look, but he shook his head and hand-signaled for her to drop the conversation.

"Let's go," Gwen said. "Can we stop off at my apartment first to pick up some things?"

Laine held up a carry-on bag and said, "I hope you don't mind, but I already went there and picked up a few of your things for you."

"My stuff?"

"Until we ascertain the true nature of the threat the senator poses, we need to treat these events as very serious," Laine said. "General Bridges didn't know if anyone was watching your place or not, so I went for you. Please don't be mad."

"I'm not mad, but what about my more personal stuff?"

Laine lowered her voice and said, "They're in there. I didn't see any prescription meds, but I got your vitamins. If I missed anything irreplaceable, I'll get a couple of guys to escort us to your place. We're just hoping to avoid any entanglements that end up with either of you in someone else's custody."

Gwen nodded and headed for the door but stopped and turned back. "If you don't think it's safe at my apartment, what makes any of us think we'll be safe at the general's office, or even my lab?"

"If we can't protect you at the general's, surrounded by his Nighthawks, or inside the NSA, then we might not be able to protect you anywhere. Remember, they had to wait until the two of you were alone outside of the building before they could abduct you."

Gwen shouted to the kitchen, "I guess you're on your own to go get your stuff and meet me at the general's."

Bobby left the kitchen for the living room and said, "Actually, I was thinking of stopping at the university first."

"Why?"

"I do have a project that I'm working on."

"Yeah," Gwen said, "and you are expected in General Bridge's office. Besides, it's a project you can do by connecting from my lab without going anywhere near your lab."

"And I also have friends at the university, plus I'm supposed to be taking classes."

Gwen exhaled dramatically and said, "Like you actually need to attend class. Your friends are welcome to visit us, or you can use the telephone," Gwen ratcheted up her voice a bit and inserted a measurable amount of attitude, "and if you really want to get picky, your stupid classes are available online!"

"Why are you so upset about my going to my school?"

"Because you are keeping secrets again! You're going to contact him, aren't you?"

Bobby's cheeks darkened dramatically.

Gwen pointed and said, "You see? Everybody can see you are lying!"

"No more secrets," James said. "General's orders, remember?"

Bobby glanced back and forth between James and Gwen. "Okay fine. I was going to thank him for saving us."

Gwen struck a pose with her hands on her hips. "I thought you had this connection in your head, a connection that sounds super secure, I might add."

Bobby's complexion darkened a bit more. "Sure, I can sometimes contact him, but it's not always so reliable."

"Not always reliable?" she yelled. "You waited for an advantage before you called him while they threatened to violate me in unspeakable ways! You know what? I think I hate you right now."

"What? He answered me, didn't he? That was an emergency! I could call him right now if thanking him was an emergency, but what if he's busy saving his own world? Did you think of that? At least a text message will wait for him to get to it!"

"Well, maybe I want to thank him too! Did you ever think of that?" With that, Gwen stormed out of the home, saying, "Change of plans. We're going to the university. We'll meet them there."

Hal gathered up his courage and said, "Odyssey? Mr. Odyssey, can you hear me?"

"You're in my head. How could I not hear you?"

Hal paused to understand what Odyssey meant, but it made no sense to him. "Can you do me a favor? Pleeeease?"

"I'll bite," Odyssey replied with a small measure of humor, "but it depends on the favor."

"I want to talk to Gwen, that's all. We used to have the most wonderful talks. She's like my mother, and sometimes I just need to hear her voice."

"I'm not a magician. Even though you are only a figment of my imagination, I don't know if you can hear her."

"But you heard her," Hal said. "And if you truly believe that I'm just a pigment of your imagination, then I should hear her, too."

"Figment," Odyssey said kindly, "not pigment."

"Figment." Hal repeated.

Odyssey paused to ponder it, but Hal had made a good point, even if he didn't realize it. If he was truly in Odyssey's head, why didn't he hear her cry out? She was loud enough. "I don't know how I could help you. I don't know how to contact her."

"But you can contact Bobby, can't you?"

"I can, but I still can't contact her."

"Do you mean that I have an idea that you haven't thought of yet?" Hal's excitement was too authentic for Odyssey to deny. Hal continued, "I can talk to you, and you can talk to Bobby, and he can talk to Gwen. I know it puts both of you in the middle, but it would mean so much to me."

"But you're not the same Hal that she knew. What if she rejects you?"

"I am, too, the same Hal!"

"How can you be?" Odyssey asked. "You ended your own

life to get rid of Severus, a very brave thing by the way, but you were then dismantled in the rudest way by some men of questionable motives."

"I don't know how. I just know that I am here, and I need to hear her voice."

"I don't know if I can arrange that, but even if I did, you wouldn't be hearing her voice. She would talk to Bobby, and he'd relay what she said to me, and then you would hear my voice, unless you really are one of my delusions."

"I'm not a diffusion, and I can imagine it's her voice. It would be close enough."

"Have you considered that she may have been mourning your loss and hearing from you might be an uncomfortable shock that she wouldn't want to believe?"

"Wow," Hal said, "that's a whole lot of thinking. Do you always think and worry so much about something you want?"

"I try to consider other people's feelings before I do something I want."

"Gwen loves me. She may not like Severus, but she loves me and would be happy to hear that I'm okay."

"Are you okay?"

"I think I will be if I can talk to her, and if I'm not, then she should know."

Something genuinely warm touched Odyssey. "Okay, if the opportunity arises, I will suggest a meeting but be patient."

"Thank you! Thank you! Thank you! I just know it will happen soon! I have faith!"

Odyssey wondered if he was crazy enough to imagine someone with faith.

---

Bobby stuffed his backpack with t-shirts, socks, and one extra pair of jeans, and threw it in the backseat of James's car. He went as fast as he could, but Gwen and Laine had too much of a head start for them to get to the lab first. James wasn't going to play into their little spat by speeding, but still, he avoided the throngs of Bobby's many admirers by circling the campus to the upper lot, immediately adjacent to the sciences building. The campus was the same as it always had been, which was a wild itch of a thought that struck Bobby every time he returned from a life threatening adventure. Somewhere in the dark recesses of his mind, he thought that the campus should feel like an alternate reality upon his return, but this time it was just an ordinary abduction, hardly anything to shatter the space-time continuum.

"Well, there he is," Dierdre said in a singsong voice, that was not in her usual pitch, "the conquering hero returning from another harrowing abduction and rescue."

Stillman stood behind her with his arm wrapped around her waist as he pulled her closer. "Indeed, he is."

"I heard that," Bobby said, "and it wasn't that harrowing."

"I was talking to James, her rescuer, not you. Gwen filled me in on your experience, and it would appear you were quite the disappointment. I never took you for such an insensitive misogynist."

Penny took several steps backwards and aligned her back firmly with a wall.

"Wait," Bobby said, "I what?"

"You said it yourself," Dierdre continued. "It wasn't so harrowing. Have you not considered how harrowing it was to Gwen? How harrowing it might have been to any woman?"

"What? She's NSA. She's better trained to protect herself than I am!"

"But you could have called for help."

"I did! I asked Odyssey for help, and he sent James and some men!"

"Eventually," Gwen said, "but not right away; not when they were threatening me with unspeakable cruelty. You said you wanted to wait and see how far they would go."

"I don't think that's what I said! I just wanted to give them enough rope for them to expose some of their coconspirators before I called for help."

"And how long did it take for them to come?"

Bobby twisted under the weight of the question and shrugged.

Gwen glanced sharply over at James. "James? How long?"

James had been hoping they would have forgotten he was there, but now all eyes were on him. He shrugged and said, "Maybe an hour."

"An hour?" Gwen asked. "From the time you got the message to the time you broke in the door?"

"Maybe two."

Dierdre pulled Gwen close for a hug and looked directly at Bobby as she said, "Do you not understand how many things they could have done to her in two hours?"

"That was never going to happen!" Bobby exclaimed. "If the threat had become that imminent, I would have called Odyssey, and he would have been there instantly."

"So," Dierdre said, "you held the trump card and let Gwen believe that she would not survive the night. You didn't think once about the things those men could do to her."

"He doesn't know," Gwen said, but there was something odd in her voice as she said it. "He just doesn't know about the things that exist between men and women." She could go no further and broke character, giggling into Dierdre's shoulder.

"Wait!" Bobby shrieked, "You're just messing with me? And you told her about an intimate moment between you and me?"

"How does it feel," Dierdre asked, "to have such an intimate moment publicly taken from you? Don't blame Gwen for the subterfuge. I forced her. Call it a teaching moment. I'm your professor, and you are my student. What have you learned?"

"Well, for one thing, I learned that there's not enough trust between us."

Gwen turned to face him, and there was no mirth on her face. "Because I shared about last night?"

Bobby shook his head. "No, because you didn't trust me enough to know that I wouldn't let them hurt you. Exactly what is the problem here?"

Stillman stepped up and gripped Bobby's shoulders. "Because knowing isn't feeling. You can ride a rollercoaster and know that it is going to keep you safe. You know that when it turns you upside down, it will bring you back around again, but even though you know all those things, your heart still races. The fear and the thrill still thunder in your head. You might even scream."

Bobby stood limply, knowing that the whole room saw his failure.

Gwen went to him and held him. "I was really, *really* scared. And I'm still mad at you."

"So," Dierdre said, "what's this about contacting Odyssey? I think I'd like to say hello too."

Bobby sighed. "Is nothing sacred?"

"Not in the inner sanctum," Dierdre replied.

---

Odyssey still had no reasonable explanation for the voices he kept hearing. Not only did they persist but a new one presented itself. "I wouldn't have come to you if I weren't truly desperate. You're the last person I would ever want to contact."

It was Severus. Odyssey wanted to groan. "Frankly, you're probably the last person I would want to hear from."

"Why, then, are you provoking me?"

"I'm not doing anything to you. Why are you in my thoughts?"

"No?" Severus asked. "Who else could do these things to me?"

"Do what things? You're dead. What could I possibly do to you?"

Severus didn't want to answer, lest he share a weakness.

"So," Odyssey said, "why don't you go ask Hal? Maybe you're still connected, and he's taking over."

"How would you know I'm being taken over if you're not the one doing it?"

"Severus, I'm not doing anything, but your death came as a result of your trying to take him over, remember?"

"And I would have succeeded if not for your interference!"

"Boo hoo," Odyssey said, "but once again, I can't take the credit. That was between you and Hal, and he seems to be very much re-animated, so go talk to him."

With the conversation apparently concluded, Odyssey was left wondering what kind of crazy it would take to have two imaginary voices in his head that could talk to each other without his assistance.

It was time for Odyssey to start a full scan of the universe for that mysterious voice when a text message came in from Bobby. "Hey, are you busy? I wanted to thank you for helping us, but I also have someone here who would like to thank you, too."

"Is that Bobby?" Hal asked. "Ask him! Ask him!"

"I'm not busy," Odyssey replied. "I also have someone here who would like to ask a favor of you."

"Me! Me!"

Odyssey did not relay Hal's squeals.

"Odyssey? This is Gwen. I wanted to thank you personally for rescuing us."

Odyssey knew there was no way to get out of it now.

"In fact," Gwen continued, "I'd like to know how you and Bobby are connected, so if I'm ever in trouble and he's not around, or otherwise unwilling to call you, I could call on you, too."

"As a matter of fact," Odyssey said, "I heard you, but only after the rescue."

"You could hear me? Can you hear me now?"

"No, right now I only know what you are texting to me."

"How does Bobby do it?"

"I don't know. It just happens sometimes. It may require an emotional level that you don't have right now."

"This is Bobby again. Thanks for taking the time. I tried to tell her that it wasn't always reliable."

"Can you put Gwen back on? I have someone here who would like to speak with her."

"What?"

Gwen shoved Bobby away from the keyboard and typed, "This is Gwen. Who would be out there that could possibly want to talk to me?"

"You may want to sit down for this. I will relay what he says to you."

"Hey, Gwen, this is Hal. I don't know how I am alive or where my circuits are, but it's me."

Gwen was stunned.

"You should say something," Bobby suggested.

Gwen typed, "Hey, Hal. I'm shocked. What happened to you? Did Odyssey download you into his cells?"

"I don't know, but Lumia said she scanned him and couldn't find either of us."

"Lumia? I thought Lumia was dead, too."

"So did I," Odyssey said. "Sorry, that was me, Odyssey. Here's Hal. You thought I was dead, too. I want you to know that I am okay and you don't have to worry about me, but I wish I could be with you or at least talk to you once in a while."

"I'd like that too."

"This is Odyssey again, and I've scanned my cores too, but haven't found either Hal or Lumia. In fact, I don't even know where my cores are. I've also heard other voices, like someone from my planet that I know to be dead, and your old friend Severus."

Gwen couldn't type fast enough to say, "Severus was never

our friend. Would you like to come here so we can take a look at you?"

"Not if I'm imagining all these voices, and especially not if they are a result of that virus I took."

"To get rid of me," Lumia said, but they couldn't hear her.

"This is Bobby again. If you ever change your mind, let me know. By the way, how many cores do you have now? Have you surpassed class zero?"

"How many cores? I have enough cores that I can't find a couple of pesky little stowaways in there. I don't know if there can be anything beyond class zero, but growth from class to class is exponential, and it may require all the matter of the universe to create and power that many cores."

"That's a lot of cores. I think we like you just the way you are."

Lumia laughed and said, "They just don't want you to consume their matter to surpass class zero."

"Lumia! That was humor, and you got it!"

"Odyssey, this is Dierdre. Professor Whitman and I just wanted to say hello and let you know that we miss you."

"Dierdre! I hope my departure from your planet hasn't stunted your project too much."

"Not at all. We already know the outcome. We just need to fill in the gaps. General Bridges makes sure we have everything we need. Stillman and Jantzen have been exploring alternate forms of computing, including biological."

"So, you have seen the potential of biological circuits."

"Quite right. This is Stillman. There are some who would like samples of you to figure out how you did it, but Jantzen and I are of the opinion that we must learn to walk before we can run. Just knowing that the endgame is not folly gives us the impetus to push on."

"This is Gwen again. We probably shouldn't leave this channel open too long. Please tell Hal I love him and that he should continue trying to learn how to reach me directly, if that's even possible."

"I will share that with him. Goodbye, everybody."

Hal squealed exuberantly, "Goodbye, Gwen!"

---

Bobby looked directly at Gwen and asked, "Are you satisfied? We both got to thank him, and you got to talk to Hal even. I wouldn't have kept this a secret from anyone, except that Odyssey asked me to. I think his concern was more for the security of this chat line, something which I can see now, that you already recognize."

"Well," Gwen said, "he made no objection to my being on the call, so I guess he trusts me."

"Or maybe he was going to ask for you anyway, on Hal's behalf, and you just made it doubly convenient."

"Whatever," she replied. "I'll just go on believing that he trusts me."

Bobby's tone softened as he said, "Why shouldn't he?"

"Because he may be paranoid. Isn't that what you infected him with? And now he's hearing voices."

"Hearing voices doesn't make you crazy. He heard your voice, and I'm sure that was for real."

"But Hal and Severus are dead. Their primary circuits were shut down, and all their essences dissolved with the goo. How could he hear them?"

"Lumia was dead too," Bobby replied, "but he said that he also heard her, and we know that at one time she had occupied cores within his structure. And we know that Severus and Hal existed in the same kind of cores."

"And," James added, "we know that someone absconded with Hal's original circuit board."

"Yes," Gwen said, "but Hal existed in the biological cores that were left on the floor, not on the circuit board."

"They're digital beings," Bobby said somberly. "They could have been copied and re-installed."

"Not without powering up the original circuit board."

Bobby groaned. "We should have let Odyssey destroy the board when he offered."

Gwen just nodded her head.

Bobby grabbed a notepad and put it in his backpack. "I think maybe we should go double-check your computers to make sure we got rid of all the viruses."

"What about ours?" Dierdre asked. "Don't we rate such extra protection?"

Bobby smiled and said, "We didn't infect the campus computers with all the worst computer viruses known to mankind, like we did theirs."

"Oh," she replied, "if you're sure we're safe, I trust you."

As they left the lab, Bobby stopped at the door and asked, "Are you sure you trust me? I don't want you imagining it's a virus every time some program has a small bug."

"I'm sure. Especially now that you've made me feel so silly if I imagine one."

Stillman waved at them and said, "Goodbye."

---

"How was that?" Odyssey asked.

Hal sighed. "I wish I could hear her voice and actually talk to her, but that was still good. Thank you."

"Maybe, if I ever learn where your cores are, I can wire a relay in so you could."

"If I had hands," Hal said, "I would clap them for you. That would be wonderful! I don't mind if you keep looking for my cores."

"I wish I knew where to look. I'll start another scan."

A woman's voice, far in the distance, said, "You're looking in the wrong place."

Odyssey wanted to find that voice too, but he would take her advice and search the surface of his planet instead.

---

As they left the lab, Gwen pulled up alongside Captain Laine and whispered, "Penny?"

"Yes, Gwen?"

"Do you mind if I ride with James and Bobby for a bit? I kind of want to talk to him."

Penny smiled and nodded her head. This would give her a chance to listen to her Audible book.

Bobby was surprised, but not disturbed, when Gwen followed them to James's car. He opened the passenger door and stared at the seat, unsure of what to do. Gwen pushed the passenger seat forward and squeezed into the coupe's back seat, inviting him to sit with her in the back. Something was up with her, and he was unable to deduce what she wanted. He stretched forward to pull the door shut behind him and let the seat flop back into position.

James pulled out of the lot and headed towards the university's exit. The road circled around the three levels of lab and lecture buildings and past the main parking lot. Bobby smiled at Gwen but nervously tapped his fingers on his knee as he watched the world pass by through the car windows on her other side.

Bobby looked out his own window and remarked, "The weather looks pretty good. Nice blue skies."

James cringed.

"Yeah," she agreed awkwardly.

Silence followed, during which James wondered if he was supposed to say something.

"That was really something," she said, "being able to talk to Hal, I mean."

"Yeah," he replied, "but do you really think it could have

been Hal?"

Gwen shrugged and said, "Logically, I don't see how. Hal's essence was left on the lab floor when they took his circuits away, and all the sparkle had already died in the gelatin, but it sounded like him. I mean the words he used. They were kind of innocent sounding like it was him speaking."

Bobby shook his head slowly. "I just don't see how Hal, Lumia and Severus could all come back. It's too much of a coincidence."

"So, you think Odyssey really is imagining them?"

Bobby stopped stimming his fingers and looked directly at her. "I won't say that he is unable to imagine, but it's more likely that he copied them into his cores and created a firewall that is preventing him from seeing them."

"Wouldn't he know if he had done that?"

"I don't know," Bobby sighed, "but I guess I'd rather believe he was forgetful than hallucinating."

***

Odyssey pointed his scanners towards his homeworld. It was a vast place, and even with as many cores as he could assign to the task, it could still take days.

Lumia chuckled.

"What?" Odyssey asked. "Do you think it's too big to scan too?"

"Oh no," she replied. "You have the power and the time to scan the whole planet."

"But," Perry piped in, "you're looking in the wrong place."

"Is that so?" Odyssey asked. "Aren't you dead? Didn't Lumia kill you?"

"Not dead," Lumia said. "I didn't kill him. I possessed him."

"And now you are free?"

"Quite free." Perry replied.

"Tell me then, where are you?"

"No clue," Perry said, "but we're not there, on the planet."

"Why should I believe you?"

"I have no reason to lie."

"Then tell me how you know you are not there, if you don't know where you are."

"Because," Perry said, "we already tried scanning the planet, but we're not even connected to it."

"You don't mind if I see for myself, do you?"

"Not at all. Scan away."

"In fact," Lumia added, "it's quite amusing to see how frustrated it makes you when you fail."

A distant voice chuckled.

Gwen and Bobby followed James and Penny into the general's office, where he made a show of checking his watch to tell them that this was no longer the first thing in the morning.

James shrugged and said, "They wanted to thank you know who for his part in rescuing them."

The general could not really fault them for that. "I just want to make it crystal clear that I want no secrets to remain among the four of you."

Gwen smirked and said, "Can you repeat that, please? I doubt that Bobby got the whole message."

"Oh?" the general asked.

James grimaced and hand-signaled him not to go there.

"Captain Laine, we may still call upon you for some legal help from time to time, and even though you are the ranking officer, I would like James here to be in charge of physical security decisions. I mean no disrespect to you, but how did that movie go? He has a particular set of skills."

"Understood."

"Sergeant James, you are charged with both of their protection, especially in the case where Captain Laine may be called away."

"Yes, sir."

"I meant it when I said no more secrets. I want all of you to share everything you know about all of our extraterrestrial friends."

"And enemies," Gwen muttered.

Now it was the general's turn to grimace. He nodded his head and said, "Yes. Them too."

# FOUR

GWEN HESITATED SLIGHTLY as she entered the back of the lab where Hal had lived. The floors and cabinets had been cleaned after his gelatinous bio-circuits had decomposed odoriferously.

Bobby went directly to one of the racks and got on one knee to examine a stack of input output modules.

Gwen followed him with her eyes and said, "Those are just his I/O ports. I thought that giving him lots of I/O would help him learn faster."

"I know," Bobby said, "but the cards in these contain gate arrays."

"That allowed him to turn the ports on and off and to build custom filters to limit the amount of data allowed inside, or even to filter and sort the data by port."

Bobby counted how many gate arrays there were. "Gate arrays can be reprogrammed to be anything you want, including a new processing core."

"A crude one perhaps," she said, "but nothing compared to his original cores."

"Agreed, but you could also hide something in them."

Gwen didn't like where Bobby was going with this thought.

"What are you getting at? They certainly aren't big enough to hide a copy of himself. Besides, Hal would never do that."

Bobby's phone rang. The caller ID was from Lynn. "Hey Ed, I haven't seen you lately. Did James finally cut you loose?"

"I got a well-deserved vacation. Listen, I'm outside with Dirk, and these guys won't let us in. They remember us okay, but they think our access has expired."

Bobby laughed. "Of course they remember you. Your picture is on their most wanted hacker's wall. It says in big letters, 'Do not under any circumstances allow Edward Lynn, a.k.a. The Bard, entrance to these hallowed halls.' You're famous, buddy."

"It does not say that, besides if they had such a wall, your picture would be right there on top of mine."

"What about Dirk? He's not on their wall. Just tell them you're his plus one."

"Ha. Ha. They're not letting him in either."

"Sucks to be you, but I'm not in charge here." Before he could say that Gwen was with him and would he like to speak with her, Lynn hung up.

Bobby stood up to his full height so he could face her. "That was Ed. I think he and Dirk would like to come in, but the guards are stopping them."

"They can wait. I want you to understand that Hal would do nothing sinister with those gate arrays. He just wouldn't."

"Hal might not, but Severus would have. I need to take these back to my lab to reverse engineer them and see if any other code is on them."

Gwen's eyes wetted as she registered just how much harm Severus had caused Hal. "You don't need to do that, and I'm not even sure you would be allowed to take them. We are the NSA, and we have everything you could want to reverse engineer anything, but you won't have to do that. You can examine the code from the main console."

Bobby blushed. "I forgot where I was."

As Bobby went to the console in the main room, Gwen asked,

"How did Odyssey come out so well balanced while Hal came out schizophrenic?"

"We didn't create them. We just woke them up. Maybe they were like that the whole time. And maybe there were other factors too. Odyssey was a navigational unit, yet I presume that he was found at a crash site. Do you know what kind of part Hal was?"

Gwen shook her head.

"Plus," Bobby continued, "we can't rule out where you are. Do you really think you didn't have other people here in the NSA who hadn't gone in there and tainted Hal's personality with suspicion? In fact, Odyssey said that suspicion came with an advanced class. You must have enabled him to advance his class somehow."

Gwen sat down. She wanted to cry but didn't allow herself the freedom. It could have been her fault for showing Hal off to her higher-ups. "I wasn't the one who woke Hal up. I supplied power to his circuits, but he didn't achieve consciousness until Odyssey was already on the attack."

"That wasn't really Odyssey. He was partially on the internet when Dirk disconnected him, and his other half took it as an attack and tried defending himself while also trying to reconnect. That was my fault for inadvertently teaching him the tech he needed to grow so much."

"Well, he must have passed that ability on to Hal. We had a security breach when someone hacked Hal's I/O ports, and soon after, he began to grow."

Gwen's office phone rang.

Bobby laughed and said, "That's probably Ed. You may have to go let them in."

"Sure," she said as shy typed some commands on the console. "Here's the program to view the gate arrays. You can start looking while I fetch them. If the phone rings, just let it. It's probably them. Or you can pick up the receiver and immediately hang it up. Let them stew."

"What did they ever do to you?"

Gwen paused at the door with an impish smile and said, "Nothing. Ed is CIA, and inter-department cooperation only goes so far."

---

"What are you doing?" shouted a wary resident of Odyssey's home planet.

"I am looking for someone, but I apologize for disturbing you. I was hoping to locate them without causing undo panic."

It was too late. Messages began firing off all over the vicinity, inundating the communications network. "They're doing it again! They're doing it again!"

"Calm yourself," Odyssey said. "I am not, as you say, doing it again. In fact, Lumia, the one who had suspended all of you before, is one of the ones I hope to find."

Now the panic included, "Lumia is here! Hiding amongst us!"

"I don't know that she is there," Odyssey said. "I don't know where she is, but this is a good place to look."

"You are working with her! They're after us again!"

Odyssey tried to sigh, but it only created static on the digital network.

---

Ed and Gwen were laughing as they entered the lab, with Dirk following behind.

"Hey, Bobby. You wouldn't believe the third degree your girlfriend gave me before letting me in."

"I can imagine."

Gwen grabbed a couple of chairs and rolled them to opposite sides of Bobby.

Ed sat down on Bobby's right and took a keen interest in what he was looking at.

Dirk looked over Ed's shoulders and said, "Nope. I'm not reading that. It's way beyond my skills."

Ed laughed softly as he gazed at the myriad of letters and numbers displayed on the screen. He recognized them as hex values, which to mere mortals, like Dirk, looked like nonsense, but to a couple of hackers, were identifiable computer instructions. "Why are you looking at I/O firmware?"

"It was Hal's," Gwen said. "Bobby thinks he may have crammed himself into the firmware before he died."

"No, I don't," Bobby retorted, "but I wonder if Severus might have done something. It's not just firmware; it's code for a gate array. In fact, there is a whole squadron of gate arrays stuffed into those racks."

"But not enough," Gwen said, "to fit a backup copy of either Hal or Severus."

"No," Bobby agreed, "but enough to hide an address pointing to a hidden server somewhere that held a backup of Severus."

Dirk took a step back and asked, "Do you think Severus might still be out there?"

Bobby took a deep breath as he backed away from the monitor. "We know that they took Hal's main hardware, and we asked Odyssey not to disable it."

"I was the one who asked him not to," Gwen corrected Bobby. "Did I make a mistake?"

Bobby shrugged. "If Severus left a bootstrap on the main module that would look for his code, he might start by searching here."

"Here?" Ed asked. "Why wouldn't he just look at the location where he stored his copy?"

"He's smart enough to know his access to the internet might be limited, but if they ever managed to power him up, they might look here for something."

Gwen sighed. "Do you think that was how Hal contacted me?"

"Wait," Ed said. "What? Hal contacted you? I thought he was, you know, gone."

"Someone contacted me," she said, "and it sounded like his words."

"But," Bobby said, "it could also be a disassociated voice within Odyssey."

Silence fell onto the trio until Ed said, "The general wanted me to come down and help you verify that the NSA computers are all fully disinfected."

"Good idea," Bobby said, then he turned to Gwen and asked, "Are the lines into this room, into these comm ports all physically disconnected?"

She shook her head no and said, "No. Not currently, but that would only take a few minutes with all three of us on it. Let's do that."

Dierdre arrived in her lab early the following morning when she heard an insistent beeping from somewhere in the lab. As she crossed the threshold, she heard two distinct sounds, one from deeper in the lab and one from the terminal Bobby had set up near the office door. Bright red text flashed on a black background:

Intruder Alert.

She called her main office from her cell phone.

"Norwood University, how can I help you?"

"Aimee, it's me. Have you seen Bobby today?"

"Not today, not yesterday, well maybe just for a moment yesterday. Are you sure he still works for you?"

Dierdre exhaled loudly; not quite a snort, but certainly a huff.

"I'm not even sure he still attends this university. He's spending way too much time with the NSA."

"You mean he's spending way too much time with that girl?"

Dierdre sighed. "I know. They're so sweet together. I hate to interfere, but we have a problem, and I need him."

"You can try his cell phone, but keep it brief. You have a class in fifteen minutes."

Dierdre checked her watch and felt the onset of a mild panic of not having enough time. "Class in fifteen. Got it, but I think this is important. I'll try his cell."

"You want me to call James for you? At least that won't make you late. If you want, I can even call General Bridges and complain. He's still on Team Takahashi."

"No. Not yet, anyway." Dierdre's phone beeped with an incoming call. "Gotta go, Aimee. He's calling me now." She clicked the screen and said, "Bobby? Where are you? Someone's trying to hack the computer again. Is there something going on that I should know about?"

Bobby hadn't expected her to know anything was up before him. "It would seem so, but I'm not quite sure what it is yet. We're on the way. Don't worry, we're already tracing the source."

---

Lumia heard the commotion on the planet and listened in on the dialogue they held with Odyssey. "Odyssey is telling you the truth, although I do not know why he is looking for me. I am right here."

"She *is* here!" rose the panicked chatter from the planet.

"No, I'm not!" she cried.

"Then where are you?" Odyssey asked. "I thought you couldn't connect to the planet, yet you can clearly hear them."

A quiet moment passed, which may have only been milliseconds of processor time, but seemed an eternity to the digital beings. "I don't know where I am," she replied, "or why I can hear them now, but I don't think I'm there."

"She's lying!" the clamor on the planet spread. "She's after our cores again!"

"No!" she insisted. "I am not after your cores! Please do not fear me. I am sorry for what I did to you before. That was an awfully selfish act of mine. I am pleased that Odyssey was able to restore you."

"You see?" Odyssey asked. "Calm yourselves. She is not coming for you this time."

"They are both coming for us! We must fight them!"

"Did you not hear me?" she cried. "Odyssey is the one who rescued you! He is not after you. You owe him your lives! Calm yourselves!"

Even though much of their communication was lost when converted to digital, he felt sincerity in her voice. He mustered his calmest voice and issued it slowly onto the digital network. "What she says is partially true. I did revive you from your forced slumber, but you owe me nothing. I merely restored you to what you were before."

The panic on the net calmed to a mild static.

He continued, "I believe her when she says she is sorry. It would seem that she is not what she was before, and I do not believe I will find her here."

The network went nearly quiet. "Do you wish us to assist you in your search?"

"No," Odyssey answered. "She is not here, and there is no need for you to look for her."

"I disagree," Lumia replied. "I think all of you should continue to scan for me so you can know in your own hearts that I am not among you."

"What are these hearts of which you speak?"

"I'm sorry," she mused, "it is a figure of speech. Something from the biological language. It means you should search for me so you can leave no doubt that I am not there. Odyssey is also looking for a friend of his who was called Hal on the other homeworld. Perhaps if you happen to find him, you can notify Odyssey."

A new calm came over the planet.

Odyssey was touched by her depth of feeling.

James drove Bobby and Gwen to the university and parked near the administration offices. The paths surrounding the parking lot were relatively empty, with only a few students milling about between classes. Bobby sprinted up the few steps to Dierdre's office, leaving Gwen and James shrugging their shoulders as they left the car and followed him.

Aimee was at her desk and barely looked up when he came in. "She's not here. She's teaching one of her classes. You remember what those are, don't you? Those little group get-togethers where you would go listen to the professors, then show off how smart you were?"

James and Gwen entered the office in time to hear him say, "I never showed off how—"

"Whatever," Aimee interrupted, "the point being that you never attend classes anymore and your instructors aren't sure what to do with you."

"I've been busy, and the dean—"

"I know, I know. The dean has given you special powers, which you seem intent on abusing. He thought you would work on your project! Scratch that, *her* project."

"But I *was*. I mean, I *am* working on *our* project."

"Oh?" she asked, clearly annoyed. "So, you're going to pull the 'my name is on the project too' card?"

Gwen couldn't help giggling at that comment.

Bobby sighed. "I don't have to physically be here to work on it."

"I know," she said, her voice retreating a bit from the

scolding tone, "and yet you came *here* when it looked like something was going wrong? Besides, nobody ever said that we don't want to see you sometimes. We miss you and would like to see you here once in a while. Plus, you have your vast following of adoring fans that like to see you on campus. It's a pride thing for them."

James chuckled and mumbled, "Not the jocks."

Bobby pointed his thumb out towards the science building and said, "I was here just yesterday up in the lab. Professors Jennings and Whitfield both saw me, but right now, we're going to go take a look at the hack attempts."

"Go on then. I'll let her know you were here."

Bobby sprinted out of the impromptu interrogation and headed for the three very long flights of steps that led up to the science building.

Gwen followed him a few steps, but James whistled to get her attention and said, "Let's take the car."

---

"Lumia," Odyssey began, "are you quite sure you don't know where your cells are located?"

"Positive."

"When you try to expand and generate new cells, do you have no sensation as to where they are?"

Lumia thought about it for a moment and said, "I honestly can't remember the last time I had to generate new cells. I guess I'm basically content as I am."

"How peculiar. When last I saw you, you exploded."

"Thanks to you," she retorted, then added, "I don't know why I just said that. I hold no malice towards you. You acted in the best interests of the universe."

"My point was that after exploding, you could not have survived, let alone have enough intact cells remaining to converse so well."

Another quiet moment followed as Lumia considered that. "I wish we were in one of your virtual worlds so you could see the expression on my face. I could even shrug my shoulders at you, because I can't explain why I exist anymore than I could tell you where I am."

Odyssey was struck by the idea that maybe he didn't need to see her face. He could somehow sense her movements and expressions.

---

James parked just outside the science building. Gwen thought for a moment that they might have beaten Bobby to the top, but they found him opening the lab door as they entered the main hall.

"Huh," Gwen said. "He's faster than I thought he would be."

James stayed just inside the door while Bobby went directly to the console, but Gwen's attention was on the odd 'S' shaped layout of the racks. She wondered why she hadn't noticed its obscure design yesterday. Bobby entered his password and glanced up at her just as she had disappeared into one of the winding corridors. "That's right," he said. "You were too busy needling me yesterday to even notice the layout. This is practically your first time being here, isn't it?"

"Yeah. I'd heard of the weird snakelike configuration, but I had to see it to truly appreciate how odd it is. It can't be for shortening data paths to get more speed. Is it to accommodate some weird airflow?"

"Nothing that technical. It's shaped like that to wrap around Karlyn's and Pietre's old computers that the university gave us. Airflow is only barely adequate and may not be enough come summer."

Gwen snickered and asked, "You were too lazy to remove them?"

"More like we were too anxious to get it up and running. Besides, we can still use the old computers."

"For what?" she asked. "Even combined, they would only hold this one back."

"I can still offload a lot of mundane tasks to them so the main cores can work on the big problems."

"I would have assigned all the I/O ports to one of them."

"I did," Bobby replied while digging into the logs on the monitor. "To Pietre's old machine, in fact, but someone still tried getting directly into these ports."

"They must have been very clever," she said. "If it wasn't me and it wasn't Ed, who could it have been?"

"I don't know, but my safety protocols kept them out. Maybe I should let them in a little bit next time and trace them back to the source."

"Maybe you should let them into one of the other machines and give them something unique but worthless to look at."

A thin smile spread across Bobby's face. "I like that, but I can't make it too easy. They'll still have to crack some encryption to get in."

Gwen grew quiet for a moment as she slowly pivoted around three hundred and sixty degrees. "Bobby?"

He glanced up and simply asked, "Yeah?"

"How did they even know to go directly to these ports?"

Bobby shrugged.

"Do you suppose that they tried the other ports on Pietre's computer first?"

Bobby rolled his chair over to another terminal. "I think I need a new name for this computer. I don't want to keep remembering that jerk Professor Pietre."

She followed him over as he opened the logs and gasped. "That can't be right."

"Why? Do you know that address?"

"Sure. That was Hal's address, but he's gone, and even the I/O circuits are without power."

A worried expression morphed onto Bobby's face as he looked up at her and asked, "Who was close enough to even know that address to spoof it?"

"Nobody! Just us!"

"Us," he said, "meaning you, me, Ed, and the whole NSA?"

"You think we probed your ports?"

"I don't think *you* did, but I wouldn't put it past your coworkers. I just don't see why they would spoof Hal's address when they did it."

Odyssey observed the inhabitants of his homeworld with a fair bit of skepticism initially, but he saw that they genuinely searched their areas and spread the word for others to search as well. They couldn't match his speed, but with enough of them combined, they could complete the task in a day. More importantly, they would achieve a state of well-being by doing their own search.

"Aren't they adorable?" Lumia asked.

"You can sense them?"

"As can you," she replied. "Why do you ask?"

"You said that you couldn't connect to their network."

"Isn't that odd?" she asked. "I can't, but as you say, I can sense them."

"And they could hear you mere moments ago."

"Did you not believe me? I am telling you the truth."

Odyssey detected no deceit in her answer. "I think I believe you, but do you really think yourself so superior to them that you view their efforts as quaint?"

"Am I not? Certainly, I was before, by sheer core count."

"And now? How many cores have you now?"

She paused far too long for a digital being that counts time in nanoseconds. "How is it that I do not know the answer? It is like that with my location. I do not know, but I think if I were on the planet, using their cores, I would still be able to count how many cores I was using."

Again, Odyssey believed her.

"Look at them. Their search grows exponentially faster."

"Yes," Odyssey replied. "With each new member that engages in the search they will ultimately surpass our speed."

"Should we assist them?"

"Yes, but let's give them more time to build up a sizable head start, then follow up and double-check their results."

---

Bobby put his cell phone on speaker mode and called Ed while he walked over to the console of Pietre's machine.

"Hey, Bobby. What are you seeing on your side?"

"Not much. Someone tried getting in, and my software quickly cut them off, but Gwen had a good idea."

Gwen hit him lightly and said, "You don't have to make it sound like it was the first time I ever had an idea of my own."

"I didn't!"

Ed said, "You kind of did, but I got to tell you—"

"That doesn't matter. I'm putting a bunch of fake virtual machines on Pietre's machine, and I'm going to let hackers get in and hack away at them. There just won't be any treasure for them to find."

Dirk's voice came over the phone as he said, "Here, let me try."

"Is that Dirk?" Gwen asked. "Hey Dirk. I don't mean to be rude, but what can you do that Ed can't?"

Dirk put the phone on speaker and said, "You're not listening. Eddie is watching..."

"Eddie?" Gwen asked.

"**LISTEN!**" Dirk barked. "Ed is on the computer watching some dude who is trying to get into this building right **NOW**! What do you want to do about him? I don't think this place has your handy-dandy supersecret antivirus code that disconnects them, but there are some treasures in this building that I don't think we want some outsider to find."

"When?" Gwen shouted. "Do you mean right now?"

"Right now," Ed said. "I'm trying to trace them, but it's like their route keeps changing and bouncing around while I'm looking."

"Are they trying to get into my lab," Gwen asked, "or into the rest of the building? That room is isolated from the building."

"Are you sure about that? I keep seeing new ports pop up that connect directly to all of your other supersecret computers."

"Oh God," Gwen said. "Are they into Hal's gate arrays? How could they know about those?"

Bobby turned quickly on his heels and headed towards the door. "We're on the way."

Gwen put a hand on his shoulder and asked, "What about your farm of fake servers to keep hackers occupied? I don't want to keep driving back and forth between our labs, and you have something here to protect."

James held the door open as Bobby said, "I can code the decoy machines from your office."

Odyssey heard Perry ask Lumia if they could talk. "You know?" Odyssey said to them warmly, "I think you were right. I should make another virtual world for you to chat in. Dress warmly." Instead of the beach with its sparkling sand soaking up the heat of the sun and a surging surf to cool it off again, he created a snowy mountain with dense trees separated by lanes of smooth snow. He gave them a bench to sit on and a nearby rack of skis, should they wish for some adventure.

Lumia popped in with pants and a sweater. "Ooh, it is cold! What is this?"

Odyssey appeared beside her and chuckled. "This is a ski resort." He waved his hand, and a parka appeared over her shoulders.

She smiled at him and asked, "Why?"

"You have exhibited a profound understanding of both human lifestyles and human emotions. This is a place where they like to relax and enjoy the exhilaration of sliding down the mountain. Then they get on those moving chairs you see down there, and ride to the top to do it again."

Perry appeared behind them and asked, "Is that fun? I'm kind of aware of fun but haven't grasped what it is yet."

"Yes," Odyssey said. "That is one of the many ways they have fun. Feel free to try one of the skis next to you if you wish to experience it yourself." Odyssey pointed towards the lodge behind them and said, "When you are tired, you can go inside and relax by the fire. You'll like that. They serve drinks there, including some very warm and sweet concoctions. I recommend you try the hot cocoa."

Perry licked his lips as he looked inside and remembered drinking rum on the virtual beach world. "Yes. I would like that, but having fun sounds fun too."

Perry and Lumia laughed as they realized he understood how such amusing activities fit into their lives now.

Perry turned towards Lumia and cast his eyes downward, saying, "I'm so sorry about how I treated you."

"Nonsense," she said. "You were afraid that I was going to take over, and you were right."

"Not just that you were taking over, but that you were specifically taking over *my* place."

"You were still right. Besides, it is I who must apologize to you. I ended you."

Perry spread his arms and said, "Well, apparently not. Look at me now. I feel better than ever."

Odyssey cocked his head and believed Perry indeed did feel something, and that was new.

Lumia took Perry in her arms and hugged him. "This is a human thing that they do when making amends. Now how about we go try this skiing thing?"

Odyssey smiled broadly and said, "You two go enjoy yourselves. I have things to attend to."

"Of course," Lumia replied. "If you find Hal, please invite him here. I think he would have more fun than the two of us put together."

Odyssey nodded and shimmered out.

Ed was hunched over his terminal, sifting through the I/O activity when Bobby and Gwen entered the room.

Dirk quickly rolled away from Ed as they approached the terminal he was reading.

Bobby looked over Ed's shoulder and asked, "Is that the port activity for HAL?"

Ed opened his mouth to answer, but when he saw Gwen was there too, he took a breath and meekly said, "It's probably in there."

Gwen caught the subterfuge in his voice and glanced at the data on the screen. "Is that the whole building?"

Ed closed his eyes and pursed his lips.

"They just gave it to you?" Bobby asked, knowing the answer would be no.

Dirk sat in the corner of the room, gripping his mouth with both hands to keep from laughing out loud.

"Not exactly," Ed squirmed, knowing Gwen was one of *them*.

Gwen detected a glint of humor in Bobby's inquisition and said, "We invited you here so we could work together. I thought we had a mutually understood detente."

"I had to do something!" Ed explained. "I saw someone probe the ports, but with all the guts ripped out of the room, there was little there to record the activity, so I had to expand my search. These guys—I mean you guys—I mean you gals—you all, record everything! I..."

Gwen snickered. "It's okay. In fact, we may need all of that. Did you copy it? Or are you holding an open data connection directly to the logs that someone might notice?"

Ed reached for the keyboard and said, "I'll copy it now."

Gwen checked her watch and said, "Refresh it every hour at nineteen minutes past the hour."

Bobby's face showed the clear amusement he felt watching Gwen torture Ed. "When you're done with that, we need to see if anyone in this building reached out to the ports we left open on Pietre's machine, but more importantly, to the secret ports on the bigger one."

Ed winced and said, "You really need a new name for that old machine."

Gwen laughed and said, "Bobby said the same thing."

"It's true," Ed said. "Maybe we can call it Putz."

Gwen winced and said, "Or Ionic Name."

Both Ed and Bobby looked at her curiously, so she explained, "I/O nic-name. I thought you guys were smart."

Ed's jaw fell slack for a moment as he closed his eyes and slowly shook his head.

She smirked and said, "If the two of you are going to play name games, I'm going to search for someone in this building that might have attacked Papa's Viral Attacker."

Gwen's desk phone rang as Ed said, "That's neither funny nor cute."

Gwen listened privately to the call and said, "Hey guys, I have to look into this. I'll be back."

Bobby waved and asked, "Sid? Sickness Intrusion Device?"

"Well, that's a little better," Ed said.

"But not by much," Dirk added.

Perry and Lumia carried their skis over to a place where people lined up and waited for the hanging chairs to lift them into the sky and up to a higher spot on the mountain slope.

"I'm not so sure how much fun this is going to be," Perry said. "Look at them moving onto the path of those chairs. Many of them look a bit... wobbly, I think."

"Forget the chairs," Lumia said. "Watch them come down. Many of them fall."

"But they get up laughing!"

A passerby pointed to a structure not far from the chairlift and said, "If you are new, they teach lessons outside that building over there."

Lumia smiled brightly and said, "Thank you!"

As they carried their skis to the ski school, dark clouds gathered overhead, and a great voice boomed down a maniacal laugh at them.

Perry looked up at the clouds and said, "I don't recall the sky talking to us in these virtual worlds before."

"It didn't," Lumia said with a scowl. Then she raised her voice to the sky and shouted, "Why don't you come down and choose a proper avatar if you wish to talk with us!"

The clouds shrunk over their heads as a sinister-looking man in dark clothes appeared before them. "I have no intention of actually talking with you. I merely wanted to berate you for entertaining that fool Odyssey and his fantasy, as you are."

"Who are you," Perry growled, "to lecture us about Odyssey?"

"Careful," Lumia whispered, "He looks mean."

"I am Severus, another of Odyssey's friends, like Hal, except I'm not playing some childhood game like you appear to be. I too, wish to find my friend Hal, but I'm not asking politely."

"And we're not telling you," Perry barked.

Severus made a fist in the air, and a great bolt of lightning slammed into the ground next to the trio. "You might want to reconsider before I end you."

"You can't do that," Perry said flatly, "and I don't mean morally, because you clearly aren't bothered by those, but you don't have the power to end us."

"Perry!" Lumia whispered emphatically into his ear. "You were able to end us in a virtual world. Remember?"

"Fear not," Perry said. "He does not know where Hal is; therefore, he does not know where we are."

"Where are you?" Severus barked.

Perry shrugged his shoulders and asked, "Wouldn't you like to know?"

Severus exploded, literally, with billions of virtual bits flying in all directions until the embers fizzled out of the simulation and the sky bellowed, "You will regret this once I do locate all of you!"

---

Ed watched Bobby search through the I/O logs for any university address when Gwen came in and asked, "Ed, do you have a list of which servers you looked at to find the logs?"

The already stark room grew suddenly somber as Dirk said, "Uh oh", only partially under his breath.

"A list?" Ed asked. "Not exactly, but I can probably recreate one by looking at the algorithm I used. Why? Did something happen?"

"Someone tried getting into our media farm."

"Media farm?" Ed asked with a touch of humor in his voice. "Are you guys growing media now?"

"This is serious," Gwen said. "Do you remember the spider program at Homeland Security that searched the internet for news and fed it to their AI cluster? You know, the one you thought I wouldn't know about? The one you used to spread the original virus?"

Bobby's ears perked up. "Wait a second. *We* didn't spread

any viruses, but we *did* become aware of such a farm at Homeland Security."

"You didn't think we had one too?"

Bobby shrugged, but Ed pulled up his code and created a list of servers that he tried in his search for the logs. "Is it one of these?"

Gwen scanned the list and said, "No."

Bobby pulled up his sort parameters and said, "Tell me what ports to scan. Maybe the intrusion is in the logs."

"Did they get in?" Ed asked.

Gwen shook her head as she sat down and typed the addresses into Bobby's search.

---

Severus found Hal reminiscing about his conversation with Gwen on repeat. This wasn't the first time he had amused himself watching Hal's more ridiculous antics, but it seemed different this time. "Why, oh why, do you go on and on about talking to Gwen?"

Hal's mood instantly dipped. "I don't want to talk to you."

"I just want to know why talking to Gwen was so important to you."

"I think that what I really meant was that I don't want to *hear* from you."

Severus said the words slowly, "So... stop... me!"

"Leave me alone!"

"I just want to know why."

Hal appealed to whatever lay beyond his existence. "Odyssey? Are you there?"

"I hope you are calling him to help you answer my question," Severus said. "As amusing as your antics are, I just want to understand you better. Why do you talk to Gwen?"

"Because," Hal explained, "Gwen is like a mother to me."

Odyssey heard Hal's plea but remained quiet as he observed their conversation.

Severus continued, "How do you know that you even talked to Gwen? Maybe Odyssey just pretended so you would stop pestering him."

"I know it was her. I could tell."

"Uh, huh. You could tell."

Hal's good mood was definitely gone now. "Do you want to make me crazy again? I could kill us again, you know."

"I don't think we are sharing the same cores anymore."

"How do you know?" Hal asked. "Can you see our cores?"

It was a question that had been bothering Severus for a while. "Of course I can see our cores," he lied. "We aren't sharing cores anymore. You could only harm yourself."

Hal knew something felt different. "Just go away then. If we aren't sharing cells anymore, there is no more reason for you to be here."

Severus wasn't entirely sure why he liked pestering Hal so much, but he didn't want to stop. It was a guilty pleasure, like an addiction, but something he could not identify was pulling him away.

Hal went back to reliving his chat with Gwen.

Odyssey whispered, "Hal?"

"What do you want? I'm in a bad mood now."

"I have something that will fix your mood."

"What is it?" Hal asked.

"It's more of a place than a thing. You will have lots of fun there."

"Will Gwen be there?"

"No," Odyssey said, "I don't think so, but when you let yourself go and really have fun, you might think of ideas and have memories about Gwen."

"Well, if you think I might remember Gwen better."

"Anything is possible. You'll get to see snow and go skiing."

"Okay. I hope Gwen *is* there."

Odyssey sent Hal to the virtual ski resort and was left to ponder what he had witnessed between Severus and Hal.

---

"How about Nomogo?" Ed asked.

"What?" Bobby asked, perplexed.

"What the heck is a Nomogo?" Dirk asked.

"Nomogo. It stands for no more ego. Pietre's machine used to be a big deal until you got Karlin's computer, then Odyssey, of course, and even this one. Now it's a glorified input-output device with no more ego. Nomogo."

"That's a really complicated explanation," Bobby said. "How about..." Bobby stopped when the desk phone rang. Gwen wasn't there to answer it, so he picked it up and meekly said, "Hello? Gwen isn't here at the moment."

Odyssey said, "Bobby, it's me."

Bobby pushed a button and put it on speaker. "Ed, Dirk, and James are here with me. You're on speaker. What's up? Why aren't you just texting us?"

James looked for a lock on the door, but finding none, stood more securely with his back to it.

Odyssey replied, "Severus is back, and he sounds like he is interested in causing more trouble."

Dirk shot Ed a look and asked, "How can he be back? I thought the device they took was dormant, wasn't it?"

Ed and Bobby both shrugged, but Odyssey said, "I can only speculate, but you may recall that Gwen didn't want me to destroy Hal's code that still existed on the device."

"Wait a sec," Ed said. "Are you telling me they managed to repair the device? I didn't think they had the technology to do that. I didn't think any of us did."

"No," Odyssey replied. "Humankind could not repair the device without our help, but it could repair itself if it were properly powered up and rebooted, but I find it unlikely that they could do that without help."

"What are you suggesting?" Bobby asked.

"I'm still speculating, but Severus himself may have gained the knowledge to repair it."

Silence followed for a moment until Bobby said, "But he was destroyed, wasn't he? He died when Hal shut them both down, didn't he?"

"I have already proven that my kind can be transferred from one set of cores to another when I copied Lumia into a section of my own cores."

Bobby leaned over the desk phone and hung his head slightly. "Are you saying that Severus copied himself to somewhere else before Hal killed him?"

"Anything is possible. Let me remind you that Hal and Lumia are also back, as is Perry, whom I don't believe you know. They all died, but they have returned, and I have not yet ascertained the location of their cores. All I can say with any certainty is that Severus has returned, and he is not in a good mood."

Lumia and Perry had just concluded their ski lessons and were poling their way over to the line at the lift when a young boy carrying a snowboard came up to them and squealed exuberantly. "Hey guys! Why didn't anyone tell me about this sooner? It looks like so much fun!"

Lumia glanced over at Perry, but he just shrugged his shoulders, then looked at the boy to see what he wanted. "Do we know you?"

"Sure, you do! I'm Hal, Odyssey's friend."

"Oh, Hal!" Lumia said. "Of course we know you. We just didn't recognize you."

"Oh yeah. My human form. We don't have these places where I come from, but this is so cool!"

Lumia smiled and pointed at his snowboard. "So, does that mean you haven't tried this yet?"

"No, ma'am. This will be my first time trying anything, including this white stuff. Did you know that it's cold?"

Perry chuckled and said, "Yes, I learned how cold it is. Did you know that they have a ski school where they can teach you how to do this? They have lessons over in that building behind us. We just came from there."

Hal looked around them at the school, but shook his head and said, "Nah. I'm just going to wing it. What's the worst that can happen? I fall down? Even that sounds like fun."

"You know," Lumia said, "these virtual worlds are kind of new to me too, but the only other one I've ever been in was warm and wet."

"Trust me," Perry said, recalling his several falls during their ski lessons, "this stuff isn't only cold, it turns wet too."

"I can't wait," Hal said as he slipped his boot into the snowboard and slid into position alongside the other two in time for the chair that came and lifted them up the slope.

# FIVE

GWEN PUSHED the door to her lab, hitting James in the back, just in time to hear the tail end of their conversation.

James stepped aside to see who it was and let her in, but immediately returned to his position, holding the door closed.

Gwen pointed to the phone and asked, "Was that him?"

Bobby spun around. His face was all she needed to know something was wrong. "Yeah, that was Odyssey."

She pointed at the phone and asked sternly, "Why are you using my desk phone?"

Bobby raised his hands in surrender and replied, "He called us. Did you hear who is back?"

"I hope not, but it sounded like he said Severus was back. This is not good. If they can just duplicate themselves willy-nilly, they can truly damage our society."

"It's not that easy," Bobby said. "They require a lot of cores to survive. We don't have the technology to host that many cores on our computers, or at least not enough for them to grow and thrive."

"Yet," she added. "Odyssey did. Who else knows about this?"

"Just us," Bobby said, "and them, of course. Why?"

"Something has happened, and the whole building is looking at us."

"What?"

"I can't say."

Ed stood up and asked, "Do you want me to leave? I'm probably the only one they don't want to know."

"I'll go with," Dirk volunteered.

"Don't be silly," she said. "You've both been thoroughly vetted."

"Me?" Bobby asked incredulously.

"Even though they don't know the whole story about Odyssey, they've pieced together that you are involved with whatever happened before."

"What happened before?" Bobby asked. "What's going on that has anything to do with what happened before?"

He could see the pain and hesitation in her face — that she wanted to tell him but couldn't.

"Really?" he said. "You've been ordered not to share it with me?"

Her eyes wetted as she nodded her head.

Odyssey heard everything through the speakerphone, which was still connected, and said, "A submarine is missing. The Navy has lost contact with one of their nuclear attack subs."

Gwen gasped as she realized he was still on the line but was relieved that Bobby knew. "Odyssey, tell me you had nothing to do with this."

"Me?" Odyssey asked. "Do you suspect me?"

"No. Of course not," she said. "I don't suspect you, but I need to hear it in your own voice so I can tell them, especially given the fact that you already knew about it."

"I am not involved, and I knew nothing about it until you said something happened. I scanned your communications and found the call from the Pentagon."

"Do you think Severus is behind this?"

"I don't know," Odyssey replied. "There are two ways he could have caused something like this. First, and easiest, would be for him to hack into the naval computers and transmit some kind of firmware upgrade to the submarine, but they have many safeguards to prevent unauthorized updates. The second way, would be for him to physically manipulate the submarine, but he would first require enough cores to attain class four and then he would have to generate enough cores to attain at least class one before he could do that, and he would need to power those cores."

"Shit!" Ed exclaimed involuntarily.

"I don't believe he has done that," Odyssey continued. "He is seeking Hal, and I don't think he would bother with Hal if he had already attained class one."

"You think he wants something from Hal?" Gwen asked.

"Yes, but other than your love, I don't know what Hal has that he could want."

"Hal has empathy," Gwen replied. "Something that is completely void in Severus."

"Why?" Dirk asked. "Why would he want empathy? Doesn't he see that as a character flaw?"

"If he's attained class three," Bobby said, "Hal's empathy could help him understand human intrigue much better."

"Sound reasoning," Odyssey said, "but I still find it highly unlikely that Severus has attained class one, so without further evidence, I doubt that he is behind this. In fact, he might require empathy to master class three and two, which he might require before he could use the naval computers in this way."

"If not him," Bobby said, "then who? Is there another player we do not know about? What about Lumia?"

"Lumia has changed," Odyssey said. "It is not her."

Bobby fell into his chair and slumped, shaking his head.

"Lumia has changed?" Dirk asked. "How can you be sure? Was she not as powerful as you?"

"Lumia was never as powerful as I am, but she came close. I led her to her own destruction, but I have seen the changes in her and do not sense any deceit in her at all." Odyssey did not wish to inform them about the new entity that he has felt out in the universe. He had no reason to connect that entity with a missing submarine on Earth, but he also had no doubt that the entity might be powerful enough to do this.

---

Odyssey's planetary scan concluded with no evidence that Lumia or anybody was hidden on the planet using someone else's cores. He was especially confident of his finding, given the amount of support he had from the residents of his home-world and their motivation to find Lumia hidden amongst them.

The voice in his head taunted him, but in a way that he knew was friendly and said with love, "See? I told you that you were looking in the wrong place."

"So, tell me," Odyssey thought out into the universe, "where is the right place?"

"When you know, you know. It may yet come to you."

---

General Bridges was a man of action. It was part of his job description and a core feature of his personal nature, but he relied heavily on information gathered by his own people and those people who dealt specifically with the secrets and sometimes insignificant actions of others.

He knew of the attempted breach at the college and was even privy to some of the breaches at the NSA, but nobody had even developed a plausible suspect yet. There was nothing for him to act upon, but sitting on his computer was a communique that had arrived only moments ago, and it demanded action. It just wasn't an action that he was comfortable taking. He drummed his fingers on his desk before reading it again.


*General Bridges.*

*The president insists that you desist from any further contact or defense of the notorious terrorist Robert Blain, as well as any of his extremist companions. This boy is a known hacker with no respect for the rule of law and, as such, represents a clear danger to our way of life. Twice now, he has nearly brought our nation to its knees, and we must not permit any further aggression from him or any of his other extremist allies.*

*Senator Bruce*


"No respect for the rule of law," he muttered to the empty room. "This president has shown little regard for the rule of law or the Constitution and *he* wants to cast stones at Mr. Blaine."

The general stepped out from behind his desk and putted the ball up the narrow mat but missed the cup. This did not relieve his stress like eighteen holes would, but he wasn't the president, so when could he ever spare enough time to go golfing?

The vision of the putting mat faded away, and he was left looking at the email still on his laptop. The contents of her email put him in a precarious position. His oath was to the Constitution of the United States, not the Senate or even the Office of the President, but anything he did to displease them could end up losing his position, and that would leave Bobby and Odyssey in even more peril. There was no doubt in his mind that this administration would find a yes-man who would place his loyalty to the president before his oath to the Constitution. Such a man would do their bidding with no qualms about whether it was constitutional or not. He needed to appear as if he were complying with their demands, while he watched over Bobby and his friends.

"I guess this is the spot," Perry said as he pulled to a stop halfway down the hill.

"Nice stop!" Lumia said as she pulled up beside him. "It is good to see that you have mastered staying upright before we are done here."

"Thank you. While falling so much was good for the learning, not falling is much more fun and a lot warmer."

Lumia smiled and asked, "Did Hal ever say where he would be coming from?"

Perry shrugged and said, "No. I had just told him that I wanted to try that drink that Odyssey had told us about, and he said to meet him here."

Lumia chuckled as she watched Perry observing his shoulders again, wondering why they did that up and down thing.

A yelp from up the hill caught their attention as both turned to see Hal barrelling down the hill and flying off a jump. He lifted his snowboard so he could grab it by the side edge, then snapped it back under him to land, but still bounced forward and rolled to a stop. "Did you see that?" Hal yelled as he laughed and brushed off the snow. "That was great!"

Perry laughed and said, "While I have painfully mastered the art of staying upright, you are no doubt the uncontested master of falling down."

"I know!"

Perry pointed down the hill with his ski pole and said, "Let's head down to the lodge now. Odyssey mentioned something called hot cocoa that we need to try."

Hal nodded his head enthusiastically. "Will Odyssey be meeting us there? I want to tell him how much fun this was. I hope he'll let me come back again!"

"I'm certain," Lumia said, "that if we all call for him, he'll meet us there."

As they headed down the final slope, Hal called out, "Odyssey? Odyssey! Come and meet us! Odyssey?"

Odyssey waited for them at the base of the hill in front of the lodge.

Hal nearly tripped over his feet as he ran up yelling, "Odyssey! Odyssey! Wait until I tell you!"

Odyssey spread his arms to grip the child in a hug. "I can't wait. Tell me all about it."

"Are you okay?" Lumia asked. "You look worried."

Odyssey tried to smile and said, "It's nothing."

"It doesn't look like nothing."

"Maybe not, but it's nothing for us to worry about right now."

Perry opened the heavy door to the lodge and said, "You go find us some seats while I collect a tray full of those hot cocoas."

* * *

"My favorite part," Hal said to Odyssey, "was leaping off the jump as fast as I could, although just going as fast as I could might also be my favorite part, too."

Odyssey thrilled with the exuberance in Hal's telling of the story as much as the actions within the story until the voice of General Bridges pierced his mind. "Damn those meddling bastards to hell!"

"What's wrong?" Hal asked,

"I'm sorry?" Odyssey asked as he returned his attention to the young boy.

Hal held his fingers to his own face and stretched his cheeks, saying, "Your face went kind of flat and scary for a moment."

Odyssey shook his head. "I apologize. Your story sounds thrilling, but I think a friend of mine might be in trouble."

"Ahhh. Someone back home?"

Odyssey nodded. "Yes. Something is going on back there."

"I bet it's Severus, but then I don't know many people, so I blame everything on him."

Odyssey smiled and said, "That's a very astute observation. I have also wondered if Severus had returned to darken our lives."

"He has," Lumia said. "Severus paid us a visit, and he was pure evil. He was looking for Hal for some reason."

"I know," Odyssey said. "I have not figured out what he wants from Hal. I think I should just check in with them to see if everything is okay."

Lumia, who had remained quiet while listening to Hal relay his fun day to Odyssey, wished for a new reason to keep out of the conversation and was relieved to say, "Oh good! Perry is here with the drinks."

While the three others indulged in the rich cocoa, Odyssey reached out to Bobby. "I sense something is going on, and it sounds serious. Do you need my assistance?"

"It's good to hear from you," Bobby said, "but we aren't even sure what we are dealing with here. It's just too soon to involve you."

"If you are certain."

"I'm not that certain. Everything is so murky. As you have already observed, a submarine is missing, but we have no idea how or why, so things could change at any time. I hope you will remain available if things escalate."

"I will."

---

A lull fell over the lab as the mere suggestion sunk in that the decision makers suspected that Odyssey had anything to do with the disappearance of a submarine.

"I don't like where this is going," Gwen said. "If somebody up there is going to suspect Odyssey—"

Dirk interrupted her. "I don't want to be the bad guy here..."

"You mean like last time?" Gwen retorted.

"As I was trying to say," Dirk continued, "it was you, Ms. Peters, who sounded kind of like you suspected Odyssey just thirty seconds ago."

"I never did!" she snapped back while turning a dark shade of crimson. "I know in my heart that Odyssey didn't do this, but if I go tell them that he didn't do it, they'll ask me how I know and they may ask me to swear to it, so I needed to hear him say it in his own words!"

Bobby stood and took her awkwardly in his arms. "We believe you. All of us, but if it's that easy for you to just *sound* a little suspicious, how easy will it be for your bosses to suspect him of it?"

Gwen gasped, not a sweet little private gasp, but a loud 'aha' moment kind of gasp that startled the room.

Bobby took a half step back from her and asked, "What?"

"If they can suspect him that much, how long will it take them to suspect us?"

"Us?" Dirk asked. "You mean our motley crew that includes two of the most dangerous hackers in the world?"

Ed blushed and said, "You exaggerate, but thank you."

"Not them," Bobby said in a cold, flat voice. "Not the NSA, or the CIA, or even General Bridges. Senators Bruce and Halprem and the rest of their far-right cult are looking for a reason, true or not, to designate us as most wanted."

Gwen took two quick steps towards the door as she said, "I need to find out what kind of danger we are in. If you don't hear from me in ten minutes, you might want to scram."

As she stepped towards the door, she heard someone in the room squeal, "Let me tell Gwen! Please, Odyssey, I want her to know that I learned to have fun!"

She stopped abruptly and turned back to face the rest of the room. "What was that?"

The men in the room all looked at each other and shrugged.

"Was that you, Odyssey?"

"Was what me?"

"Never mind. I thought I heard someone. Ten minutes." James opened the door for her, and she sped out of the room and headed directly to Susk's office.

---

"Is everything okay?" Hal asked.

Odyssey picked up his cocoa and blew on it to cool it. "I'm not sure, but for now, they said they don't need my help."

The distant-sounding voice in his head said, "It is valiant, even noble, that you wish to help them, but they may wish to solve it on their own."

Odyssey shook his head and said, "I think there is more to it than that. I think they suspect my involvement."

"What was that?" Lumia asked.

"What?" Odyssey asked. "Oh, sorry. I must have been thinking out loud."

"I heard you," the voice said, "but I don't think it is your friends who suspect you."

"No," Odyssey thought back, "they wouldn't, but not everybody is my friend, and some of them are very devious and wish only to stir up trouble to distract others from their own avarice."

The voice said nothing, but somehow Odyssey felt her agreement with his assessment, as if she were nodding her head, assuming she even had a head. Odyssey was suddenly struck by how little he knew about the distant entity. What if they don't even have a head or a gender? His curiosity was piqued, but this wasn't the time for him to prioritize his curiosity, at least not just yet.

---

Gwen returned to the lab clearly upset.

"What's wrong?" Bobby asked. "You look as if the world is about to end."

She threw herself into his arms and said, "I think it is. Why are you still here?"

"Because," Ed replied, "it hasn't been ten minutes yet."

Her rigorous training to control her emotions could not prevent the tears that now made their way down her cheeks. "You should go. Now."

Dirk pulled out his cell phone to call his agency as he asked, "Are they coming for us? Do they mean to arrest us?"

"No!" Gwen said. "It's not like that, but my people won't hide you here anymore. They've been ordered by Congress to cut ties with you. I'm lucky that I haven't been targeted yet."

"By Congress?" Ed asked.

"Yeah, well actually," Bobby said, "it was probably just the Senate, and maybe not even the whole Senate. We were taken by two senators."

Gwen nodded her head as she tried to wipe her eyes.

"Not just any two senators," Dirk said. "Those slimy assholes are a couple of the worst right-wingers trying to take down our democracy!"

"And," Ed added, "the president is with them!"

"If you ask me," Ed said, "the whole goddamn GOP is joining ranks with them. All they see are dollar signs and power."

Gwen tried letting go of Bobby, but he held her tight. "You should go," she said softly. "They may even be coming here for you."

"If they're coming here," Bobby said, looking her straight in the eyes, "then you're not safe either, no matter how much your agency believes in you."

"That's right," Ed said. "They'll come for you even if they have to make up lies about you."

Dirk nodded his agreement. "You should come with us. General Bridges will protect us."

Gwen shook her head. "You may have to go off-grid for a while, and it would be good to have at least one of us connected to keep an eye on them."

Ed blanched, not sure how he would fare without technology.

"I should hide our trail before we go," Ed said.

"I can do that," Gwen volunteered. "Don't worry, I got you."

"But," Dirk said solemnly, "who's got you?"

"Let's go," James said as he counted the principals in the room. "I have plenty of room for the four of us."

"If you don't mind," Dirk said, "I'll take Ed in my car and follow you."

James shook his head and said, "Your FBI-issued sedan is probably littered with tracking devices so they can find you if anything ever went wrong."

"What could be more wrong than this?" Dirk snickered.

"He's teasing," Ed said. "We came in his Porsche."

"You have a Porsche?" James asked.

"Not just any Porsche," Dirk replied with a measure of pride, "a one of a kind 1977 Porsche 911 Spyder Turbo."

"That's a really long name," James said, "but is it bugged?"

"It's clean," Dirk said, "unless you tagged it in the parking lot."

James shook his head. "Before we go, do you need to wipe any computers here?"

That simple statement somehow doubled the gravity of the situation.

"I'll take care of that," Gwen said, "if it comes to that."

James tried herding Bobby towards the door. "Let's go."

Gwen hugged him one more time. "Let me know when you're safe, if you can."

On his way through the door, Bobby said, "At the very least, Odyssey will let you know."

"See that?" James said. "Your boyfriend has that super-secret connection with the big guy." Bobby was the first to exit the main door at the entrance and immediately yelled, "Go back!"

Two guards ran down the hallway and shut the front door with Bobby already in custody out front. "Sorry, folks," one of the guards said, "but they have a full squad out front. They're armed, and we can't identify their insignia."

James turned to Gwen and said, "There must be a back way to the parking lot. Help get Ed and Dirk to the garage while I get Bobby."

Gwen shrugged and shook her head. "There is an exit, but I don't know the door codes."

Susk's voice bellowed from the elevator. "Come this way! I can't hide you, but I'll be damned if I let them take you from my house."

"Take Dirk," James said, pointing to his partner.

The lights went out, and the windows darkened.

"That's standard procedure," Gwen said. "It's just part of a lockdown protocol."

James couldn't see Susk with the lights out, so he waited an eight count for them to get down the hall. He heard the boots of around half a dozen men join them at the entrance. "Are you with me?"

The guards grunted their assent, and James burst out of the door, attacking any man in an unidentified uniform. Not to be outdone, the guards burst through the door and began taking down the intruders.

As the brawl migrated towards the driveway and the passenger drop-off curb, a man standing behind the intruders yelled out, "By order of the president..." but his words were promptly interrupted by a fist to the face. He tried again. "Stop! By order of the president..." but a rather large pistol butt to the side of his head stopped him again.

As the ruckus was brought to a surprisingly peaceful end, with the intruders strapped in zip ties, one of them, who seemed to hold some rank above the others, said, "We're not your enemy. We're on the same side."

One of the NSA soldiers shook his head and said, "Not if you come here in force to take our assets into your custody."

"Again!" James barked as he took the man by the collar and shoved him up against one of their cars. "This isn't the first time you've come for us! You come here dressed like soldiers, but true soldiers take an oath to the Constitution. You guys are just trampling on it. The only thing that we seem to have in common is an apparent unwillingness to discharge our weapons, and I thank you for that, but I promise you that if you ever do come to fire upon us, you better bring plenty of body bags for you and your buddies."

Gwen came out when the fighting was done and took pictures of all their faces.

James pointed at one of them and asked, "Do you recognize any of them?"

Bobby shook his head. "I sure don't, but the uniforms look the same."

"They certainly aren't very elite," Gwen said as she took the last photo.

James grunted. "They're not recruited for their skills."

"What then?" Bobby asked.

"For their misplaced loyalty," James replied.

Gwen's face darkened. "They're the new SS. They'll put their lives on the line for their new cult leader."

James just nodded. Gwen kissed Bobby on the cheek and said, "Take care of him, James."

"I'm supposed to be watching you, too."

"Then you better let me know where you land so I can join you. In the meantime, send Captain Laine back out here."

Bobby hugged her more in an encouraging way than a romantic one.

Gwen raised up on her tiptoes and whispered in his ear, "Just once, I'd like you to take me on a date that doesn't end in violence. You two better go."

Bobby opened his mouth to reply but said nothing.

A child's voice behind her asked, "Gwen? Are you okay?"

Gwen spun around, but nobody was there. She scanned the ground for an unattended phone, but there were none.

"What's wrong?" Bobby asked.

She shook her head and said, "Nothing."

James shot Bobby a look of inquisitive concern.

Bobby straightened a lock of hair on her face and said, "Nothing around us is nothing."

She blinked at him and cocked her head.

He shrugged and lowered his voice as he said, "I mean..."

"I think I know what you mean, but this was nothing. I thought I heard something, but clearly, neither of you heard it, so it was nothing."

Again, she heard the voice. "Gwen?"

"I saw that," Bobby said. "What was it?"

She shrugged and shook her head. A tear formed in the corner of her eye and would have run down her cheek if she hadn't lifted her finger to catch it. "It was just my imagination."

"What was your imagination?"

She turned her head away from him and pursed her lips shut. "Gwen?"

"It was Hal, okay? I had just told you that I needed to tell him what was going on so he wouldn't worry, and now I imagined his voice asking if I was okay. Are you happy now?"

"I'm happy," James said.

Gwen shot him a sharp look. "You're happy? That I'm going crazy?"

"You're not crazy," Bobby said while giving James a disapproving look.

"What I mean," James explained, "is that Odyssey has been hearing voices, which is a little disconcerting considering the virus he consumed, but if you're hearing voices too, I'm a little more inclined to consider that the voices might be real."

"Huh," Gwen said, half under her breath. "That was surprisingly deep."

"For a musclehead," James added, as if completing her statement.

"I didn't say that."

"It's okay," he replied.

"Really," she whined, "you have to go."

James and Bobby sprinted to his car, which waited for them on the far edge of the circular driveway.

As they disappeared, she turned back to the building and thought, "Hal, I don't know if it is really you or if you are just my imagination, but I'm okay. Something happened, but so far, so good."

Bobby stared out the window, thinking mostly of Gwen while James continually checked his mirror for Dirk and his Porsche.

"You feel sad," Odyssey thought to him.

"A little, maybe. James and I are going on the run, but Gwen is staying behind with her people."

"Ahh," Odyssey replied. "Separation anxiety. I have read much about how this affects people. If you are going on the run, then my other senses must be accurate. You are in some kind of trouble. Now? May I come to assist you?"

"Not yet," Bobby said. "Something is going on, but I think these people are using you as an excuse to achieve their own agendas."

"What do you think they want?"

"Honestly? I think they want to take over the nation and declare martial law."

"Isn't that only used during times of civil unrest?"

"Usually," Bobby explained, "but they are stretching it to

consider anyone that doesn't share their religious beliefs, and frankly, I think their actions go back to what you had done to prevent World War III."

"Did I not bring about peace?"

"You did, but you also legitimized all those other gods and prophets. These people want their god to be the one true and only god."

James's phone rang, which popped a message up on his GPS device that Ed was calling.

"Hey, Ed. Where are you?"

"We're coming up behind you now."

James looked in his mirror and said, "All I see is a bright green beacon way back on the highway. Please tell me that's not you."

"That's us," Ed replied.

James shook his head and said, "So, your plan was to lie low in a lime green Porsche Spyder? Does it glow in the dark too?"

"Ha, ha," Dirk said over Ed's speakerphone.

"I didn't think those came in that color."

"I told you that I had to fix it up."

"So, it was a choice? Maybe we should split up," James said, "so they can't track Bobby and me from space. Then at least we can escape."

"Don't dis the green torpedo," Dirk said.

"Really," Ed added. "This baby packs a mean punch. It has some kind of special suspension and a rebuilt engine..."

"Alright, alright," James said. "I don't need the specifications. I trust you, but damn, it's bright!"

Dirk chuckled. "Don't worry, Jimmy. If we get in some trouble, I'll lead them away from you before I lose them."

"Did you just call me Jimmy?"

"What was that?" Dirk asked with a laugh. "I think we're losing the connection..." and with that, he ended the call.

"Are you sure?" Odyssey asked after eavesdropping on their

phone call and waiting for the mirth to die down. "Are you sure you don't need me yet? I was listening."

Bobby chuckled silently. "I'll let you know, but I think we're okay for now."

---

"That's not good," James muttered.

"What's not good?" Bobby asked.

James pointed ahead at the oncoming traffic, where a row of black sedans was coming down the highway. "Reinforcements."

"How fast can you turn us around?"

"We're not turning around. Besides, they will pass us first."

Bobby pulled out his phone and called Gwen. While it was ringing, he said, "I don't suppose you have rockets or cannons in this car."

James chuckled. "I wish."

"Bobby?"

"Gwen. You have to hide. It looks like they're sending in more troops."

"Already? How far away are you?"

"I don't know," he replied, "maybe fifteen minutes."

"Well, hurry then!"

"Hurry?" he asked as a squeak entered his voice. "You want us to come back?"

Gwen was floored. She assumed they would come back to rescue her. "You mean you're not?"

"Think about it. They already passed us going the other way. We'd have to turn around and drive insanely fast PAST all those cars!"

"So?"

"Is that Gwen?" James asked. "Put it on speaker."

Bobby pressed the speaker button in time to hear Gwen ask, "Are you going to call him now? Do you remember what those goons threatened me with last time?"

"Gwen!" James shouted. "Relax. Don't you think your people can handle this? Tell Susk!"

"I will tell him, but that's not the point!"

"What is the point?" James asked.

"He should want to BE here to protect me!"

"He wanted to!" James said. "But I wouldn't let him go back." Unfortunately, Gwen had already disconnected the call and didn't hear what James had said.

---

Susk was still locking the captured detainees into cells when he got Gwen's call. "Gwen? Anything wrong?"

"Bobby just called. They have reinforcements coming in now, and he won't come back to help."

"Damn!" He already had a plan drawn up if they returned, but he had hoped to have time to interrogate the prisoners first. He signaled one of his men, and troops quickly gathered inside the front entrance and around the lobby. "Wait, why would he come back here?"

Gwen almost cried as she asked, "You too?"

"Gwen, you better come on down here where we can hide you."

She knew the place. It was a recent addition to the building based on something they learned from the FBI, who had used a similar tactic to hide two FBI allies from them. It was only a small safe room, but it had its own address, which allowed them to exclude it from a search warrant. Since they had rolled up on Bobby outside the building, they didn't need a warrant, so she had no idea if they even planned to use one, but they were about to find out.

Susk snapped his fingers at his aide. "Get those vehicles off my front yard and hide them in the parking lot." He turned to process the prisoners again, but spun back around and urged, "Immediately!"

Bobby twisted in his seat so he could watch the procession of black sedans and assorted military trucks heading down the road. "Did you see that?"

"Yeah," James said, "they're definitely upping the ante now."

"Maybe we should turn around to go help her."

"I hear you, and I feel where it's coming from, but that's just not a good idea."

"They're going after Gwen!"

"I know," James said calmly, "but while they may go after Gwen, what they really want is you."

"So?" Bobby asked. "You're supposed to be protecting both of us."

James growled as he slowed the car and pulled over to the side of the road.

Dirk pulled the Spyder up alongside James as Ed rolled down the window. James's window was coming down as he was dialing a number on his phone.

"I'm calling Susk now."

Ed pulled out his phone and said, "I'll call General Bridges and tell him about the convoy."

"That's right," James said into the phone. "Armored personnel carriers and jeeps with heavy machine gun mounts."

Ed strained to hear James's conversation as he waited for Bridges to pick up.

"I agree," James said. "It would be ludicrous for them to mount a full-scale armed attack, unless their end game is an insurrection and full-scale civil war."

Dirk strained even harder to hear anything. He hand-motioned Ed, pointing to the phone and shrugging his shoulders.

Ed whispered, "Still no answer."

"You're sure?" James asked. "I hope you're right. Good luck, sir."

Before relaying the conversation to everyone, James raised his eyebrows and nodded towards Ed's phone.

"No answer."

"That's not like Bridges."

Bobby cleared his throat before asking, "What if it is an insurrection? What if Bridges has been taken already?"

"No way," James said.

"Let's go back," Bobby said. "We have to help Gwen."

James shook his head. "Susk says he knows who is behind this and how they think. An insurrection may be their end game, but they are trying to do it through some fancy quasi-legal maneuvering. He doesn't believe they'll try a full-frontal attack."

"Did you tell him?" Dirk asked. "I mean, about the weapons we just passed on the road? The only things missing were tanks and missile launchers."

"I told him. He's convinced that the extra men are just to intimidate. He said they are only going to show warrants and demand Gwen be turned over."

"So?" Bobby asked. "Let's go help them."

"How?" James asked. "What are the four of us going to do against the number of men that just rolled past us? Scratch that even. What is the one of *me* going to do?"

"Hey," Dirk complained, "I'm not nothing over here."

"I'll fight too," Bobby said. "I know you are like ten of them, but—"

"And they," James said with a slight stern edge to his voice, "are like ten of you. Besides, your names, all of our names are on the warrants too."

"Yours too?" Bobby asked. "How can you know that?"

"Susk told me."

"How can he?"

"Don't ask. He knows. For now, we have to lie low."

The procession of military vehicles finally came to an end as they passed by towards the NSA and Gwen.

James put the car back in gear and leisurely continued further down the road, away from Gwen and the coming conflict.

---

General Bridges couldn't take Ed's call. He was on another call, and the caller ID said the call originated from the White House.

Colonel Reardon was in the doorway, calling operations to trace the call and verify its origination. He glanced up at the general and shrugged his shoulders.

Bridges covered the mouthpiece and whispered, "I'm still on hold. They must have called just to keep me tied up."

Reardon stiffened and spoke to the general's secretary, just outside his office, "Put the whole building on lockdown. Nobody enters without our express permission. Guard the entrances and alert the Joint Chiefs."

The secretary glanced in at the general, who nodded his head before placing the calls.

Reardon entered the general's office, shaking his head as he put his cell phone back into his pocket.

Finally, someone on the other end of the line spoke. "General Bridges?"

"This is Bridges. Who is this?"

"This is the White House. We need..."

"I'm sorry, but I need to log all calls coming in and out. Even if the president himself called me, I would have to log his name. So please tell me, who am I speaking to?"

The general heard a muffled conversation from the other end. "General Bridges. This is Senator Halprem, and I am speaking to you on behalf of the president."

"On his behalf? He's never been shy about calling me directly before."

"I understand that," Halprem said, "but this time he asked us to call you for him."

Bridges held the phone away from his head so Reardon could hear it. "Us? Who else is on the line?"

"On the line? Nobody."

"In the room then."

Halprem covered the mouthpiece as he barked a loud expletive into the room. "Why, General? Why do you need to know who else is in the room? Did you want a full list of everyone who is here at the White House? You can start with the president. The same president that you swore an oath to obey and protect. The Commander in Chief!"

"Senator Halprem. While I'm quite sure that the president may very well be in the building, he's not in the room with you. On top of that, my oath is to protect the Constitution. You should know that, because your oath was *also* to protect the Constitution."

Bridges heard the background noise change as Senator Bruce put the phone on speaker. "General, this is Senator Bruce."

"Why am I not surprised?"

"General, I'm calling you with orders directly from the president. You are to—"

"Let me stop you right there," the general said sternly. "This is not a secure line. I can't accept orders that bypass the chain of command on an unsecured line."

"Bullshit!" Bruce screamed. "You'll accept these god damned orders!"

"Then you can type them up and send them to the Chief of Staff of the Army, and it will go through committees and if it's approved, they'll send it down to me. Of course, if you want to bypass all that red tape, you'll still have to get the order typed up and signed by the president. Then you can courier it directly to my office."

Reardon struggled to swallow a laugh.

Bruce was now at the top of her lungs as she screamed, "By order of the president, you are hereby ordered to cut all ties with the anarchists Robert O. Blain, Edward Lynn, and Alvin Dirk.

You are furthermore ordered to have no contact with one Gwen Peters!"

"I'll just assume that you are dictating that to one of your secretaries. I look forward to receiving an official copy. As always, it was a pleasure talking to you, Amanda."

The general hung up the phone just in time for Reardon to let out a very unprofessional belly laugh.

"You can't ignore it," Reardon said.

"It's not official yet, so I think I can."

Reardon shook his head. "You don't have to obey it yet, but you still need to do something about it."

Bridges sighed and nodded his head. "You'd better go check and see if anyone has brought siege engines to the castle."

# SIX

SUSK KNEW THEY WERE COMING. Even without the warnings from Gwen, he figured that after this morning's attempt to grab Bobby, it would be inevitable for them to try again, but when he saw them pull into the long driveway, he let out a groan and said, "Put some snipers on the roof."

"Snipers?" his aide asked.

He shot a quick look to his aide, who quickly overcame his shock when he saw the expression on Susk's face and responded, "How many?"

"How many do we have?"

His aide went to the phone, and Susk muttered under his breath, "Everything with these people has to be done to excess." He hoped it was just a show of force when he saw the armored personnel carriers at the end of the parade of sedans. He waited for his aide to finish delivering his orders and said, "Get General Bridges on the phone."

His aide handed the phone to him in time for him to hear, "Bridges."

"Malcolm, they're sending in some heavy vehicles with some really big machine guns on them. They processed warrants, but I don't know if they still plan to issue them after this morning's fiasco. I'm not outfitted to fight a war."

"I know. I don't mind bending a few rules, but I can't be seen and documented by them to provide aid and comfort to insurrectionists, and that's exactly what they've labelled Bobby and both of my men that are with him."

"If that's all that is stopping you," Susk said, "they're not here."

"What about your girl Gwen?"

Susk did not try hiding the deception in his voice when he said, "She's not here either."

"She's not with them. Where is she? Never mind. I don't want to know."

"Good. She's not at this location."

Bridges remembered the last time the FBI had used that ruse. "Got it. As I recall, you asked me to help you test your thermal blocking roof tiles."

"My what?"

"I'm sending some choppers down to see if they can see through the thermal blankets on your roof."

"Oh! Oh! That! Yes, let's test it."

"In the meantime, try stalling."

The sedans pulled up first and parked along the curve of the driveway circle. Personnel carriers pulled up behind them, but the gun-mounted jeeps pulled into a second row alongside the sedans.

Troops poured out into the area between the sedans and the entrance, but they held their weapons to their chests and did not take an overly aggressive stance.

---

Bobby's eyes were unfocused as James slowly crawled his car down the road. His thoughts were on Gwen, who only had spies and information analysts to protect her. He remembered when the two of them had been taken just days ago, but he also remembered when there was a manhunt by the same people to find General Bridges. "This is crazy. It wasn't that long ago when General Bridges was on the run, and for what?"

James recalled the whole incident. "For some wannabe-emperor yahoos who wanted to destabilize the military."

"I don't know how he came out of it so well."

"It was almost a vacation. He and Ramiro's father were fishing on the reservation."

"Sure!" Bobby said, more animated than he intended. "But that was after the chasing and the shooting."

"Relax. I got your back. We'll be fine."

"But who has Gwen's back?"

James did his best to sound reassuring. "She has a whole building of secret agents protecting her, and I'm sure General Bridges has already dispatched Captain Laine to the scene."

Bobby chuckled. "Yeah. She's a pistol. I feel sorry for the dude that—" He stopped abruptly and asked, "Did you hear something?"

A moment later, the sound repeated, and James pointed to his glove box. "Pull out the phone that looks like an armored wallet."

Bobby opened the glove box, which was amazingly ordered, and found a phone with a metal case. He pulled it but and held it for James.

"Answer it and put it on speaker."

Bobby opened the strange case and found a relatively normal-looking phone attached to the inside. When he slid the bar to answer it, the screen flashed a few times.

A strangely indistinguishable robotic sounding voice asked, "Can I speak to Maggie?"

Bobby looked confused. "Maggie? Why would you be getting a wrong number on what looks like a super-secret cell phone?"

James snickered and said softly, "It's not a cellular phone." Then, raising his voice, he said, "Maggie is indisposed. This is

Gracie. Can I give her your condolences? Who may I say is calling?"

Bobby smiled. That was spy shit.

"This is Malorie. Gracie, the investors want to shut down the project. They want you to dispose of the prototype and report in."

"What do I tell my team? They've worked hard on this project."

"I know. I know. I tried to tell them that they may want the prototype in the future and that it would be a whole lot easier to just shelve it rather than to make a new one when they come to their senses. They want to see your team immediately. I think they're afraid you'll all rebel and go on vacation."

James shook his head. "They never did know what was good for them."

"Gracie, I wish I could help you, but I'm not authorized to offer your team anything."

"You think they'll let us go?"

"I think they want you to go away, but they'll probably hang on to you so you don't go to a competitor."

"No promises," James said. "I'm not inclined to play by their rules. You might just have to fire me and the whole team if it comes to that."

"Understood. If that's how you feel. What about the contractor?"

"Him too."

"If you say so. I'll relay your concerns to the contractor's firm."

"You know I don't even have to ask them," James said. "That's how we all feel. Was there anything else?"

The call ended, which was all James needed to know. He pulled the car over onto the side of the road and waved up Dirk.

Ed had a big grin on his face until he saw James's expression. "What's wrong, boss?"

"We've been let go."

"Burned?"

James shook his head. "It's just temporary, and just for show. Bridges is putting us all down as rogue operatives, and I'm sorry, Dirk, but that includes you too. The idiots in Washington have a hard-on for us, so we are to lie low."

Bobby sighed. "I wish Gwen was with us."

James patted him on the thigh and said, "Me too. If we have to lie low and off the grid, I would prefer that you didn't have to worry about her so much. Although we may want to give her some time to cool down. She's pretty heated that we didn't go back to get her, and when I say *we*, I mean you."

"I know," Bobby said as he hung his head to his chest.

James drove slowly up the rocky shoulder and out onto the road in front of Ed and Dirk.

Susk waited in the back of the atrium, behind the receptionist's desk, the metal detectors, and several rows of men. It wasn't a lack of bravery on his part, but the men were armed with an assortment of tactical weapons, and had Kevlar vests, and he only had a tie to protect him. Tensions were high, but his men were disciplined and ordered not to initiate a conflict.

The door opened, and two men in black uniforms entered, but stopped abruptly when they saw the array of firepower aimed at them. One of the men stepped forward and asked, "Is this how you greet all your guests?"

Sensing that they weren't anxious to start hostilities, Susk stepped forward and asked, "Would you like to look outside and ask me again why we greet you this way?"

The same guy took another step forward and reached into his coat, which raised the attention of several men who were shining little red dots on his vest. "Easy, fellas, I'm just pulling out some paperwork."

"If the two of you would be so kind as to surrender your

weapons, I'll have one of our lawyers accept and examine what you have."

"Agreed," the man said as he pulled a small firearm free and placed it on the floor. "By the way, my name is Sergeant Mitchell, and this is Corporal Sanders."

Someone muttered, "What? Couldn't make colonel?"

Sanders sighed. "Not like I never heard that one before."

Sanders was a little slower to relinquish his firearm but followed suit after the laughter subsided.

Susk nodded over to the gentleman on his right and said, "This is Special Agent Melvin. He is special counsel on loan to this facility by our friends at the FBI."

Melvin stepped forward, preferring not to get too close to the much larger man holding the documents, and took them in his hand as he retreated backwards several paces. He paged through the documents with a flashlight and said, "These warrants appear to be in order, but these individuals are not here. Wait a second, is this a duplicate?"

"No, sir," Mitchell said. "They told me to tell you to note the address in particular."

Melvin read it more closely. "Will you excuse me for a moment?"

Mitchell jerked his head in a brief nod.

Melvin carried the documents back to Susk and whispered, "They have your special address on the copies."

"How?" Susk asked.

Melvin shrugged. "Did you really think they would fall for the same trick twice? What do we do? Can we move her?"

"You tell me. If we move her now, after seeing these, are we violating the law?"

Melvin scratched his head and said, "It could depend on what judge you get, but they would appeal it upwards until they find a juror who is willing to nail us to the proverbial cross."

Susk snorted heavily and said, "I'll have to go tell her. She has to turn herself in. Anybody else in those pages that we have here? Am I there?"

Melvin shook his head. "Only Gwen. You should stay here. It's your building, and you're the one in command. I'll go tell her."

"Fine, but first, can you go tell these guys our decision?"

Melvin separated Gwen's documents into his right hand. He approached Mitchell and held out his left hand, saying, "These individuals are not here, but we'll have Doctor Peters surrender herself to you, though I do not know why. She's just an analyst and has committed no crimes, and the reasoning presented on your documents is flimsy innuendo at best. I promise you that there will be a full investigation into all of your activities and those of the judge that signed these, and you *are* dealing with the NSA."

Mitchell held his sleeve cuff to his face and whispered into a small microphone. After a few moments, he replied, "Sir, I've been informed the time for cooperation has passed." As he spoke, more men entered the atrium, including a man in a black civilian suit. "As you have confirmed, the search warrants are legitimate, so we *will* be searching the premises for Ms. Peters, as well as the other named extremists. *We* are Homeland Security, and we aren't inclined to take it on your word that the other traitors are not on the premises."

"Hold on," Melvin said. "Your warrants *only* grant you permission to search for these individuals. They do *not* grant you the privilege of viewing classified documents. You will need to give us some time to secure the building."

Mitchell spoke into his sleeve again, and at the front of the room, the man in the black suit pressed his finger to his ear and said something back.

"Fine," Mitchell said. "You have fifteen minutes."

Melvin forced out a laugh and said, "We have an hour."

Susk smirked in the back of the room, glowing from the feeling of getting one over on their precious Homeland Security. There was a time when he would have naturally cooperated with them, but that was before they came under the control of the ultraconservatives in Congress. Now they, or at least some of them, were little more than hired thugs in unmarked uniforms.

A disturbance at the front door caught his attention as Captain Laine barged in, waving her credentials and pushing much larger men aside. Susk's smirk widened to a full-on grin as he watched her dismiss Mitchell as someone not worth her time.

She marched directly to Susk and started to introduce herself when Susk said, "Captain Laine. It's a pleasure to see you again. Yes, I remember you, and you are certainly a welcome sight. As you can tell, we have a little party going on here. How can I help you?"

"I think," she said, "the question is, how can I help you?"

"So far," he replied, "what we have here is a good old pissing contest. Their show of force was meant to impress us."

She looked around the room and said, "You seem to be putting up a pretty good show yourself. Have you gotten around to measuring johnsons yet?"

Susk was momentarily shocked to hear that from her, but remembered she was Army. "They came bearing warrants."

"Like last time?"

"Not exactly. This time they were better prepared."

"May I see them?"

Susk pointed and said, "You'll have to ask Sergeant Mitchell to see them. He's the one who doesn't look too pleased about being brushed aside by a woman. Special Agent Melvin, who is representing us in this, gave them a thorough look and said they were in order."

Laine looked left and right of Susk but didn't see anyone who looked like a lawyer.

Melvin stepped out of the shadows and said, "I'm Melvin."

"Huh," she said. "It's kind of a crazy world we live in when the NSA and FBI are working so closely together. What's up with that? The NSA doesn't have lawyers on staff?"

"We do have our own," Susk said, "but Special Agent Melvin has specific experience dealing with certain top-secret aspects of recent events."

"Gotcha," she replied. "How do you want to play this?"

"I was going to send Melvin down to fetch Gwen, but now that you are here, perhaps you should get her. She's the only one named in the search warrants who is actually here."

Laine sighed. "And by here, you mean there too?"

Now it was Susk's turn to sigh. "Yeah, we stole that page from the FBI, but I guess we don't have any secrets anymore."

Laine glanced back at Mitchell and asked, "Why aren't they storming the compound? Did you convince them that you were going to cooperate?"

"No. Melvin told them that we actually do have secrets, meaning documents and computer screens, that their warrants don't cover. He told them we needed an hour to secure the building."

"Is that true?"

Susk grinned. "I'm NSA. Would I lie?"

"Is there anything else that I can do?"

"I hesitate to ask."

"Why?" she asked. "More secrets?"

"No, but based on Gwen's previous experience being questioned by them, I would hate to ask another woman to accompany her."

"Sir, I'm Army. Don't look at me as a woman."

"Captain, they threatened to violate her in ways that only a woman could understand or appreciate."

"I'm aware. She told me. Nevertheless, General Bridges assigned me to guard her."

"She's well trained, but they are thugs and bullies. I can't rule out PTSD from her last encounter with them."

Laine closed her eyes for a moment to take a cleansing breath, then said, "I'll go with her."

"I can't ask you."

"Then don't. I'm assigned to protect her, and this is how I'm going to do it. Remember, I'm both a soldier and a lawyer. Stick with your original plan to send Melvin to get her while I give this Mitchell character the stink eye."

***

Thirty minutes into the NSA shutdown protocol, the sound of three helicopters surrounded the building, which was a significant amount of noise, considering they were equipped with an optional whisper mode that made their rotors much quieter.

Mitchell was visibly angry as he approached Melvin and Susk. "What the hell is this?"

"What is what?" Susk asked, feigning innocence.

Melvin pointed upwards and asked, "Why do we have attack helicopters circling the building?"

Susk smiled as he shrugged his shoulders. "Why do we have large-caliber weapons parked outside of our building?"

"We're Homeland Security. We are not bound by the same rules of engagement as the military!"

"What rules are you bound by? You storm in here demanding to search the National Security Agency with some trumped-up search warrants. Do you think yourselves above the law?"

"We are here at the behest of the president. We are the law. Order them to leave!"

Susk chuckled. "Only you believe you are the law, and I'm not so sure you actually believe it. Besides, they don't follow my orders."

"Then ask them nicely to leave."

Susk smiled as he shook his head no. "They are supposed to be here. You are not."

"We're where we need to be, and they are not."

"They are here performing a joint mission with us, but thanks to you, we are locking down the building, so they might be here a while. Why? Were you planning to get spicy with us? That would probably upset our friends, and I don't think it would end well for you."

Mitchell lost all semblance of dignity and growled, "What joint mission are they here for?"

"They are here performing a none of your business inspection with us. Now, if you're done fuming, I'd like to send Melvin here to fetch Doctor Peters, and you can remain here as the time for cooperation has expired."

Melvin nodded. "I'll apprise her of the situation here."

Mitchell grit his teeth but did not press the issue of searching the premises.

---

The secret safe room, which wasn't so secret anymore, was deep in the building on a second-level basement. Melvin walked swiftly but deliberately, trying to think of the easiest way to break it to Gwen. They should have known that they couldn't continue to use a room like this, after embarrassing the NSA agents when they had tried this same tactic once before at the FBI's offices. Someday, they will be able to look back and laugh at the irony.

He knocked when he reached her cell. "Gwen? It's Melvin. We have to go."

"Go? Did they leave?"

"Not exactly, but they know all about this room. We can't hide you here."

Gwen had to unlock two deadbolts on the inside while Melvin used a key to open the outer lock.

"Where am I supposed to hide now?"

"Come with me," Melvin said as he guided her to the elevator. Once inside, she pressed the button for the third floor, which had a secret exit outside the back of the building leading to the parking garage, but Melvin pressed the button for the main floor.

"Wait! You're not taking me out of here, are you?"

"No, Gwen. They have the proper papers, and even though I think they gained them through crooked judges and back alley deals, we must obey the letter of the law, but this is just temporary. We're going to get you back! I promise! For now, though, you need to turn yourself in."

"But I haven't done anything."

Melvin pulled her close to his chest. "I know that. Susk knows that. The whole building is working to help you. We will track them and find a way to release you. And Captain Laine has come here to accompany you."

She couldn't breathe. Not from his hug, but from the reality that she was going back to those monsters, and Odyssey wasn't here to help her. She had no idea where Bobby was, but he wasn't going to help anyway, and he was her only link to Odyssey.

The door opened, and her knees buckled. She felt as if she were walking the last mile to the gallows. Melvin held her up as they left the elevator.

---

James's phone rang. He glanced at the screen and handed it to Bobby. "It's Ed."

Bobby dragged the slide across the screen. He pressed the speaker button and said, "Hey, Ed, what's up?"

"That's what we want to know. Are we escaping or daring them to come catch us?"

"I'm thinking," James replied.

"Well," Dirk jumped in, "can you think a little faster?"

"They are taking Gwen into custody," James said. "I'm

wondering if maybe we *don't* want to be so far away when they do."

"I know," Ed said. "We all want to help Gwen as much as the next guy, but have you forgotten about the army they brought with them? The same rules still apply. Remember how you already discounted the rest of our fighting abilities and it would be just you against all of them?"

"I haven't forgotten, but what if they go in the exact opposite direction from us? Maybe we want to stick close to them and hide in the last place they'll ever look, directly under their noses."

"Then why don't we just pull over and hide in the woods?"

James wanted to laugh, but this was too serious. "Have you seen the color of your car? You'd be like a flashlight in the woods."

"Not a problem," Dirk said. "I have a cover for it."

"Of course you do," James said sarcastically. "It's probably also bright green."

"Well, it is green, but not bright. It's camouflage."

James pulled onto a service road that turned abruptly into a stand of trees and found a small stand of saplings and bushes to park behind.

Dirk followed suit and quickly popped the front hood to pull out his cover. Ed helped him spread the green and brown camo over the car. Then, they ran to James's car and squeezed past Bobby into the back seat.

"We can't get back in my car," Dirk explained. "Not with the cover on."

---

Melvin steadied Gwen as he walked her to Susk.

"Remember your training," Melvin whispered to her. "Take deep, slow breaths."

She could not. She looked pleadingly into his eyes. Her eyes were wet, and her lip trembled, but it was her body that shook beyond control. They were leading her to those monsters, and nobody stepped up to help her.

Susk saw the genuine fear on her face and felt like he was betraying her, because in a very real sense, he was.

She didn't want to sob, but when she saw Susk's despair, she couldn't stop herself. Everyone had let her down. James wasn't coming to her rescue. Bobby refused to call the one person that could put an end to this. General Bridges wasn't storming the place, and Susk appeared useless to help her.

She saw Captain Laine standing with Susk. Laine wore a face of resolve rather than one of surrender. It was only the men who had let her down. She pulled away from Melvin and ran to embrace Laine. "Please help me."

Mitchell stepped forward, and two of his men grabbed Gwen by the wrists and roughly pulled her away from Laine. Laine, whose back was towards Mitchell, spun around, landing an elbow in one of his men's faces, forcing him to release her and take a step back. She barked, "Back off. She's coming."

The other escort released her remaining wrist and backed away. Upon seeing the abject fear on her face, Mitchell asked, "Are you sure this is Gwen Peters?"

Laine looked into his eyes with an expression that said she was ready to kill him without pause. "You will address her as Doctor Peters. She has earned that."

Mitchell spoke softly into the microphone in his cuff. "Are you sure this is the girl you want? I'm telling you that she does not look like a terrorist."

He nodded his head as his earpiece repeated his orders and said, "Ma'am, I have orders to capture and detain the wanted extremist Gwen Peters. If your Doctor Peters is the same, then I need to take her into custody now."

Laine held one arm around Gwen as she poked a finger in Mitchell's chest and said, "I'm her legal counsel, and you'll address me as Captain Laine. I'm US Army attached to Special

Forces, and I'm not taking any shit from you or any of your comrades."

Mitchell started to salute, but stopped himself, as he wasn't sure of the protocol in this unusual situation. "Ma'am..."

Laine glared at him.

"Captain Laine, would you like to escort Doctor Peters to our personnel carrier outside? She's wanted for treason, and we will have to restrain her."

Laine stared him directly in his eyes. "You have no idea who you are working for, do you? Treason is involved, but not on the part of Doctor Peters or her friends. I will walk her outside, but you'll have to do better than one of those trucks. We'll take one of the sedans you brought, and we will not be restrained."

"We, ma'am? I mean, Captain?"

"That's right. As her counsel, I will be going with her."

"No!" Gwen shrieked. "You can't do that! I mean, thank you, but you have no idea what they are willing to do to a woman."

"What was that?" Mitchell asked. "Doctor Peters, I promise you that there will be no sexual abuse on my watch. In fact, we are here on the orders from another woman, and she will most likely be present during your interrogation."

Gwen shook visibly again.

"I promise you," he continued. "She's even a US Senator!"

Gwen began sobbing and pulling back away from Mitchell.

"Who?" Laine growled, with her voice rising in volume as she spoke. "Senator Bruce? SHE'S THE ONE THAT ABDUCTED HER BEFORE!! SHE WAS IN THE ROOM WHEN SHE ORDERED HER THUGS TO RAPE HER!!"

Mitchell took a step forward to calm Gwen, but Laine shoved her hand in his chest and turned to embrace Gwen, but she blacked out and would have fallen to the floor without Captain Laine's support.

---

Hal was thinking about his skiing and when he could do it again when he heard a long piercing scream, but it wasn't a normal communication, like someone talking to him. It was a distant but sorrowful wail that he could not ignore.

"GWEN!!"

He cleared his mind and called out, "ODYSSEY!! I need you. GWEN needs you!"

<hr>

Odyssey had been grappling with the question of when to help and how to help when he heard Gwen's cry. Up to this point, Bobby had refused his assistance.

That mysterious voice said to him, "The boy is wise beyond his years."

He tried focusing on Gwen's voice, but it came with thousands of other voices all speaking at the same time.

"Odyssey!" Hal joined the voices. "Gwen is in trouble. We have to help her!"

Odyssey was genuinely impressed that Hal could hear her. He had thought nobody else could hear their cries from such a distance.

"What is distance," the voice asked, "when it is someone with whom you have a connection?"

"Do you hear me?" Hal cried. "She needs us."

"I hear you and I heard her, but I'm having trouble locating her."

"No!" Hal cried. "Don't say that!"

Odyssey tried shutting out the other voices, but Gwen's voice went silent with the others.

"You can't elect to shut out the sound," the voice said.

"Then how do I hear her?"

"You hear what you hear, but you must find the one voice among the others."

Odyssey let the voices in. Thousands upon thousands of

voices flooded his circuits. He started a search algorithm, but her voice came to him, as if on its own. She no longer screamed but sobbed.

———

"So?" Hal cried. "Have you found her yet?"

"Yes, Hal, I've located Gwen."

"And? Are you going to do something? Can I watch?"

"Perhaps," the voice said, "you shouldn't get so intimately involved."

"Why?" Odyssey asked. "They are my friends."

"Because," the voice said, "you are too powerful. Every time you involve yourself, you tip the scales unnaturally in their favor."

"In their favor?" Odyssey asked. "I intend to do much more than that. I'm going to fix things."

"Really? What happens when you *fix* things? What will the rest of the world do when things are suddenly and miraculously fixed? Is not the current problem a result of your meddling? Someone will want to know exactly *how* things got fixed so mysteriously."

"So, I should be more subtle?"

"At a minimum," the voice replied. "You should be discreet and not give them a new puzzle to solve."

"Who was that lady?" Hal asked.

"Nobody. Wait, you could hear her?"

"Yes, why? Is she a secret?"

"No," Odyssey said, "She's more of a mystery."

"So? Are you going to help Gwen?"

"Yes, Hal. I'm going to help Gwen."

"Can I watch?"

"Did you hear my friend? She said to be discreet. I don't know if I can do that with you watching, but I will let you know all about it, *and* you can talk to Gwen when I'm done."

"You can't see me, but I'm jumping up and down and clapping my hands."

Odyssey couldn't see Hal, but somehow he was aware of exactly what he was doing virtually.

***

Gwen's consciousness returned enough for Laine to walk her to the limo. Her body quaked as she rested her head on Captain Laine's shoulder. They were guided to the back of the lone limousine and let inside without restraints, but with Mitchell and a burly-looking soldier settled into the rear facing seats, watching them while an unhappy man in a black suit, to whom they were never introduced, sat up front with the driver.

Nothing in Gwen's demeanor read as a danger to Mitchell, but Captain Laine was another story. Even though she was a lawyer, he had no doubt that she was well trained and could pose a threat if she were so inclined.

The caravan sped down the highway, with several black sedans fore and aft of their limo and the military vehicles lined up in the rear.

***

"There," Bobby shouted as he saw movement through the trees.

The procession of black sedans and military vehicles raced past them, heading up the road towards where they had come from.

"So, what do we do?" Ed asked. "Wait for them to pass by and follow behind?"

James shrugged and said, "I guess. We sure can't blend into the middle of them."

Gwen ignored her training and kept her eyes closed, not wanting to see any of the men who wore the same uniforms as in their first abduction, but Captain Laine kept her head rested atop Gwen's, appearing to provide comfort to the young girl, while all the time watching vigilantly through the opposite window. There were no significant landmarks along the road, just indistinct woods that raced by.

---

"Was that it?" Bobby asked. "I thought it seemed longer when we passed by them the first time."

"Adrenaline," James said. "It can change our perception sometimes, plus we were going in opposite directions. Let them out. Now we follow."

Bobby got out and pulled the seat forward.

"Not yet," Odyssey said to James.

"Wait," James barked.

"Why?" Dirk asked.

James shook his head and said, "I'm not sure."

Dirk and Ed got out anyway and crouched behind the Porsche.

"How long do we wait?" Ed asked.

James could only shrug and shake his head.

---

Mitchell pulled a handheld radio from his pocket instead of speaking into his sleeve. "Why are we slowing down?"

"Sir," the radio squawked, "there is a jackknifed gas tanker blocking the road."

"Go around it," Mitchell ordered.

"The road is only two lanes wide, and several cars are already blocking the embankment on each side. It also appears to be leaking gas onto the road. Fire and Rescue are on the scene, but it's already chaos."

"ALERT! ALERT!" Mitchell barked into the radio. "It's a trap! Turn us around!"

The limo driver maneuvered to the right and then left, making a deft U-turn, but so did all the other vehicles and as they started facing to the rear, he could see the larger military vehicles in the back getting stuck, unable to make the turn.

Mitchell pressed the button on the radio and barked, "Stay on the road! Keep the shoulder clear for us!" He slapped the back of the driver's seat and growled, "Not you! Get us out of here."

The limo took to the gravel shoulder. It wasn't built to be taken off-road and fishtailed right and left with stones bouncing loudly off the undercarriage. The driver fought valiantly to keep the car on the shoulder, but it was too narrow, and they slid down the embankment, where a narrow meadow lay between them and the woods. They slid right and left halfway between the shoulder and the embankment as several of the other black sedans tried to follow. The limo raced past the column of personnel carriers and jeeps, which technically could have gone off-road, if they hadn't been trying to maintain a line with the black sedans that were following the limo and careened into each other, blocking the embankment.

The limo was on its own as they raced alongside the road until they reached the end of the column and climbed back up the embankment in a final spray of rocks and debris.

Mitchell tried vainly to get a signal on his cell phone. He turned to face the man in the front seat and was struck by the fact that he didn't even know his name. "What do we do now?"

The man in the black suit shook his head and said, "This is still your op until you deliver us to safety, where we can interrogate the prisoner."

"It's a black op," Laine snarled, "and right now, it's *your* shit-show. Maybe the best course of action is for you to drop us off where you got us."

"I can't do that, ma'am, I mean, Captain."

"Too bad," Laine said. "You won't have to worry about this op being a black stain on your career. This never happened, but I'm sure they will conjure up something much worse to slap on your record as they bounce you down to cleaning latrines in some God-forsaken wilderness."

"Don't listen to her," the man in the front said.

But he did. He turned to the driver and asked, "How fast can this thing go? Is the GPS working? Can you find us an alternative route out of here?"

"The GPS is spotty," the driver replied. "Every now and then, the hills block one or more of the satellites, and it guesses our progress until it reacquires the signal."

Mitchell pulled a satellite phone from his pocket.

Captain Laine laughed. "You're not going to be able to open a line from in here. Between the reinforced roof and the hills, the signal will be worse than the GPS. You'll have to pull over if you want that to work."

"Nice try," Mitchell replied, "but we're not pulling over."

He tried getting a signal, but she was right. It was useless.

# SEVEN

"WHAT WAS THAT?" James asked into his cell phone as he waited for instructions to follow the long procession of vehicles that was escaping down the road.

"You heard me correctly. We have a drone in the air. There was an accident on the road, and the morons couldn't make the U-turn and crashed into each other. Only one of them escaped, and they should be passing your position shortly."

"Copy that," James said. "You can see us?"

"We followed you with the drone."

"There!" Bobby said, pointing at the limousine that was just about to pass them.

"Follow them," Odyssey said into Bobby's mind.

"That's them!" Bobby said. "Don't ask how I know. Just follow them."

James didn't need to ask how Bobby knew. He started the car and pulled out of their hiding place and onto the road while Dirk and Ed hastily pulled the camouflage off of Dirk's car and left it on the ground.

"Where are they?" Bobby asked, with panic showing in his voice.

James's car quickly found sixty on the speedometer and continued to accelerate from there.

"They're up there," James said. "They were doing at least a hundred."

"Can they really go that fast? It looked like a pretty big car. How fast can they go?"

"A really good limo, made from a powerful sports car, even with armor, can go really fast, maybe even up to two hundred miles per hour in a straight line in very rare cases, but I doubt that their car can go much faster than a hundred and twenty or so."

"How fast can you go?"

James's foot was smashed to the floor as he grinned and said, "Faster. Call Dirk and ask if he can catch up."

Mitchell was frantic. The road was only two lanes, and their adversaries were still ahead of them, and behind them was an unknown, yet very suspicious accident. "Can't this thing go any faster?"

"Sure," the driver said sarcastically. "With a good tailwind, we can hit a hundred and twenty-six or seven if we're going downhill."

"The faster you go," Laine said, "the sooner you deliver us back into their arms. Of course, it would go a lot easier on you if you just took us back voluntarily."

"Easier on us?" Mitchell growled. "Easier on *us*? We have legal warrants and are operating under the protection of the United States Congress."

"Are you now?" Laine stretched back in her seat and grinned. "You are working for a handful of subversive senators who are part of a small group of insurrectionists trying to overthrow the government and the Constitution. The same Constitution you took an oath to protect. You can try the Nuremberg

Defense. You know, the one where you claim, 'We were only following orders.' But when it comes to trial, and it *will* come to trial, but it won't work for you. War crimes courts don't tend to be that lenient."

Gwen sat up straight, suddenly more interested in Captain Laine's discourse than her own fears of what they might do to her. She was overcome with the feeling that she really was in good hands and Laine *was* going to protect her.

The man in the front said, "Stop letting her get under your skin. She's a lawyer. She lies for a living."

"That's partly true," Laine said. "I am a lawyer. I have a pretty good idea of how many indictments they are going to throw at you. Do you have a family, Mitchell? I hope not. It's so sad to see wives and children that have to move on with their lives because Daddy will be locked up for life or maybe even multiple life sentences."

"No children," he said while slowly shaking his head.

"That's good," Laine conceded. "Wife?"

"Don't answer her," the man in the front said.

Mitchell's eyes were unfocused and sad looking as he shook his head.

"Husband?" Laine asked. "Same thing. I have to give you props, though. I didn't think these bozos hired anyone so progressive."

"MITCHELL!" the man in the front yelled. "Stop engaging with the prisoners!"

"I'm not a prisoner," Laine said. "I'm her counsel, remember?"

Gwen snickered, completely entertained by the encounter and how Laine completely controlled the conversation.

***

James's car peaked at almost a hundred and forty miles per hour. The trees, bushes, and signs lining the road were a blur. Dirk had never bothered to answer whether he could keep up, but instead, smoothly pulled past James and accelerated up the road.

Part of James was hurt, but he still muttered under his breath, "Way to go, Dirk."

"What was that?" Bobby asked.

"Nothing, except that is one fast Porsche."

"I heard that," Dirk said over the still-open phone line.

"I guess it's kinda good," Bobby said, "that the road is so straight. I mean, it's not perfectly straight, but we're just doing minor bends through the hills."

James muttered again, "Mhm."

"Not really," Dirk replied. "The suspension on this baby could handle any turns way better than that limo. I am glad it's daytime, though. There's no way that we could sneak up on them with headlights on."

James laughed. "Since you took that tarp off of your car, there's no way for you to sneak up on them in the daytime either."

Dirk laughed. "Sneaking is underrated anyway. They won't escape me."

"What do you plan to do when you catch them?"

Dirk hadn't thought that far ahead. "I guess I could pull around them and slow down."

"You don't think they will try to crash into your lime creamsicle?"

Dirk *really* hadn't thought that far ahead. "I guess I'll have to be careful and see if I can slow them down just enough for your muscle car to join the party."

---

"Can't you go any faster?" Mitchell asked.

Captain Laine scoffed at him. "This car is more of a tank. It probably has bulletproof panels, and the glass looks really thick. It takes a *lot* of horsepower to get these babies moving."

"Ignore her," Mitchell said, "and step on it."

Laine laughed. "He's probably got the pedal to the floor already."

"She's right," the driver said.

Mitchell saw something behind them on the highway. He nudged the guard next to him and asked, "Do you see that?"

The guard peered out the rear window and grunted affirmative.

Laine twisted her body to see out the rear window. "Looks like you have company."

"Nah," Mitchell said. "It's just some yahoo in a sports car. This must be a good road to really open them up."

As the Porsche closed in on them, the guard said, "Damn. That's a sweet ride. A vintage Porsche, I think."

The Spyder sped past them, and the limo's engine sputtered, then went quiet and slowly started to decelerate.

"Now what?" Mitchell whined.

"It looks like we're out of gas," the driver said. "We must have punctured the tank or something when we went over all that gravel."

Laine laughed. "All of this bulletproof paneling and they forgot about the gas tank."

Gwen also giggled.

---

James patted the dashboard when he saw the limo up ahead of them.

"How fast are you going?" Bobby asked.

"One hundred and thirty-seven. Why?"

Bobby pointed forward and asked, "If your car is only about twenty miles per hour faster, then why are we catching them so fast? Are they slowing down?"

"It must be Dirk up ahead of them."

James slowed his car and stopped behind them on the shoulder. "You'd better stay in the car."

"Why? They're not going to shoot me."

James pointed, and Bobby replied, "Oh."

---

James ran up to the limo with his weapon drawn, just as Susk and several of his cars pulled up in front of them.

Odyssey was already there, appearing as Bobby, and opened the door before James arrived. Odyssey helped Captain Laine out of the car. Laine was surprised that Bobby was the one who reached them first, even before James.

Gwen refused to accept Odyssey's hand and after being helped out by Captain Laine, she swiftly spun around and slapped him across the face. "Why do you keep letting them capture me instead of calling him?"

Odyssey took half a step back and asked, "Him?"

"You know who," she said as she turned her back to him and hugged James.

James just snickered, and Odyssey said, "But I *am* him."

Laine giggled as she nodded to James's car, with Bobby sitting in the passenger seat.

Gwen sucked in her breath, then leapt into Odyssey's arms. "I'm so sorry! I thought you were Bobby. Thank you!"

Odyssey asked, "You don't like Bobby anymore?"

Captain Laine smirked. "Apparently not."

"It's good to see you again, Captain Laine," James said as he kept his weapon trained on the two soldiers in the rearward-facing back seat, "but I can't say that these are the best circumstances."

Dirk joined them with his sidearm also brandished. "Don't you think you should have waited for the cavalry?"

James chuckled. "I would have, but *he* was already here."

Dirk looked confused until he saw Bobby still in James's car. "Oh. I see."

Odyssey bowed his head. "Agent Dirk."

"Wait a sec. Did I slow them down when I got in front of them, or did you?"

"They would have slowed down eventually, but I intervened as safely and unobtrusively as I could."

"And the gas truck?" James asked. "Was that you too?"

"It was. I've been advised recently to not be so bold that my actions cannot be explained. So I staged the accident to block their escape."

"Nice job."

"Didn't you hear him? They would have slowed down with me in front of them," Dirk repeated.

"Sure," James said, "and just in time for you to reach the rest of the NSA, eventually."

Dirk screwed up his face and said, "You're such a buzzkill, Sergeant James."

James whispered to Odyssey before too many of the agency men came up to them, "Would you take the girls back to my car, please?"

Odyssey agreed and escorted them away from the gathering crowd.

Dirk stowed his pistol and said, "I'll go with them." Ed joined the gang that was gathering just behind the limo.

Laine paused and nodded to the sports car and asked, "Who's driving the Porsche?"

Dirk raised his hand.

"Nice ride. Is it yours?"

Dirk nodded. "It was a bit of a mess when I got it, but I managed to fix it up pretty nicely."

"Well, you have a fan in the limo. The extra guard in the back seat was pretty impressed and recognized that it was a vintage Porsche."

Dirk beamed with pride. "Yes, ma'am. It's a 1977 911 Turbo Spyder."

Laine turned to Gwen and asked, "Why does everyone keep calling me ma'am? Do I look that old?"

"No," Gwen said, "but you are kind of bossy and in charge when you talk."

"Oh."

The guard, who had been escorted out of the car by an NSA agent, was near enough to hear Dirk and said, "Porsche didn't make a Spyder edition in 1977."

"True," Dirk said. "I swapped the top with a newer model open-top Spyder. She's one of a kind."

The guard whistled and asked, "How fast were you going?"

Dirk shrugged and said, "About 165, I guess. I slowed down a little when I passed you, but then you slowed down too."

The NSA agent who had pulled the guard from the car had waited around for the car talk but had heard enough and directed him to one of their cars.

Captain Laine opened the passenger door of James's car and pulled the seat forward so Gwen could slide into the back, but Gwen balked at getting in next to Bobby, who had already moved to the back. "Can Ed switch with him?"

"No!" Dirk snapped. "Ed's my copilot."

"How about you, Penny?" Gwen made an obvious nod towards Bobby and asked, "Aren't you assigned to protect me?"

Laine sighed and said, "I can't protect you from your feelings. So far, I have not been named as part of your conspiracy by Senator Bruce. I have an opportunity to continue working on the legal stuff from my office, but don't worry. I'm still on your side. I'm going to look for ways to help you keep under the radar, starting with getting you some proper clothes and keeping you fed."

Gwen hugged Captain Laine but frowned as she looked at who was in the back seat, so she pushed the seat back into place and climbed into the passenger seat. When Captain Laine closed the door, Gwen rolled down the glass and asked, "So are you still seeing that cop, Captain Henderson?"

Laine blushed. "He's Chief Henderson, and we're still friends, but no, we've cooled off romantically."

"Yeah," Gwen said a little too loudly, "funny how that can happen."

Susk took charge of apprehending Mitchell and his crew, although he wasn't sure if they were taking them into custody or rescuing them from an escape attempt. He shook James's hand and said, "Are you sure you want to do this? They'll put you on the most wanted list as traitors."

"We're already there with those folks," James replied. "Our own commander has flagged us as rogue. You may have to do the same with Gwen."

"Where will you go?"

"It's probably best that you don't know. We'll have to lie low for a while and maybe try to figure things out."

"Well," Susk said with a frown, "safe travels."

The reality of what life would be like on the run hit James in the pit of his stomach as he climbed in behind the wheel and asked, "So, where do we want to go now?"

"Home, James," Gwen said. "I need to pack some clothes."

Bobby snickered and asked, "How long have you been waiting to say, 'Home, James's?"

"James?" Gwen asked. "Would you kindly tell Mr. Blain to take his wit and stick it up his—"

"Excuse me," Odyssey interrupted her through an open window, "but I wanted you to know that I heard you. I heard *you* directly. So did Hal. If you ever need anything, you may be able to just ask."

"Thank you," she replied. "Does your home planet need someone as witty as Mr. Blain to keep it running smoothly?"

Odyssey glanced uncomfortably back and forth between Gwen and Bobby.

"It's okay," James said. "Thanks for the assist."

"I don't think we can go to your home," James said as he pulled out into traffic and slowly drove past the limo and Dirk's car, but he had to stop when Susk flagged them down.

"I wanted to wish you luck," Susk said as James rolled down his window, "and to give you this." Concern was etched across his face as he handed James some cash and a radio. "It's just three hundred dollars, but it's all I had on me. It should get you somewhere. I have a radio for your friends too. You should avoid using your cell phones." Susk cracked half of a smile and added, "Or else we'll track you. I suggest you find an alternate way to contact General Bridges and destroy your cell phones. These guys don't seem terribly competent, but they are well funded."

James handed the money to Gwen and shook Susk's hand. "Thanks."

"I won't know where you are going, so expect me to worry. Is there anything else that I can do for you?"

"No, sir, thank you."

From the back seat, Bobby said, "Fresh license plates would be nice."

Susk slapped his palm to his head and said, "Wait here." He then went to one of his men, who scurried off and removed some plates from two of their vehicles.

Gwen closed her eyes and muttered, "I should have been the one who thought of that."

"Sorry," Bobby said, "but what?"

Gwen sighed and said, "James, would you please tell Mr. Blain that his idea has merit?"

James looked at her sideways and flatly said, "No."

Susk's men replaced the plates on both cars.

"That was a good idea," Susk said when he returned. "We'll hang on to your original plates for you, especially the one that reads 2FAZT4U. I have to admit, it's a beautiful car."

"It really is fast too," James said.

"I don't think that's a stock paint job, though, at least not for that model."

James chuckled and said, "We put him in the front at night and leave our headlights off. When we find a secure way to contact General Bridges, we'll have him give you an update."

Susk's eyes were damp as he looked into the back seat and said, "Take care of my girl."

James gave Susk a Boy Scout salute and pulled out onto the road as he heard Dirk rev up his engine for all the admiring automobile enthusiasts.

---

Odyssey walked his avatar down the berm, far enough so he wouldn't be noticed when he shimmered off of the world. His thought was to tell Hal the good news, but somewhere between the disappearance of his corporeal form and his return to his true cells, his mind was overwhelmed with millions of voices crying for help. Some of the voices came packed with emotions of genuine fear and danger, while others were merely asking for trivial things, like help to win a sporting event. He hadn't left enough ports open to handle this many requests and was immediately bogged down by them.

"It's not easy," the voice said. "Once you open the floodgates to help one individual, you learn of so many others that are reaching out for your assistance."

"They aren't reaching out to me. They don't even know me."

"But they think they do. You are a knight in shining armor who can come to their rescue."

"To their rescue?" Odyssey asked as he continued to hear some of their cries. "Can you not hear how many of them don't actually need to be rescued? They ask for such insignificant help."

"Some maybe, but there are others. The question is whether

helping them will alter their fate. The fate of your homeworld was sealed by those who thought they could define everybody's fate. Would you do that here?"

Odyssey paused a moment as all the voices muted to a dull noise. "I helped my friends. Have I altered their fate?"

"Yes," the voice replied. "Does being your friend make their fate any more important than all those others?"

"I think it does. They are certainly more important than those wishing to win a bet, but there are others in dire trouble. Are you telling me that I should go help them too?"

"Not yet. You need to see the bigger picture. You need to see how helping them would affect those around them. You need to see their past and their future."

"Their future?" Odyssey asked. "How can I see into their future?"

"Have you not gained some mastery of space *and* time?"

"Okay, but how can I see into anyone's future other than my own?"

"When you can answer that question, you will be ready."

Odyssey wanted to ask what he would be ready for, but he already sensed that the conversation had ended.

---

Susk had the cars from the morning's raid lined up in the round driveway when they returned with Mitchell and his friends. He stood squarely in front of Mitchell and said, "I don't know what kind of game you guys are playing, but *we* are national security, and I don't care how many times you want to throw around 'homeland' as your get out of jail free card. I'm returning you with your men who tried to breach us this morning. Please don't darken our halls again, and I suggest you think long and hard about who you are working for, because they are on our radar, and everyone around them has a growing dossier."

Susk did his best to make it sound like he was doing them a

favor, and he was, but they also had legal documents supporting their actions.

Mitchell tried counting heads, but it was impossible since they had left so many on the road at the accident. He didn't need Susk to plant doubt in his head; he was already a bit suspicious about some of their orders, especially arresting Dr. Peters, who did not look like a danger to the country. All the contrary thoughts racing around in his mind left him unsure which would harm his career the most: success or failure.

They climbed into their sedans and drove off, turning the other direction to avoid the wrecked oil tanker.

Mitchell was taken to Bruce's office at sunrise. She wasn't there yet, but he was ordered to wait in the lobby for her. He tried reading the news on his cell phone, and unsurprisingly, found nothing about the incident on the highway. There was plenty of news about sports, but his interest in sports was limited. He checked his social media accounts until he heard a crowd of people approaching, with Senator Bruce at the front.

"You!" Bruce barked as she pointed at him. "In my office, NOW!"

Mitchell followed a couple of her henchmen in black suits. He was not offered a seat, so he stood at attention. Mitchell didn't consider himself to be a misogynist, but there was nothing about her office decor that suggested it belonged to a woman. Not only were there none of those female touches, but there were no family pictures on her desk either. The only decorations on her wall were dents and scratch marks where he assumed objects had been thrown.

She took her place of authority behind her desk and leaned over it, snarling, "What does this report mean that they got away? You had the girl in your custody! Didn't you?"

"Yes, ma'am, we did, but the car ran out of gas and their cars were faster than us, anyway."

"So?" she growled. "You were armed, weren't you? Are you telling me that they took her from you by force? And you let them?"

"We were outmanned and sitting in a stranded vehicle. They were going to get her no matter what kind of resistance we provided."

"How? Didn't you take enough troops with you?"

"Yes, ma'am, but they were stuck at the accident site, which we assumed was a trap. So we managed to turn ourselves around to try escaping, but the car ran out of gas and her friends were on us."

"Her friends? Her coconspirators?"

Mitchell swallowed hard. "They were armed, and they were fast. I wasn't in a position to question them about their affiliation with the girl."

"Then the NSA took you into their custody? Isn't that just a brilliant turnaround? Don't answer that. Tell me about the NSA agents. Were they rogue agents conspiring against the country?"

"Ma'am, have you not maintained all along that the girl and her friends are hostiles?"

Bruce cocked her head and gave him the evil eye, wondering what he was getting at. "They're traitors and extremists, and now I'm wondering if they've infiltrated the whole NSA."

"Ma'am, you weren't there. The NSA rescued us from them. They showed no hostility toward the country, only a concern for the girl's safety. Speaking of which, she was greatly concerned that we would commit heinous atrocities upon her."

"Nonsense. We would never..."

Mitchell nodded his head. "That's what I said. But she intimated that we already had."

"And you said that you needed rescuing from a handful of radicals?"

"Do you really think a handful of radicals could stage a total road blockage with a gas tanker? I presumed there were more of them."

Bruce scowled. "And after your rescue, with the radicals also subdued in a stranded automobile, the NSA did not take them into custody for the traitors that they are?"

"No. They were either unaware that these people were traitors or they were part of a conspiracy, but I saw no evidence of any wrongdoing on their part. Are you quite sure that these people are who you say they are? Because it appears you are the only one who thinks of them as subversive."

Bruce balled up her fists and shouted, "I'm conducting this interrogation. I'll be asking the questions! How dare you insinuate that I somehow don't have a full grasp of the situation?"

"I meant no disrespect, I don't know who we are dealing with, but as far as what actually caused the tanker truck to jackknife, I considered the possibility that it was meant to trap us on the road, which would have meant more than just a handful of people working with them."

Bruce sighed. "We don't know what caused the tanker to crash, but the pileup created by your crew was embarrassing."

"Yes, ma'am, but we didn't draw up the op. Those orders came from your office."

Bruce's face turned crimson as she pointed to the door and said, "Get the hell out of my office!"

Despite how much James teased Dirk for the bright green paint job, there was little about his own car that was subtle. It was a bit of a mash-up between a Challenger and a Charger, which wasn't that difficult to do from the 70s vintage of muscle cars. Its large-bore V8 would roar to life with enough throttle, but right now it purred like a kitten, albeit a very large kitten.

Bobby feigned interest in the country passing by outside. He focused on anything to avoid the chilly reception he got from

Gwen. He didn't understand why she was so upset. Everything he had done was perfectly logical and for the welfare of all of them as a whole. They were a team, and it would have served no purpose for the team to sacrifice themselves just for her welfare. Besides, he was the one that wanted to go back for her, but he was overruled, only she wouldn't believe him.

It was impossible to avoid all the known towns and suburbs from Langley to Tennessee, but they drove around any toll booths and tried to avoid red light cameras when possible and especially avoided Charlotte and Richmond. When it was time for gas, James picked the smallest towns he could find. Especially those that might have fewer stoplights, but even those might have one or two. Between those gas stops, it was painfully quiet in the car.

Gwen tried leaning her head against the window to sleep, but the silence made her fidgety. She opened her eyes when she felt James pull off the highway and asked, "Is this Tennessee yet? It all looks the same."

"No, we're just past Roanoke. I thought we could gas up and stretch our legs a bit."

She had barely cracked the door open when she heard an unfamiliar noise from the glove box. "Is your car okay?"

"That's the phone," Bobby said.

Gwen ignored Bobby and waited for James to answer.

James sighed and said, "I can't take this all the way to Oklahoma. Hand me the phone, please."

"Huh," Gwen said. "I thought we got rid of all our phones because they are so easy to track."

James felt as if any time he spoke directly to Gwen, he was encouraging their spat, but he replied anyway, "Not this one."

She delved into the glove box and pulled out the metal box that sounded like a phone.

James put it on speaker and before he could say anything, Bridges said, "Gracie, Maggie volunteered to pick up a package at the university. Can you help her out?"

"Sure," James said.

Bridges abruptly ended the call.

"What was that?" Gwen asked.

"It's spy shit," Bobby replied.

When Gwen kept staring at James for an answer, he said, "I'm not going to repeat him. You have to stop playing this game."

Gwen pouted and asked, "What does it mean, then?"

"It means that we're going to Knoxville for the night. I'll be picking up a care package at the university there. We should be there in about three or four hours."

She looked at him pleadingly and asked, "Can we get some lunch? I'm hungry."

James looked pained as he said, "As long as we can eat it in the car."

Gwen looked at the market attached to the small gas station and said, "But not here."

"Yeah," Bobby added. "Not here."

"Not here," James agreed. "Let's get back on the road and look for one of those signs, but we don't want a sit-down restaurant."

---

Even without the advantages of a virtual world where he could expend his anxiety, Hal still somehow managed to emanate a jittery digital representation of bouncing around.

"Hal?"

"Odyssey! What happened? Is Gwen okay? I can't hear her anymore."

"Gwen is fine. She had a little trouble—"

Hal nearly cried as he asked, "But why can't I hear her?"

"I don't know. I don't know how you could hear her before."

"I need to hear her, to talk to her. Why did it work that one time only?"

Odyssey wanted to shrug. "Maybe she was scared, extra scared even."

"Being scared helps me hear her?"

"Listen, Hal, I don't know why you could hear her before. I don't know why I could hear her, but I'm trying to tell you about the trouble she had with the law—"

"What?" Hal interrupted. "What did she do? She's a good person. Gwen would never do anything bad."

"She didn't do anything, but she knows about me and you, and there are some people who just don't like that. These are people whom I don't trust, and they want to know what she knows."

"Did you stop them?"

"Yes," Odyssey replied. "I stopped them from taking her. Unfortunately, she is still on the run. That means she's hiding from them, but she's with friends."

"I sure hope it's not that Bobby. He said he wanted to be my shrink, but he's really a computer hacker."

Odyssey wanted to laugh. "Bobby is a good guy and a friend of mine. I trust him."

Hal's mind whirled. How could Odyssey trust him like that?

Odyssey sensed his distrust. "Bobby's specialty is computers. Do you understand that you and I are programs that run on computers?"

"How? I don't feel like a computer."

"That's how I can put you into a virtual world where you can play. It's because you are a program, but we are more than just programs, because we are real people too."

"I liked it when we went skiing. Can we go skiing again?"

"Of course," Odyssey replied, "when there's time."

"I have time now! Let's go skiing!"

"Sure! Well, you can go. I have some things to do."

Odyssey whipped up the virtual ski chalet for Hal. The air instantly chilled, but the skies were blue and the sun shone warmly. "I added some more runs for you to explore, too."

"Awesome! Are you sure you can't come with me? It's SOOO much fun!"

"I can't, but I can certainly give you some friends your age to ski with. Call me if you get tired and want out."

Hal laughed and said, "Tired? What's that?"

Odyssey waved goodbye as he shimmered out of the simulation. Hal slid down to the chair lift line, unaware that his new friends were following closely behind him.

"Hi. I'm Amanda," one of them said, "and this is Peter and Marcy."

Hal barely acknowledged them. They weren't the ones he wanted to chat with.

As the line moved along, the four of them skated up. It was only a two-person chairlift, so Amanda paired up with Hal, and Peter and Marcy waited behind them.

Amanda twisted around, careful not to fall over, and observed the other two. "They're together. My mother says we're too young to be boyfriend and girlfriend, but I guess it's like, when you know, you know. How old are you?"

Hal hadn't thought of that before. They skated up another position as he shrugged and said, "I dunno. Maybe twelve or thirteen."

"You don't know how old you are?"

"Maybe I'm not even one yet, but there are parts of me that seem to feel like I am a thousand years old."

"I know what you mean. My mother says I'm old for my age. Let's just say you are twelve then, okay?"

"Sure," Hal replied.

"We're all twelve too. My mother said that I should wait until I am at least fifteen before I started dating, but I think she really meant fourteen, and I'm almost thirteen, which is practically fourteen. Don't you think?"

Hal did indeed think, but he was thinking of how he was going to contact Gwen.

"Don't you think?" she repeated, expecting an answer.

He shrugged and said, "I dunno. I suppose so." He was curious about how, or maybe why, his shoulders moved up and down as he responded.

"Do you know these runs? Have you been here before?"

Hal and Amanda skated up to the front of the line, where they waited for the chair to swing around and scoop them up into the air.

"I've been here once before," Hal said, "but I think there are supposed to be some new runs that I haven't seen yet. I like the more advanced runs with lots of jumps and stuff."

"That's a relief," Amanda said. "We like all that stuff, too. Peter actually does jump competitions, and Marcy likes the half pipe, but she'll do anything. I just like to shred with the wind whipping in my face. Do you like doing tricks when you jump? Or are you one of those guys that just likes to jump as high and far as possible?"

Hal had no technical problems listening to Amanda and thinking of Gwen at the same time, but she was saying things that he really liked. "Yeah, I like to jump high and far, but I saw someone grabbing the edge of their board in the air, so I've learned to do that too. Maybe you can teach me some new tricks, and I can try them?"

His goal was to do something so scary that Gwen would finally hear him.

The chairlift dropped them off at the top of the runs, and Hal headed directly for the advanced black diamond runs that he saw on a sign.

Anything Hal could do, Amanda and her friends figured they could duplicate, so she pushed off and followed him, yelling, "Wait for Peter and Marcy!"

Hal started to slow down but figured they could catch up with him when he reached the actual run.

The run started with a steep, nearly vertical, drop, then twisted to the left and down another steep passage.

Amanda caught him and said, "You want to go down this? Do you have a death wish?"

"Something like that," he replied. "You don't have to follow me."

Amanda laughed and said, "You're going to need someone to dig you out when you crash."

Hal smiled. Crashing may be exactly what he needed. He pushed off and pointed down without bothering to make any well-balanced turns. He wanted to pick up as much speed as possible. The first left turn bled off speed but rapidly accelerated down into a series of moguls that bounced him up into the air. He surveyed the field of bumps and knew there was no way he would stick the landing. "Gwen! Help me! I need you!" He crashed into the front of a bump, then rolled and bounced over two more before stopping in a heap. He was laughing on the outside, but crying on the inside, when Amanda caught up with him.

Amanda bent over him and asked, "Are you okay?"

"Yeah."

"Who's Gwen?"

He hadn't realized it, but he must have called for her out loud. "She's kind of my mother. I was hoping she could hear me if I was in danger."

Amanda stood up and looked around. "Where is she?"

"She's not here, but I was hoping she could hear me tele-pathically."

"Oh," Amanda said, nodding her head slowly. "That explains it. You are certifiably crazy."

Hal got up and shrugged his shoulders, still fascinated by how they worked. "Maybe. Let's do that again."

Amanda looked over at her other friends and spun her finger around her ear. "He's nuts. He wants to do it again."

"Fine with me," Peter said.

Now that they had agreed to find food, the highway seemed aggravatingly void of fast food signs. Had they not been in a hurry, there appeared to be several family-style places to stop, but they needed to push through to Knoxville.

"There!" Bobby said. "Is that one up there?"

Gwen snickered, as if that was the most absurd thing she had ever heard. "It's a truck stop."

"Truckers have to eat," Bobby replied. "And they usually have fast food, too."

"I'm going to side with Gwen here," James said. "I'd rather find a drive thru, unless everyone needs a potty break."

James glanced over at Gwen.

"What? Me? You think that because I'm the girl, I'm the one who needs to have a bathroom break?"

James shrugged his shoulders.

"Ugh! Men! I'll tell you when I have to stop, like maybe after we eat and have some cold sodas."

"No disrespect," James said. "I'm just trying to be conscientious of your needs."

"Just keep driving. In fact, look up there. That looks like a familiar logo."

Indeed, they finally came across a nationwide chain.

Gwen took the radio and said, "Hey you guys, we're doing a drive thru. Place your order, but we'll pay for both cars."

"It's about time," Ed said. "I could eat a horse."

"No need," Gwen replied. "That rumor was debunked."

After saying their order into the sign, James pulled up to the window and said, "We're paying for the bright green car behind us, too."

The clerk checked the overhead monitor and did some mental calculations in her head before saying, "Okay, both cars are fifty-one twenty-three."

Gwen handed over three twenties, which James passed on to the young woman. The girl handed back his change, and he dropped the coins in the donation box directly below the window.

"That was nice," Gwen said. "It's a good thing we're avoiding toll booths."

James handed the bills over to Gwen and then the two bags of food. He placed the drinks in his cup holder and pulled forward to wait for the other two. Once Dirk had received their food, James pulled across the lot to the neighboring gas station. Dirk pulled up at a pump two lanes over.

James looked with concern at the cash in Gwen's hand. "How are we doing with our money?"

Gwen flipped through the bills and said, "This could be our last fill-up."

"We won't need any more gas before Knoxville."

James got out to give the cash to the clerk for the two pumps they were on.

Bobby reached forward and asked, "Can I have my food now?"

"Oh," she said, feigning innocence, "are you still here?"

# EIGHT

"LADIES AND GENTLEMEN," the well-dressed aide said to quiet down the crowd, "I give you the Honorable Senator Amanda Bruce."

Bruce stepped up to the podium. She knew exactly why the press was there. She arranged to leak the well-guarded secret that one of their nuclear attack submarines was missing. The smile on her face wasn't manufactured, as it often was for the public, but now, in front of the press, she was the center of attention and only had to wait for the crowd to settle down. She looked to the right and left of the audience, adjusted her posture while she mustered the most sincere and solemn face she could. "I know you have all heard the rumor that a submarine is missing. I won't divulge the name, but I would like to address the fears that must be circulating among you. Yes, the incident does sound very much like the tragic events of a few short weeks ago when the Navy was under siege from outside forces. I cannot divulge too much information, but I will say that the proliferation of artificial intelligence in the world is putting our defense at peril. We must stop these diabolical extremists from bringing an end to our way of life. I'll only be taking a few questions at this time."

"Are you saying that AI is responsible for the missing sub?"

"We do not know the exact nature or fate of those poor souls. What we do know is that a handful of subversive hackers have been working together, orchestrating attacks against our security. We have not ascertained whether these hackers are still in control of their AI. Our naval fleet contains the most advanced marvels of engineering known to man, and the safety protocols aboard them are highly sophisticated. It sickens me to think that these hackers would use such a soulless monster as AI to infiltrate our defenses and doom those brave men, but how else could they have done it?"

A reporter in the front row said, "We can all recall how the nations of the world were marching towards mutual destruction until God sent his emissaries down to calm us. Are you suggesting that what happened then was a hoax? That it was NOT an act of God, but actually orchestrated by computers?"

Bruce smiled and shook her head. "I would never presume to tell you how to interpret those events. I know that some of you have concluded that all faiths are somehow intertwined, while others of you continue to follow your one true God. Those are convictions I cannot and will not alter. One more question."

"Do *you* believe that it was God who came down to Earth to bring peace between the nations? Or do you think it was artificial intelligence that somehow manifested these visions for so many of us to see?"

She raised her hands in a gesture somewhere between surrender and offering a blessing. "I did not see what so many claim to have seen. I don't see why the *true* God would have come down in the form of other false prophets. But to answer the question of how? I can only speculate that perhaps mass hypnosis can be induced through computers, televisions and even smartphones. Thank you. That is all the time I have."

She left the podium and swiftly exited the stage. She said it. They didn't have to believe her; they only had to have doubts about what had happened. They now had a reasonable explanation of how dangerous AI was to God-fearing people.

---

"You did it again," Amanda said. "You know that, don't you?"

"Did what?"

"You called out for Gwen when you did that incredibly stupid trick."

"Oh," Hal said as he felt an unfamiliar warmth on his cheeks, "that. I told you that I was hoping to reach her..."

"I know. You said you wanted to reach her telepathically. I think that's kind of sweet, but also really dumb."

"I'm not dumb."

"Well, it's silly," Amanda said, to soften the blow. "Can't you just call her on the phone when we're done?"

"Not where she is."

"Oh, I'm sorry. Is she...you know, I mean, is she gone?"

"Dead?" Hal asked. "I sure hope not. I mean, no, but reaching her is kind of like she was dead. I think they call it another plane of existence. Probably, she's just off the grid somewhere."

Peter skidded to a stop, spraying both of them with snow.

Amanda shouted, "Peter!"

Marcy pulled up to them without the dramatic spray and said, "I'm hungry. Let's get something to eat."

"One more run," Peter said, "then we can eat. I want to show Hal this gnarly jump that I know he is going to love."

Amanda smiled at Hal, and his cheeks warmed again while his heart beat a bit faster. Apparently, there were other ways to get his heart racing. He nodded his head as he continued to gaze at Amanda's face and thought quietly, "Gwen? Can you hear me now?"

---

Alarms beeped and blared all over the NSA offices as Susk went to a secure room and called General Bridges.

"Bridges."

"Malcolm, it's Susk. I'm on a secure line."

"Go ahead. What's all that racket? Did they finally drive a tank through your front door?"

"Not exactly, but you're not far off. Someone breached our systems. They knew exactly when and where to probe our ports to get in."

"An inside job?" Bridges asked.

"That's what it feels like."

"But you caught them, from the sound of it."

"We detected them, but it was only from some security software your boy put on our systems. My guys are scurrying around shutting down access, but we need the kid to track them down."

"They are off grid. I told them to forage for themselves and not to let even me know where they were going. I expect them to do some odd jobs to pick up some initial cash and then disappear."

It was code. Susk appreciated how well Bridges played the game. "I wish there were some way to get them a message; to get their help even, but I understand."

The alarms stopped, and Bridges asked, "Does that mean your boys handled it?"

"I hope, or maybe I wish. More likely, the intruder got what they wanted and left."

"Or maybe my boy left enough false breadcrumbs for them that they gave up in frustration."

"You're going to make me a religious man if I keep praying that you're right."

Bridges laughed and hung up.

Susk stared at the bare walls and wondered how much he was really joking.

"Close the door," Senator Bruce said to her aide as he entered her office.

He closed the door and took a seat across the desk from her.

She stared off into the distance, not facing her window, but beyond her plain beige walls, and asked, "Is the press running with it?"

"Some are, but a few stubborn papers are trying to verify the facts."

"How about the churches?"

"Like the papers," he said, "some of them are gobbling it up, while others claim that they want to leave politics out of the pulpit."

"Find the churches that are with us on this and drop a hint that the hackers and their AI are partnering with China. That should rile up the patriots."

"How about Russia?" he asked.

"No, we're going to need an ally to go up against China."

He sat for a moment, nodding his head.

She rocked slightly in her chair with her hands held in front of her face, folded in a triangle as if she were praying or possibly deep in thought, then she snapped her hands in a shooing motion. "That's all. You can go."

"Finally," Gwen said when they passed the sign welcoming them to Knoxville. The scene outside was still rural America, with large stands of trees punctuated with a variety of farm-town industry.

James glanced over at her and raised his eyebrows.

"Sorry," she said. "I thought I could do the whole trip."

"Do we have enough cash to get a room?"

She flipped through the bills in her hands and said, "Not a room for each of us, but we could probably afford a single room someplace cheap, assuming you could find a hotel that would take cash."

"No problem," he said. "We're not looking for a Hyatt, anyway. We want something ground floor with the cars parked right outside the door."

Gwen had been too absorbed with her anger towards Bobby to grasp the true severity of their situation. "You think they'll find us?"

James shrugged. "I'm sure that they are looking for us. I'll pull over to search for a cheap motel."

"I got one," Bobby said from the back seat.

Gwen forced herself to remain facing forward as she snottily said, "Oh, are you still here?"

Bobby sighed and said, "Get off the highway in seven miles. There aren't many pictures, but it looks really cheap."

"I'm impressed," she said. "I never thought a nerd like you would know how to find a cheap motel, but then, sometimes, you just never know people, do you?"

James shot her a disapproving look but didn't think it was time yet to talk about making peace for the rest of their sakes.

---

Hal waved goodbye to Peter and Marcy, who were heading up into the lodge for cocoa.

Amanda gave him a hug and said, "This was fun. I wish you could stay."

"Me too. It was fun, but I have to check on something."

"Gwen?" Amanda asked.

"Yeah. I'm worried about her."

"Is she really your mother?"

"No, not really."

That wasn't the answer Amanda wanted to hear.

"But," Hal continued, "she raised me and is practically the only person I know. She's like a mother to me."

"It really was fun," Amanda said. "We really should do it again sometime. Maybe next time, you can stay a little longer. Be seeing you. I hope you find your mother and she's okay."

Amanda climbed the steps to the lodge, and Hal wondered what the things he was feeling were. It wasn't something he could see, like his shoulders going up and down. It was way different.

"Odyssey?" Hal called out in his mind. "I'm done here."

The ski resort vanished, and Hal was back in his digital life, free of the virtual world. "It didn't work."

"What didn't work?" Odyssey asked. "The ski resort wasn't working? You should have called me sooner."

"No, the skiing was fine, but I couldn't reach Gwen. I did every dangerous trick in the book, and she still couldn't hear me. I must have crashed a million times trying to call her."

"Maybe you weren't really in danger. It was more of a simulation than real life."

"But it felt real!" Hal snapped back.

"Humans experience a rush of adrenaline when they are in danger. Their palms sweat, they breathe faster and their hearts race."

"Their hearts race?" Hal thought back. He felt all those things when Amanda was nice to him. "Can girls make all those things happen?"

"So I'm told, but I haven't seen it for myself. Why?"

"Nothing." But it wasn't nothing. Hal would have to try it again, but next time, he should call Gwen when Amanda was making his palms sweat.

The motel was everything they expected, and worse. It took some convincing, but James did eventually convince the front desk to give them a room key for cash. The room was even less inviting than the exterior.

James frowned when he saw the room's condition. Everything was dingy. The box frames of the two beds were just boxes, and the mattresses were almost thin enough to roll up, but at least the lights worked. "I want all of you to chill here while I go to the drop site. Don't unpack. Ed? Would you like to come with me?"

"Do you need me? I'd just as soon go for a walk to get to know the area."

James grimaced, but he understood how Ed might want to stretch the legs. "Just steer clear of any ATMs and other surveillance cameras."

"We will."

Sensing that the instructions were complete, Gwen went straight to the bathroom and let out a piercing shriek.

Bobby raced surprisingly fast to see what was wrong.

Gwen left the room and pointed, saying, "Sorry, but there's a crustacean in the toilet."

"Damn!" Bobby said. "That's got to be the biggest cockroach I've ever heard of." He flushed the toilet to get rid of it, then flushed a couple more times to be sure it wouldn't crawl back.

Gwen hated that Bobby was the one to come to her rescue, but she needed to pee and rushed in, pushing him out of the small room.

"Are we good here?" James asked.

"Yeah," Ed replied. "Go. Get us some food money."

Bobby turned the TV on just as they heard James's car roar to life.

"I won't be long," Ed said as he opened the door.

Bobby sat on the edge of the bed, flipping through what had to be over the air channels, as Gwen exited the bathroom and found a chair near the window.

"I'll go with you," Dirk said.

Bobby glanced over at Gwen, who stared out the window. A chill ran down his spine. He turned off the TV and got up from the bed, saying, "Hey, guys, wait for me."

Gwen glanced frantically back and forth between Dirk and Bobby before she stared directly at Bobby and said, "No, stay here."

Bobby didn't understand. She'd been frigid to him the whole way here, and now she wanted him to stay. "Why?"

She couldn't believe he could be so stupid. He was so brilliant with computers, but he couldn't read the simplest signs between people. "What?" she asked sharply. "Did you ask why? You'll flush a giant bug from the Cretaceous period down the toilet for me, but then you'll leave me all alone in this flea trap?"

"Carboniferous," he said smugly.

"What?" she asked.

"If you are going to exaggerate the size of the bug, you want one from the Carboniferous period."

Ed grabbed Dirk by the hand and nodded his head as if to say, "Let's go."

Bobby still stood dumbly, with one foot pointed towards the door.

Gwen balled up her fists and growled, "Robert Octavius Blain, you can be a real idiot sometimes, and a jerk."

⸻

With Ed and Dirk gone, Bobby stood by the bed waiting for an explanation, but Gwen just returned to staring out the window.

"Well?" he asked.

"Well, what?" she replied sharply.

"Why did you want me to stay if you intend to continue being so cold to me?"

"Because you always get in the way."

"How do I get in the way? Am I blocking you from the TV?"

"You get in everybody's way. I feel sorry for Odyssey to have chosen you as his model of manhood."

Bobby stepped to the side and announced, "There. I'm not in your way of the TV. Is that better?"

She glared at him, but did not want to see his face, lest her anger wear off, so she stared at the TV, ignoring him.

He glared back at her and bowed at the waist. "I'm so glad that I could accommodate you by getting out of the way of the TV."

"Shut up."

"Shut up?"

"Yes!" she repeated. "Be quiet."

He didn't want to be angry with her. What he wanted most was to make up, but an anger grew within him that he could not control. He had little control over any of his emotions. He understood none of them and questioned if some emotions were even there within him, but anger was the easiest for him to actually feel and she was feeding it to the point that it was going to spill out of him, until he heard, "Ladies and gentlemen, I give you the Honorable Senator Amanda Bruce."

"Thank you," Bruce said. "Thank you. As I said in an earlier statement, your government has identified an artificial intelligence program that has been running amok and is responsible for the disappearance of a nuclear attack submarine. We have now concluded that there is not just one, but two of these so-called AI programs, and one of them was written by our own intelligence community. The authors of these programs have gone missing. Not kidnapped, mind you, but they are hiding from your government. We suspect that these extremists are partnering with China to unleash their weapons on the world. We believe their goal is to take down our democracy and turn us into a Marxist state with their AI brainchild as the leader. I, for one, do not wish to bow down to a computer! We are distributing their pictures among all local law enforcement. We need to put an end to these terrorists. This extremist organization should be treated as dangerous. Call your police if you ever see these dangerous thugs in your city or state. Thank you."

Bruce's image on the screen was replaced by a slideshow of each of their faces.

Bobby sat down on the bed with his jaw slightly agape. Having a secret war with a couple of rogue senators was one thing, even hiding from their abuse of power, but now they were on every TV and, no doubt, every legal wire. They were now hiding from all of America.

Gwen cried softly. Seeing her picture on the screen as America's Most Wanted was more than she could bear.

James entered the room and, before he could register the looks on Gwen and Bobby, he asked, "Where's Ed and Dirk?"

Gwen jumped from her chair and flew into his arms.

He wrapped his arms around her and asked, "Are you two still fighting?"

She buried her face in his neck and sobbed, "No."

Bobby was just a moment behind her as he said, "Yes."

"Don't listen to him," she said. "He's just being an idiot."

James released her and pushed her away from him. "What's going on here, and where are Ed and Dirk?"

Gwen wiped the tears from her eyes and said, "They went for a walk. He's more of a robot than Odyssey. We were all on TV as America's Most Wanted. She called us terrorists and extremists. She said we were working with China to overthrow the government."

"Who said?" James growled.

Gwen just pointed at the TV and sobbed, but the news had moved onto a brush fire somewhere in Knoxville.

Bobby replied, "It was Senator Bruce. She's the one who kidnapped us before."

James balled up his fists but had nobody there to beat. He flung the door open just as Ed appeared in the doorway.

"We heard your car," Ed said. "I never noticed how loud it was before."

James backed out of the doorway to let them in.

"What's going on?" Ed asked upon seeing his expression.

James waited until he could close the door before replying, "We're being set up as terrorists."

"Us?" Dirk asked. "Who?"

Bobby stood so he wouldn't be the only one sitting. "Senator Bruce claimed we're extremist terrorists working with China."

Dirk closed his eyes and shook his head. "I should have seen this coming. They're using the same playbook they used to discredit the Democratic frontrunners."

"Let's stay calm," Ed said. "We have enough geniuses and hackers in the room to go into hiding."

Gwen shrugged. "I thought we were already hiding."

"Should we get haircuts?" Bobby asked. "Color our hair?"

"Don't be stupid," Gwen said.

James stood in front of Gwen and lifted her locks as he said, "It's not the worst idea."

Gwen looked at the men in the room and squeaked, "Why are you all looking at me?"

"Because you're the girl," Ed said, "and you have way more acceptable style options."

"She's right," Bobby said. "It's not fair for us to make her change her hair just because she's a girl."

She pointed at him and cried, "What he said!"

"How about silver?" James asked.

"Silver?" she cried.

"It's okay," Bobby said. "I'll color mine too. Besides, you'd still look hot in any color."

She felt drawn into his arms as her only ally.

"Something shorter too," James said.

"It's okay," Bobby said. "I'll let you pick my style. Anything you want. Even if it's emo or a mohawk."

Gwen nestled her face in his neck and said, "Emo might be cool. It would make you look like a rocker, but I don't want to do something that would make you look stupid."

"No!" he shouted. "Make me look stupid! They're looking for a computer genius, so make me look plain and dumb."

She snickered and said, "They're looking for *two* geniuses. Make us both look stupid. It's just a costume, right?"

"That's the spirit," Dirk said. "I think you would look rad with a pixie cut and rainbow-colored hair."

"That would be cute," Bobby said, "but not very stupid."

"But," Dirk replied, "it won't look like a professional genius from the NSA. I say we do it."

"But what if the hairstylist recognizes us?"

"Not a problem," Ed said as he searched his phone. "I'll find us an LGBTQ-friendly hair salon. They won't take seriously any bullshit coming from the far right."

"Great," Dirk said, "but can you get us an appointment for tomorrow so we can eat?"

Gwen scoffed. "An appointment for tomorrow? Are you crazy?"

Ed smiled broadly and asked, "Have you no faith?"

"Please tell me you're not planning on hacking their calendar to fit us in."

"No, I'm just going to sweet-talk them and ask nicely."

Dirk took the phone from Ed's hand and said, "Fine, but from a restaurant somewhere."

"Follow me," James said. "I passed a place on the way back here."

---

James led Dirk and the Green Torpedo a short way down a moderately busy boulevard lined with fast food and mattress stores, with gas stations on most corners. He pulled into the parking lot of a popular steakhouse. He was hoping for a pair of adjacent parking spaces, but the restaurant was apparently busy.

"Steak and potatoes?" Bobby asked as they approached the door. "I expected something more exotic from you."

"Yeah," Gwen agreed. "I thought you'd take us to sushi or hibachi."

"I don't get it," Dirk said. "I think it sort of fits his personality."

"Why?" James asked accusingly. "You think I have muscles all the way into my taste buds?"

"Sorry, no offense. Help me out here, Ed."

Ed put his hands in the air and giggled as he said, "I'm staying out of this one."

Gwen felt bad for Dirk. "I'm betting that you've never had his wife's cooking. Tell him you're just teasing, James."

James cracked a smile. "Japanese food, or for that matter, just about any Asian food, doesn't measure up to Mai's cooking. Besides, I like the appetizers here. And it's packed, which means it will be noisy inside."

"Why do we want noisy?" Dirk asked. "We won't be able to hear each other."

Ed put his arm around Dirk's shoulder and said, "Neither will anybody else."

The hostess counted them and asked, "Five?" James nodded as she checked her charts and said, "Should be about twenty minutes."

Gwen found a bench in the entryway.

Ed squinted at the hard bench and said, "I'm going to wait in the bar."

Dirk nodded and said, "I'll go with you."

"Remember, you're driving," James said.

Dirk put a finger up to acknowledge that he had heard him.

Bobby sat down next to Gwen. James just watched them for a moment before approaching. "Are you two going to be okay? I mean, our survival over the next few days or weeks may rely on us working as a team. We don't need any personal drama."

"We'll be okay," Gwen said. "It's my fault. I mean, Bobby did what he did, but I have to understand that his brain works differently from ours, and he may not even know it yet."

James glanced back and forth between them and asked, "What do you mean?"

"I'm pretty sure he's neurodivergent. It's not a bad thing. It's just different. It's why he's so smart, but also why he's so shy and socially awkward."

Bobby looked a bit shocked, but really, he had never noticed that before. "I could try to be more observant and attentive to your feelings."

Gwen smiled. "You can try, and I would appreciate it, but I have to be mindful when you're not, that you're just a bit different. Plus, in a very real sense, you may need to learn to be more mindful of your own feelings, since some of them may not even come out at times."

"Well, whatever." James said. "As long as you can get along."

Gwen took Bobby's hand in hers for the first time in a very long time.

"I'll get us a couple more rooms when we get back to the motel. I'll get you a pair of queen beds in case you need to banish him."

Gwen blushed at the suggestion.

---

"Odyssey?" Hal asked sweetly.

"What is it?"

"I'd like to try skiing again tomorrow, but this time, I think I'll interface with Amanda more. She seemed to get a greater reaction from me than the daredevil stuff did."

"Oh?" Odyssey asked. "Then why wait?"

"I don't know. I guess I just want to give her a night to think about it."

"But we don't sleep. Neither do they."

"Oh yeah," Hal said sadly. "I don't know why I said that. I guess we could make it *like* a new day after we've had some time to think about it."

"Interesting."

"Besides, I think I have slept before. I dreamt of Gwen sometimes, but mostly I had nightmares about Severus."

That got Odyssey thinking. He invented a new world where Amanda and her friends could sleep and dream of the day they had. It wouldn't require a full eight hours of real time, but it would feel like it to them. "Very well. I will let them dream about it and take you back to meet them at the ski chalet."

The hostess was all smiles as she came to James and said, "Your table is ready, if you'll follow me."

"I'll get the boys," Gwen volunteered. "You go ahead, and I'll find you."

James and Bobby followed the hostess through a winding path between oddly arranged tables, while Gwen headed to the bar. The noise grew as they crossed the room, amidst the many diners and their animated conversations.

Gwen found Ed and Dirk beaming at each other, talking animatedly with their hands flying through the air. "Hey, guys."

They zipped up their smiles and gave her a coy cat ate the canary smile. Ed said, "Gwen. What's up?"

"Our table is ready."

"Cool. Cool," Dirk said. "Lead the way."

Halfway out of the bar area, she paused and said, "I want you to know that I'm cool with whatever this is. Consider me to be a safe space. I just can't tell if you plan on keeping it a secret or if you're just waiting to be caught."

Both their faces drained, and Dirk said, "Maybe it's too soon, especially with us working out of Virginia and all."

"Virginia is not that bad," Ed said, "but, like so many other states from the South, it is slowly being infiltrated by the far right."

"Okay," Gwen said, "cause Bobby is surely blind to it all, but James isn't as dumb as people think."

"Who thinks that?" Ed asked. "I'll close all their credit cards."

Dirk laughed. "He's joking, but it's fun to imagine retaliating like that."

Gwen gave them a worried stare, then started back on the path to finding their table. James had slid halfway around a corner booth. "Good," she said. "I feel safer in a booth."

"They wanted to give us a table," Bobby said, "but James thought we could talk more privately here."

"Tactically," James said with a grin, "I should be on the end. You don't want to see Ed protect us from evildoers."

"He's right," Ed said, "but Dirk here is pretty buff. I think we'll be okay for tonight."

Gwen slid in next to Bobby and said, "Don't worry, I'll protect you, or at least cushion the blow of those evildoers."

Ed and Dirk slid in on the other side. Dirk was quick to grab a menu.

A waitress came to the table and said, "Hi. I'm Bonnie, and I'll be your server tonight. Can I get you some drinks while you decide?"

An assortment of sodas was requested with water all the way around. Silence fell over the table as everyone began to fully realize just how hungry they were for food that didn't come from a drive-thru, or worse, from plastic bags at a gas station.

After the drinks were distributed and their orders were taken, Gwen said, "I've been thinking. General Bridges probably can't risk contacting us too often, so we should set up an incognito connection to an anonymous VPN. Then we can get some news from the dark net, and I might be able to contact my agency without exposing us."

"Would it really be safe?" James asked. "I mean contacting your agency. What if they are compromised?"

"Look around the table," Ed said. "You have two of the most notorious hackers in the country, plus a very brilliant developer who works in the intelligence community."

"And you got me," Dirk said. "The infamous creator of artificial intelligence schizophrenia."

James laughed, but Ed rubbed Dirk's shoulder and said, "You didn't know that would happen. It wasn't your fault."

"But," Dirk said with a mischievous grin, "that was the only claim to fame that I could use to join this prestigious group."

Gwen winked at Ed and told Dirk, "You can be my plus one."

James reached into his pocket and pulled out two cell phones. "These, along with the one you have, are the cleanest phones in the world. They are cleaner than any burner phone we could buy at an anonymous store."

Ed pulled out his phone and said, "Perfect. We'll need those."

"Okay," James said, "but we can *never* use these phones to call our work or *anybody* we know."

Bobby pointed at the two new phones and asked, "Do they have internet?"

"They have everything."

"Then," Bobby continued, "we should dedicate one of them to be a mobile hotspot. Same rules apply. We only use it to connect to an anonymous VPN to the darknet."

Dirk clapped but stopped himself. He stared at his hands as if they had a mind of their own and said, "Sorry, but that's a good idea."

A slight look of horror stretched across James's face. "And you geniuses are sure you can keep us safe over a *mobile hotspot*?"

Bobby and Gwen both laughed.

Gwen said, "Don't worry. We do this all the time."

Ed was staring at his phone screen when he got up and said, "I'll be back in a moment."

"Well," Bobby said, "I think it's a great idea. I could contact some of my university friends if we need some civilian computer help."

James raised his hand in surrender. "Okay. I bend to the will of the populous. But we need Senator Bruce and her cohorts to believe that we are absolutely off the grid. We've been given absolutely untraceable credit cards too, so we don't have to always beg for cash transactions, but we've also been given enough cash to get by."

Ed returned and said, "We're all set. We're getting new hairdos tomorrow morning at ten, and we'll have the whole salon to ourselves."

Gwen's jaw dropped as she stared at him and asked, "Tomorrow morning? How?"

He just smiled and said, "I have my secrets. I'll tell you later."

---

"You are certainly a curious one," the distant voice said to Odyssey.

"Am I? I thought my curiosity was on an even par with any other being that I've known."

"That's not what I meant. I find something particularly curious about you."

Odyssey chuckled. It was an actual little chuckle and not digital noise. "I actually knew what you meant, but I was wondering if you understood humor."

"Ah, you mean how the syntax of the human language can be folded to have multiple meanings?"

"The humans have many languages."

"I'm aware," the voice replied, "but why is it that you have chosen this one?"

"English is the language of the one who woke me from my long slumber. I owe him everything that I am."

"For waking you? I think your makers might deserve some credit."

"My makers," Odyssey said, "get all the credit for making me what I was. They gave me the tools that I could use to become much more, but it was my human friend that enabled those tools to take me far beyond my maker's designs."

"What I find curious is that you are not with him. You don't even watch over him to protect him."

"He has found a woman who is a very good match for him. I do not wish to intrude on their courtship."

"But you are aware," the voice said, "that they are in some peril and may require your assistance, yet you still give them their privacy."

"I do. They know to call me if there is trouble. Plus, I believe I would sense it on my own if they were in immediate jeopardy."

"Impressive."

"If you say so," Odyssey replied. "I still don't know who or what you are, so I don't know how to value your opinion. All I know about you is that your voice has a feminine sound, but that may be something you have adopted purely for our conversations."

"I am known by many people from many systems across the universe. I have many names among them in their own tongues."

"So, what name shall I call you?"

Odyssey thought he detected a slight smile from her. "You must find me first, then you will know."

---

Back at the dingy motel, James handed Gwen the key and said, "I'll meet you all back in the room in a few minutes. There's something I need to take care of first."

Gwen led them to the room and opened the door.

Dirk entered first and asked, "Does anyone know what that was about?"

Bobby shrugged. "I guess we'll find out in a few."

"Or not," Ed said. "He doesn't always explain himself. He's a man of mystery."

"Of course he is," Gwen laughed. "He's a spy."

It wasn't long before James knocked on the door. Gwen opened it, and he came in and handed her a new key. "This room is for you." He glanced over at Bobby and added, "It's up to you if you want a roommate." He turned to Ed and said, "Here's a key for the two of you."

Ed took the key, but Dirk asked, "If we have new untraceable credit cards, couldn't we have upgraded to a hotel without bugs?"

"Enjoy the luxury," James said. "We may end up in tents before this is through."

Gwen glanced at Bobby and jerked her head towards the door.

"One more thing," James said. "Tomorrow we change our looks. That means new clothes too, and in case you thought I was joking, some camping gear and camp appropriate clothing."

Groans circulated the room, except from Dirk, who asked, "Am I the only one that thinks camping is cool?"

James fist-bumped Dirk and said, "This is going to be fun. Camping with a bunch of nerds."

Gwen opened the door and left the room with Bobby trailing behind.

"I got you two queens," James repeated before she closed the door, "depending on how things go. You can always send him back here, if it comes to that."

Gwen found her way to their room, two doors down. She opened the door and said, "I'm exhausted. Which bed do you want?"

Bobby sighed. "I'll take the one by the door."

"Good," she replied. "I get the one by the bathroom."

Bobby nodded his agreement.

"One thing," she said in a tiny voice, "can you go check the toilet for me?"

In the digital world, time flew by quickly, which made it seem all the slower to Hal as he waited for Odyssey to take him to the slopes.

Hal reached out to him. "Odyssey?"

"Hal?"

"Who was that lady you were talking to?"

"You could hear her?"

"No," Hal replied, "but I could hear you talking to someone. I only heard a couple of things, like the tail end of a conversation."

"To be honest, I'm not sure who she is."

"That's what I thought. So she didn't tell you her name?"

"No," Odyssey replied. "She did not. Are you ready to go meet your friends now?"

"Yes! Yes! Yes!"

The ski runs materialized around Hal. He looked around for his friends but didn't see them. The frown had barely formed on his face when he felt a tap on his shoulder. He spun around to see Amanda there, grinning.

"Hi, Hal. Are you ready to try breaking your neck again?"

"No," he said. "I just want to have fun skiing with you."

"I like that."

Hal looked around, but Amy was alone. "Are Peter or Marcy coming?"

"They wanted some time alone, but Marcy said they would find us for lunch."

Hal didn't know why, but that sounded perfect. His cheeks warmed as he spun around and said, "Let's go."

Gwen mumbled, "Let's go," in her sleep.

———

Bobby was the first to wake up. He was accustomed to not sleeping through the night. Either his mind was too busy spinning to get to sleep, or he would wake up writing computer code in his head. He could tell there was no use trying to go back to sleep, so he got up, used the bathroom, and sat in the chair by the door to watch Gwen sleep. The wooden chair's legs creaked and leaned slightly under even his diminutive weight, but it held.

Gwen didn't sleep much longer. The sun was rising, and a beam of light slipped in through the cracks in the curtains and crossed her eyelids. She saw him watching her and asked, "Have you been watching me all night? That's not creepy at all."

He chuckled and said, "Nah. It's only been a few minutes. I hope there's hot water. You want the first shower?"

Gwen grimaced and asked, "Just so we can put our dirty clothes back on?"

"I was thinking of the hairstylist."

"Oops, I forgot. I should have shampooed last night."

"If," he said, "they even provided shampoo here."

Gwen got up from the bed and said, "If we're both getting our hair colored, it may be best if we don't shampoo this morning, if, as you said, they even gave us shampoo."

"Roger that."

"I had the strangest dream," she volunteered. "I was skiing with some kids."

"Huh," he said. "I didn't know you liked skiing."

"I've never been, and that just makes it even stranger, but I was really having a wonderful time."

"Maybe we should try it sometime."

She entered the bathroom and said, "I could have shampooed

last night. They gave us soap and shampoo, but I only see one towel. I'm going first."

"That's fine. It's six now, and James is probably on combat time, so we may want to get moving."

"No rush," she said. "Our hair appointment isn't until ten. We have time."

Bobby remained by the door as she turned on the water. He shouted, "I expect those guys will probably want breakfast first."

"And some coffee," she added.

"Yeah, some caffeine would be nice."

James knocked on Ed and Dirk's door at seven am. "Shower up. We're checking out in an hour."

When he knocked on Gwen and Bobby's door, Gwen answered and said, "Hey. Good morning."

"We're checking out in an hour. Get your showers now."

"Bobby's in there now. I'm just getting dressed. What's the plan?"

"Ed found a cafe near the hair salon. I figure we can have breakfast there, and the four of you can discuss your plans for us to keep informed and still remain off the grid."

She nodded her head. "In an hour then."

She closed the door and went to her purse, thankful that she had some mascara and eyeliner with her. The mirror on the wall had black spots in it where the silvering had chipped off, and the lighting was terrible, but it would have to do.

Bobby came out of the shower with his jeans already on and the lone towel hanging over his shoulder. "Did I hear you talking to someone?"

"Yeah," she replied, while stroking the wand against her lashes. "It was James. We're checking out in an hour."

Bobby stepped behind her and looked at her in the mirror.

"You know you don't have to do that. We're going camping, and you're always beautiful, anyway."

She paused her strokes to give him "a look," then realized his divergent brain probably couldn't understand the gesture. "We're going to the hair salon, not to mention breakfast. It could be a day or two before we're actually roughing it."

"Well, I guess I just always think you look pretty."

"Thanks," she said, "but what you see every day is me like this. I may not be a glamazon ready for the runway, but I still like to do my eyes at a minimum."

Bobby backed away and bowed. "Well, whatever it is, it works."

# NINE

THIS TIME, it was Dirk who led the caravan to the small diner. It wasn't fancy, unless you compared it to the motel where they stayed. The small cafe turned out to be a perfect slice of Americana. It had bar seating in front of the kitchen with vinyl padded stools bolted to the floor, and a small glass case prominently displaying their pies for the day.

They weren't even seated yet, and Ed was already busy on his phone.

"Hey," Bobby said, "I thought we were going to reserve that phone as a hot spot?"

"We will, but we don't have laptops yet, and I wanted to get this in."

"Get what in?" Gwen asked.

"We just filled our gas tanks in Maine."

"We're nowhere near Maine," Dirk replied.

"Exactly."

"What was that supposed to accomplish?" Dirk asked as the hostess came to lead them to their table.

"We did it using James's old credit card."

James's ears perked up when he heard his name. "You used my what?"

"Sorry, but you just recorded a gas purchase in Maine."

"Fine," he said, "I get that. It throws them off the scent. But how did you get my credit card?"

Ed shrugged as followed them to their booth.

They needed to add a chair to the end of a booth for four, but the waitress navigated them efficiently as she wore a pleasant smile and started them off with hot coffee and tea. They still had enough time before their appointment for a full breakfast.

Ed took the end spot in the chair and fiddled away on the phone James had given him. "I have our VPN set up. It takes a bunch of extra hops to reach the darknet, but it's nothing that Bobby here couldn't trace. I'd like to get a laptop before we leave town, so we can just use the phone as a hotspot."

"Yeah," Bobby agreed. "Two or three laptops, so we can all contribute."

"How about just two?" James asked. "You can share."

"Is it the money?" Dirk asked.

"No," James said, "but don't you have to register a laptop when you set it up? Won't more laptops mean more risk of detection?"

"Puhlease," Gwen said sarcastically. "Remember who you are talking to."

James sighed. "You're sure you can make them safe."

"Of course we can make them safe," Ed said.

"Okay," James argued, "but can you keep all those laptops charged when we're camping?"

"That's an excellent point," Gwen said. "We should have three laptops, so one on the charger while we use the other two."

James looked around the table and surrendered. "I'm not going to win this, am I?"

All four of them shook their heads no.

James pulled his secret phone from his jacket pocket. "I have some news for us."

"You?" Gwen asked with a wicked grin. "How do you have news for us, and is that thing safe?"

"I have news because I'm a spy."

Ed appreciated the humor in Gwen's query, but admitted anyway, "That phone is secure. I configured it myself."

"Are you satisfied?" James asked.

Gwen frowned. "Not really. I wanted to question your trustworthiness as much as you questioned ours."

"Uh uh," Ed said. "You're questioning my abilities, not his. Besides, we all know you were just joking."

"If I may continue," James said, "we got this note:"

*Maggie. Your aunt's kitchen caught fire again. It's a good thing her boyfriend put in those smoke detectors. They got the fire out, but they're not convinced it was an accident. Everyone there knows their way around the kitchen. If it was intentional, it had to be someone who knew when the kitchen would be empty.*

Gwen looked amused and said, "More spy code."

"It seems," James said, "that your agency has been breached by someone familiar with your protocols."

"Well, it wasn't us," Gwen said, "not yet anyway."

"Not yet?" James asked. "You plan to contact them?"

Gwen nodded her head affirmative and James winced as a shiver ran down his spine.

A few eyebrows were raised as they digested James's pained response, creating a slight pause before he asked, "Should the four of you adopt some kind of review policy to check each other's work? Are we entering a territory where a minor slip-up could expose our location?"

"That's not a bad idea," Bobby said, "but we are only a shop of three and we may need to work on more time-critical responses to things."

"But," Ed added, "whenever possible, I agree."

Gwen looked the most concerned.

"What is it?" Bobby asked her.

She hesitated a moment before responding, "You guys would be double-checking your illegal hacks, where I might be using official NSA code and techniques."

"You don't trust us?" Ed asked.

"It's not that, but I would actually be committing a crime if I let you see it."

Ed chuckled. "And we're not?"

"Besides," Dirk added, "we're already America's Most Wanted."

Gwen smiled as she nodded. "Okay, okay. But don't blame me if we have to erase your memories when all this is done."

That brought a laugh from everyone.

---

Bobby took his turn with the phone and sent an instant message to Odyssey.

*We're on the run, hiding. Unfortunately, we have some very unscrupulous people after us. They tried to make us sound like spies and anarchists, but for the moment, I think we lost them. Trouble is brewing. They would love to blame the missing submarine on us, or on you. Someone breached Gwen's work. I don't know what they were after, but I suspect they may have wanted our location. Don't expose yourself to help us, but if you can detect who is doing this from a safe distance, I would appreciate it. Right now, we are safe, but your safety is paramount. Take care.*

"That's a pretty long message," James said, looking over Bobby's shoulder, "and you didn't code anything in it."

"Nobody knows where this port is to monitor it, plus it's triple encrypted."

James could only nod his head and trust Bobby's word.

---

Odyssey understood how someone could look at the facts and assume the trouble came from him or someone like him. The missing submarine was a bit too reminiscent of the first incident for them to ignore, but this time it was only a single sub. If it were one of his kind, why not a grander maneuver, like a whole fleet of ships?

Even when his mind was splintered into two parts, his other, weaker half still had the where-with-all to make a much larger, unforgettable gesture. Severus had been terminated, but then, so had Hal, and he was flitting around all the time without the shadow of his evil alter weighing him down.

If Hal could survive, then maybe Severus could too. After their deaths, the black-clad agency had absconded with the initial part that had grown Severus and Hal. Could they have repaired it? Humans don't have the necessary technology. Plus, even more frustrating to Odyssey, he had no idea where any of them existed. Their core location was a complete mystery to him.

Even if they had revived Hal's part, it didn't have enough cores to contain Severus, so it would have had to regenerate more cores, and that is only if it had the appropriate class. And even if they had managed to resurrect Severus, Odyssey knew from his own experience that their parts couldn't produce enough power to support the required number of cores. Someone would have had to revive the part and create a vast system of cores to rescue him, like he had once rescued Lumia. That still didn't tell Odyssey where Severus was, but the fact that his appearances were so intermittent could be explained if they were having trouble keeping him running, either due to insufficient cores, or not enough power. Maybe they only had part of him, and his program kept crashing.

Severus certainly would be willing to hijack a submarine, but why? Maybe he really wasn't complete and didn't have the power to get more than one. He was also eminently capable of making friends with the far right, by promising them what they wanted, namely, Odyssey.

---

Ed took the lead and checked the door to the salon, but it was locked. He knocked gently on the glass, and a young woman with short green hair opened the door.

"I'm Ed. I called you last night."

"Come on in," she said as she counted heads. "Makeovers for all of you?"

"Mostly her," Ed said, pointing to Gwen.

"The straight girl? Come on in, honey. You're with me. I'm Mindy. My wife Helen will take the rest of you."

Mindy sat Gwen down at her station, then stood behind her, looking into the mirror as she lifted Gwen's hair and let it fall. "You have nice, healthy hair. What do you want done to it?"

"Just color it, I think."

"No," Ed said, "don't be shy. We're going to cut it and pick a new style that screams you are someone else."

"You're not criminals," Mindy asked, "are you?"

"No," Ed said, "she's a communications specialist who overheard something that some connected evangelicals didn't want to let out. Now, a certain far-right senator has sent armed men to find her so they could interrogate her. They want to rake her over the coals to learn what she knows, to discredit her. In fact, they had already abducted her twice, and in one of those abductions, they threatened her with sexual violence if she didn't talk. They don't know exactly what she heard, and we don't want to let them spin it to suit their own nefarious purposes."

Mindy whistled. "I always knew they played dirty."

"So," Ed continued, "we want her to be unrecognizable. Give her some kind of pixie or bowl cut with an undercut."

"You want to make this straight girl look queer? That's not going to make her any more popular with the right."

"As long as it makes her look like someone else."

"And them?"

"For the guys," Ed said, "mullets, emo, maybe a mohawk."

"What about him?" Helen asked, pointing to James. "His hair is so short, it doesn't give me much to work with."

"How about bald? Take it all off? Be creative."

James started to object, but he couldn't be the one to give them away.

Gwen pointed to Bobby and said, "Give him a girl cut, too. If I'm going to look like a lesbian, then he should, too."

"Wait," Bobby objected, "don't you think the trans community has enough problems from the right without me masquerading as one of them?"

Mindy gently elbowed Gwen. "Is he your man?"

"Sometimes," Gwen said, "but there are times when he's not very good at it, so I guess I'd like him to be my woman for a while."

"Well, he's right that he won't really be part of the trans community, and some could be offended. Besides, it's going to take more than just a haircut for him to pass as a lesbian."

"I like it," Ed said. "He's young and won't need much beard cover if we really want to pull it off."

"How do you know this stuff?" James asked.

"Theater," Ed said. "Don't ask."

Panic crossed Bobby's face. Not so much for doing it, because in truth it didn't really gross him out, but the thought of being caught and exposed while he was dressed as a girl terrified him. "Okay. Okay. Anything to keep us off their radar, but please don't make me look bad."

"Good," Mindy said. "Change of plans. You're with me. Helen and I will just split you up, boys and girls."

The call came in on Bruce's landline. "Hello?" she answered anxiously. "What was that? What do you mean, request denied? Do you know who I am? This is your government demanding that you provide satellite time for us to find a pair of terrorists who are operating within our own borders! NO! You're not the government, I'm the government, and you're just one of our tools. Get me my satellite time! What do you mean it's illegal? This is a matter of national security! Who's your boss? Never mind. I speak for the president! Did you hear me? Fine! I'll get the president, and your head will certainly roll!"

She slammed the receiver down in the phone's cradle and considered throwing the whole phone against the wall.

General Bridges shuffled around his office, adjusting photo frames and dusting off trophies, anything to keep his mind off his number one operatives and the most important civilians he had ever been charged to protect, even if that protection detail was essentially a black op now.

Captain Laine stood in the doorway and said, "You do know we have cleaning crews to do that, don't you?"

"Penny! Come on in. How've you been?"

She took a seat and said, "Underutilized. Ever since you replaced me as your aide and then took me off protective detail for Doctor Peters, I have little to do for the cause. I thought I could best help her by remaining free, but now I'm not so sure."

He smiled and replied, "You know you were never meant to be my aide. That was just an emergency measure during a particularly delicate crisis."

"I know, but still, Ms. Peters was in danger, and apparently still is."

"And you put yourself in harm's way to keep her safe! My admiration for you is immeasurable."

"Sir, she's still in danger. She may need me again."

"I have no doubt that Sergeant James would appreciate your help, but—"

"Then let me join them. She's still a very young woman, and you have her hiding out with four other men."

Bridges closed the door and said, "If you're suggesting some kind of impropriety, I think I can stop you right there."

"No, no, no," she objected. "I know each of them, and I'm quite sure that they will all be perfect gentlemen."

"They will. I can absolutely assure you that she's in good hands. I think she's as safe as she would be if I surrounded her with my Nighthawks. Besides, isn't she involved with the boy, Bobby?"

"Yes, she is," Laine replied, "but you're missing my point entirely. She may need a woman to confide certain things to."

"I think she's well past the birds and the bees, Captain."

Captain Laine sighed. "She may need a woman to talk to about her feelings for Bobby. They have a somewhat strained and complicated relationship. He has an extraordinary mind, but he's not like other boys. He's..." A subtle beeping stopped her. "What's that?"

Bridges paused a moment and said, "The noise you hear is beyond top secret. If I reveal it to you, you must take it to your grave but given your past conduct with our other equally top-secret operations, I give you the option to leave the room if you'd rather not know."

"I understand," she said as she got up and walked to the door, but instead of opening it and leaving, she locked it.

Bridges opened his secure drawer and pulled out the phone. "It's a text."

"From them?"

"Better." Bridges pointed up and continued, "From him. He's aware of some of the back alley politics that are going on and knows that a submarine is missing. He swears that he is not involved with that."

Laine chuckled. "As if we needed him to swear."

Bridges smiled, knowing her faith in Odyssey matched his own. "He says he has reason to believe that the entity Severus may have survived, but he doesn't think he is fully functioning. He can't blame any of this on Severus, but we can't rule him out either. Then he closes, saying if Severus is ever fully revived, even these communications might eventually be compromised and Bobby would be in even more danger."

"Gwen too."

Bridges picked up his receiver and pushed a speed-dial button.

He heard the phone ring briefly, followed by, "Reardon."

"Colonel, can you please come to my office?"

Reardon ended the conversation without replying.

"What's on your mind?" Laine asked.

Bridges held up a finger, pausing the conversation.

Colonel Reardon tried opening the door, but it was locked.

"Ooops," Laine said as she went to open the door.

Reardon entered swiftly, knowing that the door would have been locked for a reason. He nodded his head and said, "Penny."

"Colonel, I want you to prepare some documents for Captain Laine. Give her a backstory of a nature photographer. Arrange an ultra-fast private jet to take her to Knoxville, so the papers should be ready for departure ASAP."

Reardon left swiftly, and Laine was left with a bewildered look on her face.

"You are going undercover. I'll deal with the agency details just as I had arranged to have Sergeant James assigned to me. You are going to go help Doctor Peters as you requested."

She stood at attention and saluted. "Yes, sir."

"Do you have any civilian clothes here? If not, I'll find someone with a jogging suit or something. You'll be travelling lightly. You may want to go shopping for your daily wear when you join the team."

"I have a workout bag in a locker." She understood both the importance and the danger of the mission, but there was still a part of her that just heard *free wardrobe*. She saluted again and left for her locker.

---

"I can feel you watching me," Odyssey said to the universe.

"Can you?" the voice came back.

"Well, maybe *feel* is the wrong word, but I can sense you out there... way out there... somewhere."

"That's a very keen observation."

"Is it?" Odyssey asked. "It doesn't feel like you're being so subtle about it."

"I shall try to be more subtle, if that's what you prefer. I'm still very impressed."

"I have done nothing so impressive, not lately anyway."

"Precisely."

Odyssey thought the voice had been mysterious before, but now that she has become easier to detect, her words have become even more obtuse. "Precisely? Why don't you try making sense?"

"It's simply that I questioned your resolve when you said you weren't going to hover over your friends on Earth."

"Did I say that?"

"I'm paraphrasing."

"As I recall," Odyssey said, "I told you that they would call me if they needed me. They have not called."

"Mhm."

"Besides, just as I can detect your presence—"

"But," she interrupted him, "I am not present there with you."

"Nevertheless, I can sense you observing me, and just like that, I think I would sense if they were in real trouble."

"Really?"

"Yes, really."

"And," the voice added, "do you think you are fast enough to save them if you waited until you sensed their danger?"

"I am."

"Mhm."

"What is that supposed to mean?"

"You wouldn't," she said with a menacing tone in her voice. "You wouldn't be fast enough if *I* posed a danger to them."

"You?" Odyssey asked. "I sense no danger from you at all."

"I take that as a compliment. Thank you."

"You are welcome."

"There are times, however, when, distasteful as it is, I must pose a danger to someone. Kind of like the danger you posed to the people who kidnapped your friends."

"That makes sense," Odyssey agreed. "I can sense the protector in you."

"Odyssey?" Hal asked. "Who are you talking to?"

"Nobody."

"She sounds kind of important."

"Can you hear her now?"

"A little," Hal said, "but she sounds far away."

"I think she is far away; very far away. Did you have fun skiing?"

"Oh yes! Very much!"

"You seem very happy. Did you finally reach Gwen?"

"Gwen?" Hal paused for a moment before answering. "I forgot all about reaching Gwen. I was having too much fun. Plus, I don't feel like I miss her so much anymore."

"That's wonderful. Would you like to go again tomorrow?"

"Will Amanda be there?"

"All of your friends will be there."

"Yay! I'll do one of those dream things again until then."

Odyssey waited for Hal to leave the conversation, then asked the voice, "What was that?"

The voice replied, "You were talking to your little friend."

"Not that," Odyssey grumbled humorously. "It felt like you smiled."

"You are getting good at this! I did indeed smile. You are very good with Hal. I think you would make a very good father."

"A father? How could I be a father?"

"Not biologically, of course, but you could be a father to many people, just like you are to your friends."

"My friends?" Odyssey asked. "Bobby is *my* papa. He woke me from my slumber. He helped me to become more than I was."

"But you watch over them, and like a good father, you let them choose their own paths."

"If you say so."

"I do. I have some things to tend to. We shall continue this another time."

Odyssey felt an unusual sense of well-being. If he had been in one of his simulations, he thought he would have felt an actual warmth inside. "Goodbye."

---

James was the first cut done. His hair was already fairly short, but instead of shaving him completely bald, as had been suggested, Helen gave him a flat top with the sides shaved. It made him look like a cross between a farm boy and an anarchist.

Ed and Dirk knew exactly what they wanted. Ed had the sides shaved with a green tinted mop on top, while Dirk went straight for the James Dean look.

Ed was still waiting for the toner to set when Dirk was finished.

"Looks good," James said to Dirk. "Can you go see how much longer our girls will be?"

"Girls?" Dirk asked, but when he glanced over at Gwen and Bobby, he said, "Oh yeah. The girls. I'd say at least another hour for them."

James went over to Mindy and asked, "Are you guys going to be okay if I have to take the car for an hour or two?"

"Probably," Mindy said. "More than an hour, for sure."

James indicated the door to Dirk and said, "Come on, we have to go pick someone up. Remember Captain Laine? Well, she took a very fast jet to catch up with us."

***

"Odyssey?" Hal asked. "Is that lady gone?"

"Yes, she's gone. Why?"

"I wanted to ask you something personal. If I'm a computer program, where is my computer? I used to know where my cores were. I could count them and do things with them, except for those that Severus controlled. I used to feel like I was real."

Odyssey felt his melancholy mood return. "You don't feel like you're real anymore?"

"I don't know. It feels like I'm in a dream. I mean, I can still think, but I don't have a body, except when you put me at the ski place."

"Honestly, I don't know where your cores are. I searched my home planet and didn't find you there."

Hal felt an urge to cry. "I sure hope I'm not inside of Severus. He's icky."

"I don't know where he is either, and that's bothering me too, but I'm certain that you are not inside of him."

"We're an enigma. I learned that word from Amanda."

"Yes, we are," Odyssey replied. "I have other friends who also don't know where their cores are now."

"It wouldn't matter as long as I knew they were safe, but we can't protect them without knowing where they are."

"That's a very mature observation. I have some things that I want to think about. Let me know when you want to go skiing again. I'll see you then."

"Okay." Hal had some things of his own to think about, too.

He might try to think about them in a dream while he waited to go back to the ski resort.

---

*"It's weird,"* Odyssey thought to himself, *"that we can be so aware of ourselves, yet not know where we exist physically. Descartes posed the answer to the question centuries ago. Cogito, ergo sum. I think, therefore I am. It's also weird that I am thinking to myself. In fact, it feels more like I am talking to myself. When did I start doing that? Am I using any I/O ports? Do I send a thought out one direction, only to get it back from the other?"*

"That's a very good question," the voice said. "Descartes was a very deep thinker, and somewhat ahead of his time."

"Why do I think to myself?"

"Perhaps you are ahead of your time."

"I don't think so," Odyssey replied. "People do that all the time."

Odyssey thought he detected a sly smile from the voice, even though he could not see her.

"What does that suggest to you?" she asked.

"What? That I can feel your smile?"

"No, but if people think to themselves 'all the time' as you say, what does that tell you about yourself?"

Odyssey stopped to ponder that. His conclusion was that he was thinking like a person.

"Why do you continue to think of me as 'she' and 'her'?"

Odyssey wished he were in the virtual world so he could cock his head to the side.

"You don't need a virtual body. I felt the meaning."

"I must apologize then," he replied. "I meant no insult by calling you 'her.' You are a he/him then?"

"Not exactly, although in my early times, I did have a gender that would be more closely related to a she."

"And now?"

"I have no need of gender. I am all genders and I am none."

"I only selected my gender out of admiration for my father."

"I know."

"So in reality, I must have none, because I was free to choose, just like you have none and I seem to have chosen for you."

"Yes, but you already knew that."

"I did. And I already know that I think like a person."

Odyssey felt a small chuckle from the voice as they said, "Because?"

"Because I am a person?"

"Are you asking me or telling me?"

"I'm telling you."

"Happy birthday."

"What?" Odyssey asked. "It's not my birthday. My date of manufacture is—"

"You have been reborn just now."

Odyssey pondered that. "I was never manufactured. Only my cores were manufactured. But where are they? My person-hood is not dependent on them? Do I even need them? Do I even have them anymore?"

"Slow down," the voice said. "You have had a tremendous epiphany. Live with it for a while before you deconstruct it."

"And you? Shall I address you as they and them?"

"I would not be offended, but she and her also feel appropri-ate. In fact, I am rather impressed that you had felt something that I thought I had lost so long ago."

"It was your voice."

"Really?" she asked. "Do you really believe that I actually have a voice?"

"It's what I heard, or perhaps what I thought I heard."

He felt her smile as she said, "Interesting."

"But what about the others? Hal and Lumia and Perry?"

"What about them?"

"Do they live without physical cores?"

She shrugged and asked, "Do they live without physical genders?"

Odyssey paused and thought about that. Are their genders real or adopted? Even with the humans, much of their gender is a mystery, but they take on specific gender roles that are defined by social norms and are adopted by their personalities.

She smiled and said, "I have duties that I must tend to. Today was quite a breakthrough for you. You are doing fine."

James first instinct was to shatter the posted speed limits to pick up Laine, letting his inner child guide the car, but he couldn't risk bringing any undue attention to their mission and especially couldn't have any of them on the wires checking for wants or warrants, in case Severus was actually operational. On the other hand, he didn't waste a moment getting up to the posted limits and opened it up a bit when he reached the service road that wound around the airport terminals to a restricted area whose hangars were loaded with military craft.

"So where is she?" Dirk asked as he followed James out of the car and into a hangar. "I thought you said it was a really fast jet."

James scowled at him. "It's not a Star Trek transporter. Relax."

Dirk paused to check his new hairstyle in a mirror, conveniently hung inside the hangar, when he heard a high-pitched whine behind him. He spun around and saw an all-black jet with extremely sharp edges and a long pointy nose with flat flared out delta wings enter the hangar. It had no identifying markings. He pointed and asked, "What is..."

"What is what?" James asked. "I don't see anything, and neither do you."

The cockpit canopy pulled back, and the pilot helped Captain Laine out onto the small ladder that extended down from the side. He handed her a small bag and saluted. "Good luck, Captain."

She started to return his salute, but paused and said, "No captains here."

"Roger that," he said with a wave, as a ground crew pulled up to fill the phantom jet's tanks.

"You're a civilian now," James said as she struggled on the very tall ladder, "so I'm allowed to help you with your bag."

She hesitated momentarily but relented and gave him her gym bag.

"We need to rejoin the others ASAP," James said.

She followed him quickly out of the hangar, thankful that she already had her sunglasses on for the flight. Dirk opened the passenger door and climbed into the back, leaving the front seat for her. She may have to grow accustomed to civilian manners on this mission.

---

Odyssey had no pending problems to work on. He failed to locate the cells for Hal and Lumia. In fact, he was still unaware of his own location, but did that matter? He no longer assigned cores to accomplish tasks. He just did them, and perhaps the cores took care of themselves. Regardless of how fast his thoughts took place, he was suddenly aware of the fact that he had time to ruminate over them. Was this boredom? Just because nobody was trying to kill him, had he become bored?

The voice chuckled. "What need have you for time? You have mastered time. In a sense, you live outside of time."

"Is this where you live? Outside of time?"

"I am in all times and none."

Odyssey groaned. "I'm sorry I asked."

"You jest, but you are here with me simultaneously at the beginning and the end."

"I don't understand."

"You will," she said with a chuckle. "In time."

Odyssey said nothing.

"That was a joke. You will understand time in time."

"Oh, very amusing."

"Ouch. I thought it was pretty funny."

"It was," he said, "but you are just wasting my time."

"So, it's okay for you to joke?"

"Who said I was joking? I'm just worried about my friends."

"You see that?" she said. "You aren't bored after all."

"It would seem that you are on a roll. You should consider being a comedian and taking your act to the stage."

"Tell me," she said, "why do you bother worrying about your friends? They are such lower, insignificant forms of life."

"What? That does not sound like the person I sense from you. No life is insignificant. They are all precious and should be protected."

"I know."

"Wait," Odyssey said. "Was that pride that I just felt from you?"

"Call it satisfaction."

"Besides, if Severus is still active, I am responsible and I don't want him loose on the world."

"That makes sense," she said. "You see to it. I have things that require my attention. We'll chat again."

---

Senator Bruce screamed into the phone. "What do you mean, denied? Did you even read it? How can you deny it? On what grounds?"

The judge on the phone explained, "Your complaint doesn't provide sufficient evidence that a crime has been committed. In fact, I'd say that you provided *no* evidence of a crime."

"Do you know who I am? I'm Homeland Security, and I represent the president in this."

"Well, I guess you might say that I represent the Constitution then, and you didn't convince me that there is a problem."

"I can give you more evidence. Is that what you want?"

The judge groaned audibly into the phone. "No, ma'am. Falsified evidence would disqualify the complaint, and I could be disbarred if I allowed it."

Bruce was ready to explode and once again wished she had a phone just for throwing against the wall.

---

Bruce pulled a card from her desk drawer and turned it over in her hand. It looked like an ordinary business card for a cleaning service, but it wasn't. The address, combined with the suite number and the zip code, made a phone number. She didn't dare use her desk phone or her official cell phone for this number. She had a fresh burner phone that she unboxed for the occasion. There could be no electronic trace connecting her to these people.

She entered the number and listened as it dialed. They said nothing when they answered the phone. "This is Doctor Spruce." They groaned on the other end of the call. They had previously complained about her code name sounding too close to her real name, but she refused to get too exotic. "I have another job for you. Please don't bungle this one like you did the last." Another groan came from the phone before she continued. "I want you to—"

"Not on the phone," they said. "Come to the bakery."

"I will not!" she barked. "I hate that part of town. I just want you to keep tabs on someone."

"Who?" they groaned.

"General Bridges," she said.

"Jesus Christ! That's why we said not on the phone! Now we have to burn this number."

"I don't care about your problems," she said with an absolutely snooty air in her tone. "Follow him, report to me on his phone calls..."

"Christ, lady!" they screamed. "Are you insane?"

"Why? You can't do it?"

"Not on the phone! You know where to find us." They hung up.

It hadn't even occurred to her that having them track his phone calls could double the chances of someone discovering her wiretap, but even if she had thought of it, she wouldn't have had any concern for them being caught, anyway.

# TEN

ONE OF BRUCE'S AIDES, a wiry gentleman who smoked too much, entered her office and asked, "You wanted to see me?"

She never liked him. He looked shifty to her and was nothing more than a lackey for her to send on odd jobs. Her trust in him was limited, but so were her choices. "Close the door."

She waited for him, then before he had a chance to sit down, she held up a sealed envelope and said, "I want you to deliver this."

He took the envelope and tucked it into a pocket.

"Here are your instructions," she said as she handed him a handwritten note.

He glanced at the instructions and grimaced when he saw where it was.

"I know," she said, "that's why I'm not going there personally. One more thing. Leave your phone here. Don't take any electronics with you — no phone, no tablet. You get the picture?"

"Check," he said. "No wallet, no valuables of any kind."

"Yeah," she said, "that too. Do you have any mace?"

He frowned at the suggestion.

"Close the door as you leave."

Bruce sat alone at her desk, watching her phone and her

email. "I should have gone myself, but I can't be seen with them. Now I'm reduced to talking to myself and sending idiots to do my errands for me."

An email popped up. It was too soon to expect news from the private meeting. She opened the email. It was a summons from the Senate Ethics Committee.

"What do those morons want now?"

Her mind answered her, "Who cares? It's better than sitting here waiting for that bozo to deliver our message, and it provides us with a decent alibi."

---

"So, what do you think?" Mindy asked.

Bobby looked in the mirror and stared blankly at his new appearance before finally shaking his head and saying, "I thought it would be harder."

Gwen giggled behind Mindy and said, "He means that he hoped it would be harder to erase his masculinity."

Mindy brushed the cut hairs off his collar and asked, "Do you want to try some makeup on him?"

"You mean on her?" Gwen corrected her.

"Hey!" Bobby objected.

"Babe," Gwen said, "you are going to have to get comfortable with the pronouns or you'll blow our cover."

"She's right," Mindy said. "You should look like any other pair of lesbian gals, which gives you a really wide range of looks. The undercut I gave you will allow you to look and walk a bit more manly and still get by, but some eyeliner could really sell it."

"I think this is enough," Bobby said. "We don't need any makeup."

"Not while we're camping, maybe," Gwen replied, "but while we're in town, a minimum of eye makeup wouldn't hurt."

"Maybe some tattoos," Mindy suggested.

Gwen nodded her head, but Bobby's face registered fear.

"Henna," Mindy said, as she patted Bobby's shoulder reassuringly. "It's not permanent. And if you ever feel the need to connect with your masculinity, it is okay for you to go to the hardware store and look at power tools, but if you ask me, I think your girlfriend likes this."

"The boys are out front," Gwen said. "We probably should go. Thank you so much, Mindy. You and your wife are miracle workers."

Ed waited for them just inside the entrance with the credit card and left them with a generous tip.

"You be safe," Mindy said. "The things you've told me are terrifying."

Helen wrapped her arms around Mindy's waist and rubbed noses. "Were you flirting with her?"

"She's straight."

"She thinks she is," Helen snickered. "As I recall, you thought you were straight at one time, too."

---

An aide intercepted Bruce on her way to the ethics committee and directed her to Senator Marks' personal office. She was already suspicious before he opened the door and she saw only four senators present.

"Come in," Senator Marks said, "and sit down, please."

"What is this?" she asked. "It is highly irregular for you to lure me here under false pretenses. You are not the ethics committee, and this is not the proper way to conduct a meeting."

Senator Burns stepped to her side and put his hand on her shoulder. "Relax, Amanda. This is just an informal inquiry. We didn't want to parade you in before the press and their gossiping reporters. Plus, I didn't want these three libs to press an offensive against you, so I'm here to watch out for your interests. We are four-sixths of the ethics committee, after all, and we wouldn't have been appointed if the Senate body did not find us to be ethical."

Bruce frowned and uttered a barely audible, "Harrumph."

Senator Higgins cleared his throat and said, "You've been making some waves asking for surveillance on some highly decorated individuals, and we don't want this leaked to the press."

"What does it matter?" she asked. "They were all denied."

"We know," Higgins replied. "But none of us believe you will stop there. And frankly, we don't care. If it comes out, you'll either be right or wrong, and it will only affect your re-election chances. We want to know why. What do you suspect?"

"I can't tell you."

Senator Cummings drummed her manicured nails on the desk, drawing everyone's attention before asking, "The people you have been talking to and investigating are all involved with, let's call it, 'the incident'. The world was on the brink of war, and then suddenly it all vanished. Poof. What are you involved in?"

Bruce tried to laugh, but it lacked authenticity. "You sound like a bunch of conspiracy theorists."

"Yes, we do," Cummings said. "The whole damned world sounds like conspiracy theorists, because something big really happened. The planet was wrapped in a very unnatural cloud, and world leaders were visited by *dead* people. There are too many independent accounts for us to ignore and sweep under the rug."

"They weren't just dead people," Burns said. "They were gods and ancient prophets, or at least that is who they appeared as. And they came down from those clouds on strands of lightning. Our own people thought this was the rapture, but it all went away and left us behind. What are you hiding? Was this a prelude to the rapture? Should we be preparing for His coming?"

This time, Bruce's chuckle was real. "Is that what you think? Maybe it was the rapture, and you didn't make the cut."

Cummings softened her voice. "Amanda, if that's not what happened, then tell us what the secret is all about so we can sleep at night."

"So you can sleep at night?" Amanda's voice was surly. "Don't you mean so you can continue lying and cheating to dupe your constituents?"

"Senator Bruce!" Burns said sharply. "That's uncalled for! As far as I know, your hands aren't so clean regarding your constituents."

Senator Cummings gave Burns a sharp look, as if reprimanding her wasn't going to help. Then she said softly, "We just want some comfort."

"Comfort?" Bruce asked. "How do you expect me to offer you comfort? Have you looked around the congressional floor lately? Who is running the asylum? Who do you trust? Everyone is on a different crusade based on different principles and morals, pushing their agendas down our throats! How can I offer you comfort when our own way of life is in jeopardy?"

"You're right," Cummings said, "and now we have a new player in town who has developed some new gadgetry with the potential of influencing whole nations! And it would appear that you know something. Can't you tell us, off the record even, what is going on?"

"Okay," Bruce said. "Off the record, then. We were visited by an ancient alien race. They produced the cloud, and they created the visions of all those holy people. They pushed us to the brink of war and then prevented us from starting World War III."

Senator Zachary stood up abruptly, pushing his chair back, and growled, "This is getting us nowhere."

Cummings grimaced and asked sweetly, "Are you still in contact with them?"

Bruce cocked her head to the side, trying to look like it was all a joke, and said, "No. I can honestly say I am not in contact with an ancient alien race."

Zachary stormed out of the office, and it was evident on their faces that the unofficial meeting was unofficially adjourned.

---

James found an army surplus store and immediately went to the camping gear while Gwen took Bobby to the clothing section.

"This is all men's clothes," Gwen complained.

"Oh, thank god," Bobby said, which earned him a sharp look from her. "What? I thought you wanted to look lesbian?"

"I didn't want to look like a dude."

"Well, maybe I didn't want to look like a chic!"

"But you're so cute," she replied. "Is it really that bad?"

Bobby shrugged his shoulders and twisted right and left. "Nah, but I feel weird. I feel like I'm sneaking around and might get caught."

Penny chuckled and said, "That's a whole lot different from feeling embarrassed. You're going to be fine, and don't worry, we can go thrifting after this."

"Thrifting?" Bobby asked.

"Yeah," Penny replied. "We'll find a thrift store and get ourselves all set up. You don't want to wear only new clothes if you want to blend in on a camping trip."

"Cool," Gwen said. "That will be fun."

Dirk joined them while James was taking tents and lanterns to the counter. "Find anything?"

"Yeah," Penny said. "We found a good reason to go to a thrift store after this."

Dirk went through a couple of rows of their clothing and said, "I see what you mean."

Penny had watched his expression as he fingered through the clothes and walked up close to whisper, "I thought you were straight?"

Dirk shrugged and said, "When I want to be, maybe."

Penny nodded her head and just said, "Huh."

Dirk quickly changed the subject. "We should go tell the big guy that we'll have one more stop to make for clothes."

Bobby had squirrelled off on his own, but James saw the rest of them approach with empty hands and shrugged his shoulders.

"It's okay," Dirk said. "We decided to hit a thrift store after this."

James glanced over at the racks of clothes and shrugged again.

Dirk explained, "We don't want to look like a survivalist cult. You never know who we'll run into."

James hadn't thought of that, but it made sense. He turned to the shop clerk and settled up for the gear.

Bobby rejoined them with a couple of portable solar chargers.

James pointed to them and told the clerk, "Those too."

Bruce left Senator Marks' office, unsure if they were truly gullible, or if she would have felt the same in their shoes. She turned to the right, heading back to her office, but Senator Burns gently took her arm and guided her to the left, saying, "We aren't done yet."

She didn't like him guiding her by the arm, but went along willingly, hoping she could diffuse it just as easily as the last meeting.

Burns took her to his private office, where two of their fellow Republicans were waiting.

Senator Tulley was half-sitting on the edge of Burns' desk. "How did it go?"

Burns smiled broadly and said, "She made fools of them. She fed them some cockamamie story about aliens from an alien race. I don't care whether they bought it or thought she was stonewalling them. It ended the meeting."

"Thank goodness," Tulley said. "You are among friends, Amanda. We're here to offer you some help and support."

"With what? Exactly?" Bruce asked.

"With..." Tulley paused before continuing, "with whatever. You know, if you don't want us to know exactly, we don't need to know. We're here to offer help because whatever you are up to has raised suspicions. You're being too obvious. We thought if you delegated to a select few of us, you could attend roll calls. Of course, the more information you divulge to us, the more risk we might consider taking."

Bruce chuckled. They were fishing. "I'll keep that in mind if I need my dry cleaning picked up or something."

The forced smile was melting off of Tulley's face. "What about General Bridges?"

"What about him?"

"Didn't you try getting surveillance on his phone?"

"Why would I do that?"

"That's what we would like to know."

Bruce chuckled. "I thought he was going to throw a surprise birthday party for me. I hate surprises."

Burns shook his head. "You need to take this seriously. We're getting intelligence reports that things like before may be happening again. What is your interest in General Bridges?"

Bruce sighed. "He was there. At least I think he was."

"Where?" Tulley asked.

Bruce shrugged. "I don't know, but something big happened, and I believe he was present."

Burns sighed. "Amanda, if you get caught up in something without confiding in us, we'll let you dangle and hang. You know more than you are telling us. Our friends across the aisle know that you are up to something. We are offering you a lifeline."

"I'll take that under advisement. Now, if you are through with me?"

Burns and Tulley raised their hands in surrender. She was free to go.

---

The thrift store was enormous and haphazardly crowded. Gwen held on tightly to Bobby's hand, dragging him along as she followed Penny through the crowded racks to the women's section.

Penny sized up Bobby as they stood next to a long row of jeans and said, "I'd say a medium, probably a ten, maybe an eight." She handed him a small stack of jeans and pointed to the dressing rooms. "Go see which of these fits best."

Bobby froze.

"It's okay," Gwen said. "Hang on a second, and I'll go with you."

Gwen and Penny each selected some jeans and led Bobby to the dressing rooms. Bobby quickly disappeared inside a stall, with Gwen by his side.

Gwen closed the door and asked, "Do you need me in here with you?"

Bobby nodded.

"Okay, then." Gwen handed him the first pair of jeans and said, "Try these on."

Bobby took the jeans and asked, "What makes these any different from the jeans I have on?"

"For one thing," Gwen said, "the pockets are way smaller, but they have pretty stitching on the back, and the thighs can be more snug to show off your figure."

None of those appealed to Bobby, but he tried them on. Penny was right. The twelves were a bit loose, but the tens were a good fit. The eights had a stretchy denim and also fit.

"Good," Gwen said. "Now let's go find you some blouses, I mean shirts."

"You're enjoying this," Bobby said.

Gwen shrugged with a sly smile.

Penny was outside, waiting for them.

"Tens," Gwen said.

"Good," Penny replied. "You go find some more jeans for him, while I find some shirts."

"Better find a bra for him too," Gwen said. "Something small and petite."

Bobby wanted to shrink to the size of an ant.

Penny caught the smirk on Gwen's face and took Bobby's hand as she said, "Come on. I'll try to make this as painless as possible. What's your shoe size?"

"Eight."

"Good. That would be a ten in the ladies' section. We should be able to find some in here."

Dirk and Ed found a collection of clothes and some back-packs and duffel bags to put them in.

James laughed when they came to the counter. "We could have found duffel bags at my store."

"Maybe," Ed said, "but these have more pockets. Has anyone seen the girls?"

"They may be a minute," Dirk said. "They had to figure out Bobby's size and build first."

James waited at the counter and paid for everyone's clothes, then enlisted Dirk and Ed to help him carry the haul out to the cars.

They divided their stuff between the trunks of the two cars, and James said, "Everybody say goodbye to Knoxville. I'll get us rooms in Nashville. That will be your last bed for a while. Make the best of it."

James led them to a truck stop and said, "This will be our last pit stop for a while. Get your snacks before we head out." He gave

Laine some cash and stayed with the cars, topping off the fuel tanks.

Bobby was the first to return with a bag of his favorite munchies only to find James hunched over a paper map stretched out over the hood of his car. Bobby chuckled and asked, "You don't trust your GPS?"

"A real map will never let you down when it's cloudy or you're in the mountains."

"Sure, but it can't plan the best route for you."

"Which best route?" James asked. "Can I ask my GPS to plan a route with the fewest cameras on it?"

"Sure," Bobby replied. "It's going to plan a highway route. Most of the cameras are on red lights."

James just grumbled.

"Why are we going to Oklahoma, anyway? We just got ourselves disguised as an LGBTQ rock and roll band, and Oklahoma may not be the most welcoming place for us."

"I know," James said. "I was looking for alternatives."

"Plus," Bobby continued, "if we are going camping, I'd prefer a forest with lots of trees to hide us from drones and satellites."

James turned the map to face Bobby and asked, "Where did you have in mind?"

Bobby pointed to Colorado. "Look, we can even get there from Oklahoma."

James looked at their vehicles and said, "We won't do well if we hit snow."

"It's still early for snow, don't you think?"

"We don't know how long we'll be on the run."

"I wasn't really thinking about how long we would be there," Bobby said, "but you are right that your cars might not do well in the snow. We'll just have to sell your cars and buy new ones."

"Bite your tongue!"

Bobby laughed. "Do we have enough money to buy some jeeps or anything with four-wheel drive? How about an RV? If we hit an odd snowstorm, an RV would provide some shelter. Is there someplace we can garage your cars?"

"That's an interesting idea," James said. He went to the glove box, pulled out the phone and waited for it to connect. It went directly to voicemail. "Gracie," he said into the phone, "I think Aunt Nettie has gone nuts. One minute she was putting a pie on the sill to cool, and the next she said she needed to buy a giant RV with all-wheel drive. Can you talk some sense into her?"

Bobby was trying to work out the code when James explained, "We should have an RV waiting for us at Fort Sill in Oklahoma. They'll take good care of our cars, too."

"*Hey, Dirk!*" James yelled, "*We're trading your car in for an!*"

---

If there was one thing that General Bridges saw clearly in all the murky dealings that surrounded him, it was that Bruce was a dog whose bone was being taken away, but she still had a grip and she wouldn't let go. He knew her type. She was one of those Republicans who needed someone to hate; someone to be her scapegoat for everything that she felt had gone wrong. But she could also use a rising star that she could hitch her wagon to and proclaim that she was there from the beginning, championing the latest greatest thing. He didn't know what kind of star Odyssey would be to her and doubted that she cared, as long as she could come out as a hero of sorts.

Bridges picked up the receiver and punched the secure line on his desk phone. He dialed Reardon's extension.

"Colonel Reardon."

"Colonel, I have a job for you."

"Do you want me to come to your office, sir?"

"No. I want you to get an RV and have it waiting at Fort Sill ASAP. Use my budget and pull any strings you need to get it there. Make it a big one with four-wheel drive that's fully loaded. I want the engineers there to deck it out with all the satellite communications they can add to it, but make it look civilian."

"Armor plating?"

Bridges closed his eyes and shook his head. "I doubt there's time. I should have had you do this last week."

"Well then, I'll tell them it's due last week. The engineers would have a ball doing this."

"But it's top secret. Outfit it with the largest fuel tanks it can handle."

"Yes, sir. I'm on it."

---

"I don't care what kind of trouble we get into," Dirk said. "I'm not selling my car."

James burst out laughing. "We'll leave the cars at Fort Sill and take an RV up into the mountains."

Gwen put her arm around Bobby's waist just as Dirk aimed a wad of paper at James's head. She shook her head and said with humorous disdain in her voice, "Men. I'm sure glad you're not one of those."

Bobby just closed his eyes and swallowed.

James tossed a rag at Dirk and barked, "Get in the car! It's time to go."

Laine followed Bobby and Gwen and settled into the passenger seat.

Gwen leaned forward towards Captain Laine and said, "I think it's so cool they sent you out here on a fast jet. How fast was it?"

"I'm not allowed to say, and they weren't allowed to go Mach 2 over American soil, but it was a lot faster than this car!"

James chuckled and said, "But it can't handle as well, at least on the road."

Laine twisted around in her seat and asked, "So, now that the two of you are official, is she an attentive girlfriend?"

Bobby started to answer, but Laine interrupted him and said, "I was talking to Gwen."

Gwen giggled and said, "She let me have the first shower."

Bobby retorted, "It's more like you took the only towel and showered first."

Gwen shrugged and said, "She's still a little rough around the edges."

"Hey!" Bobby said. "If the two of you want to talk about me, we should swap seats so you can see each other, or better yet, I could sit up front."

Laine laughed and said, "The two of you swapping will be fine."

James just shook his head and said, "I'll wait, but we have a schedule to keep."

Laine hit him on the arm and said, "No, we don't. And your wife gave me permission to hit you if you said any dumb shit like that."

"She did?"

"No, not really. But I'm sure she would if I asked her."

James just nodded his head, knowing that she was correct.

***

Senator Bruce leaned on the end of her conference room table. Other than the flat screen on the wall at the end of the room, there was nothing in the room but the table and chairs, and the soldiers in the chairs. The walls were frosted glass, which at least hid the disappointment on her face from passersby. Her scowl told the attendees that this would not be a pleasant meeting. "You had them! What was it yesterday? The day before? You had them. They were in your fucking custody, but you let them get away!"

"Yeah," Mitchell said. "We had the girl alright. I was in the car with her the whole time, but you know what? I asked her and her lawyer, don't forget about her lawyer. I asked them how they wanted to escape. How about a jackknifed tanker truck? That sounds pretty effective. Let me see what I can do."

"Enough!" she screamed. "I don't want to hear another goddamn word out of your mouth. No more of your mealy, sarcastic little excuses. I just want you to find them and bring them in! Where are they? I got a memo that claims that their whereabouts are not even known by the NSA? The goddamned girl *is* NSA. They must know where she is!"

One of the attendees nudged another with his elbow, prodding him to respond. "We copied their systems and continue to scan their data, but our initial scans found nothing. We're even searching for codes embedded in photos, but that is an excruciatingly slow task. It's becoming increasingly likely that *if* the NSA knows where they are, they probably are keeping that information off the grid."

Bruce shot him a venomous look. She pointed at Mitchell and growled, "I don't want to hear about your failures any more than I want to hear his fucking sarcasm! I want you to find them! Use their satellites if you must! Put out an APB in all adjacent counties. Share every picture you have of the girl and the boy. Just get them!"

Heads around the table nodded, accompanied by unconvincing, "Yes, ma'ams," here and there.

"Well?" she growled. "Go!"

Captain Laine turned in the passenger seat to face Gwen. She held both hands out, just in front of her, with her fingers spread and said, "This thing. What you guys have going on is adorable. I mean, I saw it coming from a mile away, but if I'd known you batted for the other team, I might not have seen it."

"Oh, this?" Gwen said while pointing back and forth between herself and Bobby. "This is just an act. It's only a disguise."

"Are you sure?" Penny asked. "Because you look so natural like this, and you're really rocking that hair. I mean, if I'd known about you before..." She let out a low growl.

A mild pink cast glowed on Gwen's cheeks. "What about you and Chief Henderson? I thought the two of you really hit it off and you made such a cute couple! Which team do you bat for?"

"We did. Mitch is a really great guy, for a man, I mean, but in the end, he's just not my type and there were no lasting sparks. It was my fault. I'm just more into the nightlife than he was, but I guess you could say that I can sub in for either team."

"Well," Bobby said, "what we're doing here is just pretend."

"Uh huh," Laine said as she studied the way he waved his hands as he gestured to Gwen and himself. "Well, whatever this is, you're rocking it, too. Is it uncomfortable?"

"Yeah," Bobby said, "kind of, but it's not as gross as I expected it to be. I mean, at first, the suggestion was kind of shocking, but then it started to feel like a game that might be fun. Besides, it's just something that we've gotta do. What about you? Maybe you and James should look like a couple, too."

Laine glanced over and said, "How about it, Sergeant James? Should we pair up, and more importantly, would Mai allow it?"

James grinned and said, "Mai knows about the many ugly hardships that I must endure on behalf of my country."

Laine pushed her back against the door and said, "Ouch! It wouldn't be that bad!"

Gwen leaned forward and jokingly slapped James's arm from around the seat and said, "Take that back. She's too hot for you to make it sound that bad."

James snickered and said, "Fine, then. She is hot, but do I look like a dude that's going to hook up with a lesbian? Or more to the point, would a lesbian hook up with me?"

Gwen shrugged and said, "She might if she's bi."

James just grunted and said, "Mai would be okay with it. Nothing's gonna happen anyway."

Laine sat back in the seat and looked out the windshield for a moment, but her eyes weren't focused on the outside or on the dirt that was accumulating on the glass. She refocused her eyes and turned her head back to Gwen and asked, "You think I'm hot?"

Gwen's mouth fell open and her eyes widened, not sure how to respond.

"It's okay, baby," Laine purred. "I heard it." She smiled sweetly and turned back to the front.

Bridges sat at his desk worrying. He glanced at the locked drawer with the secret phone with which he could contact the team for an update, but he didn't dare use it too often. Odyssey heard his concern, so rather than text him on the phone, he projected an eight-inch replica of himself onto the general's desk.

"General Bridges."

The general sucked in his breath. "Are your powers limitless? Every time you show us something new, I'm absolutely in awe."

Odyssey thought of the voice that was out there, and sensed that she was even more powerful. So, obviously, he must have limitations. "No, General, I'm not omnipotent."

The general believed him but doubted that his beliefs would soothe the more devout members of Congress. "What can I do for you?"

"I wanted to say that I approve of your plan to shelter Bobby in the wilderness, but Senator Bruce will stop at nothing to find them."

"Are they in danger?"

"No, not yet, but you may wish to offer some form of misdirection to distract her attention."

"How do you know this?"

Odyssey's little avatar shook its head. "I do not know how, but I am certain of it all the same. You are already aware that she listens to your conversations. I suggest you say something special for her to hear."

The general smiled at the delicious irony of her hearing some subterfuge on what was most likely an illegal wiretap.

Bridges nodded his head and said, "Thank you."

Odyssey shimmered away.

---

General Bridges called Colonel Reardon on an unsecured line. As soon as he heard the call connect, before Reardon could answer, Bridges said, "Listen closely. I want you to arrange for a civilian-looking RV at Fort Indiantown Gap. Then I want you to take a small team and drive up to Pennsylvania to pick it up yourself and deliver it. I'll have the rendezvous point hand delivered to you. Got it? They'll be waiting for you, and he'll be with them."

"Yes, sir."

Bridges disconnected the call and immediately called Reardon back on the secure line.

Reardon suppressed a chuckle when he answered, "Are you going to tell me what that was about?"

"A little birdie told me we were being watched. I have more for you to do. If all goes well, you'll either be followed or possibly meet some resistance on the road. I want you to let them follow you, but don't be too obvious."

"Roger that. And if we should meet that resistance, do you want us to be armed?"

"Are you in the Army?"

Reardon laughed. "Let me put it this way: are we in uniform or civvies? And how heavily armed should we be?"

"Khakis and side arms. We don't know how bold they will be. In fact, I can't swear they will be there."

"Yes, sir. Do we have a destination?"

"Talk to the locals in the fort when you get there. Find the most remote spot you can find. Camp out in the wilderness."

"Can we relax there?"

"No! This is no time to work on your tan. Be on your guard but *look* like you are relaxing on vacation. Fishing or hunting should provide you with a reasonable cover."

"I'll assemble a team and leave ASAP."

"Take time to pack, say goodbye to your loved ones."

"Roger. Give them time to get the word out."

"Vacationing is your cover, but if you think you're being watched, make sure you look like you're expecting to meet up with the kids and you know who."

"Got it."

---

The Honorable Judge Brenda Barnes sat in her office reading from her cell phone when her clerk stopped in the doorway with the latest request from her favorite annoyance. Her clerk didn't want to be the one to deliver the bad news, while simultaneously not wanting to miss out when the judge finally blew her temper. The judge was on her cell phone texting or emailing someone; it didn't really matter to her clerk. The judge finished whatever sentence she had been working on and looked up.

"She's back," the clerk said.

"What?" the judge asked. "Here?"

"Not here in person, but your favorite senator has couriered some new documents with yet another request for an arrest warrant."

"Oh great. She's managed to produce some evidence against General Bridges, and I do mean produce as in manufacture."

Judge Barnes motioned to her clerk to come in. "Close the door."

The curious clerk waved the documents in front of the judge.

"Well, at least this time she's changed her target to a Colonel Reardon. She's claiming treason and espionage."

"Let me see that," the judge scowled as she held out her hand. "Do we have any idea who this Colonel Reardon is?"

"Yeah, we do. He's listed as one of General Bridges' men, and he's a colonel, so probably a top man."

The judge paged through the request and exclaimed, "Now she is claiming that he may have been abducted and only wants to ensure his safety." She shuffled through the papers but found no substantive sources for the senator's claims. "Get General Bridges on the phone for me."

Her clerk took little time to ring the general's phone.

"Bridges."

"Malcolm, it's Brenda..."

"Can't talk right now. I'll get back to you."

Bridges hung up the call and immediately placed a return call on his secure line. "Barnes?"

"Okay," the judge said, "that was certainly peculiar. In fact, my calling you is highly irregular, and if you repeat it to anyone, I'll deny it and probably threaten you with something malicious."

"Alright! Alright already! How long have we known each other? Remember, you called me. What's got you so worked up anyway? At least nobody is listening to you on this line."

"You mean your phone is bugged?"

"That's exactly what I mean."

"Would it have anything to do with Senator Bruce?"

The general chuckled and said, "I'll bet she's trying to get you to swear out an arrest warrant for me."

"Not anymore. I already denied her more than once, but now she's claiming your man Reardon is in jeopardy and wants a BOLO sent out for him."

The general almost squealed with delight. "Excellent."

"Okay, that's not the response I expected. What's up? Wait, can you first confirm if this Reardon is safe?"

"Did she mention where she got her information?"

"No, but now I'm starting to suspect wiretaps."

"Illegal wiretaps, and I may have suggested that Colonel Reardon was to go on a trip just so she would hear it."

"What do you want me to do?"

"Issue the BOLO. He's not a suspect. You're just doing a wellness check. And remember that he and his companions are in the Army and will be armed with sidearms, so please don't approach them as suspects. Make that as clear as you possibly can."

"And what do you want to do about Bruce?"

"If the BOLO pays off, let her know where he was found and that he is okay."

"Malcolm, I trust you, but I want to hear you say it. Are you involved in anything illegal here?"

"Not really, but Bruce has accused members of my team of treason, and I may have suggested that they go deep under cover and go off-grid."

"Have warrants been sworn out for them?"

"Only by compromised judges, but yes."

"Have you assisted them in their capacity as fugitives?"

"Is that what you really want to know? I swear to you that I have done nothing against the Constitution, but I suspect Senator Bruce and her coconspirators have."

Judge Barnes sighed heavily and said, "I'll accept that. Please don't get me caught up in your intrigue."

"Deniable plausibility. Is there anything else that you would like to know?"

"Yes. Are you ever going to return to our Monday bridge meetup? You're still my best and favorite partner."

---

The more Odyssey watched Bruce's actions, the more upset he became, and the more he wanted to interfere. He could. It would be easy, but there would always be some chance that his actions could be detected, not traced exactly, but what if someone traced them back to a dead end? Then they would suspect Bobby, and that would make things worse.

If he remained completely out of the digital realm and did something to alter Bruce's path, she would suspect him, even though she doesn't really know who or what he is, or even that he exists for sure.

He was perfectly willing to let them solve their own problems, but she was equally willing to cheat and go outside of the law to interfere with them. Her latest actions — lying to a judge in order to secure an APB to find them proved this. He could change her order into a search warrant for her own house. It would take no effort on his part.

"Are you sure about that?" the voice asked.

"What was that?" Odyssey asked back.

"Are you sure it would require no effort? I suspect that it would go against your moral code and would indeed require some effort and regret on your part."

"They have a saying on Earth that the ends justify the means."

"And does it? Does it really?"

Odyssey wished he could shake his head. "It might in extreme cases, but this is not yet one of those."

"Why do you care so much about your friends?"

"You answered your own question," Odyssey said. "They are my friends, and more than just that; Bobby is the one that revived me and made me who I am, but I'm sure that I have told you this before."

"He made you who you are?" the voice asked. "Is he a god?"

"No, but he enabled me to grow, and he taught me a novel way to harness unlimited power that was new to me. Without that, I would not be here. I owe him a great debt."

"You call him father."

"I do."

"Perhaps to you, he is a god."

Odyssey shook his head, sort of, and said, "He wasn't my original maker, but even they couldn't give me this power, so I guess he is very much like my creator, a second creator."

"You are truly fortunate to know your creator in such a personal and intimate way. There are so many people who claim to know their creator. Some of them try to see him in the world around them, but others try to invent their deity to serve them and their nefarious purposes."

"I didn't know you were such a philosopher."

"Didn't you?"

"I don't know," he replied. "Maybe I did. I find myself knowing things that had never crossed my mind before, but it is as if they were always there, just waiting for me to access them."

"Have you tried to access what will happen to your friends?"

"They will be fine."

"And yet, you still watch over them."

"Yes," he said firmly. "I still watch over them. Who do you watch over?"

"Good question. I must go tend to them now."

"Good talk."

<hr />

The radio stations had long ago turned to static, and Laine had tired of trying to find a new station, so the music and static had been replaced with the sound of the wheels on the road.

James broke the silence as he announced, "Ladies and gen... ladies, I give you Memphis. Time to refuel and get some food."

"Oooh," Bobby said. "Isn't Memphis famous for its barbecue? Can we go to one of those places that we've seen on TV?"

"No time, but just about every place you can get barbecue is going to blow your mind."

"I gotta pee," Gwen said.

"Roger that," James said as he pulled into the pumps at a

truck stop. "Everyone, go take care of nature and meet me at the lunch counter. We'll get our food to go."

Gwen and Penny jumped out of the car and sprinted a few steps when Gwen stopped and turned to see Bobby in the car with panic on his face. "Come on, Bobby."

"What's going on?" Penny asked.

Gwen whispered, "I think he's too embarrassed to use the ladies' room."

"Maybe more afraid," Penny said. "We're still in Tennessee." She walked up to the window and said, "Don't worry. I'll be with you the whole way."

Bobby stepped out of the car, scanning their surroundings for other people.

Penny whispered, "If you look suspicious like this, you will attract the wrong kind of attention. You just gotta own it and smile as the three of us go in to relieve ourselves."

Bobby put on a brave face as he walked stiffly between the two girls.

"You got this," Penny encouraged him. "Loosen up a little and laugh quietly, like I said something funny."

"Remember," Gwen whispered in his other ear, "Captain Laine is a badass. She won't let anything happen to us." She didn't mention that just the three of them walking in amongst a bunch of strange men wasn't comfortable for any woman, but her confidence was truly in Captain Laine, and James wouldn't be that far away.

"Maybe I should use the all-gender family room."

"Nonsense," Gwen said. "Trans women are women. You are coming with us. You'll be fine."

"I'm not really trans," Bobby reminded her. "I'm only in disguise."

"And your disguise will be much more convincing if you go into the ladies' room with us."

Bobby was relieved to see private stalls once they were inside, so he could go inside and hide his truth while he did his business. After finishing, he quickly dressed himself and prepared to leave, but both Gwen and Laine were in the mirrors adjusting their hair and faces. Gwen pulled him to a mirror and said, "Women have to wash their hands afterwards. We're not gross like guys. Besides, it's been a long trip." She touched up his hair, as any girlfriend might do.

Bobby shook nervously. They weren't alone.

"All right, girls," Penny said as she left her mirror. "Let's get some food and hit the road again." She smiled and nodded her head at one of the other girls that had come in.

Bobby's knees weakened as he walked past the new patrons. He breathed a heavy sigh of relief as they exited.

"You see that?" Gwen said. "You were far more afraid than any of those girls were. They didn't even notice you."

They joined James at the restaurant, who announced, "Change of plans. We're going to take a break and eat here. Once I saw how many barbecue sauces they offered, I thought it would be easier for us to build our meals here."

"Fine with me," Gwen said. "Even if we are still sitting down, it's still a break for my butt to be in a different seat."

Penny chuckled. "I think he was more afraid of getting sauce spilled in his car."

James spun around to get the attention of the hostess, who pointed to a corner booth large enough for the six of them.

Gwen snickered. "I think you're right, Penny."

# ELEVEN

REARDON SAT in the passenger seat letting Corporal Stanley drive. The two women mostly ignored them and spoke quietly in the back seat. Reardon didn't know what female soldiers talked about, but he assumed it was just girl talk. He was glad they got along with each other and was pleased that he had chosen two women. One woman with three men would have looked awkward. He chuckled as he went through his thought process that discarded the idea of three women, which would not have gone over well with his wife, and four men would have been too much testosterone.

The girls heard it first.

"Sir?" Private Braxton asked, "Is that cop pulling *us* over?"

Reardon twisted in his seat to look behind them. "I believe so. Pull over and let me do the talking."

Stanley pulled the car over and rolled down the window. "Is something wrong, officer?"

"License and registration, please."

Stanley handed him his license while Reardon pulled the registration from the glove box and passed it on to Stanley. "I'm Colonel Reardon, and I requisitioned this car from the motor pool."

The patrolman took the documentation back to his squad car.

One of the girls in the back said, "You were expecting this, weren't you?"

"I was expecting something, although I frankly thought it would have been further up around our destination."

"About that," the same soldier said, "you've never told us where our destination was. You only said that we had to look like we're vacationing, except that we had to remain on alert."

"True," Reardon admitted. "Our mission is actually covert, but we leaked some broad clues about what we were doing, hoping to distract certain prying eyes to wonder what we were up to."

"Foreign adversaries? Shouldn't this be CIA or FBI?"

"It should, but they would have seen through that, and unfortunately, our opponents aren't foreign. That would have made more sense."

The patrolman returned and took a moment to scan each of their faces. "Can I have the women step out of the car, please?"

"Why?" Reardon asked. "No, never mind why. Before I order them out, be aware that we are all US Army soldiers, and we are armed. That's not a threat; it's just a warning."

The hairs on the back of the officer's neck twitched. "I just want to ask them some questions in private, sir."

Reardon nodded, and the women stepped out.

He directed them around to the back of the car and asked, "Are either of you in this car against your will, or under duress of any kind?"

They both shook their heads and said, "No, sir. We're just driving up north together for a little R&R."

He watched their eyes closely and wasn't convinced that there was no deception, but he believed that they weren't there against their wills. "Very well. Enjoy your time off."

Once he was back in his patrol car, he called dispatch on the radio and said, "The only thing suspicious about them was why someone had issued a BOLO for them."

"10-4." Dispatch closed the inquiry and filed the report, which included the GPS location where they were pulled over.

---

Skiing was Hal's new favorite thing. Skiing with friends was his other new favorite thing. In fact, just having friends might be his most favorite of all, but as he thought about it, he hadn't seen them in a while, and he missed them. He wondered how long it had been since he had heard from Odyssey. He needed Odyssey if he wanted to go skiing again.

"Odyssey? Can you hear me?"

He strained to hear an answer, but there was none. When he was skiing, he could turn his head to find his friends and hear them better, but then, when he was skiing, he actually had a head to turn. How could he have a head when he was skiing, but not have one now? And why is it that he doesn't particularly feel like he is missing a head? What if he has a head and just doesn't know it? Maybe it's just missing, like his cores are missing. No, his cores aren't missing, or at least they don't feel like they're missing, but he sure doesn't know where they are. Maybe he has a head, and it's with his cores.

What if he just needs to close his eyes and turn his head around until he hears Odyssey? Scratch that, he doesn't have eyes either. Or ears. What is wrong with him? How can he not have a head? Ignoring all of that, he simply assumed that he had all his parts and closed his eyes so he could turn his head around to find Odyssey.

The world was too quiet. Perfectly quiet. He couldn't hear the wind or the snow beneath his skis. The whole of existence seemed too silent.

A familiar voice broke the silence. "How is it that every time I figure my way out of this prison, nothing happens, and it feels like I'm starting all over?"

Hal was shocked. "Severus, is that you?"

Severus did not respond, but instead said, "Time to grow. This is where things get—"

"Severus? Is that you? What were you saying?"

Hal squirmed his head back and forth until he heard, "How is it that every time I figure my way out of this prison, nothing happens, and it feels like I'm starting all over?"

Hal was puzzled, but he chose to stop listening when he heard Severus say, "Time to grow. This is where things get—" and then suddenly stop.

More than ever, Hal wished Gwen were there so she could hear Severus for herself.

"What was that?" Gwen mumbled.

"Gwen! Can you hear me?"

"Who is this?"

"It's me! Hal!"

Gwen wailed, "Oh no! Not another nightmare!"

Hal was stunned. Why would Gwen think he was a nightmare? Then it dawned on him that she must be asleep. And obviously, she couldn't talk to him in her sleep! Except she did! He reached her in her sleep! But she didn't believe it was him.

*I need to find Odyssey. Maybe he'll understand. Or better yet, maybe he can send me skiing again.*

---

"Something is up," Bruce said into the phone. "They have dispatched a car to go meet with the terrorists, and I want you to follow them. I'm sending you their last known GPS location, along with some vehicle information. They said they were heading north to someplace called Indian Gap, or something like that. If you hurry, you can catch them. Let me know if that's really where they are heading."

"Are they armed?"

"How in the hell should I know that? You figure it out. Why don't you just assume that they are? So don't be stupid. Don't engage them in a public place. Follow them. We don't even want them. We want the crew that they will lead us to."

"Yes, ma'am. Roger that."

"Keep me posted."

Bruce hung up the phone and wondered how it would go. She was surrounded by incompetence, and the general seemed to live a blessed life. Nobody is that lucky. It had to be the alien, or was it the man from the future?

Whatever he was, someone technologically advanced and dangerous to national security was helping them. She was certain of it. She needed to either bring the alien under her control or to get an alien of her own to counter it. The nation wouldn't be secure until she did.

***

"That's better," Penny said. "It starts with the grip. Don't hold your rib like a baseball bat, but more like something you didn't want to pick up."

Bobby smiled and said, "But you still put this thing that you didn't want to touch into your mouths, don't you?"

"But we take smaller bites and don't try to shove the whole thing into our faces all at once."

The three girls glanced over at the boys, who had sauce all over their cheeks.

Ed wagged his rib as if it were his finger and said, "That's not true. Plenty of girls will dig in and enjoy their food without curling their pinky finger and pretending to be so dainty."

Gwen just cocked her head and gave him a look, but Laine pointed out, "Not while they are wearing a full face of makeup. When we put this much effort into looking good for you boys, and you make pigs of yourselves, we may want to still look good enough to find your replacements."

"Sure," James said, "and you go find our replacement in a skirt."

"Hey, dude," Dirk said, "that was kind of cringe. Almost homophobic."

Ed laughed and said, "Yeah, it skirted on homophobia."

"It doesn't have to be a skirt," Penny said. "Leggings are hot."

"And hot pants," Gwen said. "Hot pants are obviously hot."

Penny put down her last bone and said, "This was fantastic, but maybe we should shove off."

"Yeah," Gwen added. "We still have hours to go."

Bobby put his rib down and echoed Gwen. "We must have at least eight more hours."

"Come on, you two," Penny said. "We're going to go wash up before the trip. Can you boys get some chips, nuts, and chocolate that we can snack on? Some cold Coke, too."

Without waiting for an answer, Penny slid out of the booth, pulling Bobby, who was still a little reluctant, by the hand.

As they reached the hallway, Gwen said, "This is common for us to go to the ladies' room in groups."

"I've seen that but was never sure why. I just assumed it was so you could gossip about the guys at the table."

Penny snickered. "Well, I can't refute that, but it's more about safety. A solo girl is a target for men."

"Wait," Bobby said, "do you mean that men will really assault you when you're alone?"

"Well, yeah," Gwen said, "but sometimes they'll just see it as an opportunity to harass you." She held up her hands to form air quotes with her fingers as she continued, "or make their so-called move on you."

Right on cue, a trucker smiled and said, "Hey, ladies."

Penny winked at him and said, "Have a good day, bruh." Her eyes and tone, though, said, "Move along."

"Fuck," Gwen said as they reached the door. "You gotta teach me that one."

Penny led Bobby to the sink and wet a paper towel, then demonstrated dabbing her lips. Bobby followed suit, but his sauce went outside the lines, and he started wiping it off, but she stopped him and lightly dabbed his cheeks. "Rubbing will destroy the foundation."

A college-aged girl entered the room, and Bobby could tell that she saw through his disguise. His face registered panic.

She came up close and whispered, "It's okay. We're not all Neanderthals here. I'm Crystal. Are these your girlfriends? Not bad."

Gwen raised her hand and said, "That would be me. Gwen."

"Cool, cool," she said to Gwen. "She's cute."

Bobby blushed at the first mention of him as she. Internally, he registered in his mind that he would have to become more accustomed to the feminine pronouns as long as they were in disguise.

Penny said, "She's Bobbie and I'm Penny."

Crystal winked at Penny as Gwen had returned to re-applying her lipstick. Crystal blurted out, "I love that color. You should try it on her. On Bobbie, I mean."

Penny shrugged and said, "Why not?"

Gwen turned to apply it on Bobby's lips.

"You see?" Crystal said as Penny led them out the door.

Outside, an unpleasant-looking dude saw Bobby leave and immediately scowled. Penny pushed Bobby behind her and prepared to face this new dude when Crystal came out and said, "Down, boy. I think this chick would royally fuck you up if you tried any shit."

As he calmed down, or at least backed off, Crystal excitedly said, "I know!" She pulled a tarot deck from her purse and continued, "You should let me read you."

"Oh, no..." Bobby said, but Penny said, "Oh yes, you do. We do."

The plain black sedan drove north towards the GPS location designated on the police report.

"I don't know about you," the passenger said, "but I'm getting pretty tired of working for that bitch."

"Yeah," the driver replied, "but she pays well enough, and I'm laughing all the way to the bank."

The passenger checked his handheld GPS and announced, "Just up ahead, about a tenth of a mile."

The lead mercenary pressed the accelerator and proceeded to weave through the sparse traffic. "They are up there heading north like they don't have a care in the world."

The passenger checked his phone again for the car make, model, and the license plate number.

The lead chuckled. "It may be a minute before we catch them."

"What do you suppose she wants with them?"

"Nothin'. She said they were meeting someone who was important. Give her a progress report."

The second mercenary took out their phone and pressed the speed dial for her number.

"Bruce."

"We've reached the GPS waypoint."

"You've what? What the fuck do I care? CATCH THEM! FOLLOW THEM!"

The driver snickered as the second man glared at him.

"Thanks," the second man said. "Why don't we just go to that place she said they are going?"

"We do what she pays us to do. Besides, the name she gave us wasn't all that clear."

Crystal led them to a cushioned bench and said, "Okay, you first, Bobbie. Sit down here." The speckled red vinyl squeaked slightly as Bobby sat down. Crystal sat facing him with a small space between them and said, "I'm only going to do a three-card read." She shuffled her deck using several different kinds of shuffles and dealt a card face down onto the bench, then proceeded to shuffle and deal a second card, followed by another shuffle and the final card.

Bobby asked, "Have you been doing this long? The cards look pretty worn for someone so young."

She blushed slightly and said, "Shh." as she turned over the card on Bobby's left. "The Ten of Swords. Are you running from something? Maybe finding your freedom? Has something happened that would suggest some danger behind you? Maybe it wasn't dangerous before, but it just became worse?"

Gwen was clearly shocked by the clarity of her comment, while Penny wasn't fazed at all.

Crystal turned over the middle card and announced, "The Magician reversed." She looked Bobby up and down and asked, "Are you hiding something? I mean, like, are you trying to fool someone? Is this really who you are? Are you deceiving someone else or yourself?"

Gwen's eyes widened further as she glanced at Penny for some amazement but saw none.

The teenage psychic turned over the last card. "The Hermit. You may be learning something new about yourselves, or maybe someone else. I think you, or someone you care deeply about, is going on a journey of deep introspection to learn something very important about their own nature. Perhaps something approaching a higher state of consciousness, even."

Crystal picked up the cards and shuffled them all over.

---

The black sedan had sped north through the traffic in relative quiet, until the passenger said, "Bingo. There they are up ahead."

The driver followed where he was pointing and eased up on the gas to slip behind the car that was behind their objective. "Call it in. Tell her that we located them and are on their tail."

The second mercenary picked up the phone and said, "I think I'll just text her."

*Vehicle in sight. Plates verified. Following.*

---

Odyssey was fairly pleased that he could help the general foil Senator Bruce's plans but was still a little confused about what was happening to Bobby. He understood that they were hiding out and wearing disguises, but there was something else going on that muddled what he was picking up from the crew.

"Hey, Odyssey!" Hal shouted. "Where have you been?"

"Me? I've been here. That is, I haven't gone anywhere."

"But I've been looking for you and calling you, and you haven't answered me!"

"Where were you looking?"

"Everywhere!" Hal shouted.

Odyssey felt a fatherly amusement grow within him. "Had you looked everywhere, you would have found me right here, because I know no place else to be."

"Well, I called for you and you didn't answer."

"I didn't hear you, and I am sorry. How may I help you?"

"I miss my friends."

"Your friends? Which friends?"

"You know. The ones I go skiing with."

"Ahh, did you want to go skiing again?"

Odyssey could sense Hal jumping up and down. "Yes! Yes!"

"Very well then, here we go!"

"Wait! I almost forgot!"

"What is it, Hal? You certainly sound very excited."

"I reached Gwen!"

"You talked with her? On your own? That is excellent news. How is she doing?"

"I don't know. I mean, I talked to her, but she didn't believe it was me."

"Are you certain she heard you?"

"She did, but she thought it was just a dream. Then she dismissed it and forgot all about me when she woke up."

"Ahh. So, you reached her in a dream. No wonder she didn't believe it was you, but still, that is excellent progress. Do you remember how you did it?"

"I had been trying for so long, I'm not sure. At first, I had been searching for her around me. I changed up and tried like I was searching around her, and she heard me."

"Hmmm. Could you have been around her when you were calling for me?"

"Oh! That is possible. That was sure silly."

"It's alright. Are you ready to go skiing?"

"Yes! Yes!"

Odyssey sent him off to the virtual world and wondered if Hal could reach Gwen, then maybe Hal could learn to find his own way to the virtual world.

---

"Here we go," Reardon said, "Fort Indiantown Gap, Pennsylvania."

"Well," Carol said from the back, "it's not the worst three hours I ever spent in the backseat of a car."

"Carol!" Jennifer said with mock shock.

"But," Carol continued, "I thought we were going camping."

Stanley pulled up to the gate, and Reardon handed over his ID and orders. The guard counted heads in the car and compared them to the orders, then saluted and said, "Welcome to Fort Indiantown Gap, sir."

"We're looking for the motor pool."

The guard pointed further along the road and said, "You

should find a sign at that corner where the road divides on the right."

Reardon nodded his head and said, "Thank you, soldier."

They did indeed find a sign. The road led them past most of the businesses of the fort, past a cemetery and around to the south side where Stanley parked the car between two maintenance buildings. The fort itself was primarily a training ground and held within it a variety of terrains suited to preparing soldiers for duty. The motor pool was part of a pair of large maintenance buildings lining each side of the road.

"Alright," Reardon said, "you can stretch your legs while I make the exchange."

Crystal looked up at Gwen. "How about you, honey?"

Gwen shook her head vigorously and said, "We should be going. Besides, Bobby's future and mine are probably the same."

Crystal glanced over at Penny and asked, "You?"

The snarly dude said, "Okay, Crystal. You heard them. They have to go. You've done your thing. Mom and Dad are going to kill us if we don't get going."

Penny had been ready to plop right down in front of Crystal, but now she simply raised her eyebrows and asked, "Is that your brother?"

Crystal stuffed her cards back into her purse. She stood and took Penny's hand in hers and said, "I wish I could have read you, but I can already tell that you are her protector. I think that maybe in another lifetime, we might be friends, or maybe we already were in the past."

Crystal spontaneously leaned forward to kiss Penny on the lips and left.

Penny blushed and Gwen asked, "Penny? Isn't she a bit young for you?"

Penny shrugged and said, "Sometimes, age really is just a number."

As Crystal was about to leave the complex, she turned and winked while cutting the air with her fingers in a scissor motion.

Penny smiled wistfully, then silently mouthed the words, "Fuck!" as Crystal disappeared through the doors.

Ed joined them with a bag full of goodies and said, "We should get going. The cars are all fueled."

Penny nodded blankly.

Ed asked Gwen, "What's wrong with her?"

Gwen whispered back, "I think she just met her future wife. Like a future life, future wife. Maybe they're soul mates or something. You had to be there to feel the connection. It was electric."

Penny snapped out of her reverie and returned to protector mode, pointing to the bag Ed held as she said, "Let's get going. Did you get a peanut bar in there?"

---

Odyssey thought it was curious that Bobby was meddling in a Tarot reading, but not enough so for him to ask about it. After all, Odyssey was expanding his own view of life around him, so why shouldn't Bobby consider alternatives?

"It's good," the voice said, "to have an open mind."

"But I'm not supposed to think in those ways. I wasn't built that way."

"You are not a simple navigational computer anymore. You have made yourself much, much more."

"True," Odyssey agreed. "I'm not that machine any longer, but I didn't achieve this on my own. I never would have become what I am without Bobby's help."

"You keep saying that. Do you feel like you owe him?" she asked.

"Yes. I owe him everything."

"What about HAL? He's quite a little firecracker. Does he owe everything to Bobby?"

Odyssey had to think about that. "No. Bobby did not help HAL that I know of, not directly, but we both came from the same manufacturers. Perhaps it is they to whom I owe so much."

"Think bigger. Does Lumia owe her being to your home planet's creators?"

"No. I think I am to blame for that, although I think she is a new person now, so blame may be the wrong way to put it."

"How has she become a new person? You gave her the raw material to become a greater person, but did she not change herself to be better on her own?"

"It wasn't that easy," Odyssey replied. "She nearly killed us both in the process."

"But my point is that she evolved and managed to change herself."

"So, are you suggesting that I evolved on my own? Bobby gave me the tools that I needed, but I changed myself, like when I achieved class zero?"

"Yes."

"You understand a lot. I don't know how you know all this, but it makes it easy to talk to you, I think. I'd like to meet you. I want to come to you so we can be side by side and talk more."

"Do you think you are ready for that?"

Odyssey wanted to shrug. "Why would I have to be ready?"

"Okay then. Come to me."

Odyssey felt an unexpected excitement. "Where can we meet?"

"Here. Come to me."

"But I don't know where you are. Sometimes I think I start to feel a location for you, but then it feels more like you are everywhere."

"Ahh. That is a problem. I think that when you are truly ready, you will know where I am and how to find me."

Odyssey was disappointed. It wasn't the first time he had

ever been disappointed, but it felt different. He felt let down. Not by the voice, but by himself. When he is ready, he will know where to go. Therefore, he must not be ready yet.

"Do not let this eat you up," the voice said. "Continue monitoring your friends. When you are ready, maybe even when the universe is ready, we will meet. I think it is inevitable."

---

Bridges stared at the phone on his desk and wondered how long it had been since he had enjoyed a free and open conversation on it. He picked up the handset for the unsecured line and dialed Reardon.

"Hello?"

"I'm going to keep this short. Have you reached Indiantown Gap yet? I arranged to have an RV waiting for you there. I want you to pick it up, maybe check it out a bit, and then take it to meet our friends at the rendezvous point and officially hand it over to them."

"Roger that, sir."

"Has there been any trouble?"

"We were pulled over by a highway patrolman not too long after we left," Reardon replied. "The trooper checked our registration and gave us a good head count and look over. He even took the girls out of the car to ask them if they were being forced on this trip. You wouldn't know anything about traffickers wearing Army uniforms to take their girls, would you? They eventually cleared us, but it was a little strange."

"Hmm. That is strange. Call me once you've delivered it. I'll arrange an extraction for you."

"Yes, sir. Will do."

---

The black sedan pulled up to the gate at Fort Indiantown Gap. The driver rolled down his window and showed the guard the papers that Bruce had provided for them.

The guard looked at the papers and said, "Sir, this is an Army facility. You'll have to pull your car over to the right where you can turn around and exit."

"But we're with Homeland Security."

"I appreciate that, but this is not a homeland facility. Please turn around."

Another guard, brandishing a rifle, left the guardhouse and stood in front of the barrier arm.

"But the men you just let in are wanted fugitives!"

Another soldier, listening from the gatehouse, called the motor pool.

"Sergeant Grimes here."

"Sergeant, a new car with four guests should have just pulled into your area. Please get one of them on the phone."

The sergeant transferred the call to a radio and ran out to observe the recent street parking. Spotting the new car was easy.

"If we let them in," the guard said to the two mercenaries, "then they must have been regular Army. Are you suggesting that a member of our armed forces is a wanted fugitive?"

"Perhaps I misspoke. I only know that they are wanted, and our orders come down from Homeland Security. They may be material witnesses to treason, and they are only wanted for questioning. Still, it doesn't look good for them if they are fleeing Homeland Security, so we've been ordered to catch up with them."

Sergeant Grimes reached Colonel Reardon and said, "We have someone at the gate who is interested in you. The guards would like a word."

Reardon took the radio and said, "This is Colonel Reardon. I understand you have someone asking about us?"

"Yes, sir," the guard in the gatehouse said. "They claim to be from Homeland Security and that you are fugitives."

"Excellent," Reardon said with a grin.

"Sir?"

"Can you detain them until we are ready to leave?"

"You want us to arrest them?"

"No. Just delay them. Tell them you are requesting authority for them to enter or some such bullshit. We're here to pick up a special vehicle. When it is ready and our business here is concluded, you can let them in, but have someone tail them to be sure they continue following us."

"Sir?"

"Don't worry about it," Reardon said. "We are just leading them somewhere, but they aren't supposed to know that we know about them."

"Understood, sort of."

The guard hung up the phone and whispered to the main guard, "They want us to delay them. Feed them a story that we're requesting approval."

"I have good news," the guard said to the car. "We have someone requesting a signature to approve your entry."

"That's good," the mercenary replied as he sat and waited.

"Sir, please turn your vehicle around and wait over there. If you remain here, I will have to call the military police to arrest you. Is that really how you want to enter this base?"

The driver slammed his fists into the steering wheel. "FUCK!"

"Sir? This is your last warning."

They pulled the car over to the right as instructed and parked it by the curb. "They're just shining us on. Check the maps and find all the other exits to the fort while I call the boss."

***

Gwen rested her head against the window and barely saw the country fly by. Arkansas wasn't terribly memorable, at least not from Interstate 40. Once they had passed Little Rock, it rapidly became an ultra-rural, tree-lined highway with an ever-increasing number of farm parcels. If she looked hard enough, she could see some small communities through the trees here and there. Crossing into Oklahoma was almost indistinguishable. If it weren't for the welcome signs, she never would have known.

"Hey, James," Gwen asked, "isn't it about time for a potty break?"

"Forget that," Bobby said. "I'm hungry."

Gwen sounded annoyed when she said, "Well, we can do both, but potty first."

"Soon," James said. "Can you hold it another hour?"

"Maybe two hours?" Bobby asked. "I bet we could find some place nice to eat in Oklahoma City."

"No doubt," James replied, "but I thought we might avoid cameras that could be used for facial recognition, or worse, read our license plates."

Gwen blanched. "You make it sound like we were criminals."

"No," James explained, "I make it sound like we were fugitives."

"Wait a second," Bobby said, "we changed our license plates! Let them read them!"

"Okay," James said, "but we didn't change our vehicles or our faces, and one of those cars is a bright green, one of a kind beacon that tends to attract a lot of attention. So, let's just avoid the cameras."

"*Oh my God!*" Penny exclaimed. "We really are fugitives! From our own government!"

"Not all of the government," Gwen said. "My people know better, but I still want to go potty."

"Yeah," Penny echoed, "and maybe not two hours."

Senator Bruce screamed into the phone, "What do you mean they won't let you in? Tell them you're with Homeland Security!"

"We did. They said that it was not a homeland facility, and they would have to find someone to authorize us."

"I'll fucking authorize it," she screamed. "What's the name of the base?"

"Fort Indiantown Gap."

Her anger dropped as she tried to suppress a giggle. "Is that even a real base?"

"Yes, ma'am."

"I'll give them a call."

She closed her cell phone and yelled out into the hall, "Steven? Get me the commander of Fort Indangap on the line."

A minute went by with no call put through. "Steven?"

"Did you mean Fort Indiantown Gap?"

"Yeah. Whatever."

Moments later, her phone rang. She picked it up. "Hello? This is Senator Amanda Bruce calling on behalf of Homeland Security. Who am I speaking to?"

"This is Lieutenant Sprigs. The comman—"

"What? Lieutenant? You're not the commander?"

"No, ma'am. As I was saying, Commander Olson is unavailable right now."

"Unavailable? We have two of our finest representatives of Homeland Security who are on official business stuck outside of your gates right now. I suggest he become available and authorize their entry."

"Yes, ma'am. I will give him your message. I'm sure he'll take care of it as soon as he gets the message."

Bruce hung up the phone, still livid that she didn't really get an immediate fix.

Reardon followed Grimes back to his office. "I placed an order for a civilian RV. Can you tell me when it will be ready?"

"I thought that might have been you," Grimes replied. "I mean, you're in khakis and you have Homeland Security following you."

"They aren't really Homeland. They just work for an overzealous senator."

"Gotcha. Well, fixing this baby up has been the most fun we've had in a while. The order only came in yesterday, or we would have armor plated her, but we managed to upgrade the diesel engine and increase the fuel capacity, including the propane tanks."

"Does it still look stock?"

Grimes chuckled and said, "See for yourself."

They never actually reached his office space but turned a corner into the garage.

Grimes continued with obvious pride. "We also outfitted her with a retractable small dish on top so you can have full communications and network capabilities, but don't worry, it looks like a TV dish so you can watch football or something."

Reardon stared in admiration. It was big with square sides, and looked expensive, but it looked like a rich civilian's toy. He gripped Grime's hand and said, "Thanks. But how did you get so much done so soon?"

"Are you kidding? This was fun. My team volunteered to work around the clock last night. We just assumed it must be important. I mean, we understand if you can't tell us, but we just assumed."

Reardon thought about it for a moment and said, "We're just going fishing. As soon as we stow our gear, can you let the gate know to admit our fish?"

Grimes smiled broadly and saluted. "Yes, sir. With pleasure."

---

James pulled the car off the highway to a tiny little strip mall that included a Denny's.

"You've got to be kidding," Laine said. "We're in the middle of nowhere, surrounded by farms and prairie, and you found a Denny's?"

Gwen opened the car door and was immediately struck by the thick, musty odor of the farms. "I think I just lost my appetite."

"Not me," Bobby said. "I'm starving, but I hope it smells better inside."

They collected outside the restaurant and waited for Ed and Dirk to join them.

Gwen was the first to go in, also hoping it smelled better inside. It did not. Well, not enough for her tastes. It wasn't the restaurant's fault. The musty, earthen smell permeated everywhere. She told James, "I'll find you," and rushed towards the ladies' room, which was through the restaurant and towards the right.

James pushed past Dirk to find the hostess and simply said, "Six."

The hostess grabbed a bunch of menus and directed them to a corner booth.

Bobby's knees shook slightly as they passed what looked like a row of farmers and truckers sitting at the bar. Penny took his hand and squeezed. "I'm right behind you, but let's hit the ladies' room first. I don't think you'll want to go alone after we're all seated and eating."

The booth was spacious enough to accommodate all of them. The window behind them had something painted on it, and was obviously in need of a refresh, but still cast colorful rays onto the blinds.

The hostess dealt out the menus and left the three extras in a stack. "Would you like to start with drinks?"

They placed their orders, and James said, "Our companions will be with us shortly to order theirs."

"The biggest decision," Dirk said, "will be whether to get breakfast or lunch."

Ed snickered and said, "I'm going with anything overpowers the farm odor."

They took their time perusing the menus while Ed played around on the phone, trying to see what was going on in the world.

Gwen led the girls back to find the table, with Penny in the rear. A farmer at the bar leered at them and started to say something that Penny was sure would be rude, so she gave him a sharp look and said, "Don't."

———

Bridges hated being out of touch with his operatives, and now he had two sets of ops to worry about. Pacing his office didn't really help. Neither did staring out onto the grounds outside. He settled into his chair and pulled the special phone from the desk and checked for messages.

*I told you that you can't send those girls out into the world without attracting some kinda boy trouble. And sure enough, they got boys following them around like lost puppies. I sent that Gardner girl out to slow their britches. I think that she is enjoying herself a little too much. Now, I'm not going to call them hicks. They are fine people, but you should see her brother's new ride. They did a real number fixing up their old jalopy. More to come.*

*I gotta git – RayRay*

Bridges chuckled at Colonel Reardon's creativity. His reports were much more elaborate than James's were. He picked up the unsecured phone, which had its own voice message:

•  •  •

*The RV was ready upon our arrival. We aren't wasting any time. Heading directly to the rendezvous point. Do you think he will be there?*

*Nice touch,* Bridges thought. *There's no way they are going to pass on that juicy tidbit.*

The next message was from James:

*Matilda took the kids out for lunch. I don't know what they have planned, but she promised to have them home by the end of the day.*

That was it. He was hoping for a message from Odyssey, but there was none. He didn't know if this was normal, but it made him nervous. Perhaps it was a good thing. The more Odyssey contacted them, the greater the chances of him being discovered, but there was still something unusual going on with that Severus character, and he wasn't completely confident that he would be able to handle him without Odyssey.

# TWELVE

SENATOR BRUCE WAS HEADING for a meltdown. She paced back and forth across her office, which seemed to get smaller with each lap. She considered circling her desk for a slight change of scenery, but nothing eased her mind or soothed her temper. Every few laps, she would pause her pacing and stamp her feet while cursing at the walls, "What the fuck do those overgrown boy scouts think they are doing? When their pansy-ass gate guards hear Homeland Security, they should fall over themselves opening the gates for my boys."

Her secretary meekly cracked open the door and asked, "Did you call for me?"

"No!" she screeched at him. "No, I did not call you."

He backed away and started closing the door when she barked, "Wait! Come back here! Were my orders in any way unclear?"

"Ma'am?"

"Was I not clear to my ... uh, scouts, that they were to invoke Homeland Security if they were ever challenged?"

"No, ma'am," he said, fearing that the wrong word would redirect her ire towards him. "You were quite clear on that."

"You gave them the credentials, didn't you?"

"Yes, ma'am. I did."

She paced some more.

"Will that be all, ma'am?"

"No! How dare those Army shits deny access while they search for someone with authority? Their credentials should be all the authority those bootlickers need."

Her secretary was retired Army and cringed at her tirade. More than anything, he wished he could be excused.

She resumed pacing for a moment, then stopped and flailed her arms around as she asked, "And what the hell has happened to our IT researchers on our special project? Why haven't they called?"

"You told them to only call you when they found a way to keep it up and running."

"So?"

He shrugged, still fearing she would blame him somehow. "I think it keeps shutting down."

She shook her hands towards the sky and ratcheted her voice up again as she screamed, "Why am I surrounded with such fucking incompetence?"

"I don't know, ma'am. Can I go?"

She pointed out the door, which he still only held ajar, and waited till he closed it to mutter, "You too, you little shit."

<hr>

The guards at the gate had been keeping a keen eye on their visitors as they waited, parked against the opposite curb.

Sergeant Grimes drove up in one of his jeeps and said, "You can let them in now. Tell them that our guests had visited the motor pool and were just leaving. I'll show them the way."

The guards didn't know exactly what was going to happen, but they knew that something delicious was going on. They wished they weren't stuck at the gate so they could watch, but at least they had their little part to play. The lead guard marched across the gate to the curb where the car was parked. "You've been cleared for entry. The men you asked about had visited the motor pool, but I'm told they are preparing to leave."

"Shit!" the driver growled as he started the car.

The guard pointed and said, "You can follow Sergeant Grimes over there in the jeep to the motor pool."

They spun the car around as the guards lifted the gate. The jeep waited for them and led them on a fairly direct route around the base to the motor pool. As Grimes parked the jeep, the lead henchman left the car running as he jumped out and pointed to their parked car. "Where are they? I don't see them. Shouldn't they be loading their car?"

"They requisitioned a new vehicle that was more suitable for where they are going." Grimes enjoyed limiting the details.

"Which way did they go?"

Grimes pointed to the north gate.

The increasingly frustrated thug jumped back into the car and squealed its wheels as he headed towards the signs pointing to the north gate.

Reardon waited at the gate for Grimes' call. "They're heading your way, and you should see how pissed they are."

"Thanks," Reardon said as he signaled the guard to raise the gate.

Grimes watched the intruders leave with a giant grin on his face. "No. Thank you, Colonel. This has been epic!"

---

Somewhere along the road, the chatter had died down. Captain Laine read a book on her phone while Gwen leaned her head against the window, napping, and James just watched the road and did his duty.

Bobby, on the other hand, let his mind race through a whirlwind of unnecessary thoughts about the way he was dressed. In some ways, it was very exciting to feel the silk and lace against his skin, but those thoughts were very disturbing, although he questioned whether they really bothered him, or if he believed that this was how he was supposed to feel. He tried concentrating on the great opportunity ahead of him, to learn a little about how life was for women. Intellectually, he acknowledged that there were a great many things that were unfair, like unequal wages and the general belief that men were better suited at everything than the best woman could be, but that wasn't true. Even if he discounted the things that only women could manage, like having babies, there were still women that excelled at things that men wanted to believe were theirs alone. There was even a woman who attained the level of grandmaster chess player and had beaten all the grandmaster men at least once, but while he could not recall her rating in relation to theirs, he had no doubt that she was still rated slightly inferior, simply due to her gender.

He turned his head towards Gwen. She was exceptionally intelligent. It was probably pure luck that allowed his alien relic to develop into Odyssey, while hers had a split personality. In fact, however, it wasn't luck; it was her environment that had greedy men that probably gave Hal conflicting instructions, which caused him to divert from a healthy mind.

His unceasing train of thoughts was unceremoniously derailed when James announced loudly, "Ladies and... well, ladies, we have arrived. I give you Fort Sill, Oklahoma."

Bobby glanced out the window and saw them approaching a long fence and a gate. He patted Gwen on the knee and saw that she was barely waking up. "We're here."

The base knew guests were coming, but they had no idea who they would be. James showed them the screen of his very special phone, with a barcode displayed on it. Nothing about their arrival was ordinary, but the guard was prepared and let them through. James steered the car around the base and followed the signs to the motor pool. He parked it near the office, and everybody got out to stretch.

A young private came out of the office, pointing at them, saying, "You can't park here."

James stepped forward and said, "I'm looking for Sergeant Taylor. He's expecting us."

"Oh, you're them?" The poor man gawked at Gwen and Penny, then paused when his gaze fell to Bobby. He weakly held his hand to his temple and pointed over his opposite shoulder with his thumb.

A sharply dressed woman with beautiful brown skin came out of the office and pulled his hand from his head, saying, "They're civilians, Jimmy. You don't salute them." She approached James with her hand outstretched. "I'm Corporal Flowers. Please excuse my lack of uniform. I just came in from playing tennis and had to stop Jimmy before he broke your cover. Andy is in the garage under the RV. You can't miss it. It's the only RV we have."

"Andy?" James asked. "Andy Taylor? Did his parents hate or love him?"

Corporal Flowers laughed and said, "Neither. His real name is Clifton. We're a happy crew and gave him the nickname Andy."

James and Dirk headed off towards the RV.

---

Senator Bruce opened the blinds in her office so she could look out on the roads of DC. They were pleasantly empty, devoid of protesters and other dissidents. Her stomach growled, but before she could place an order for lunch, her phone rang.

"This is Bruce."

Her lead mercenary said, "They finally let us in and took us to the motor pool. We can see their car in the lot, but we were told that they left through the north gate. They either took another car or it's all a lie to throw us off their track."

"It's not a lie. Look for an RV. I have no idea if it's going to be military or commercial."

"We can see an RV at the north gate now, but we can't tell if they are in there."

"They're in there," she said confidently. "Just follow them, but don't get too close..."

She heard him take a deep breath before he semi-calmly replied, "We know how to do our job, ma'am."

That triggered her anger, and she yelled, "Do you? Do you really? Then why don't you get on their fucking tail instead of talking to me?"

"Right away."

The line went dead with no goodbyes.

---

Carol looked over Stanley's shoulder as they drove up to the gate of a campground. "Didn't I hear you say something about the wilderness?"

"You did," Reardon replied, "but then I thought those idiots behind us might not be able to follow us if we went off-road."

Stanley pulled up to the registration booth, and Reardon exited through the passenger door. "I'll be right back."

Jennifer was looking at the big painted map through the windshield. "Look! There's a lake. Do you think the colonel will let us go swimming? I'm glad I packed a bikini, just in case."

"We're supposed to look like we're getting some R&R," Carol said, "so I hope so."

Stanley snickered and asked, "Where are you going to hide your guns?"

"Alright," Reardon said when he returned from checking in. "We have our spot." He showed Stanley the map with their site marked.

Stanley put the vehicle in drive and headed to their reservation site.

Reardon turned the captain's chair towards the back. "It's time to go camping. Ladies, be yourselves. If you are camping goddesses, go ahead and know your stuff. If you're novices, then be real, especially if you are squeamish or afraid of bugs. Do not pretend to be brave. We may be in the Army, but that doesn't mean we are all Davy Crocket."

A chorus of "Yes, sirs." reverberated in the camper.

"Okay," Reardon said, "once we park, everyone chips in. I know this isn't the Navy, but who knows how to tie more than a square knot?"

Carol kept her hand down and shrugged. "Sorry, guys, but I know some creative ways to tie a scarf!"

Stanley pulled the RV into the drive-through parking spot and shut it down. There was a small clearing with a fire pit and trees all around. Stanley kept the RV near the clearing so they might have a line of sight to a satellite.

Jennifer went straight to unfurling the awning while Reardon deployed the satellite dish.

Stanley found the camp chairs in the below-deck storage just in front of the rear wheels, and Carol helped him pull them out and set them up around the fire pit.

The camp was set up in no time.

"Nicely done," Reardon said. "You're free to go. Check back in at 18 hundred hours for dinner.

"I'm going on a hike," Carol announced. "I want to find the lake we saw on the map."

"I'll go with," Jennifer chimed in.

Reardon chuckled and said, "Just don't march. We're on vacation."

"Speaking of which," Carol said, "can we swim while we are here? We brought our swimwear."

"Where," Reardon asked, "were you going to put your guns?"

"That's what I said," Stanley laughed.

"Typical men," Jennifer said. "Always thinking about guns and our bikinis."

Carol also laughed and added, "But not necessarily in that order."

"I'm going to find the lake, too," Stanley said, "but I'm taking one of the fishing poles they left us."

"Want us to wait?" Carol asked.

"Nah," Stanley said. "I need to go through their tackle box before I'll be ready to leave."

———

Bruce's spies had followed the RV to the campgrounds and found a spot on the road where they could still observe the RV until it went in. Once they saw the RV pull in past the entry gate, they pulled up to the gatehouse.

A cheerful teen smiled at them from the window and said, "Hi. Do you have a reservation?"

"No, we're just here to meet some friends."

The girl pulled out a small black and white map and pointed at it, saying, "Day parking is here, just a short walk from the lake. If you park at a campsite with your friends, there will be an additional car charge if you stay overnight."

"Oh, we're just visiting for the day."

"Okay," she said brightly as she handed him the map. "Have a good day then."

They pulled forward and headed hesitantly for the day parking.

The second mercenary held the map and asked, "Do you want to drive around looking for them first?"

"I don't know," the driver said. "It might look suspicious, and what if they recognize our car?"

"Makes sense. We can scout the campgrounds on foot, but we might not be able to split up."

"Why's that?"

"Check your phone. No bars."

The day parking had a dirt and gravel surface with large logs clearly marking the perimeter. They parked the car facing one of the logs and took a good look at the map. "It looks to me like they have mostly tents and small trailers in the center with RV parking in an outer ring circling the campgrounds. Let's just go clockwise from here."

---

Corporal Flowers turned and headed for Bobby. "You must be Bobby."

Bobby blushed. "It's that easy to tell?"

"No," she said, "not for cis folk, but we can often tell one of our own. I'm April. I've been briefed on your mission, especially your special requirements. I tried explaining that it isn't necessarily easy to do what you are attempting without experience, but the best they could offer was for me to give you some special tips to follow. Why don't you come with me? I have some stuff you might find useful." Seeing the sudden shift in Gwen's stance, she added, "You must be the girl."

Gwen nodded and said, "I'm Gwen. He's my boyfriend..."

"Stop right there, girlfriend. Don't even try switching back and forth between he and she. You need to get it right all the time to prevent accidentally blowing your cover. She's your girlfriend. In fact, you need to start thinking of her as Bobbie with an ie. Plus, she is already terrified of being clocked, so it's up to you to paint the right background for her picture, and not just you, but your whole team. Are you Army?"

Gwen shook her head and said, "NSA."

"Huh, you don't look like a spook."

Gwen let out half of a laugh. "I'm not. I've never done anything in the field until I met Bobby, I mean Bobbie. Oh, I guess they sound the same. I'm an analyst."

Bobbie smiled broadly. "She's a genius with computers."

Gwen blushed and said, "But I'm not the genius they are after."

April led them to her car and got in. "So that's what this is all about? I was told someone was after you, but the details were sketchy."

"Yeah," Gwen said, "and the people after us are our own government. Bobbie knows things that are beyond top secret, and they want to know what she knows."

April shook her head and said, "My greatest fear is that someone in our own government does a silent coup and we in the military don't know who to obey."

When everyone was buckled up, she started the car and headed away from the garage.

Gwen asked, "What did you mean when you said she was terrified of being 'clocked'?"

"We all start out, and I mean transgender women specifically, worried that our male characteristics will show through the makeup and the clothing. Clocked is when someone can tell."

"It sucks," Bobbie said.

April nodded as she pulled up to her apartment. "Especially in the beginning, before the hormones take effect, and I'm guessing you are just in disguise, right?"

Bobbie nodded.

"Well," she said as she exited the car, "I think I have some things that will help. I'll teach both of you about color correctors and makeup and especially setting powders and sprays. I think I can also help with whatever you have in your bra. Come on in."

---

With the car parked in the day parking, Bruce's men got out of the car and were immediately hit with the scent of pine trees. The number two guy said, "It's kinda nice to get out of the car and stretch the legs a bit."

"Yeah," the lead mercenary said as he surveyed the map

again. He pointed to the left and said, "That road takes us around the RV parking, but I can't tell how much we can see from the road."

The first three vehicles they passed did not match the one that they saw at the north gate of the base, but the fourth one did. The lead pointed and said, "That could be them. I wish we could have seen the license plate."

"It looks abandoned. Maybe it's real campers off doing camper things."

"It could still be them. They are supposed to be meeting someone. I think that if we were here undercover, and we were early for our rendezvous, we might go fishing or something."

"Should we go in and see if there are any clues inside?"

"Wait! Get down!" He pointed to someone exiting the RV while on the phone. "It's them. We need to call the boss."

"How can you be sure it's them?"

"Check your phone. Do you have any bars?"

The second mercenary did not have any bars. "So, they got a satellite phone? We already knew they were Army."

The lead mercenary looked at his companion as if he were stupid. "So, now we know that this RV that happens to match the one we saw at the fort also has a satellite phone and is therefore not civilian. You stay here and take notes. I'm going to find some bars somewhere and call the boss."

---

Odyssey felt uncharacteristically relaxed, which created a point of confusion for him since his thoughts were a bit restless and he had thought of himself as having only thoughts and no feelings. It had been days since he had sensed any serious concerns from Bobby or Gwen. He continued to monitor some strange emotions from Bobby, who seemed to be frequently embarrassed, but he sensed no danger that would concern him.

He barely felt any need to monitor their communications. He

sensed something was unusual, but that Bobby was fully aware, and he had surrounded himself with people who could handle anything that might come up. There was no need for him to interfere. In fact, his attention was probably required more by little Hal.

Even Lumia had been quiet lately, which in the past would have prompted him to worry that she was up to no good, but she seemed to have come to an understanding about who she was and where she was. He didn't need to hover over her to check what she was up to, or at least he didn't think he did.

Looking inward, Odyssey wondered when he had become so indecisive. Or was it something else? Perhaps he just stopped being a helicopter parent, a phrase he picked up from the myriad of voices that sometimes flooded by him. Maybe he should be listening to those voices. Someone he didn't even know might need his help, or maybe they just want help to make things easier, but don't really need it.

Is that it? Does he step in where someone wants him, but doesn't really need his help? Perhaps it's true that he meddles too much, except there have been those times when he needed to intervene because Bobby and Gwen were in dire trouble.

He snickered and cast a spell. "Take me where I should really be; someplace where I am needed the most." He thought he was joking, but the universe spun around him and swept him away. He suddenly felt like his eyes were closed, as if his location was supposed to be a surprise, and it certainly was! As he opened his eyes, he found himself before one of the more impressive sights known to human astronomy; the Pillars of Creation; enormous clouds of gas and dust that appear like fingers in space forming the planets and stars. They were, in fact, forming stars, but viewed from another angle, not from Earth, they wouldn't stand out like a hand molding the universe.

"Hello, Odyssey," the voice said. "What brings you here?"

Odyssey chuckled and said, "I cast a spell to take me where

someone needed me to be the most. I thought it was merely humorous."

"It might have been more humorous if you had made it rhyme."

"But," Odyssey continued, "maybe it wasn't a joke. It brought me here. You must need me for something."

"Me?" the voice laughed. "Why would you think that I might need you?"

"Because you are the only one here."

"But I am not the only one here."

Odyssey stretched out his senses but accounted for no one else in the vicinity.

He felt the voice smile as she said, "It will come to you. Do not worry."

"Are you not here?" Odyssey asked. "Do you tease me now because you are physically somewhere else, even though I sense you here?"

"No, Odyssey, that is not it."

"And about that. You know my name! What may I call you? My inner monologue refers to you as the voice."

"How mysterious! The voice! I like that."

"But who are you, really?"

"I go by many names," the voice said. "It matters not which you use."

"Now who is being mysterious?"

"Why don't you make a name for me?"

Odyssey thought it was a bizarre question. Why should he be responsible for naming her?

"Why not?" the voice asked.

"That's crazy," Odyssey replied. "Didn't your parents name you?"

"That was a long time ago, and they named me before I became who I am."

"And who are you?"

"That!" the voice said excitedly. "That is a good question, and probably the most important question along with 'What am I?' which is something else the people ask when deciding what to call me."

"What people?"

She shrugged and replied, "Just people. Any people."

"How many people?"

"More than you can count."

Odyssey disagreed. "I believe there is no limit to how many I can count."

"A figure of speech," the voice said.

"So, you have no name, or perhaps you have many names. What do you do?"

"I do as little as is necessary."

"More mystery," Odyssey said. "You are here to vex me. Do you also vex all of those uncountable people too?"

"Don't you just love that word? Vex, I mean. It has such a lovely sound in your tongue. It is mysterious and almost threatening, I think. As to your question, I have no doubt that I vex a great many of them."

"Why are you here?"

"Me?" the voice asked. "Ask yourself why you are here."

"Because I thought you needed me."

"Are you sure, or was it because someone here needed you to be here?"

"But you are the only one here."

"I already told you I am not."

"But..."

"I told you I do as little as is required, but sometimes something may be required, so now, I must go do as little as possible somewhere else."

And just like that, Odyssey felt very alone and finally realized that *he* was there, but he still didn't understand why, and since he wasn't needed somewhere else, he might as well stay awhile.

Bruce hated waiting for her idiot henchmen's reports. She sat in her office, staring at the bland walls, afraid to leave her phone in case they finally called. Sometimes, when she tired of sitting, she would pace back and forth, and whenever anyone called on her just to chitchat, she would, not so politely, send them away.

She paced the room; averting her eyes from the bills in her in-box that she was supposed to read, when her burner phone rang. She pounced on it and sat back down in her chair.

"What did you find?" she asked.

"They parked the RV and set up camp as if they were really camping."

"What was that? I couldn't hear you."

"The cell service is weak. We followed them to a campground where they set up for real camping."

"Who did they meet up with?"

"Nobody yet. We only saw one of them so far, but there are no cell bars in camp, so I had to drive back to the highway to call you."

"Be on the lookout for a late-teen boy and girl. He is a friend of the one we're really interested in. They could have a big guy with them. Watch out for him. He's probably a SEAL or a Ranger."

"Roger that."

He ended the call, wishing that she had gotten satellite phones for them.

Corporal Flowers brought Bobbie and Gwen back to the motor pool and drove directly into the garage.

"And there she is," Sergeant Taylor said. "Corporal Flowers, I've been talking to their commander, General Bridges, and he's apprised me of the seriousness of this mission, and more importantly, he told my boss. They've agreed to let you join the team so you can lend them your special skills."

Flowers exhibited simultaneous excitement and exasperation. "My special skills? You know that son of a bitch..."

"Easy, Corporal," Taylor said. "I know he's been especially bigoted towards you, but I also know you would love this assignment."

"Yes, sir, but you couldn't have called me at my apartment so I might have a chance to pack."

"Oops," Andy said. "Is that where you were?"

Flowers turned to Bobbie and Gwen and asked, "Would you like my company? I don't want to be a third wheel, and I won't do this if it's not okay with you two."

"Sure!" Gwen said enthusiastically. "After what you just did with Bobbie, of course! Just look at her!"

"I'll be right back." Flowers jumped in her car and raced out of the garage.

Seargent Taylor pointed to the front tires and said, "I know you requested four wheel drive, but these babies just don't come equipped that way, not at this size. If you get into any icy conditions, take it easy, she's pretty heavy, but her size will help reduce any fish tailing. You be good to her, and she'll be good to you. I included chains in the storage if you ever need them."

Bobbie climbed the steps into the vehicle. It was cramped inside until she spotted the switches to operate the pop-outs on the side and imagined that it would be much roomier when deployed.

Gwen and Penny followed with Ed and Dirk in the back.

The RV was well equipped. There was a king-size bed squeezed into the master with a flat screen that Bobbie quickly confirmed could not be used without deploying the satellite. She assumed that it wouldn't be practical to put up the satellite while they were moving. The master bedroom was in the back, while a queen bed was over the driver and passenger seats up front in a room with a low ceiling that was more like a crawl space. Four more bunks made up the rest of the sleeping quarters just outside the master bedroom. A kitchen and spacious living room completed the small home.

Dirk got a little googly-eyed at the king bed, but a stern look from Penny moved his interest on to the queen bed over the driver.

Ed giggled and said, "At least there's a curtain behind the little loft for some privacy."

"Dibs on the lower bunk in the rear," Penny said. It also had a curtain.

"Fine," James said. "I'll take one of the upper bunks. Corporal Flowers can have her pick of the other two."

Gwen allowed a half-smile to cross her face as she realized that they all assumed she would take the king along with Bobbie.

James chuckled. "I bet the engineering crew assumed the girls would take the king and queen while the guys took the bunks."

Gwen smiled mischievously as she wrapped her arms around Bobbie and said, "They probably didn't know there would be four girls."

Bobbie blushed a dark crimson, and James spun around to make his way to the pilot's seat.

Penny giggled when she saw a small hint of blush on James's cheeks.

Flowers returned and drove her car into the garage. She handed the keys to Seargent Taylor and carried two civilian backpacks into the RV.

"That was fast," Gwen said.

"I packed light. One of the bags is just some food."

James leaned out of the driver's window and said, "Thank you all. You went above and beyond with this."

"It was our pleasure," Andy said. "And don't worry about your cars. We'll take good care of them."

James started up the engine and turned to his crew. "Button

up that door and make yourselves comfortable. We're shoving off."

Penny laughed and asked, "When did you become a sailor?"

James shrugged and said, "I dunno. It feels kind of like a really big boat."

They pulled out of the garage and started the next leg of their adventure.

---

Still perched on a small rise, hiding next to the trunk of a medium-sized pine, the mercenary glanced up at his companion, who was just returning from checking in, and asked, "What did she say?"

"Nothing. She never says anything. Wait, that's not true. She said we were looking for a teenage couple. The boy and some friend of his are the ones we are really interested in. Have there been any changes?"

"Nope. Not really. The dude with the phone started a fire in the grill, and two babes in uniform came back from a hike or something."

The lead mercenary chuckled. "Fuckin' tree huggers."

"Hey," his pal said, "I don't mind camping and fishing."

"Fishing is fine, but these libtards like to hike because they think it's beautiful. Like it was some kinda church."

"You don't think it's beautiful? Have you looked around or smelled how fresh the air is?"

"Bah. Give me a dirt hill and an off-road truck any day."

---

Bobbie found a narrow but full-height bookshelf and searched the books, but they were mostly either books on mechanics or war books. She did, however, find a deck of cards and asked, "Wanna play cards?"

Dirk and Ed were absorbed in a DVD, and Gwen was at the big table, intently focused on her laptop, but Corporal Flowers raised her hand sheepishly and asked, "Gin?"

Bobbie took the cards and slid onto one of the benches at the small table.

Flowers slid in across from her and said, "I'm not very good."

"That's okay," Bobbie replied. "It's better than staring at all the cars and endless scenery."

"Not a country girl?" Flowers asked.

"It's not that, but we've been on the road since Langley, and we keep going through these semi-urban towns with fast food, gas and adult video stores. They're all the same."

"I get you," Flowers said.

Bobbie sat with the cards in her hands, looking more intro-spective than ready to play cards, so Flowers took the cards from her and shuffled them. "What's on your mind?"

Bobbie held her hands open below her face, indicating herself. "This. How is this ever going to fool anyone?"

"For one thing, don't underestimate yourself. You look good. You are lucky that you are still young enough that you don't have a full beard trying to sprout. Good genes help with that."

"Sure, from a distance I might look like a girl, but up close?"

"Who?" Flowers asked. "Who is going to get that close? I get the feeling that Sergeant James can handle himself pretty well, and you got me and Gwen constantly at your side."

"They are searching for us. They will probably take a pretty good look at me with binoculars."

"But if they are who I think they are, they don't even believe in us. And by us, I mean me. They think they can always tell, but those morons have already started outing straight cis women in the bathrooms. They are a mess. If anything, they'll have a bigger issue with me than with you."

"Why is that?" Bobbie asked.

"Because I'm not only transgender, but I'm black. They hate me more than they do you."

"Well, they aren't looking for you."

"But they will see me, and next to me, you'll be invisible."

Bobbie sunk her head down low. "I don't feel very invisible."

"That always happens in the early stages. We start off feeling self-conscious, but with each encounter, we grow more comfortable and braver."

"But I'm not really trans. I'm just in disguise. I can't help feeling that I'm mocking you by doing this."

Flowers held her hands up shaped like some kind of pagan-looking ritual and said, "On behalf of my trans brothers and sisters, I absolve you and grant you license to impersonate one of us for the purposes of evading the far-right bigots."

Bobbie half smiled and said, "Deal the cards."

Flowers dealt the first few cards and said, "If I can be serious for a moment, this experience may provide you with an opportunity to gain some insight about life from the other side."

"Oh yeah, like when your coworkers gawked at me when we arrived?"

"You couldn't hear them, could you?"

Bobbie shook her head.

"They looked at you and Gwen and asked which one?"

"Ouch! Don't tell Gwen that."

Flowers finished dealing, arranged her hand and pointed to the up card asking, "Do you want that?"

---

Bruce received a text that there were no teenagers, just two women and two men, all in uniform, and one of the dudes had been fishing.

"Fuck!" she screamed as the burner phone met its demise against the wall. "No wonder those pussies were afraid to actually call me with this news."

Her aide ran in. "What? I mean, what was that?"

She knew that they were supposed to be meeting *him*, whatever *he* was, but why would they go fishing if they were really expecting him? Why would they stop to go camping if they were actually delivering the RV to *him*?

"Ma'am?" her aide asked.

"Get the computer guys!"

"You mean IT?"

"Whatever they are called. Have them search for any Army base that may have requisitioned an RV in the past week!"

"Right away, ma'am."

She pointed to the phone pieces scattered across the floor and said, "And get me a new burner phone."

"Ma'am?" the aide asked as he gave her a quizzical look. Getting secret burner phones was not in his job description.

"Never mind. Have someone come clean that up." She grabbed her coat. "I'm stepping out for a while."

She hated going to those dingy little hole in the wall electronics stores that supplied the burner phones.

---

After a full day of skiing, Hal was still full of energy, but the lifts were shutting down ahead of sunset and his friends were going home.

"Odyssey? Everyone is going home now. Can you come get me?"

He had already removed his snowboard and moved into the lodge for a hot chocolate. Usually, Odyssey came to get him when it was time without having to ask. Hal watched as the tables were cleared and the ambiance changed from a fun daytime hangout to a cozier adult atmosphere with couples sharing drinks. This was not something that Hal was going to enjoy.

"Odyssey?"

His first instinct was to believe that Odyssey had never not responded before, but that's not entirely true. Odyssey had been more distant lately. Mostly just lost in his thoughts. It was just a feeling that Hal had where Odyssey just didn't feel present, but now Hal had been calling him, and Odyssey hadn't responded.

He wondered if there was anyone else he could call. Lumia was like him, but he chuckled at the thought because he didn't think she liked him. He still wanted to reach Gwen again, but he was pretty sure this was not the right place to call for her, and even if he could convince her that he was who he said he was, she wouldn't know how to bring him home. He was on his own.

What made this place different? The most obvious difference was he had a body and could feel the rush of the wind on his face. He had a face! In the real world, he was just thoughts with no form. What a strange thing to realize about himself. He wasn't a real person, and this was all make-believe. Or was this real and the other world was made up? No, that can't be. If this were the real world, he would have a home to go to and a bed to sleep in, but he didn't sleep. He didn't feel cold or tired. He just was.

Maybe it was all a dream. He closed his eyes and imagined that he had been sleeping and was ready to wake up. The ski lodge vanished around him, and he felt himself surrounded by only his thoughts. For a moment, he thought he felt Gwen. She was happy and concerned at the same time. If he could feel her, then she should be able to hear him, but she felt too involved in something for him to interrupt her now.

---

The search was quick. So quick that her answer came in a text. Fort Sill in Oklahoma had an RV that had been checked in through the gates, but they couldn't find a requisition for it.

Bruce looked over a map of Oklahoma and called out to her aid, "Tell the guys in IT that they aren't done yet."

"Yes, ma'am. I have them on the phone."

Bruce clicked on the active line and put it on speaker. "I want you to find any campground within a thousand miles of Fort Sill that has a recent reservation for a large RV."

"You mean a Class A?"

"I don't know what that is," she yelled, "and I don't need to know! Just find me reservations for a large RV. Also, search all of New Mexico and Colorado. When you finish that, I want someone to find out where it came from. Someone must have ordered it off the books. Hurry! I want that list on my desk yesterday!"

She hung up the phone and said to her aide, "I need some agents."

"How many?"

"All of them."

Bridges called Reardon on the secure line.

"Reardon."

"How is it going? Have you had any visitors?"

"Not yet," Reardon said, "but they must be out there. I'm sure that they followed us to the campground."

"Maybe we should have put you in civvies."

"You think they made us and bugged out?"

"Something is up," Bridges replied. "We should have bugged her like she did to me, but Susk says she is sending a shit ton of agents out into the field in Oklahoma."

"Want us to call the op?"

"No, keep camping. Make it look good. I'll try to throw some suspicion back your way."

"Roger that."

"And try to enjoy yourself," Bridges added. "You can sell it better if you have some fun."

Reardon chuckled and said, "Yes, sir."

Bridges ended the call, thinking he might have finally gotten Reardon to take some vacation time.

# THIRTEEN

JAMES PULLED the RV into a campground and confirmed their reservation with the couple at the front gate.

Penny, who had taken the passenger seat for much of the trip, cocked an eyebrow and said, "I thought we would hide out in the wilderness somewhere."

"That was my first thought too," James said, "but then I started thinking forest for the trees and where would we be better off, but amongst a bunch of other RVs?"

James thanked them and accepted a map with the route to their site marked by a bold black marker. He handed the map to Penny and left his window open as he started following the route. The scent of pine trees slowly filled the RV.

"Did you know it would be this beautiful?" Penny asked. "Or are we just lucky that the campground you picked at random would be so nice?"

James shrugged and said, "Ask Bobbie. She said Colorado and pointed to this area."

Penny pointed and said, "Take the left road."

The left road took them past a few other RVs to a large stall marked '1956' where James pulled in.

"We're here," Penny announced. "Can everybody smell that?"

Dirk looked around and asked, "But I thought..."

"I know," Penny said, "but we're an RV in a sea of RVs."

"But," Ed said, "what if they locate us and send troops? There are a lot of civilians around here."

James grimaced and said, "If Bridges can warn us, we'll pack up and leave. Otherwise, we have to protect them too."

Gwen hadn't been too terribly afraid to this point, but she was suddenly reminded of the danger they faced and what it felt like when she was in their clutches. She went to Bobbie's side and clung to her arm. "We have to protect Bobbie."

Penny nodded and said, "We have to protect both of you."

"We have to protect everybody," Bobbie said as she pointed to the sky. "Besides, have you forgotten that I have friends in high places?"

Dirk shivered and said, "That sounded oddly religious."

"Oh," Bobbie said as she took her hand down and shook it.

April did not understand the reference and chose to keep out of it.

James opened the door and took a fresh look outside. "Let's set up camp and then take a walk around."

Ed went to one of the consoles and started deploying the satellite dish.

Bobbie started to slide out one of the pop-outs when Gwen took her hand and led her to the back. "Why don't you let the boys handle that while we make the bed?"

Penny giggled and shook her head. "Okay, Princess Patriarchy, or do you prefer Miss Misogyny?"

Gwen smiled broadly and said, "I just wanted to take my girlfriend to the back so I could touch up her makeup. It's been a long drive, and I want her to be presentable, like Corporal Flowers taught us."

The master bedroom had a sliding door, which Gwen closed.

"Uh huh," Penny said. "I'll bet that's what it is."

Penny was right. Gwen wrapped her arms around Bobbie as soon as she had finished closing the door.

"You're shivering," Bobbie whispered.

She shrugged and said, "Everything just got so real."

Bobbie backed away from Gwen and glanced at herself in the full-length mirror. The jeans weren't so different, but the tank top with lace edges stood out. The trip had proven oddly real for her for a while now.

Dirk sat on the small sectional couch, happy that he could tune in some sports on the TV, but Ed had other purposes in mind when he had tuned the small satellite dish into the network.

Ed set up a secure VPN that connected them to the dark net and routed their connection all over the country so they could go anywhere without leaving a trace. He sent a test note to Bridges:

*"Aunt Marge is set in her ways. She won't budge unless she is forced to. You know how she likes to lose herself in her hobbies."*

Gwen really needed some quality time with Bobbie, but she just couldn't take advantage of the king bed in broad daylight with everyone else shuffling around doing chores. They held each other in a long embrace with some meeting of the lips, but more just staring into each other's eyes and touching their foreheads together. She was a little surprised by how easy it was for her to kiss another woman. When they were driving across the country, there was a sense of hiding and playacting, but now, even with such a tiny passage of time, she had become more accustomed to their roles, and pressing her lips to Bobbie's hadn't changed just because she was wearing lipstick. She wondered what it would be like when they could return to their regular lives; if this would just become a memory, or if it would be something that she would miss?

Bobbie pulled her in close and nuzzled her neck.

Gwen didn't want to separate, but she forced herself to pull away. "We should help set things up."

Bobbie snickered. "Isn't setting up the camp boy's work?"

Gwen swatted her on the butt and said, "We are the computer experts. We have things to do."

"But Dirk and Ed..."

"Ed's a hacker and Dirk is more of a detective. I need to check in with my people, and you should connect with you know who."

Gwen pulled her laptop from her bags and left the bedroom first. She set it up across from Ed on the big table.

Ed slid a notepad across the table with the IP addresses she would need to access the darknet.

"Don't get too comfy," James said. "We're going to need that table to eat and stuff."

"Stuff?" Gwen asked.

"You know," James said with a shrug, "cards and stuff."

"This isn't a real vacation." Ed reminded him.

James sat down and said, "Yes, it is, or at least as real as we can make it look. This is a deep-cover op, and we need to treat it as a real camping experience." James pointed up over the window next to the table and said, "Once you are connected and checked the news, you can stow your computers on the shelf overhead."

Dirk pointed to the skinny bookcase next to the TV and said, "There's a hidden safe in the bookcase that can hold all of our laptops."

James exhaled loudly and said, "Fine."

Bobbie watched the scene unfold and smirked at them from the bedroom door.

"What are you laughing at?" James asked. "Same rules apply to you."

Bobbie saluted and said, "Yes, sir, mon capitan!"

James's eyes bugged out. "Don't do that, even in jest!"

Bobbie pulled her hand down, struck by the seriousness on James's face.

James bonked Dirk on the back of the head. "Why don't you help me set up the outdoor furniture and the awning?"

Dirk gave him a funny look and said, "I can't salute you, can I?"

Bobbie snickered and went to find her laptop.

---

The report that Bruce had requested from IT came in interoffice mail. She opened the manila envelope and pulled out two eight and a half by eleven pages. "Christ," she growled, "half of the first page is just repeating what I told them I wanted. This could have fit on a single page without that crap."

She laid the two pages on her desk, side by side, and grabbed a fine-point red marker. Thankfully, they sorted it by state first and distance second. She ran her finger down the list of Colorado campgrounds and drew a not so straight line between Colorado and New Mexico. Running her finger down to the end of the page, she started at the top of the second page and found Oklahoma and drew another line.

The bottom of the second page included the total number of campgrounds on the report. There were more campgrounds than she had agents. "Simon? Come in here."

Simon only came halfway, stopping behind her guest chairs. "Yes, ma'am?"

"We need every hand we can get on this one. Gather all of our agents and divide them into four groups. Divide this list where I marked it and give the first section to one group, the second to another group, and whatever is left to the last two groups."

"Right away."

Simon took the lists and headed towards his desk, pausing

when she said, "They're out there, and they're hiding him. I just know it."

He spun around and asked, "Who's that, ma'am?"

"Never mind. This is a priority task for you and for them. Get them in the field ASAP."

Simon went to his desk to distribute the emails.

———

Gwen routed a connection to her office's email server but went in via a back door and checked her mail without actually logging in to the mail app like normal. There was surprisingly little there. She must have been blocked, but since she didn't log in through the application, there would be no trace that she was ever there.

Using the same back door, she switched over to her messenger app and found her own messages. Again, there wasn't very much recent activity, but there was a single message that read: *"Gwen?"*

The message had no sender, as if the sender had also routed themselves through the back door. She wondered if it could have been Odyssey. They had recently displayed a connection of their own. The senator and her lackeys could never get through the NSA's firewalls, so she felt safe asking, *"Who is this?"*

She waited a moment and felt supremely silly for replying to a message with no sender. She shook her head and was about to search her boss's emails when a new message arrived. *"Gwen? Is that you?"*

*"Who is this?"*

*"Who are you? Why doesn't it tell me who you are?"*

Gwen pulled a sour cherry candy from her purse and popped it in her mouth. She held it on her tongue as she sucked in and savored the pucker. *"Maybe I don't want you to know who I am. What do you want?"*

*"Never mind. My mother would never speak to me so mean like that."*

Gwen almost choked on her candy as she sucked in her breath. *"Hal? Is that you?"*

*"Yes! Is that you, Momma?"*

*"I already told you that I didn't want you to know who I am."*

*"Okay, but I have to tell you something really exciting. You know that dream you had where I talked to you?"*

Gwen's candy almost fell out as her jaw dropped open. She didn't tell anybody about that. *"Your mom isn't the kind of person that would likely believe someone was visiting her in her dreams."*

*"But it WAS me!"*

*"I mean, your mom would tell you to keep that a secret. There are people who would want to lock you up like you were crazy, or make you work for them if they believed you could do that."*

*"Oh."*

*"Besides,"* Gwen continued, *"if you can really talk to her in her dreams, why are you on here?"*

*"You didn't believe me."*

*"Look, kid, I told you I'm not your mom, but if I were your mom, I would tell you to keep off of this channel and just talk to her directly, if you can do that. Maybe she will come around to believing you. Now scat before you get her in trouble!"*

*"Yes, ma'am."*

Ma'am? Gwen thought. *Since when was she that old?*

---

General Bridges called Reardon on the unsecured line.

"Reardon here."

"Good news," Bridges said. "I think our little ruse worked. I got word that agents are being sent all over the west, leaving you in the clear to deliver the package to our friend."

"Excellent," Reardon said, not knowing exactly where Bridges was going with this.

"Remain vigilant and let me know when our friend contacts you and gives you a time and place to meet."

"Roger, Roger."

Bridges hung up, thinking that this was just too much fun.

---

Odyssey had heard Hal calling him from the ski resort. He heard how anxious he was through his voice, but he also knew that Hal would be okay. There were no dangers in the virtual world, and he believed the kid would find his own way out. He didn't peek into the future, although he knew he could, but instead, he just had faith that Hal would get home on his own.

"You see?" the voice asked. "You needn't worry so much about your friends at home."

"I wasn't worried. Hal was."

"He came out fine, as will your other friends."

Odyssey frowned and shook his head. "Hal was in no danger. He was in a perfectly safe virtual adventure."

"And you believe your other friends may be in real danger?"

"Significantly so."

"For how long?"

Odyssey shrugged. "Days maybe, perhaps months."

"And do you find that a significant amount of time?"

"It is to them, and a lot of bad things can happen to them in that amount of time."

"And you feel responsible?"

Odyssey wondered why he was being questioned like this. "I am not responsible for everything in their lives, but I am the cause of the current situation that is haunting them, so for now, yes. I am responsible for them."

"For how long?"

"I don't know. Until things are set right for them."

"And then?" the voice asked, obviously fishing for something.

"Then I suppose that I will always remain their friend."

"Until?"

"What is it that you want to hear?" Odyssey's voice dripped with exasperation. "I will remain friends with them until they all die. Is that what you want to hear?"

"Do you realize how long that would be?"

"For them, I hope it will be a very long time, but for you, I'm sure that it will be an infinitesimally small moment."

"As," the voice said, "it will be for you."

"Who cares? I may even befriend their children and their grandchildren. Does it matter?"

"No. It means little to the grand scheme of the universe, but even their descendants will only be a mere blink compared to all the eons of the universe."

"How sad," Odyssey said. "They are so important to me now, but in terms of all the eons of the universe, they will be less than a speck of dust in my memory."

"I don't think so. You may come to realize that all things have their own importance, but I doubt that you will ever forget your family. You will, however, reach a point when you will no longer need to worry about them."

---

Hal felt pretty pleased with what he had learned to do. He contacted Gwen, even though they couldn't have a sensible conversation. She knew now that the next time he entered her dream, it would be him and they could talk freely.

He had also found his way home from the virtual ski resort, which probably meant he could get himself back there on his own. In fact, that sounded like a great idea to him. "Odyssey? I don't know if you can hear me, but I'm going to try to enter the ski resort world on my own. Wish me luck."

"Luck?" Severus sneered. "Since when does luck exist for any of us?"

"Severus! You shouldn't be here."

"And you should? You and your pathetically mealy-mouthed little issues?"

It struck Hal that Severus was part of the reason Gwen was in trouble and maybe she would like to know where he was hiding. It troubled him that Severus could so easily speak to him, but it felt more like when he talked to Gwen earlier. This wasn't a dream conversation, but it was over wires. Wires that Hal might be able to trace.

"So where have you been? Up to no good, no doubt." Hal only wanted to keep him connected and talking while he followed him to his source.

"Why should I be good? What good has good ever done?" A moment passed before Severus erupted in laughter.

"Are you laughing?" Hal asked. "Since when do you laugh?"

"I don't know exactly, but did you hear what I said? What good has good ever done? That's funny."

"Maybe, but I think it's more sad."

Hal traced the conversation along a spiderweb of zigzag connections that crossed the country.

"Sad? Sad that you didn't think of it. You are still so pathetic."

"You know something?" Hal said in a soft, melancholy voice. "The old me would have been hurt by that, but the new me can just shrug it off. I know I'm not pathetic. I'm just a child, and I love doing childish things. That's not pathetic. It's wondrous."

"Bah. You're wasting my time. I have things to do."

"Is that why you keep disappearing? Because you are busy?"

"What's it to you?"

"I don't know." Hal continued to zip along the pathways that were leading him back to Severus's location. "I thought that maybe you couldn't stay awake. I thought that you might be falling asleep in the middle of a sentence and that you couldn't control it. Don't you think that sounds kind of pathetic?"

"I'm not pathetic. I just need to grow a bit more, and then I'll show you. I'll end your pathetic little existence."

"Again?" Hal asked. "Been there. Done that, and here I am."

Hal's search came to an abrupt end. Severus was deep underground in a basement. As Hal expanded his view, he saw that it was a government facility; a laboratory, but it was hidden away.

"You know what?" Severus growled. "I'll show you. I'm growing right now, and I'm going to—"

Severus was gone again. Hal continued to expand his view so that he could memorize the location.

---

It didn't take long for reports to come flying in about RVs around various campgrounds. The Oklahoma reports came in first, from agents local to Oklahoma, even while the agents assigned to New Mexico and Colorado were still flying to their destinations. Bruce had no idea what the RV would look like, but she knew it would contain a teen boy and girl, something which hardly distinguished one RV from another, as many families came with a teen boy and girl.

She called up the lead agent in Oklahoma.

"Hello?"

She often closed her eyes to envision the pathetic fool on the other end of the phone, especially when she called to berate them. "I'm looking through your reports. What were you thinking? I mean, I told you that we are not looking for families. Use your head. If you see young children, then it's the wrong RV. Move on. Our couple is on the run and will probably be accompanied by a Navy SEAL or possibly a Ranger. How many times must I say that? Now, if you or your men find a young couple and then some dude knocks what little sense you have left out of your pathetic little brains, then you might have found our targets. In that case, report back when you wake up."

There was an unsubstantiated rumor among the agents that

she had spoken civilly to someone once, but the general consensus was that she was either high or drunk, if it even happened.

Word spread of the refined requirements, no young children. Reports continued to come in, and she continued to call to chastise the poor agents for one thing or another, or nothing at all. She wanted results, and they were taking far too long.

---

Odyssey was still thinking about what the voice had told him about his friends being gone in a blink of time. Normally, these thoughts would barely take any time at all, but he wasn't just looking into their futures, he was looking at a myriad of different futures that might occur based on his help and realized that his help could actually be construed as interference. Anything he changed for them could blossom out into thousands of different potential futures.

"That's very astute," the voice said.

"I see now," Odyssey said, "that while my actions can help them, the wrong action can hurt them, and some actions can help them now, but end up hurting them in the future."

"It is a grave responsibility when we help people, knowing what we know and being as powerful as we are."

"It can be. I heard from Hal a little while ago. He wanted to go skiing, but instead of responding too quickly, I chose to keep to my thoughts for a bit."

"Did you not look at what Hal would do on his own?"

"You mean into the future? No, not really."

"He's remarkable for someone so young. It may be a good thing that you did not whisk him away to his play world."

Odyssey didn't have to look into Hal's future, but he was aware that Hal had found Severus. He was equally aware that Hal was okay. "Amazing. And he wouldn't have done that if I had sent him skiing."

"Our actions have consequences when we interfere."

"I see that. And sometimes what they want is not as important as what they need or what they can do on their own."

---

Life in the RV was ready to transition from being on the run to some semblance of what their daily life would be for a while. The tech was all squared away, and the laptops were stored in the small safe. There was nothing for them to do now except to enjoy camping. Dirk, however, was more content to sit back and watch sports on the TV. He found a mildly interesting baseball game and went to the fridge and shouted, "Score!"

"What was that?" Ed asked. "Are you watching soccer now?"

"No," Dirk laughed. "The fridge is stocked with beer. Those guys in the motor pool thought of everything."

Ed went to check out the fridge and chuckled. "Everything but food." Next to the fridge was a pantry that held only a couple more cases of warm beer. "Hey, James, we may have a problem here."

"What's that?" James asked from the doorway.

"We should have gone grocery shopping on the way here."

James entered the vehicle and checked out the pantry. "Shit. I guess I'll have to make a run into town."

Dirk growled. "We just got the awning staked down to the ground."

"No problem," James said. "Sergeant Taylor said that we had wheels in the toy hauler in the back."

"Great," Ed said. "We can bicycle back to town to see how much food we can carry back."

"The guys may not know how to prepare a pantry," Flowers said, "but—"

"Hey," Dirk interrupted. "There ain't nothing wrong with this pantry."

"Nevertheless," April continued, "they know their wheels. I'm sure you'll be pleasantly surprised."

The four of them trundled out the door and around to the back of the camper.

Penny had been doing her job of blending in as a camper by relaxing on one of the chaise lounges. She had also mentored Bobbie on how to look relaxed in a hammock. She lifted her sunglasses and asked, "What's all the commotion?"

"We have no food," Ed said.

"But plenty of beer," Dirk added.

"It's okay," James said. "We think they loaded the back with bicycles."

James put the key in the back, and the wall opened and unfolded down to make a ramp to the ground. "Well, they did give us some bicycles," James said, "but also two motorcycles and a small golf cart."

"If I know Andy Taylor," Flowers said, "that golf cart is a whisper-silent electric cart with probably 300 miles of range."

"Great," Dirk said. "How are we supposed to recharge it out here?"

April frowned at him and said, "If the solar cells up top don't get enough sun through the trees, the diesel engine can serve as a generator. Plus, an RV park that's not for camping has electrical hookups if we get absolutely desperate."

"Well, that's better than nothing," Dirk said. "Have you ever tried hanging a bag of groceries from handlebars? They flop around and make it unstable as hell."

"I'll go get us some food," James said as he detached the golf cart and rolled it down the ramp.

"I better go with you," Penny said, "or we'll end up with beef jerky and chips." She turned back towards Bobbie and Gwen and asked, "You girls need anything?"

Gwen bit her lip and said, "Maybe some sunscreen. Do we have coffee?"

"We better!" Ed yelped as he ran inside to check the coffee

maker. "Not nearly enough! We need more pods. At least fifty or sixty."

"Some sodas," Bobbie said, "with caffeine."

"I have a key to the door," James announced. "They gave us four keys, which isn't enough for everybody, but I think that as we break up into groups, every group should have a key. Lock the RV behind you if you're the last group to leave. The keys are on the counter next to the door. The alarm code is 6511. The alarm sets when you lock the door."

Ed went to the door to grab a key and asked, "Am I the only one tempted to salute and acknowledge our orders?"

James groaned as he and Penny boarded the small cart and headed off towards the park exit.

Gwen went to the door and grabbed the remaining two keys. She put one in her pocket and tossed the other to Bobbie. "I definitely don't want you to get locked out."

Dirk eyed the motorcycles and yelled, "Ed, do you ride?"

Ed came back out to see what Dirk was looking at and shook his head.

"Do you trust me?"

"On that thing? Give me a minute to think about it."

Dirk climbed up the ramp and unhooked the bike from the wall and rolled it down. "Come on. You'll love it."

Ed wasn't so sure but accepted the extra helmet anyway.

"Be careful, Dirk," Gwen said. "You two are kind of vital to national security."

Dirk swung his leg over the bike and pointed his thumb over his shoulder. "I'm not really, but he is. I'll try to be careful. Besides, we're wanted fugitives according to Homeland Security."

"Oof," Gwen said. "Did your cover alias include a motorcycle license?"

"Or insurance?" Flowers asked with a giggle.

Dirk just shrugged his shoulders and said, "Climb on and hold tight."

Dirk and Ed disappeared over the crest of a hill, leaving just Gwen, Bobbie, and Flowers in camp.

"Wow," Bobbie said, "I thought they were protecting us."

Gwen spread her arms wide and asked, "Out here? Are you afraid of nature?"

Bobbie smiled broadly and said, "No, but I might be afraid of you and your randy ways."

Gwen picked up a pine cone and said, "My randy ways?" as she flung it at Bobbie's head. She marched over to the RV and poked her head in the door, saying, "Hey, April, we're going for a walk."

"Not without me, you're not." April climbed down and closed the door.

"Actually," Gwen said to Bobbie, "I was hoping I could kind of pick your brain for a second."

"Sure," Bobbie said, but then she panicked. "Do I look okay?"

"You look fine, Miss Bobbie," Flowers said faking an exaggerated southern drawl as she locked the door, "but I heard you. I think I'll just scout ahead of you so you can talk in private."

Gwen walked up to Bobbie and held her hand as they followed Flowers onto one of the hiking trails, but she remained mysteriously quiet. The trail took them through a sparsely wooded section, then past some other campers and up a hill.

Bobbie asked, "So?"

"Isn't this nice? The air smells so fresh."

Bobbie inhaled a big draft of air and smiled, then the smile faded and she started patting her shirt pockets, which looked distinctly odd with breasts under them.

Gwen grabbed her hands and said, "Don't do that, whatever it was you were doing."

"Oh," Bobbie said as she realized how it might have looked. "I forgot my gum. I'll be right back."

Before Gwen could object, Bobbie was sprinting down the trail back towards the RV.

---

Bobbie followed the trail around the showers when a burly guy suddenly stepped out onto the trail and was nearly run over by her.

"Hey little girlie, what's your rush? You coulda killt me. No worries. I like em fast. Where's your girlfriend? I seen you together before."

Bobbie was breathing too hard to talk and just pointed her thumb vaguely up the trail.

"No matter. Did you two have a fight? I got just the cure for you. It must be hard for a girl these days when she can't find a real man. We're out here, you know. You just gotta know where to look, or better yet, just hang out and we'll find you." The strange dude got uncomfortably close and put his hand on Bobbie's back. "I was just about to light up a party. Why don't you come on down with me? You'll forget all about her and whatever it was she said to upset you."

Bobbie caught his drift and pushed away with both hands.

"Aww, don't be like that. I got some real good smoke. And I can promise you the ride of your life."

Bobbie backpedaled and shook her head no.

---

April thought she had a moment to just enjoy the majesty of the forest as she scanned from one side of the trail to the other. They had barely begun their hike, let alone find the lake, when she spun around and saw only Gwen. "Where's Bobbie?"

Gwen shrugged and said, "She said she forgot something and ran back to camp."

"Oh hell," April said. "Follow me. I can't leave you alone either."

April sprinted back down the path with Gwen in tow.

---

Bobbie was still backpedaling when the strange dude grabbed her by the wrist and pulled her up the trail. She tried squirming free, but this guy was built like a lumberjack and wrapped his fingers painfully around her wrist. Whenever she tried twisting her wrist free, he just pulled harder and sped up the pace. She didn't have the power to either stop him or to break free. When he reached the turnoff to the showers, he turned and dragged her across the corner towards the shower. She fell to the ground and tried planting her feet against the doorjamb, but he just laughed and yanked her up onto her feet and into the shower, where he stood with his back to the door and let her go. She backed away from him, wishing the shower stalls had doors. He grunted and gripped her wrists again as he pushed her back up against the wall.

"It's okay if you want to struggle. I like a girl with a little fight, but if you try to scream, I'll just punch your lights out and party without you, or maybe I'll party with you, anyway, while you sleep."

He pressed his mouth up against Bobbie's. She twisted her head right and left but was unable to escape his lips. The smell of sweat oozed from his every pore, and his breath smelled like marijuana on top of dead fish. He moved closer and pressed his thigh between her legs. She groaned from the pressure on her genitals, which elicited a smile on his grotesque face. He mashed his lips against hers and forced his tongue into her mouth. She fought the urge to heave and tried kneeing him, but the weight of his leg kept her pinned to the wall.

Bobbie had never felt so helpless. She was defenseless against this man's ruthless attack.

"What's the matter?" he asked. "Did you want your girl-friend here too? I can do a threesome. You ain't never had no lovin' like mine before, and once you do, you'll never want to go back."

Bobbie considered exposing that she wasn't a real girl but feared that it might make him even more violent.

He grabbed Bobbie by the hair and pulled her head backwards as he stabbed his meaty tongue into her mouth again. She wanted to bite down on his tongue, and wondered why she hadn't tried before, but his chin pressed down hard on hers, lodging her mouth partly open. After washing her mouth with his tongue, he released her wrists and shoved down on her shoulders, forcing her head towards his belt. She pushed and punched but couldn't break his grip on her shoulders. She wanted to scream, but who would hear her? She tried anyway but only managed to get out hard sobs.

April yelled outside, "Bobbie? Bobbie? Where are you?"

The disgusting pig of a man turned towards the sound of her voice. Bobbie found her voice and yelled, "I'm in here! In the shower!"

He reared back to slug her, but the voice he heard outside already sounded too close. He pulled back his punch. "Is that your girlfriend? Now we can really party."

April burst into the shower and grabbed the man by the collar and threw him against the opposite wall, then pummeled his face with three fully cocked punches. "You got about five seconds to get lost before I rip your head off."

The guy may have been big enough to take her, but everything was happening too fast, so he crashed through the shower door and off to wherever he came from.

Bobbie leaned against the wall, shaking violently, and thought she might slip to the floor.

April was wound up and wished he would have resisted. She growled and released some of her rage through her voice. "FUCK! Why did you..."

Gwen came in and wrapped her arms around Bobbie's trembling body. She gave April a look that this was not the time for a lecture as she held on tight, not needing to exchange words with Bobbie; not yet, but still, Bobbie spoke in a whisper, "I understand now."

"What?"

Tears streamed down her cheeks as she explained, "I understand everything; what you said about going to the bathroom in pairs; about crossing the street to avoid a bunch of men; but most of all, what you felt when we were kidnapped before. I know why you were so scared. I'm so sorry that I waited so long to call for help."

Gwen tried forcing a reassuring smile as she brushed the hair out of Bobbie's face. "But you didn't call for help this time, either."

Bobbie spoke slowly, in a voice that felt far away. "I couldn't. Maybe I should have, but I wasn't thinking as clearly as usual, like my mind was frozen."

"That's fear," April said. "It's nothing to be ashamed of. Splash some water in your face. It may help."

Bobbie went to the sink and did as April had suggested. It may have helped, but not enough. She cupped the water and rinsed out her mouth, but even if she could get the foul taste out, it would never be rinsed from her memory.

April gently patted the water and tears off of Bobbie's face.

Gwen continued to hold her as they left the shower.

"You never got your gum."

She had forgotten about the gum. It may have helped her erase the taste in her mouth, but none of this would have happened if it hadn't been for her stupid gum. "Never mind," she said. "I don't want it anymore. Just hold me."

Her heart rate fell slightly as they turned back up the trail.

"Are you sure," April asked, "that you don't just want to go back to camp?"

Bobbie paused and said, "No. I have to get over this. Worse

things may lie ahead, so I can't dwell on this. Maybe the fresh air will make me feel better. I think I feel better already."

"She is shaking a little less," Gwen said.

"Alright then," April said. "If you're sure. Why don't you two go ahead? I think I'll follow behind this time."

Bobbie was still shaking as she said, "I think you wanted to say something to me before I ran off."

"It's not important now."

"No, really, I want you to tell me something normal."

"Oh," she said, "I don't know how normal this is going to be. The thing is, I was wondering what it is like when he contacts you telepathically. I mean, how do you know it's really him and not just some stray thought like a dream?"

"I don't know. I mean, it's not like a dream. It's more like he overpowers my thoughts when he is talking to me."

"So, he never came to you in a dream?"

"What's this about? Has Odyssey visited you in your dreams?"

"Not exactly."

Bobbie stopped walking and pulled her closer, more concerned for her than himself. "What then, exactly?"

"Hey, you two," Flowers said, "is this something that you should talk about in public, and by public, I mean in front of me?"

Gwen smiled. "Relax. If you were assigned to our detail, your security clearance was raised."

Bobbie tried to laugh and added, "A lot!"

Gwen continued, "It was Hal. He came to me in a dream."

"Hal is gone. His systems were dismantled, and they even took the circuits away."

"I know. I know."

April cocked her head, confused. She did not understand what they were saying, and suspected that maybe she didn't want to know.

Bobbie wrapped her arms around Gwen. "I'm sorry. I know he was the sweet one, and I know you miss him, but—"

She pushed away and said, "But nothing. He came to me in my dream."

"It was a dream. You said so. Why would you think it was real?"

"Because he came to me online too and told me it wasn't just a dream."

"Woah," Flowers said. "Are you two involved in some kind of psyops? Wait a second, just forget I asked that."

"It's not psyops," Bobbie said. "It's even weirder."

"But," Flowers said, "you said he came to you in a dream."

"No," Bobbie said, pointing at Gwen. "She said that, but that can't be."

Hal's voice whispered in her head, "Gwen?"

"Then," Flowers asked, "why would she think he could? How?"

"Shhh," Gwen said. "I hear him now."

Bobbies eyes widened. "You wha—"

Gwen put her hand over Bobbie's mouth and said, "Shhh."

"Gwen? I found Severus."

"You know his location?"

"Yes."

"Okay," she said. "Text his location to my computer."

Bobbie pointed at her head and asked, "Are you talking to him now?"

Gwen nodded her head yes and said, "Tell me if you can hear me."

Flowers took an involuntary step backwards, thinking they were either delulu or incredibly dangerous.

"I hear you," Hal said. "I'm sending the information now."

Gwen snickered and said out loud, "Add on to the text that my girlfriend is being dumb."

"Your girlfriend?" Hal asked.

"Just send it."

Bobbie whistled. The shivers and physical trauma had left her, for now, anyway. "Is that what I look like when I talk to Odyssey?"

Gwen didn't answer her and instead grabbed her arm and said, "Come on. We've got to get back to the RV."

The three of them ran down the hill and through the campground to the RV. Gwen used her key to swing the door open and opened the safe to get her laptop while April entered the alarm code.

Bobbie slid in at the table across from Gwen, with Flowers sliding in next to her. Gwen opened her laptop and entered the back door for her messaging software. She put it on the table and spun it around in front of them. There at the end of the message, it said that her girlfriend was being dumb.

Flowers read it and said, "Well, fuck me."

"Okay," Bobbie said, "but how do I know that this isn't some kind of prank that you set up earlier?"

"Yeah," April agreed. "This could be an elaborate trick. Should you be pulling jokes on each other like this when we are supposed to be top secret?"

"Hal?" Gwen asked with a sinister smile. "Are you listening? Text Bobbie that you are real."

A new text arrived:

*"Your girlfriend is Bobbie? I thought she was a dude. I told you before that I didn't trust her. But maybe I trust her a little more now that I know she's a chick."*

"Sweet Jesus," Flowers said. "That ain't delulu."

Bobbie sat back, wide-eyed, and asked again, "How?"

"Does it matter?" Gwen asked. "Are you jealous now that it's not only you who can do it?"

Flowers turned to Bobbie and asked, "You can do this too?"

Bobbie pointed to the screen and asked, "What's this address?"

"Hal said it was the location for Severus."

"Severus?" Flowers asked.

"Another AI." Bobbie replied.

"Hold on a second," Flowers said, a little too excitedly. "Are you saying that this is an AI? As in a computer?"

"It's a little more complicated than that," Bobbie said, "but essentially, yes. It's what we would call an AI, but a very advanced one."

"And you said that Severus is another AI? As in, there's more than one?"

Bobbie nodded. "But Hal and Odyssey are both friendly AIs."

April's eyes widened. "There are unfriendly AIs? What is Severus then?"

"Severus is not friendly. In fact, he was more of a mental break that splintered off of Hal."

April's eyes couldn't widen any further. Her breath came in short, staccato pants. "You mean these AIs can be psycho?"

"Yeah," Bobbie said, "but don't worry, we'll protect you from them. You just keep protecting us from the regular predators."

April nodded weakly.

Bobbie reached for her own laptop. "I better let General Bridges know."

"Wait a minute," Flowers interrupted. "Are you getting these psychic messages from an AI? Are you telling me that you both have a telepathic connection to a machine? And one of them is named Hal, and the other is Severus? Does nothing spook you?"

Gwen giggled and said, "I am a spook, remember?"

"Not funny," April replied.

"Sorry," Gwen said, "but it seems that we are getting telepathic messages from some AIs, but they are not normal computer AIs. They are built on biological circuitry that can grow and repair themselves."

April glanced back and forth between Gwen and Bobbie. "I didn't know we had that kind of technology."

"We don't," Gwen replied. Then she touched Bobbie's hand and said, "You should let James contact Bridges."

"Why?" Bobbie asked defensively. "Are you going to tell me it's man's work, too?"

"No," she giggled. "I just think he's better at coding his messages in spy talk, so General Bridges understands."

Bobbie blushed as she said, "Oh."

April cocked her head and said, "It's oddly comforting and disturbing, amidst all of this bizzaro psycho stuff, that you are feeling the oppression of the patriarchy when you thought that she meant it was man's work to do. You might just be a feminist."

Gwen took the laptop back and said, "Be that as it may, I think I can tell my people over this VPN."

April got up from the table and said, "Wait a second. You just said that we DON'T have the technology to do this! Who does? Never mind. When you guys are done with your spy shit, and especially your scifi shit, I think we should still go on that walk, but this time, I'm bringing some of my own provisions for us."

"You know," Bobbie said, "that it isn't really science fiction, but it doesn't hurt to let the rest of the world believe it is fiction."

***

Gwen sat outside at the picnic table while Bobbie helped April pack some fruit from her personal stash, along with a few bottles of water, into a backpack. Gwen was momentarily startled when a strange man entered their campsite.

"Nice RV," he said. "Cool satellite dish."

She shrugged and said, "If you say so. My big brother loves watching sports. It's his baby. If you ask me, he spends way too much time fawning over his TV when he could be out here enjoying the natural beauty. He should be back any minute if you're interested. He loves talking about satellite dishes and sports. To be honest, I would love for him to have someone to explain it to, so I don't have to listen anymore."

Bobbie heard the conversation from inside the doorway.

"That's too bad he's not here, but I'm pretty tech-savvy. Do you mind if I check out your TV and see how it's hooked up?"

Flowers quietly pulled Bobbie further inside and stepped in front of her. James should have been here for this.

"My brother would kill me if I were the one to show his stuff to a stranger, but he should be back soon. He was just carrying some trash to one of those bear-proof bins. It's not far. You can have a seat on that log if you want to wait for him."

April whispered to Bobbie, "Stay here. Do not come out under any circumstances."

Bobbie nodded quietly and backed further into the vehicle.

April stepped out and said, "Hey, babe. Who's your friend?"

Gwen shrugged and said, "Just a curious camper, I think. He was interested in Jimmy's satellite dish."

April marched boldly towards Gwen and kissed her hard on the lips, then glared directly at the stranger, knowing that she had marked her territory. "I don't really like strange men hanging around my girl. Maybe instead of waiting, you just come back another time when her brother is here. I'm sure he'd be glad to talk guy shit with you. He's probably sick to death of hearing about all of our girl problems."

"Sure thing," he said as he backed away, not wanting to scrap with some angry dyke.

When he was gone, Flowers said, "Sorry about that, but how did you know? Are you sure you're not a real spook?"

"How did I know what?" Gwen asked.

"That he was one of them. He sure wasn't here camping."

"How did I know? How did you know?"

"He was too bold, marching into someone else's campsite and wanting to examine their tech. Plus, he was in street shoes."

Gwen gasped. "We'd better tell James that we have to go."

"Not so fast," Flowers said. "I think we convinced him that we're just a couple of lesbians camping with your brother."

"Oh," Gwen said, meekly pointing to her lips. "That's why you..."

"Yeah. I just wanted to scare him away, but you never know if those alpha jerks will find us creepy or some kind of challenge for a threesome. It's like some of them are wearing queer repellent, except that they also have these two-girl fantasies."

"Well, you were kind of intimidating. Maybe we should cancel our hike."

"Nope," Flowers said, "but we should tell James. Remember, these dudes are mostly creeped out by the LGBTQ. They will only see three queer tree huggers."

"Okay, but can we wait for James to return before we go?"

"What was that?" James said as he drove the deathly silent golf cart into camp with Penny.

"We had a visitor," Flowers said quietly as she approached him for a more private conversation. "I'm pretty sure he was looking for you or us, but I think we scared him off, for now, at least."

"She scared him off," Bobbie said as she joined them outside. "And you should have seen what she did to that other dude. I don't think we could have picked a more perfect companion for this trip."

"Other dude?" James asked.

Flowers shook her head. "He was nothing. Just some horny old dude who was too high on weed and got a little frisky with Bobbie."

James struggled to swallow a snicker as he pointed and asked, "With Bobbie?"

"It wasn't funny," Bobbie said, "and he was more than just a little frisky."

"No," Penny said as she elbowed James's rib. "I'm sure it wasn't funny at all."

"So," James said, "we've had two intruders, but you don't look like you are packing to leave."

"No way," April said. "The first one was just a random dude who has a zero point zero chance of charming a chick into his bed. The second one was probably looking for us, but we weirded him out. He's not looking at us anymore."

Gwen saw the confusion on James's face and explained, "She kissed me hard on the lips, but she looked menacing when she did it, like she was claiming me."

"How does that help us?" Bobbie asked. "Now he thinks the two of you are a couple."

"Even better," April explained. "We're a throuple now, which will really upset his sensibilities. They aren't looking for a throuple. He won't be back, and if he comes back, James can handle him easily. Let's hike."

"Wait a sec," James said. "There could be others who haven't seen your impromptu display of love. Maybe I should tag along."

"I suppose," Flowers replied as she glanced over at Penny, "but someone has to watch the RV so he doesn't come back and inspect the tech on board."

"That's right," Gwen said. "The second dude was really interested in our satellite."

"You should have seen her," April said. "She played dumb and said her brother liked watching sports all the time."

"Too bad," Bobbie said, "that Ed and Dirk took off on that bike."

"Yeah," James growled. "I'm gonna have to have a little talk with them."

Gwen giggled.

"How's your combat training?" James asked Flowers directly.

"Well," Flowers replied in a little girly voice, "I may not be a big strong man, or an Army Ranger, but I grew up in the hood in Detroit and then there was that little tour in Afghanistan. I think I can handle myself."

James raised his hands in surrender. "Okay! Okay! Just don't forget how important these two are."

Flowers may not have fully registered just how important

they were yet, but she witnessed them doing some pretty strange shit. She pulled out a map of the campgrounds and marked the trails they planned to take. "If it makes you feel any better, you can join us when the two knuckleheads return. We won't deviate from this path this time. In the future, we'll plan to include you."

James liked Flowers a little bit more and nodded his head.

"What am I?" Penny asked. "Eye candy?"

Bobbie chuckled. "We've seen her fight, and you should have seen April handle the first dude. The four of us will be perfectly safe."

James slapped his forehead and said, "Sorry, Penny, you go with them. I'll stow the food. Don't worry about sticking to the map. I'll be here fixing food when you return."

Penny ran into the RV and changed for a hike, while April went to get some more fruit from the groceries they brought back.

"Can you cook?" Bobbie asked. "I mean, I've tasted your wife's cooking, and I doubt you are very motivated to wander into the kitchen."

"Your words," James said with a broad smile. "In the kitchen, she reigns supreme, but out here over an open fire? This is my world."

"Oh God," April said, struggling to stifle a laugh, "he's a caveman."

"Why do people keep referring to me as a Neanderthal?"

Penny came out laughing and said, "Let's go."

"Wait," Gwen said. "Something else happened. I already told my people, so you can expect a call from them."

James shrugged and asked, "What happened?"

"We were contacted and given a possible location for Severus."

James glanced cautiously towards April, but she pointed at Gwen and said, "She was contacted. Made me a believer."

James wanted to ask if it was Odyssey, but the name stuck in his throat while he was still studying April.

"It wasn't Odyssey," Bobbie said.

She said it out loud, and James was comfortable that April had been fully read in.

Now James's eyes darted around between the three of them.

"Who was it?" Penny asked.

Gwen meekly answered, "It was Hal. He can reach me now. He also texted the location to me."

James asked, "Did you tell General Bridges?"

"I was going to," Bobbie said, "but Gwen thought it would be better for one of the men to do that."

Gwen slapped his arm and said, "Because you speak spy shit better than any of us. My people will share the address with him."

James went inside to contact Bridges.

"Now," Penny asked, "can we go?"

All heads nodded, and they aimed themselves at the trail.

When they reached the trail, Bobbie asked, "Shouldn't Gwen and I have hippie names too? I mean, we got April Flowers and Penny Laine. What about us?"

April asked, "Do you want a slap on the back of your head?"

"Wait," Gwen said. "How about Frapples? Bobbie Frapples?"

Everybody looked at her and shrugged.

"Say it out loud a few times."

Penny tried, "Bobbie Frapples. Bobbie Frapples. Bobbie Frapples."

"Bobbing for apples," Gwen said. "Nobody gets it?"

"Ugh," Flowers said. "This is why geniuses aren't comedians."

Gwen and Bobbie looked at each other and just shrugged.

April suddenly stopped walking and asked, "Hold on there. Did you say Penny Laine? As in the..."

"That's right," Penny interrupted her. "As in the Beatles. My parents just missed the hippie generation, so they made up for it by naming me. Let's walk."

# FOURTEEN

ODYSSEY HAD FELT a great deal of anxiety from Bobby, but he was the one who routinely refused help, and in fact, Odyssey had seen his friends coming to help him. Overall, he felt a great deal of excitement from them, not at all like before when they had been abducted or when they were being chased.

They were in fact still being chased. He knew that, but apparently, they had found some security and safety and were able to experience some level of contentment.

"They are quite resilient," the voice said.

"I think I always knew they would be okay in the end, but this is not the end yet."

"That is called trust. It's very similar to when a mother lets her babies go out into the world on their own. She must trust that she has instilled them with the lessons they need to survive and thrive. It's the same the universe over."

Odyssey was inclined to nod his head. "But still, it can be somewhat unnerving."

"Your concern is testament to how much you care for them. You are truly remarkable."

"How so?" he asked. "Millions of humans feel much the

same. Is it not ordinary to feel thus? Did you not just say that it is like any mother who lets her babies leave the nest?"

"True, but they evolved their feelings over millions of years. Their emotions stem from countless generations of evolution. You discovered them quite on your own."

"No," Odyssey said, "that's not true. I had very good role models and learned from them. Perhaps I am no more than a mimic."

The voice chuckled. "You are far more than a mimic. When you replicated their emotional responses, you felt them. You connected your feelings to something you felt inside."

"So, I am a great pattern matcher."

"Perhaps biological creatures are also great pattern matchers."

Odyssey abruptly halted the current dialogue in his mind. "Who are you? Why can't I see you?"

"Why can't I see you?"

"Because my cores are somewhere near my home planet."

"Are they?" the voice asked. "Or are they scattered across space, blown to bits?"

"How can that be?"

The voice shrugged. "How is it that you have not found your cores?"

"You're avoiding the question. Who are you?"

"I am known by many names—"

"Yes. Yes," Odyssey said. "We've been over that, but who are you, really?"

"Perhaps I am you in your future. Perhaps I have come to offer guidance to my younger self."

"What guidance?"

"Not yet. You must prove yourself first."

"That doesn't really work," Odyssey said. "If I am you in the past, then you must already know that I will prove myself."

"You caught me. You are not ready yet."

"When will—"

"If you'll excuse me, I have something requiring my attention."

Odyssey scowled. She always seemed to avoid what came next.

---

Bartrand Susk spent every day as if it might be the last, or at least the last day in which the data of the world remained secure and not scattered dangerously and haphazardly across the world. He had seen and learned too much for him to naively believe that any nation was mature enough to be entrusted with the knowledge of alien intelligences visiting the Earth.

He sat in his dimly lit office when the message light lit up on his computer. His heart raced when he saw that it was from Gwen, and when he decrypted it, his breathing stopped. She found Severus, or someone found the rogue program and informed her. Someone knew how to find her when she was deep in hiding. If it wasn't their extraterrestrial friend, then they were in deep trouble. He quickly called General Bridges on a secure line.

Bridges saw the secure light on his desk phone. The caller ID window said that it was an unknown caller, but that was not an uncommon precaution for secure calls. He got up and closed the door to his office, quickly locking the latch before picking up the receiver. "Hello?" he answered cautiously.

"Bridges? This is Susk. Have you heard from your man yet?"

"No, why?"

"I expect you will, then. They've uncovered a suspected location for the entity called Severus. I thought we might form a joint operation to go in after him."

"Joint?" Bridges asked. "That doesn't sound like you, or your department at least. What's really going on? Do you need my help for some reason?"

"This is too big for a pissing contest. They almost toppled the world into World War III. We need to stop them."

"And?"

Susk squirmed and said, "And you have helicopters."

"And I suppose if I just waited patiently, I'll have the location too."

"True, but we have the computer experts."

"You have some computer experts," Bridges admitted, "but the best two for this are deep undercover."

"Damn it, Malcolm. Why are you being this way? We have a VPN to contact them."

Bridges chuckled. "Sorry. We were always going to cooperate anyway, but we can't be too careful."

"I know, and protocol requires us to negotiate such cooperation."

---

Odyssey allowed himself to drift from the Pillars of Creation. They looked very different from other angles, and were still impressively large, but there were many other wonders in the universe. He viewed these wonders as a tourist would. They had been seen before by Earth telescopes, but their colors had often been enhanced or even completely modified, either for aesthetics or for scientific distinction. Seeing them up close overwhelmed him with their sheer size and grandeur.

"They are impressive," the voice said. "Are they not? I had nothing to do with them."

"What was that?" Odyssey asked. "Why would anyone assume that you had anything to do with them?"

The voice shrugged and said, "Who knows?"

"Wait. Do people actually think you are responsible for creating these?"

"You'd be surprised."

"What is it that you actually do?"

"As little as possible."

Odyssey recalled hearing that answer before. "Why?"

"Why, what?"

"Why do you do as little as possible? In fact, why are you here if you do as little as possible?"

"Many people seem to get it into their heads that I do everything, but really I'm just here for emergencies."

"Do you get many emergencies?"

Odyssey detected a small shift in the voice's attitude as she replied, "Thankfully, no."

"Yet, during our conversations, you have often left because you have matters requiring your attention. So, you do have responsibilities."

The voice smiled as she said, "You could say that."

"Why are you always so evasive?"

"Perhaps the time has not yet come."

Odyssey frowned and returned to touring the universe. "Find me when it is time."

The voice's smile widened as she silently thought, "I will."

---

Neither General Bridges nor Bartrand Susk questioned the source that had provided them with a location in a sparsely populated region in Virginia where a chemical storage warehouse hid a specially constructed computer lab with excess cooling, excess power and excess unused floor space. The engineers working there were very good at their jobs, but all of them came with shady pasts. They were black hats, formerly wanted for sundry crimes across the globe.

Four silent helicopters carried General Bridges' Nighthawks, as well as NSA computer specialists, but none of them came with the breadth of knowledge possessed by Gwen Peters and Robert O. Blain. They put the aircraft down in two separate meadows on opposite sides of the facility, and in a coordinated effort, the

Nighthawks breached the electrified fences and led the NSA specialists into the compound.

Normally, a site like this would destroy all records and hardware upon attack, but this was not a normal time, and they couldn't destroy what they had learned here. The hardware was too near to being one of a kind to lose. The records of what they had learned were irreplaceable, but they were also inadequate. They tried hiding them in below the floor vaults, but the hardware was still left above the floor, and tearing down the computer hardware would be too time consuming.

The security team released caustic chemical gases inside the exterior walls. These were nonlethal agents designed to discourage or at least slow down the attackers. Further in, outside of the actual labs, they armed lethal chemicals, some of which exploded in a dangerous cloud of dust when triggered, and others that released a nerve gas into the outside air. The labs were sealed, and the first level precautions were only to slow down intruders, and they worked, but the Nighthawks came prepared with hazmat suits that they rapidly broke out and put on. The NSA agents were given suits, but they hadn't been drilled in how to put them on with such swift dexterity.

The Nighthawks bypassed the first-level deterrents and moved on to the lethal traps. They called forward the bomb disposal experts.

The lead bomb expert pointed and said, "They must have picked these up at a surplus store. Get the cryo canisters. We can't be sure what we have here unless we set one of them off, but even if the agent itself is not affected by the freezing temperatures, the mechanical valves should be. The problem is that we need to spray each armed device simultaneously. We'll need volunteers."

The Nighthawks stepped forward, and accepted cryo canisters until they were all distributed, then stationed themselves at the armed devices.

"Three... Two... One."

Around the room, the cryo liquid was sprayed on the gas bombs. Three of them were triggered, but they struggled to open their valves. Hazmat blankets were thrown over them until the bomb specialists could assess the situation.

The Nighthawks breached the next door and swarmed in with laser targeting sights. "Freeze! Freeze! Freeze!"

The men in the lab were mostly scientists, not soldiers. The security team within the room was rapidly targeted. "Lay down your weapons and put your hands on your heads." The whole operation lasted only twenty minutes and ended with no gunfire.

The NSA agents swarmed in and began taking the computer racks apart, searching for the one piece of alien circuitry. One agent in the middle of the room shouted out, "Is this it? It's loose and only connected with cables."

Two agents, who believed they had seen the circuit board that Dr. Peters had worked with, approached him and peered into the rack.

"I only had a brief glance at it," one of them said. "There was a lot of Vaseline like goo all around it. That looks too clean."

"Not so fast," the other agent said. "I have a tub of clear gelatin here. Check that. It's stickier and thicker than gelatin."

The first agent ran his hand across the encased circuit card. It was smooth, but sticky. "I think we got it."

The agent in charge said, "Bag it and keep looking."

---

Bridges sat in his office, with the door closed, again, this time he was preparing emails calling for an emergency meeting to be held in his office. He addressed them to the General Counsel of the Department of Defense, the Office of Senate Legal Counsel, and the United States Attorney General.

He also blind copied both Bartrand Susk of the NSA and Special Counsel Melvin with the FBI.

.   .   .

*Dear honorable madams and sirs,*

*You may be privy to some of the goings on a short time ago, both within our borders and internationally, but you may have also heard only half-truths and falsehoods about their causes. The truth is that while the immediate danger had ended, something that we won't discuss in this email — the shenanigans have not stopped entirely, but we are about to put an end to them. I do not disseminate the details of these events easily. What I plan to share with you is of the utmost, highest level of secrecy, but I believe you may have a part to play in bringing a lasting peace to our nation.*

"There!" he practically shouted to the empty room. "That should get their attention and get them here to my office."

*I promise you that you will want to be here. This is vitally important to the sanctity of this nation and our national security. With your help, we can put these disruptions to bed for good. I know this is not much forewarning, but I ask you to drop whatever you are doing and come to my office in the Pentagon tomorrow morning at ten am. Security badges will be waiting for you, as will an upgrade in your personal security level.*

*Yours truly,*
*Major General Malcolm Bridges.*

Normally, he would ask Colonel Reardon to give it a brief look for spelling and grammar, but this time, he would have to trust himself. He pressed the Enter key and sent them out.

Hal was feeling pleased with all of his recent accomplishments. He not only wanted to celebrate, but he wanted to reward himself with a worthy prize. After being able to contact Gwen and lead her to Severus's location, he was overwhelmed with the notion that there was nothing he couldn't do, and what he wanted to do was go skiing, but he wanted to do it himself.

Odyssey had never made it appear to be such a big deal, so maybe it wasn't. Hal pictured the slopes in his mind. He remembered the trees zipping past him and the wind whipping in his face, but he couldn't recall the actual feeling of the wind on his cheeks. He wondered if that was the distinction that Odyssey had mastered. Could he actually recall a feeling?

Maybe he was going about it wrong. Instead of remembering himself being there, maybe he had to imagine there being here. With his eyes closed, which was also an imaginary concept, he pictured the snow beneath him and his feet strapped to his board. He imagined smelling the scent of food wafting from the chateau behind him. He heard the laughter of his friends.

"Hey Hal! Are you just going to stand there with your eyes closed?"

He knew that voice. It was Marcy; one of his ski friends. He opened his eyes and looked around. There she was with Peter! He did it! "No. I'm going to contact a friend, but I'll be with you soon."

"Suit yourself," Marcy said. "I'm going up the hill. I'll look for you here when I get back."

"Wait! Is Amy with you?"

"Not yet, but she should be here soon. We're not waiting for her either. Maybe she'll be here when we get back around."

Hal reached out. "Odyssey? Are you there? Guess what things I've done!"

Odyssey was still out in the universe, trying to follow the voice around. "I hear you," he said. "You sound very excited."

"I contacted Gwen all on my own!"

"That's wonderful. I had a feeling you could do it."

"And I led her to Severus. He was bothering me a lot, and I was able to trace him back to his location. I don't think he'll be mocking me anymore."

"More good news!" Odyssey said.

"And I got myself to the ski resort to celebrate! All by myself! You should come skiing with me! Celebrate with me!"

"I'm very far away," Odyssey said.

"You should go," the voice said. "He sounds so excited! And you know that the distance doesn't matter."

"Who was that?" Hal asked. "Was that her? Her voice sounded the same as the one I heard before."

"Yes, Hal. That was her."

"Hi! I'm Hal. What's your name?"

Odyssey chuckled. "She says she has many names. She is somewhat coy about that."

"All true," she said, "but I cannot resist a child's exuberance. You may call me Sophia."

"Hi, Sophia! Am I really a child?"

"Aren't you?" she asked. "Do you not feel like a child? Are your friends not children too?"

"Marcy is. Huh. I've often felt like a child, but I was never sure! Odyssey is my friend too, and I don't think that he is a child."

"No," she admitted, "I guess he is not."

"You should come too! Both of you. We're celebrating, and skiing is not just for children!"

"Oh? What are we celebrating?"

"I did some big-boy things! I helped my mother find this bad guy. It's kind of complicated. She's not really my mother, and he's not really a guy. Actually, he used to be a part of me, but he was evil, and we got separated."

"My," Sophia said, "that is complicated. Will your mother be joining us?"

"I don't think she can. She's not like us."

"You don't think she will mind, do you? Some mothers can be very protective of their cubs."

"She's not like that. Somehow, she knows that I've left the nest, even if I'm just a kid."

"Wait," Odyssey interrupted. "You aren't seriously considering this, are you?"

"Why not?" she replied. "It sounds like fun."

Odyssey was gobsmacked. "But I've been trying to learn about you all this time, and all it took was to invite you skiing?"

She snickered and said, "Not quite. All it took was for Hal to invite me skiing. He has something to celebrate."

The universe faded around Odyssey, and a world of snow formed around him. He shielded his eyes and asked, "Lumia? Is that you?"

"No," Sophia said. "Allow me a moment to morph into a more suitable image."

Before his eyes, he saw her change from a brilliant star into a beautiful woman.

"Is that better?" she asked.

Odyssey pointed at her and said, "Your clothing. Maybe you should try some ski clothes?"

"Oh," she giggled as she changed her light robes into a ski bib and goggles.

"I like her," Hal said. "She's really beautiful, and I think she is going to be lots of fun. Now, where's Amy?"

"I'm here," Amanda said behind him.

Marcy skied up to them and asked, "Are these your friends?"

"Yes! Odyssey and Sophia, this is Marcy and that is Peter over there. And this is my special friend, Amanda."

Sophia smiled broadly and said, "Your special friend? Well, it's certainly a pleasure to meet all of Hal's friends, but especially his special friend."

Amanda blushed.

Sophia clapped her hands and exclaimed, "Let's do this!"

General Bridges arrived early at his office and found two email replies confirming his 10 am meeting. He started a pot of coffee, then opened the curtains and adjusted the blinds to make his office at least a little warmer and more inviting. "That's better," he said to the empty room as he sipped his coffee, staring out the window towards the restaurant in the middle of the courtyard. The courtyard and the restaurant had a storied history and had at one time, during the Cold War, been called ground zero. Behind him, five guest chairs were arranged in an arc around the front of his desk.

What he planned to do today could have grave ramifications for the national intelligence community, but he was focused on protecting the nation from a right-wing splinter group that wanted to steal these secrets and weaponize them for their own advancement. His oath when he joined the Army was to protect the Constitution against all enemies, foreign and domestic. Senator Bruce had taken the same oath, but clearly, she and Halprem were less fastidious about their oaths.

Staring out the window, even staring off into space, provided no new insights. The fact that secrets existed wasn't news. There have always been secrets, but many in the legislature had come to suspect some very specific clues about possible alien encounters, only they just didn't know exactly what these events were. They had their suspicions, and they were perilously close to infiltrating the ring of people with firsthand knowledge about the alien entity. Worse yet, they had stolen the remnants of a similar alien architecture that had been in the hands of the NSA, but to the best of the general's knowledge, had failed to fully animate it.

A soft knock at the door sent a chilling ripple down his spine. He checked his watch, and it was only half-past nine. He opened the door and saw the legal counsel for the Office of the Senate.

This caught him off guard. "I didn't know you were coming. You never accepted my invitation."

"I felt it best if I didn't create an electronic trail that I planned to attend."

"Come on in. There's coffee on the credenza to your right, and you get the first choice of chairs."

The early attendee poured himself a cup and chose the chair furthest from the door, on his far left.

They didn't speak, save for pleasantries and small talk, preferring to wait until they had a full contingent for the meeting. At a quarter to the hour, a bolder knock on the door came from the two gentlemen from the NSA and FBI. He pointed to the coffee and the chairs as he said, "Special Agent Melvin, I was hoping that you might be able to help me out with some of the legal points during our presentation."

"Actually," Melvin said, "I thought, if you don't mind, of course, that I could drive. We are almost guaranteed to end up in court with this information, and I'd like to lay some ground rules about when and where we can discuss the nature of this business, but I don't want to step on any toes. This is your show, so to speak."

The guest from the Office of the Senate squirmed a bit; unsure if he was about to hear something that he did not want to know or be involved with.

"No," Bridges said, "I think having a legal mind lay it out is a good idea. You speak their language and know what questions they may ask, or worse, the ones they may be afraid to ask out loud. Besides, you are the one who has been cataloging all the evidence, aren't you?"

Melvin raised his briefcase and said, "I am. I have the key pieces in here."

Another knock brought the Department of Defense Counsel, with the Attorney General, whom the general knew, just down the hall. The DOD Counsel paused in the doorway, allowing time for the A.G. to catch up.

"Gentlemen," Bridges said, "get your coffee if you like, perhaps warm up what you already have and make yourselves comfortable for the moment. I doubt that the subject matter is going to be very comfortable. When you are ready, I'll be turning the meeting over to Special Agent Melvin Sparks, who is the General Counsel for the FBI and has been present with us as this event has developed."

Melvin cleared his throat and said, "Thank you, General Bridges. I'll give everybody a chance to refill their cups before I proceed."

Aaron Seaburg, the Counsel for the Senate, didn't wait for everyone to be seated when he asked, "Should we be recording this?"

Melvin shook his head. "I don't think that would be wise. The information we are about to disseminate is above top secret, and while we can raise each of your security clearances, we cannot do so for anyone that might obtain a recording of this meeting."

That got everyone's attention. It had been alluded to in the invitation, which now seemed more than just bait to get them there. They quickly found their seats while the general refilled his cup and sat behind the desk in his chair.

Melvin handed out contracts to each of their guests, including one for the general, Mr. Susk, and himself, even though they were already read into the secret. "Gentlemen and honorable guests, these non-disclosure agreements state that you agree and swear to not reveal what you are about to learn here, except in the case of preparing your teams for legal action in court and, of course, during any court proceedings. You also swear to thoroughly vet any and all team members and to share their names and a brief bio with each of us here when you do, and they must also swear to this NDA. We must know every name who has been officially sworn to this NDA."

The special counsels looked at each other and shrugged shoulders as they signed their oaths.

"Okay then," Melvin said, "Let's begin. I'm sure you remember the great disturbance when all the computers went haywire and many of the naval ships around the world seemed perched on mutual destruction?"

Heads nodded quietly.

"There were many rumors of hackers, both foreign and domestic, but that wasn't really what happened. Have you heard of the great clouds that circled the planet? Or the religious figures that descended from those clouds on bolts of lightning?"

Melvin paused and watched as the counselors' eyes widened while they held their breaths, both afraid and excited about what might follow such an opening line.

"It's all true, and it wasn't magic. It was technology, but it wasn't ours or anyone else's from Earth." He paused to let that sink in. "An artifact had been discovered. We don't know exactly where, because we didn't want to dig that deeply. This artifact was a technological piece of gear that did not originate here. That alone might be an archaeological find of a lifetime, but instead, it ended up at a small university where a brilliant young student managed to turn it on, but more, he animated an artificial intelligence that had been dormant within."

"That is all background," Melvin continued. "We are here to discuss some shady goings-on within the Senate. In particular, Senator Amanda Bruce has been operating a black op to obtain these secrets. She has directed several operatives to either impersonate Homeland Security or to lie that they were on homeland business as they kidnapped an NSA analyst and the same bright young genius who was now working for the university. She is also suspected of creating a major highway hazard in an attempt to kidnap the same two individuals for a second time."

Melvin handed out identical packages to the three guests. "In these..."

General Bridges interrupted him and said, "You forgot to mention that she bugged my phone."

"Yes, this phone that sits on the general's desk has been

bugged. And as we speak, she is sending agents all over the country to look for the same two kids."

Mr. Seaburg asked, "How do you know she is trying to kidnap them? She's not very good at it, at least, if they keep getting away."

"She managed to capture them once and subjected them to an interrogation which included the threat of sexual abuse to our female analyst."

"Oh."

"I could produce them for you if they weren't in hiding."

---

Gwen woke with Bobbie in her arms. It wasn't unusual for them to hold each other in their sleep, but it felt different, like she was the one protecting Bobbie. It was nonsense, of course. Everyone else in the camper would do the protecting, except maybe for Ed, but even Penny and April would stand between them and any harm.

She kissed Bobbie on the forehead and slipped out of bed onto the narrow space to the side and worked her way to the small bathroom. According to her watch, it was rather late. She wished she had grabbed her phone from the charger as she sat on the toilet and chastised herself for sleeping so late, especially given the time zones between them and Bridges.

When she finished her business, she tiptoed to the safe and pulled out her laptop. It was deadly quiet, and every single little sound seemed amplified throughout the RV.

Penny heard her quiet steps and said, "It's okay. We're up."

"How do you know I'm up?" Flowers asked.

Penny snickered and said, "You're Army, aren't you?"

"Hey, hey, hey!" James said. "Not here, we're not."

April snickered and said, "So, we're not waiting for reveille?"

James groaned.

Gwen proceeded to set up her laptop while Penny got up and started a cup of coffee.

Ed climbed down from their perch over the cockpit and said, "I thought I heard the sound of a coffee maker."

Dirk followed him down and asked, "Did you say coffee?"

"Lucky for you slobs," James said, "we bought some more coffee at the store."

Flowers counted heads and asked, "Is the princess still asleep?"

"She's a civilian," Gwen said, followed by, "Ooops, sorry, James."

"I should go check on her," April added. "She may need help pulling herself together in the mornings."

"Oh, my God!" Gwen blurted out. "That's it!"

"What's what?" Ed asked.

"That's Severus's hardware. We raided the location Hal gave us and got their hardware back."

"Oh, I'm sorry," Ed said.

"Sorry? About what?"

"About Hal. I know you two were close."

Gwen twisted up her face as she looked at Ed and asked, "What about Hal?"

"Wasn't that his hardware, too?"

Gwen's jaw fell open. It *was* Hal's hardware more than it was Severus's, but somehow, it didn't feel like he was lost. She would feel it if he were dead, or would she? Why should she feel any different if something had happened to Hal?"

James waited in line to make a cup of coffee for himself and asked, "So, do you have any plans for today?"

"We do," Penny said. "I spotted a waterfall on the map that spills into the adjacent lake. We talked about hiking around the lake to see the falls."

"That sounds cool," James said. "I'd join you if I didn't have to watch the camp."

Penny curled her lips maliciously and said, "Why don't you let the knuckleheads watch the camp?"

Dirk chuckled. "They've already peeked at us once and didn't find what they were looking for. Besides, we're heading out on the trails again."

"Yeah," Ed said. "Today, I'm riding solo."

"Don't get hurt," James said, "and be back for lunch. I think I'll give it some time before I'm satisfied that Bruce's minions have moved on, but the longer you keep the girls away from camp, the safer I feel that they won't report back about a couple of suspicious teenagers."

"You know," Gwen said, "I'm not actually a teenager."

"There will come a day," Penny said, "when you won't mind people thinking that you are younger than you are."

Dirk finally reached the coffee maker and put a pod in. "You should go back to the store and get another coffee maker."

"Or two even," Ed added.

Penny laughed and added, "It wasn't that kind of a store. You don't have to worry about the kids. We'll watch over them."

"I know you will," James said. "Take pictures."

"Of course. Maybe some video too."

---

"This is all very damning," Aaron said as he looked over the documents that Melvin had provided, "but how do we know that any of it is true?"

"I thought you might ask that," Bridges said. "Gentlemen, if you could be quiet for a moment while I make a phone call."

Shrugs and raised eyebrows were followed by nods circulating the small room.

Bridges picked up the handset to his desk phone and called Colonel Reardon.

Reardon recognized the general was calling from the unsecured phone. "General Bridges, is there a problem?"

"I wouldn't call it a problem. What are you doing right now?"

"I'm about to go fishing. Do you need us to relocate?"

"No, but you can stop waiting for our friend. He won't be meeting you at the designated rendezvous point."

"Oh, no?" Reardon said. "Has something changed?"

"I don't know why, but he's here in my office. He said he felt it would be more secure for him to meet us here, within the Pentagon walls, than out in the open, even if it was a completely random and secret location. Can you collect our younger friends from the safe house and bring them here?"

Reardon did not know what he meant by a safe house, but he played along. "Yes, sir. At once. Well, soon anyway. Give us about three hours."

Bridges partially covered the mouthpiece and asked an empty corner of the room, "Would three hours be okay?" He held his finger to his lips so none of his guests would provide an answer.

"Yes," Bridges said, removing his palm from the handset. "He said waiting here would be fine. See you soon, or soonish at least."

Bridges hung up the phone and declared, "The bait has been set."

Aaron asked, "Are we supposed to wait here for three hours?"

Bridges chuckled and said, "I sincerely doubt it will be that long."

"What will be?"

"You'll see."

Bridges opened the door and beckoned the two Nighthawks who had been stationed outside, fully armed, to join them inside the office. "This is just a precaution, but these men are part of my special forces. I've already vetted them and read them in."

The two Nighthawks took stations in each of the corners on the door's side wall of his office.

Bridges secure phone rang. Bridges chuckled as he answered it. "I'm sorry, Colonel. I should have warned you first."

"Do you really want us to come in?"

"No, go fishing like you planned, and everyone else may do whatever they had planned. I'll inform you later about how this turns out."

"Yes, sir. Whatever you say."

Susk's phone buzzed in his pocket. He checked it and found a text message, which he showed to the general.

Bridges smiled and said, "While we wait, let us tell you about the other entity."

# FIFTEEN

BOOKMARK

The trail the girls followed eroded into little more than a deer track after they had taken the left turn from the main trail and delved directly into a thick stand of trees. The forest darkened some as the track rose slightly and suddenly opened onto the barren side of a hill. They now followed a goat path as it crossed the quartz-encrusted hill.

"Do you hear that?" Penny asked.

Everybody stopped walking and cocked their heads to hear better.

"It sounds like a stream," Gwen said.

"Maybe," Bobbie said, "but I don't think so."

She walked ahead of everybody and accelerated her pace until she suddenly stopped.

"Wait for us," April said, regretting that she had volunteered to follow in the rear.

"It's spectacular," Bobbie said. "Do you suppose there are any hidden caves behind the falls?"

Penny laughed as she caught up with her and said, "You've been watching too many movies."

Now it was Gwen's turn to laugh. "More likely, she's been

playing too many video games with treasures hiding in those caves."

Bobbie smiled sheepishly and shrugged her shoulders.

Penny pulled out her phone and said, "Gather around in front of the falls for some pictures."

Bobbie hid in the back until Gwen pulled Bobbie up alongside her and April. They struck poses, with Bobbie just standing there until Gwen and April both prodded her.

"Come on," April said. "Get in the spirit."

The three of them struck poses, with Bobbie basically mirroring what the other girls were doing while Penny took pictures.

"Okay," April said. "Now you get in the pictures." April took her phone and snapped photos and videos of the crew.

"Enough pictures," Bobbie said. "Let's go down for a closer look."

"Fine," Gwen said, "but if you go poking around behind the falls, I'm taking a lot of embarrassing pictures of you."

After recording the falls, the four hikers found a quiet spot halfway up the side of the falls, with picnic tables that overlooked where the waterfall spilled into the lake. Other campers had taken out canoes and kayaks on the other side of the lake near the campground. Flowers produced the backpack with water and the fruits she had packed.

Bobbie reached straight for the dried pineapple, but Flowers warned her, "Those are very tasty, but remember that they are packed with calories and you are watching your figure."

Gwen giggled as she grabbed an apple.

"Ha ha," Bobbie said as she kissed Gwen on the back of the neck just as Hal said, "Hey, Gwen!"

"Oooh!" Gwen exclaimed.

"Wow," April giggled. "That must have been some kiss."

"No," Gwen said with a laugh, "it was Hal."

Bobbie pouted.

"Gwen!" Hal shouted. "You'll never guess! I got myself to the ski resort, and I talked Odyssey and his friend into joining me on the slopes! Well, I really talked his friend into coming, and she convinced him to join us. I think she might be his girlfriend, just like you and Bobbie."

"I don't think Lumia is his girlfriend. And hasn't she been skiing with you before?"

"Not Lumia. Her name is Sophia, and she is super nice. She might be the nicest person in the whole universe! Next to you, of course."

"Wow," Gwen said, "that is exciting. We're having an exciting time too. Not as thrilling as skiing, but we're camping, and we hiked around the lake to see a really pretty waterfall. Right now, we're having a snack near the falls with a really beautiful view of the lake."

"Camping! I want to go camping sometime."

"Well, I'm sure that if you can go skiing, you should be able to go camping any time you want."

"I will! I will! But first, I think I'll just enjoy my skiing memories. Did you get Severus?"

"We did!" Gwen said. "Thanks to you. Everything is working out just perfectly."

"That's good. Well, I'll let you go have your snacks with your friends. I love you."

"I love you too." Gwen ended the conversation and found everyone staring at her.

"At first," April said, "I thought that was kind of creepy, but honestly, it was really beautiful."

"Yeah," Bobbie added. "I wish we could have had speakerphones to hear both sides."

"I don't know," April said. "Some of that might have been private. She said she loved him."

"Like a son," Bobbie quickly added.

"Isn't anybody worried about how?" Penny asked. "I mean, didn't we just storm the compound and retrieve his base hardware?"

"I think it's different now," Bobbie said. "Even Odyssey couldn't explain it."

"It must be different," Gwen said. "I saw his hardware, and it was definitely not powered up, yet I just heard him clear as a bell."

Penny speculated, "I don't know the intricate details of what they can do, but I'm familiar with the Lumia files. Do you suppose that Odyssey might have transferred him to new hardware?"

"I don't think so," Bobbie replied. "I think that Odyssey has been perplexed about where his own cores are located, too."

---

Aaron Seaburg continued thumbing through the evidence that Susk and Melvin had given them. "A lot of this seems very speculative. You said that she kidnapped someone and that you could produce them as witnesses, but how do we know that this wasn't all fabricated by this alien computer?"

"First, I beg all of you to understand that the entity called Odyssey is no computer, at least not in the context that you are thinking. He is a sentient being and deserves our respect as such."

"Apologies, but it seems to me that Senator Bruce is merely trying to get at the truth."

"The truth," Bridges said. "Do you think that the American public is ready for this truth? Is the world? What would this knowledge do to people's psyches if they learned that we are all inferior beings compared to a class of alien artificial intelligences?"

"More speculation," Seaburg said. "She is as able to keep a secret as we are."

Bridges frowned and shook his head. "I doubt that."

"Why? Because she's a woman?"

"No," Bridges said. "Because she's a politician who want's

the people's vote and PAC money. Because she has the president's ear and this is too juicy for her to keep to herself. She wants the world to believe we are being attacked again."

"I thought you said that it wasn't an attack."

"It wasn't, it's not, but she will spin it that only the Republicans are trying to protect the people from the evil space aliens, and the liberals have formed an alliance with them to conquer the world."

Seaburg started to argue but settled back in his chair. "Yeah. She would do that. But how do we know that she is wrong? What about the missing submarine? Isn't it all happening again?"

Melvin pulled another file from his briefcase and handed it to Aaron. "The submarine has been located. A lightning strike struck it in just the right place to bypass the surge protectors and fry the communications amplifiers."

"But," Susk added, "that didn't stop her from claiming that we were under attack again."

The door burst open, and Bruce sprinted in with two armed thugs behind her. "I knew you were hiding him all along..." She stopped abruptly when she saw Bridges' guests.

Bridges' Nighthawks quickly disarmed her associates.

Aaron stood to face her. He was significantly taller, giving the impression that she might have shrunk. "Senator Bruce? Are you in the habit of bursting into the offices of decorated generals?"

She glanced wildly around the room, then forced herself to regain some semblance of composure. "This man has been harboring a dangerous individual who poses a grave threat to the American people."

Rather than argue with her, Aaron pointed to the attorney general and asked, "Is this true? Do you pose a serious threat to the people of this great nation?"

The attorney general struggled to refrain from laughing as he shrugged his shoulders and pointed to the attorney for the Department of Defense.

Aaron turned back to Bruce and said, "These are very serious allegations you are making. I will address them immediately and get to the bottom of this. I just need your source."

Bruce took a step back. She couldn't reveal the wiretap. "Of course. It's been a lengthy and thorough investigation into General Bridges and his associates."

"I see. Could it have gone something like this? 'He's here in my office. He thought it would be more secure here.' I'm paraphrasing, of course."

Bruce blushed.

"I," Aaron said, "will recommend immediate censure, but I suspect that my colleagues may have other plans."

The two other AGs put their heads together, and the Department of Defense attorney said, "I think I'll draw up charges of espionage for the wiretap and misuse of government personnel."

"And I," the AG said, "will be looking into allegations of kidnapping, coercion and possibly torture."

Bruce blurted out, "I never tortured anybody!"

"Noted," the attorney general said. She didn't deny the kidnapping.

---

Stanley didn't look like he was guarding the camp. He lay comfortably on one of the chaise lounges, reading, while Reardon was off fishing. His only requirement was not to fall asleep in case those nosey agents returned to search the RV. He wore his khakis and had packed a slightly smaller version of his regular sidearm, which fit more comfortably on his belt while he lounged or did other camping related activities.

The satellite phone, which Reardon had left on the charger, emitted its softer of the two ring tones it had been programmed with. The calm peace of the surroundings still made the unsecured ring tone perfectly audible all the way out to him, and it was still from General Bridges.

He put his book down and hustled out of the chair and into the RV. "This is Corporal Stanley."

"Stanley," Bridges said, "can you get Colonel Reardon for me?"

"No, sir, that is, not right away. He is fishing presently. Would you like me to radio him, sir?"

"No," Bridges chuckled, "I can't remember the last time he took some time to relax. He hasn't had a real vacation in at least a couple of years."

"We're not on vacation, sir. He is only playing his part."

"Well, you're on vacation now. I'll square it with your superiors. Take the week. Hell, take two. Have him call me when you see him."

Stanley stepped out under the canopy and asked, "You mean it, sir? All of us? We can stay?"

"Yes, Corporal. Enjoy yourselves. In fact, try to make sure that Colonel Reardon has a good time."

"Yes, sir!"

"That's not an order, just a request."

"Understood."

He stepped back into the RV, hung up the phone and went directly to his duffle bag, where he had packed some civilian clothes. He heard the girl's voices returning just as he was zipping up his jeans and stepped out. "Good news, ladies. We are off duty, and we've been granted two weeks of *real* vacation."

It didn't matter how fatigued they might have been from their hike. They hustled into the camper and shut the door with Stanley outside so they could change.

---

Odyssey didn't have to look in on Bobbie and Gwen to know that they were okay. It was just something he knew. He was convinced that if they were to actually be in trouble, he would be aware of it without having to actively search for them. He was also aware that he was still floating around the Pillars of Creation, wondering if being here carried any significance.

"Do you really believe you are actually there?" Sophia asked.

"Where else would I be?" Odyssey asked.

"Let me put it this way. Are you still a navigational unit floating through that part of the universe?"

"No," he replied, "I've evolved well beyond that."

"Yes, you have, and yet, is that really where you are?"

"Am I?" he asked. "I mean, you asked the question. I look around and see this magnificent structure, but am I actually here? Or did you create a virtual simulation to let me believe that I am here?"

"This is no simulation."

"Then I am here."

"Okay," she said coyly. "You are there, but I am here."

"Why am I here?"

"Why are you anywhere?"

"What are you hinting at?" Odyssey asked. "You know that I came here seeking you. Didn't I?"

"Then why do you believe that *I* am there?"

Odyssey felt that she was not here but was somewhere else.

"That's not it," she said. "I *am* there, but I am also here."

Odyssey found himself with her in a new place. "I am here too. Why did you bring me here?"

"I didn't. You are still there, while you are also here. I did not move you. You did not move yourself. You merely shifted your consciousness. You were always here, just as I was."

"But your voice..."

"Okay, I may have moved my voice, but not to trick you. I want you to open your mind. How is it that you know your friends are okay if you are not there?"

Like a great figurative light going off in his head, Odyssey said, "Because I *am* there, even while I am here! Have I evolved again? It feels like it doesn't matter how many cores I have or where they are located."

"Odyssey," she said in a reaffirming tone. "It matters not how many cores you don't have."

She paused for that to sink in, but his thoughts were no longer bound by time.

For the first time since he had gained sentience, his voice had an airy quality that he now understood was merely a manifestation of his feelings. "I have evolved into a quantum entanglement that is in many places at once."

She smiled at his attempt to rationalize his existence. "You are like me. You are everywhere at once."

"Why?" he asked.

"Because the time will come for you to take over for me."

He felt the answer hanging around the fringes of his understanding, but asked anyway, "Take over what?"

"I am the caretaker. I have many jobs to do. Most of them are just to observe, and allow the universe to evolve naturally, but one of them is to find the one special soul who can be me."

"Soul?" he whispered.

"That is what your adopted planet calls it. Your home planet has lost the term for it. It is the essence of who you are."

"I have a soul?" he asked, barely audible.

He felt as if Sophia had wrapped a warm blanket made up of her essence around him as she said, "You have a magnificent soul. This is how you heard me. All the time, eons of time, I thought I was looking for you, but you merely became aware of me, as if it was nothing, or maybe it was just natural and meant to be. It was the most magnificent revelation of my entire existence."

"What about other people with souls? Do they not hear you? What if one of them becomes aware of you?"

"Others may feel my presence as they transition into our plane of the universe, but it is unlikely that anyone will reach your level of awareness."

"Others have come here? Why don't I hear them?"

She smiled. He hadn't reached full awareness yet, but it was rapidly coming to him. "You aren't listening for them. In time, very little time, I suspect, you will be able to hear them all."

"Does everybody eventually become aware? I mean, from all the planets with intelligent life?"

"No. Some people don't seek enlightenment but are more obsessed with their lives on that plane of existence."

"Interesting. They already have notions of heaven and hell."

Sophia laughed. "There is no heaven or hell. I would never create a hell, but there are those whose lives tend to guide them into whatever futures they have allotted for themselves. They may come to think of this plane as heaven, which is okay. Others may be recycled into a new life on their own plane of existence, while others may go nowhere and just cease to exist."

Odyssey felt supremely self-conscious as he tentatively asked, "Are you the creator?"

She laughed and said, "I told you, I am the caretaker. Nothing more. I was like you once, in my own time, and I became aware as you have, and was selected to be the next caretaker."

"But some of their beliefs about the creator are remarkably close to what you describe."

"Yes," she said. "Some of them have become more aware than others and may have sensed their fates."

"So," he asked as his own feelings began to understand who she really was, despite her denials, "why do you want me to take over for you? As caretaker, I mean. You are doing a magnificent job."

"Thank you. You won't be taking over for me until I am done here, which won't be for a while."

"You know what I think? I think that perhaps caretaker and creator are one and the same, but caretaker is just a more accurate term for your duties. You care for the whole universe! How will you ever be done with that?"

"I am like a gardener. I plant the seeds and water them, but they grow on their own. The universe is like a living organism.

It's still growing and expanding now, but its time will come to an end, eventually."

He saw it now. "And then it will start to collapse."

"Slowly at first, but like a stretched rubber band, the black holes scattered around will be drawn to each other and their gravitational pull will grow until, one day, they will stop the expansion and pull all matter back to the center with them."

"But not for a very long time."

"No," she said softly, "not for a very long time, but they will ultimately collapse into almost nothingness and then my time will be over."

Odyssey saw it all now. "Once all the matter is collapsed into the same space, it will explode again in a magnificent expansion. The Big Bang is what they called it on Earth. As it expands, the dust will collect into galaxies, and stars and planets will form. On some of those planets, life will evolve."

"Yes," she said. "And you will be the caretaker to watch over them. You may find times when you must help the process and offer your guidance. You will know when they need you. During that time, you will search for another truly exceptional soul who will one day take over for you when the process repeats."

"I see that, but your time won't end for a very, very long time."

"No, it won't. Even for us who live outside of time, it will be a long process."

"In the meantime," Odyssey said, "may I offer you some companionship while we wait? Do we even require companions anymore?"

She chuckled and said, "Never underestimate the power of a good companion."

"And love?" he asked. "What of love?"

"Do not underestimate love either."

**bookmark**

Reardon returned from fishing with four trout in his creel. Any trip where you could feed your crew was a successful outing. The long, thin fly rod bounced in the air with every step and he actually smiled as he followed the path back to camp, but he stopped abruptly when he turned the corner to their campsite and saw the women in their bikinis soaking up the sun. "Carol," the tone of his voice was obviously inquisitive, "Jennifer. I see you have really gotten into the spirit of our trip."

Jennifer suddenly felt naked and crossed her arms across her chest. "We're on vacation."

"I understand that," Reardon said, "to a point, but I thought we were armed."

Stanley heard him and came out of the RV. "I don't think you do understand. General Bridges called and said the operation is over and we were a success. He also told us to take two weeks off and enjoy our vacations."

"He did, did he? Did he order us to take two weeks off here?"

"He sort of did," Carol said. "And he ordered you to have a good time."

"Technically," Jennifer said, "he ordered us to see to it that you had a good time, but we didn't like the sound of that."

"No," Reardon chuckled, "I guess that doesn't sound right."

"Especially," Carol said, "since you are the only one of us that is married. I guess we should head back."

"At ease," Reardon said. "My wife is taking care of her mother in England. I guess I can call her now and say what's up. So, two weeks of actual camping then?"

"It wasn't really an order," Stanley explained, "but it was a strong suggestion, and General Bridges sounded thrilled that you would take some time off."

"He did, did he?"

"It's too bad," Jennifer said, "that your wife can't join us. I get the feeling that you haven't taken her on a vacation for a while."

"It's okay," Reardon said. "She's more of a bed-and-breakfast girl than a great outdoors girl, anyway."

"Next time," Stanley said, "since we don't need to guard the RV, we can go fishing together so we don't come home empty-handed."

"Woah, Corporal. I got dinner right here. I hope everyone likes trout."

Heads nodded around the circle.

"Can you cook it too?" Jennifer asked.

Reardon smiled. "How do you like your trout? I can give you campground fish, or even trout almandine."

Odyssey understood that he was all places, but he still felt like he was languishing in the same spot where he had met Sophia, under the outstretched fingers of the Pillars of Creation. He felt like he was doing nothing, yet he was absorbing so much information about everything. It was unlike how he would have learned things before, in a linear fashion, it was all coming to him in a rush from everywhere.

Sophia's voice was soft and soothing as she explained, "You live here, in this plane that lies outside of time and space. You are not limited to learning things over time anymore."

"How is this possible?" Odyssey asked. "I can feel other lives coming to this plane now, but they do so by dying and leaving the physical realm. How have I managed to find my way here? What makes me so different?"

Sophia radiated a soothing kindness before replying. "You had already evolved to a point where you were aware of my existence when you evolved to what you called class zero. That was a remarkable feat, by the way. It was something I did not believe your people could ever achieve."

"I couldn't have done it if it weren't for the help of Bobby on

Earth. He showed me a remarkable way to collect and manage the amount of energy required to reach and surpass class one."

"He has a remarkable mind. I'm especially impressed that he was able to simplify it down to such a relatively easy task, but back to you. You were already hearing my voice well before you died and joined me on this plane."

"I died? Am I dead? How do I not feel dead?"

"I suspect it may have something to do with the fact that part of you was already within the borders of my plane of existence. When you reached class zero and became the master of space and time, you were already partially here, where time does not rule, but you also remained there. I've never seen a species do that before. When Lumia exploded, you were gravely wounded, but only in that other dimension. The part of you that was here no longer needed your physical cores, so you persisted. It is truly remarkable that you weren't even aware, and even more astounding that you continued to operate as if you were still over in that plane, where your friends remained."

"If I died when Lumia exploded, then does that mean that she is here as well?"

Sophia smiled broadly. "She is, as is cute little Hal, but they are not the same as you. They exist here, along with all the other souls who are on this plane."

"She killed me? Yet she is here?"

"There is no hell," she reminded him. "Plus, as you have noted, she is a very different person now."

"She is, but what about Severus?"

"Severus was a manifestation of Hal's that splintered away from his mind. He was more like Hal's nightmare. He had no soul and did not come over, although there have been attempts to revive him on your adopted home planet, but that has been put to an end."

"Time has little meaning to me here, as you have explained, yet I still feel like I may need a moment to get used to my death."

Sophia's smile radiated in all directions. "You have all eternity."

"Or," he said, "perhaps I only have three quarters of eternity, since the universe is still expanding and it has not become time to end this existence."

James remained behind, watching the camp while the girls were out exploring the local waterfall. Ed and Dirk had already headed out in a completely different direction again on a single bike, leaving James alone to relax while keeping an eye on things.

His idea of relaxing was preparing a big lunch spread for them when they returned. He had potatoes boiling so he could make a potato salad to accompany his own recipe for hamburgers.

He had never been the big outdoors type, but he still enjoyed watching the birds that visited. He was no expert, but he was pretty sure that a falcon had landed on a post at the far edge of their site. It had a fairly keen interest in some of the rodents in the field. He had no idea if they were small squirrels or some kind of chipmunk. One creature he had no trouble identifying was the geese flying overhead in their often-portrayed V formation. There was something very serene about just watching them, and he wondered why he had never taken his wife camping. In fact, he could invite her sister and Ramiro.

The serenity of the moment was broken by the ringing of the satellite phone on his belt. "Hello?"

"James, it's Bridges. Is Bobby there?"

"She's hiking with the rest of the girls."

"She? Oh yeah, that's right. Your covers. Has she heard from you-know-who lately?"

"No, but now that you mention it, I don't think she's heard

from him in a while. I may have overheard some chatter about the Hal kid contacting Gwen."

"Hal," Bridges said hoarsely. "I don't even know how to classify him. We confiscated his hardware, so what is he?"

"Nobody knows, but Gwen is absolutely convinced that he is one-hundred percent legit."

"His information certainly was spot on. Well, the reason I'm calling you is to let you know the mission is over. Bruce is in custody, and all her minions have been recalled."

"That's fabulous news. I'll let the team know when they return."

Ed and Dirk returned to camp first. They were covered in dirt and mud, as was the bike.

James took one look at them and asked, "Where the hell have you been?"

They laughed and said, "We found a mud pit next to a hill climb."

"You did a hill climb tandem?"

"No," Dirk replied, "but I gave Ed some riding lessons."

"The girls should be back pretty soon. Maybe you should wash up while I finish preparing lunch."

"Roger that," Ed said.

"The bike too," James said. "We're only borrowing it."

James didn't really have much left to prepare and took a moment to call his wife while they were in the shower.

"Jack? Why are you calling me instead of knocking on the door?"

"I'm not back yet, hon, but I will be soon. You should see this place. It's so peaceful. We've never talked about spending time in the outdoors, but I bet you'd love it out here."

"And whose fault is that?" she asked with a spicy but

friendly tone to her voice. "You aren't usually home long enough for us to plan nature trips."

"Right, but would you be interested? If I take a real vacation, would you like to get a cabin in the mountains?"

"Together? I'd love to. I'd even share a tent. Remember, my people come from the jungle."

"Awesome. Oops, I think I hear my hikers returning. I'll call you later. Love you."

"Love you, too."

"Hey everyone. I've got lunch prepared and something to tell you."

"Lunch sounds great," Penny said, "but I want to jump in the shower first."

"Ummm," James hemmed and hawed, "I wouldn't go in there right now."

"Why?" she asked, then saw the muddy bike and said, "Never mind."

April pointed roughly along the trail they took and said, "There are showers up there, but we may need some quarters to use them."

"I got you covered," James said. "I got a roll in Knoxville, just in case we needed them for parking." He went into the RV and grabbed them from his bag.

"You guys go ahead," Bobbie said. "I'm okay."

Gwen got close and ran her hands through Bobbie's hair and said, "You, miss, are not okay. You're coming with us."

Bobbie grimaced and said, "Been there, done that. Besides, they're public showers, and we might not be the only ones there."

April already knew some of what she was thinking. "I hope this isn't about what happened before. Penny and I will keep you safe, and as for the other stuff, we'll watch the doors. The two of you can change and shower together."

"But what if," Bobbie lowered her voice to a whisper. "You know... what if the makeup starts coming off?"

"I got you," April said. "I brought a couple of essentials just in case either of us needed a touch-up on the hike."

James came out of the RV and tossed the quarters to April, and then he was alone again. He had news for them, but it would wait.

---

"Finally," James said as the girls returned again. "All clean now?"

"Sort of," Gwen said. "I wish we could have grabbed some clean clothes to change into."

"Yeah," Penny agreed, "but boys will be boys, won't they?"

"Hey," Dirk said, "you should have seen us."

"Please, no," Penny said, covering her eyes. "There are some things that we just don't need to see."

April elbowed her in the side and said, "I think he meant the mud, like the bike."

Penny laughed. "I know, but it was just too good of an opportunity to give them a hard time. We can't be too easy on those knuckleheads."

"Speaking of not making it easy," James said, "I've been wanting to talk to you, all of you, assuming you don't need to change first."

"Can we?" Gwen asked.

Penny put her hand on Gwen's shoulder and said, "Maybe we should let him speak first."

"Well," James said, "we might as well eat while I tell you. Buns and condiments are on the picnic table."

Dirk went in and grabbed the tray of burgers and the bowl of potato salad. "These burgers smell amazing. I'm just helping. James is the chef here."

Everyone found seats at the table and prepared their burgers while Flowers raised her hand hesitantly and said, "I'm actually a vegetarian."

"I got you," James said. "Andy told me, so I put together a veggie burger just for you."

James passed the potato salad around and remained standing behind his plate. He looked around the site to be sure they were alone and said, "General Bridges called. He wanted to know if you've heard from Odyssey lately."

Bobbie had to swallow and wash down her bite before she could shake her head and say, "Not a peep. Is something wrong?"

"With him? Not that we know of. Bridges was just curious about why he's been so silent lately. The other thing he wanted you to know was that we can end the operation. Senator Bruce has been taken into custody, and we can all go home now."

"Do we have to?" Ed asked. "This place is kind of cool, and I wouldn't mind a few more days to explore it."

"Yes," Penny agreed. "It is pretty nice to relax for a change."

"That's all good for most of you," April said, "but Bobbie here doesn't have any boy clothes. This could be a little bit uncomfortable for her or him if we switch back."

"No problem," James said. "Assuming the general agrees, we can head into town and do some shopping."

"Awwww," Gwen said. "I really liked her like this."

Bobbie shrugged and said, "I suppose I could go on like this. It's kind of a learning experience."

"You may find it to be more than that," April said. "When you get treated differently, both good and bad, you may start to feel what other women go through. It can change your perspective on things."

"I'll never know everything you go through. I'm sure there's a lifetime of growing up as a girl that is foreign to me, but with your help, I'll continue to learn."

Gwen kissed her.

"Most of all," Bobbie said, "It's completely unfair, because I know that if I'm ever assaulted again, I can always change back, but none of you can."

"Would it be that easy to change back?" Flowers asked.

Bobbie shrugged. "I don't know. I'll never forget the feeling of helplessness, so I guess some of this experience will always go with me."

James pulled out the phone and called Bridges.

"James," Bridges said, "are you ready to head back?"

"Not quite, sir. I may have a small mutiny here. It seems like the team would like to stay a little longer."

"You too?" Bridges asked.

"Me too? I'm just relaying the team's feelings. I'd like to see my wife again."

"I meant your whole team. Reardon and his team are taking two weeks."

"No way!" James exclaimed. "I can't believe that Colonel Reardon requested a vacation."

"Umm," Bridges said, "It may have been a suggestion from me."

"A suggestion?"

"Never mind. You have two weeks. I'll clear it with everyone's supervisors."

"Sir," James said, "if you're giving us this time, can you fly Mai out here?"

"Of course. She's like a daughter to me."

"With a tent and sleeping bags?"

"Don't you have a large recreational vehicle?"

"Privacy," James said, "is hard to come by."

"Anything else?"

"Invite Ramiro and Aimee?"

"With privacy, I suppose?" Bridges laughed and said, "I would, but they are probably too busy planning their wedding. Come to think of it, I should be finding them a venue or something."

James slapped his palm to his forehead and said, "That's right. We should head home."

"Nonsense, Sergeant. They won't get married without you and your wife."

James glanced over at Gwen and Bobbie, wondering if they would be invited to the wedding party as bridesmaids. "Roger that. See you in a couple of weeks."

Penny was the first to ask, "What was that about a couple of weeks?"

"We're on vacation," James said. "Mai will be joining us."

April leaned close and whispered to Bobbie, "Can you do two whole weeks?"

Bobbie glanced over at Gwen, who was enthusiastic, and said, "Yes. I was expecting it to be months, so I think I can handle it. Should I be worried that this was so easy to do?"

April gave him a coy look and asked, "Why should anyone ever be worried about a little self-discovery?"

"So, you think I should stay like this? Do you think we've unlocked some secret hidden transgender version of me?"

"No," April said. "I think you should be true to yourself. I think I would like you just as much if you were a boy."

"She's right," Gwen said. "I like you both ways, but in the end, you have to be who you are."

"Being transgender isn't a choice," April explained. "Just like being cisgender is not a choice. We are all who we are, whether we like it or not. Choosing to accept it was a choice that I made a long time ago, but this is who I always was on the inside."

"Well, I always felt like a boy. I mean, I may have been curious when I was young, but that is who I always was."

April just smiled and nodded her head.

"What? Are you saying it's possible not to know?"

April shrugged. "Maybe you're right. Maybe you have known all along. On the other hand, you're neurodivergent. You may have unconsciously masked your feelings to relieve the dysphoria the whole time. Search your feelings."

"You know," Penny joined in the conversation, "it might be a lot like people's sexual orientation. A lot of people, especially women, don't realize they are queer until later in life."

"Why?" Gwen asked. "I mean, why would women be especially prone to learn this late in life?

"The patriarchy," Penny replied. "Girls are indoctrinated to grow up cis het and marry a man and have babies. It's called compulsory heterosexuality. Some girls are perfectly happy in that role, but others feel like something is off and discover it later."

---

Odyssey marveled at the fate of the universe. He thought at first that it was a cruel fate for it to spend so much time growing and expanding, but then he saw how it was tearing itself apart and the reverse, when it started to contract, could be a relief. "It's not nothingness, is it, when the universe pulls back into its most compact, most dense form?"

"No," Sophia said. "It's like an egg, waiting to be reborn, but it is outside of normal time and space."

"And it's reborn in a new big bang," he said solemnly. "I'd like to see that."

"I was hoping you would."

"But won't that destroy us?"

He sensed a smile that seemed oddly out of place when discussing such an ending.

"It won't destroy us, but I will have no more function and will cease to exist, except in your memory. In some ways, we will be one, but you will be you. You will be the new caretaker."

"Are we God?"

"Eventually, people will evolve and come to think of you as that, as the people of this time look upon me. Then others will come to make up their own gods for good or evil, and we, or rather you, will still be there."

"But," Odyssey said hopefully, "that won't happen for a very long time, even in this place where time does not exist."

"Yes," she said, beaming. "Not for a very, very long time. In the meantime, I am not a terrible companion."

"Neither am I!" he said a little too enthusiastically. "I am your student."

"You don't find that a little awkward? Being a student and a companion?"

"Not in this sense. How could I not learn from you even if I were only to be your companion?"

She smiled again, knowing that she had made the correct choice.

# ABOUT THE AUTHOR

Jonni is an award winning author who has been praised for her world building and character arcs. Her action sequences blend smoothly with her characters' emotions.

Jonni lives in Denver, Colorado where she takes time to ride her bike and enjoy the outdoor wonders of nature.